TIMOTHY K. CLARK

Revenge of the Dragonwitch

Survival is inherited.
Revenge is chosen.
So is mercy.
Each shapes what follows.
Choose wisely.

Acknowledgments

Writing this book felt less like starting something new and more like continuing a journey that began long before these pages took shape. I want to thank everyone who contributed directly to this story, and especially those who have supported me since the first book.
My thanks to Jake of J Caleb Design for the stunning cover design on both books, and to Jennifer Bruce of Red Fox Illustration for bringing the map to life.

Special thanks to Sara Wing for your feedback and advice. And to Emeryl Williams, Matt Gabrielson, Selene O'Neal and Jill Miller, thank you for your overwhelming help and support! Tiphaine? Merci de m'avoir aidé avec mon français!

I am also deeply grateful to everyone who helped carry this story beyond these pages by sharing it, recommending it, and leaving reviews. Your generosity gave the first book a life far beyond my desk and you are the reason this story exists.

And to Karen, Emma, and Abigail Clark—thank you for putting up with all my nonsense. Love you dearly.

I'm thankful for you all, from the bottom of my heart.

JÖTNARLAND
VALHALLA
VANAHEIMR
OCEANTIS
NIBURU
DIMIAN
OPONSKOYE
MAG MELL
HYPERBOREA
AGARTHA
RELNA THUNE
THE BLACK CITY
MANANNÁN
CASTLE LEVIATHAN
NIRVANA
IRKALLA
PANDÆMONIA
EYES OF THE GODS
SHANGRI-LA
KER-IS
KUNLUN
VALLEY OF THE BLACK BONES
RIVER STYX
VULCA
HELL
SCHOLOMANCE ACADEMY
ELYSIUM
CAMELOT
OGUN
CIBOLA
QUIVIRA
SVARGA
CANELA
GODSRIBBON CASTLE
ATLANTIS
TRITON SEA
TIR NA

Prologue

Hey. I'm Finley Maguire. And, somehow, I'm not dead anymore.

If you have no idea what I'm talking about, that's fair. Unless you read the giant tome Pherric made me write about how I accidentally became the dragonwitch. (Still not a fan of the name, by the way. Dragon *Lord* would've been cooler. Or Dragon *Master.* But nope. They landed on Dragonwitch.)

Anyway, here's the short version of what happened: I'm originally from Terra—Earth, as you probably know it. Turns out there's another planet in our orbit, hidden by tech that may or may not have come from ancient aliens. Welcome to Tir Na. It's got a floating city, another city that completely disappears when you walk away from it, creatures from every myth you've ever heard about, and just slightly less gravity than back home.

I've got a theory. The ancient aliens, or maybe sorcerers from this world, used to bring humans from Earth to and from Tir Na. Because almost every myth you've ever heard seems to have originated here. There are talking apes, flying people, giants, hydras, hellhounds, and... dragons.

I was kidnapped from New York City, by Pherric, and dropped right into the middle of a rebellion. Apparently, I was their "chosen one." But... I wasn't. Pherric, an alchemist from a place called the Scholomance, had gathered a ragtag group to take down a king. Turns out the real threat was his knight commander, Kane—who wanted immortality and saw me as the perfect test subject. He knew about our little group and captured us. I was thrown into a gladiator pit and was mortally wounded. He gave Pherric back a spell book from which he used a potion to make me immortal. Only... well, one page was missing. So, I died. More than once. But each time, I came back... just a little later than the last. Ten minutes, then an hour, then a day.

Yes, I died a lot. I'm an idiot.

Eventually, we pulled together an army. There was a big battle. Dragons helped. Kane died. So did I, again—but for a month this time. When I woke up, I was Queen of Irkalla. Not by choice. Apparently killing both the king and his commander, who had no heirs, puts you on the throne.

A lot more happened. And I made a few enemies along the way. Some cowards poisoned me. Pherric thought I'd be dead for a century, but thanks to another alchemist from Scholomance, I was revived after just eight months.

Being queen isn't exactly what I want for my life. I'd rather be out in the world, having another cool adventure. Since I can't do that right now, I'm going to share what went down after I became queen.

And I've asked a few others to share their part of the story.

So, let's get to it.

(And yes, this all *really* happened. I know. I was there.)

1

My Name is Jonathan

Jonathan

I woke up face-first on a cold stone floor, which made it immediately clear I was already having a very bad day.

The chill bit into my skin, sharp enough to register before my brain caught up to the fact that I was conscious. The air smelled of dust and mildew, settled and stale, the kind of air that hadn't been disturbed in a long time. When I exhaled, it kicked up a dry, powdery plume that drifted upward before sinking back down.

I sneezed violently, convinced my allergies were going to kill me before I ever found out where I was. The sound cracked through the space and came back to me hollow and multiplied, confirming what my eyes already suspected.

This place was big.

I groaned and pushed myself upright, palms scraping against rough stone and scattered gravel. My head throbbed like I had too much whiskey and then decided to fight a truck.

Nausea didn't arrive exactly, but there was a distinct sense my insides had been... rearranged. Not painful so much as incorrect. My organs seemed uncertain about their new seating arrangement.

I blinked hard, trying to focus.

The hall stretched at least fifty feet, its ceiling supported by towering wooden beams arched overhead, thick enough to be architectural overkill. Sunlight poured through tall, narrow windows above.

The place was a ruin.

Rubble lay in uneven piles—chunks of stone that had broken loose from the vaulted ceiling or sloughed off aging walls. Ivy pushed in through cracks near the windows, green and stubborn. The cathedral or... no. Castle. It seemed more like a castle. And it had clearly been abandoned. This was not a building on campus.

And I had no clue how I'd gotten here.

I pressed my fingertips to my temples and winced. My throat was bone-dry, and more urgently, my bladder was making its displeasure known.

But neither sensation compared to the disorientation of what I was wearing. Gone were my usual jeans, T-shirt, and watch. In their place was a loose off-white linen shirt hanging past my hips, itchy black wool pants cinched with a rope doing its best impression of a belt, and stiff leather shoes that looked cut from a tire and stitched together with twine.

That sent me into panic. My brain stalled. *Was this a cosplay costume? Had I been kidnapped to a historical reenactment?* I was going to have a lot to explain to my therapist.

I stood slowly, bracing myself on a splintered wooden table. It groaned under my weight. One leg gave a loud crack, and for a brief, stupid moment I wondered if I'd be blamed for breaking antique furniture. I caught myself and steadied my balance.

I scanned the room again, hoping to find a door. My phone. A person. Anything.

To my right, a sleek metallic wall shimmered against the ancient stone.

It didn't belong. That was my first, clearest thought.

It looked surgically grafted into the castle wall—smooth, seamless, featureless. No handle or hinge. Just cold matte metal that hummed faintly when I stepped too close. Not loud or aggressive. The sound of a device idling, waiting for input.

To the left, an open archway led into a corridor lit by thin shafts of sunlight from a far window.

I chose the hallway.

The stairs spiraled downward, narrow and slippery with algae.

With every step, I felt lighter. Not spiritually—mechanically. Gravity felt reduced, dialed back just enough to notice. My feet didn't strike the stone the way they should have. There was a fractional delay before impact. In a lab, I would've said the constants were wrong.

I wandered through halls filled with rot and forgotten relics. One room held shattered armor piled in a heap, metal corroded beyond use. Another had once been a library—now reduced to dust, its books collapsed into pale outlines on the shelves.

Eventually, I found the front entrance: twin wooden doors, warped and splintered but intact. I shoved one open.

The courtyard outside was being devoured by nature. Tall grass whipped in the breeze, bending in waves of gold and gray. I tilted my head back to inspect the castle walls. Thick vines crawled up the towers. Moss mottled the off-white stone.

And everything was silent.

No birds. No insects. Just wind.

With no one in sight, I chose a wall and relieved myself, groaning as tension drained away. One small victory in a day that had already gone completely off the rails.

I tried to recall my most recent memory. There was nothing. Not even static. Just a blank where continuity should have been.

The castle was ringed by a crumbling outer wall, studded with square lookout towers. I headed toward the nearest gate. Beyond it stretched a wooden bridge over a thick moat.

"Hello?" My voice cracked. "Anyone here? Hello?!"

Nothing answered.

Beyond the bridge lay a wide field of brittle yellow grass. To the right, a forest rose—trees massive and unnaturally smooth, their trunks disappearing into a low, cloud-choked sky.

I hesitated. What you know is safer than what you don't. But my throat burned. I needed water, just not whatever festered in that moat.

I stepped into the field and stopped cold.

Arrows. Dozens of them. Maybe hundreds.

Splintered shafts stuck up from the grass. I bent and picked one up. Crude fletching. Functional. The forged metal tip was still edged. Dried blood streaked the shaft.

Blood stained the grass, too. A battle had taken place here. Recently. My heart rate spiked.

Where were the bodies?

Behind me, something shifted.

A slither. A heavy, wet dragging sound.

My spine locked. I turned slowly.

The grass rippled.

Something enormous pushed along beneath it, green-black and impossibly long. A train car made of muscle. When it rose above the reeds, my mouth went dry.

It was a snake. Or not quite. Its scales shimmered with an oil-slick sheen. Its body was as thick as a tree trunk. It lifted itself high off the ground, balanced with terrifying precision. Its face was angular. Intelligent. Its fangs were as long as my forearm, and it was looking directly at me.

I ran.

After years in classrooms and labs, running fast wasn't my strength. Adrenaline corrected that. I tore through the brittle grass, lungs burning almost immediately. I risked a glance over my shoulder and regretted it.

The serpent was closing in.

It moved with horrifying efficiency, flattening everything in its path. It was heavy—that much I could tell—and that gave me a slim advantage. Between that and the strange lightness still clinging to my body, I managed to stay ahead. Every step felt wrong, the world slightly miscalibrated beneath my feet.

I wasn't stopping to test the theory.

The serpent hissed as I veered toward the forest. I sprinted between massive trees, vaulted a fallen log, and threw myself behind a thick gray boulder just as my legs threatened to give out.

I crouched there, gasping, every muscle trembling as I strained to hear over my pulse. This wasn't panic. This was certainty. I was prey.

"Get away from here!" a voice hissed.

A hand clamped around my arm and yanked me down hard.

"What—"

"You led that thing right to me!"

"I didn't exactly invite it to dinner!"

"Shut up!" she whisper-screamed, slapping a hand over my mouth. Her grip was strong—confident, practiced. She peeked over the rock, muscles in her neck tight. "It's coming."

The grass shifted ahead of us.

We bolted.

She moved first, fast and precise. Every step deliberate. I stumbled after her, my heart letting me know it was barely up to the task.

We slid down a muddy incline, splashed through a shallow creek, and collapsed behind a big fallen tree. I braced my hands on my knees, sucking in air until the edges of my vision steadied.

She spun on me, eyes blazing.

"Who the hell are you?"

"Who am I?" I gasped. "Who are you?"

She hesitated, calculating whether it made sense to reveal that. "Genevieve."

She was tall, nearly my height, with an easy physical confidence built for motion. Athletic in a functional way. Her dark skin caught the light along intense cheekbones and strong shoulders. Golden-brown eyes tracked everything at once. She was beautiful, but not softly so. This was beauty born of control—of body, space, situation.

Right now, that control was tightly wound.

"My name's Jonathan."

She scanned the creek and treeline. "Do you know what the fuck is going on?"

Her hand rested against the bark, trembling despite her posture.

"No idea."

"Where are we?"

I took in the forest again—the heat, the humidity, the unfiltered sun.

"No clue."

She exhaled sharply, eyes glaring. She was seriously unimpressed with me.

We stayed still until the tension eased enough for me to straighten.

"Where are you going?" she whispered.

"I need water."

The stream looked clear. Dehydration won the argument. I slid down the hill and scooped a handful and drank. Genevieve followed, never stopping her scan.

The water was cold. Clean. Mineral-heavy and had a bite I couldn't name.

"We're going to regret this," I said, thinking about the bacteria in the water.

"I don't care. I feel like I haven't had water in days."

"You too?"

She nodded. "Woke up in the castle. Hangover. Field. Giant snake. Ran. No idea how I got here."

"Was I in there?"

"Yeah."

I couldn't believe it. "And you just left me there?!"

"I didn't know who you were. I've been kidnapped and you might've been one of 'em."

"Next time, maybe mention the monster snake."

"And alert it? Oh, hell no."

I gestured weakly. "For what it's worth, I think I was kidnapped too."

She studied me, then slapped my shoulder. I had passed inspection. "Let's move."

She climbed first and offered a hand. I ignored it. She snorted and disappeared into the trees.

I took one last look at the field—no sign of the serpent—then followed.

2

The Thick Plottens

Jonathan

We moved carefully through the underbrush, pushing past low branches and sidestepping roots until we came across the remnants of a trail. It was barely visible, but consistent enough to follow. Eventually, it widened and spilled out onto a dirt road skirting the outer edge of the woods.

Genevieve stopped immediately, scanning north and south with a focused expression that told me she was doing more than just looking. She was assessing patterns, risk, probability. I caught up a moment later and bent forward slightly, hands on my knees, trying to work through the ache in my sides from all the running. My lungs still burned, and my heart hadn't quite accepted that we weren't sprinting for our lives anymore.

I straightened slowly. "So... what now?"

She glanced down at the ground, then along the road again. "It's definitely not a main road. No pavement. No tire tracks. I wouldn't count on a car passing anytime soon."

The road stretched in both directions, swallowed quickly by trees and shadow, offering no signs of activity or recent use. My pulse finally began to slow, leaving behind a hollow unease.

"Okay," I said. "Which way do we go?"

She nodded south. "We go this way, John."

"My name is Jonathan."

"Yeah," she said, giving me a sideways look. "You mentioned that." Without another word, she started walking. I followed close behind, unwilling to let the forest close ranks between us.

We hadn't gone far when a sharp hissing sound cut through the trees ahead, followed by the unmistakable disturbance of something large pushing through brush.

I stopped. "Um—"

Genevieve didn't hesitate. She spun on her heel and headed back the way we'd come. "Yeah. On second thought…"

I turned and ran with her. Only I didn't hear it following us, which somehow made things worse.

We walked for at least an hour. Or rather, Genevieve walked, forging ahead with a pace that suggested this was inconvenient but manageable. I did my best to keep up.

The sun beat down relentlessly. My shirt clung to me, soaked through, and my mouth went dry again.

"Wait," I finally called, struggling to breathe. "Just… wait. I need to sit for a minute."

She stopped and glanced at her wrist as if to check her smartwatch, but there was nothing there. She looked back at me, disappointment softening into reluctant pity, and sighed.

"Two minutes." She stepped to the side of the road and stretched her calves as if this were a scheduled pause, not a concession.

I collapsed onto the ground, legs giving out beneath me. I focused on breathing while she kept her eyes on the road behind us, alert for movement. After a minute, she glanced back.

"Let me guess," she said. "Desk job?"

"Sort of," I said, still panting. "I'm a graduate TA. Working on my doctorate in chemistry."

"So, yeah. Desk job," she said with a faint smirk.

I tried to laugh. It didn't land. "Yeah. Guess so."

"What school?"

"Brown."

She squinted. "Brown University? Where's that?"

"Providence. Rhode Island." I rubbed my ankles.

The stiff leather shoes were already digging in, the straps chafing. Genevieve hadn't escaped the wardrobe downgrade either. They'd stuck her in a rough tunic and fitted leggings, the fabric stiff and practical, paired with worn leather boots built for endurance, not style.

A frown crossed her face as she turned the information over. "Rhode Island," she repeated.

"Why?" I asked.

"I live in New York. Manhattan." She tilted her head. "So... why would they take you from Providence and me from New York and drop us into this jungle?" She gestured vaguely at the empty road. "We're not even close together? How far is Providence from—"

The hissing sound returned. Louder. Closer.

I jumped to my feet, adrenaline slamming back into my system. Genevieve didn't flinch. She held out a hand and listened. Her eyes swept the road, calculating.

Then she started walking again—but not running. I scrambled after her.

"Shouldn't we be going faster?" I asked, glancing back.

"No need," she said evenly. "We're not being hunted. We're being herded."

The word landed hard. "What do you mean?"

She kept walking. "Think about it. We both wake up alone. Both times, that thing shows up. Doesn't kill us. Just drives us out. Then we find this road, and again it's behind us—enough theatrics to keep us going, but not enough to escalate."

"So, someone's guiding us," I said slowly. "Leading us somewhere."

"Yeah." She threw her head up in annoyance. "That's what I just said. And I'm starting to think we might not want to go where they're directing us."

I swallowed. "But if they can control a snake that size, maybe we should...

listen?"

She stopped and looked at me. "A snake what size?"

"Well, snakes don't get that big. Not biologically. But in mythology there's the Basilisk. The so-called king of serpents. And whatever that is... fits the description."

Her mouth twisted into a grin. "You're a doctoral student who believes in mythical monsters?"

"I'm a scientist," I muttered. "Which means I question things. That creature violates biology."

She laughed, really laughed, for the first time. "You really don't get out much."

Genevieve patted my chest as she passed me, heading north again. I sighed and walked along, aching, confused, but unwilling to fall behind.

We walked quietly for another half hour. Eventually, the forest thinned and opened into a wide field of thick, chest-high grass shimmering in the sunlight. Unlike the pale-yellow wild wheat I recognized, this grass was a vivid orange—its color off in a way that bypassed explanation and went straight to alarm.

I slowed, brushing the coarse stalks with my fingers. Nothing about this terrain made sense. The plant life, the gravity, even the quality of the light felt inconsistent with everything I knew. What country were we in?

The sun had begun to dip, softening the heat, and I was grateful for it.

We crested a small rise, and a tight grove of dark trees came into view. Genevieve stopped, posture snapping into alert focus.

"Do you see something?" I asked.

"No," she said slowly. "But this might be where we're being directed."

"That's not very scientific."

"Neither is a Basilisk," she replied. "But here we are."

She started forward. I followed.

It didn't take long before we knew she was right.

The dirt road cut straight through the grove, shaded by a thick canopy overhead. A breeze stirred the leaves, briefly calming.

And that's when we saw him.

He was waiting, sitting cross-legged in the center of the road and perfectly still.

"Uh, Gen. What is—"

"My name... is Genevieve."

The stranger lifted his head.

"Touche."

At first, I thought he was asleep. Then I noticed the tension in his frame. He wore a long green robe that shifted subtly in the wind, the fabric behaving in a way that suggested intention rather than physics. His bald head was covered in dark, intricate tattoos spiraling across his scalp, face, neck, and hands—precise, deliberate markings I'd mistaken for hair at first glance.

Even seated, he was massive.

We crept closer and closer until Genevieve stopped short and threw out an arm, blocking me.

The stranger's eyes locked onto us, intense and impatient.

When he spoke, his voice vibrated through my chest.

"Juwagget," he growled. "Be dannara ish eh grannuh!"

3

The Mystery Man

Jonathan

I didn't understand a word he said. Whatever language he spoke was completely unfamiliar. That was saying something, considering how many international students I'd worked with as a teaching assistant. I was used to hearing accents, code-switching, even half-formed English threaded through other languages. This wasn't that. There were no recognizable roots, no familiar cadence to latch onto.

Still, I got the impression he wasn't pleased with how late we were. That much came through clearly enough. Maybe it was the tone. Or the way his eyes never stopped assessing us. We'd arrived behind schedule.

The thought vanished the moment he stood up.

He was huge. Not just tall, but structurally massive. Easily seven feet, maybe more, with proportions that made my brain hesitate before accepting them. If basketball had been an option wherever he came from, he would've gone first round without question. Watching him rise triggered an involuntary step backward on my part, my body reacting before pride could intervene.

Genevieve jumped in front of me.

It wasn't dramatic. No big gesture, no sudden shove. Just a subtle shift of position that placed her between me and him. I noticed and... I didn't love it. I wasn't used to someone else deciding I needed protection, and the hit to my ego landed before I could stop it. I stepped up beside her and squared my shoulders, making a quick, conscious effort to mirror her posture despite the tension creeping in.

She spoke first. "Who are you? What do you want?"

I scrambled to add something, so I didn't seem completely useless. "Do you speak English?" I asked, forcing my voice to stay steady.

He didn't answer. Didn't even blink. He just stood there with an unreadable expression, then slowly brought his fingers together in a steeple and bowed his head. A deep, guttural sound rose from his chest. It wasn't speech, but something structured. A chant. Rhythmic. Spoken in the same unplaceable language.

The sound carried across the field with weight, humming through the air in a way that felt wrong—not louder, but denser, and the space around us was being compressed.

Genevieve's hand found my arm. Her grip tightened as the chanting grew louder and more insistent. She took a small step back, eyes darting around the grove as she searched for exits. I stayed where I was, caught between the instinct to analyze what was happening and the very real urge to run.

"We need to leave," she whispered.

"Okay."

We backed away. Slowly. One step. Then another.

And we started to turn, except... we didn't. I told my body to move. Nothing happened. The signal just stopped; the command had been intercepted. My legs stayed planted. My arms locked at my sides. For a second, I wondered if fear had short-circuited me.

Every hair on my arms stood up. Genevieve made a frustrated sound beside me, cutting and breathy, and I knew she felt it too. Whatever held of us wasn't physical. Nothing restrained us, yet movement was simply not permitted.

The tall man never opened his eyes. His chant didn't falter as he walked forward, arms outstretched, fingers splayed as he reached toward our faces. I wanted to fight. To yell. To do *something*. But my body remained obediently still.

He placed fingers on her head and then mine. My vision blurred.

Something pressed against my thoughts—not physically, but undeniably present. I couldn't describe it any better than that. My awareness folded inward, distorted, and my mind was no longer a closed system.

Panic surged.

And everything went black.

Waking up wasn't exactly a relief.

The first thing I noticed was the new headache—sharp, throbbing, concentrated, like someone had struck the inside of my skull with a tuning fork and left it ringing. The second thing was that I was face down on packed dirt. Not ideal.

Groaning, I shifted my weight and pushed up. The sun was lower now, casting long shadows through the trees. We couldn't have been out for long, yet my body felt heavy and sluggish, out of step with the passage of time.

Genevieve stirred beside me, sitting up with a wince and brushing black curly hair from her face. I followed her lead, slower, careful, trying not to trigger another wave of dizziness.

And there he was.

The same man—tall, bald, composed—sitting cross-legged a few feet away as if nothing had happened. His head was bowed, hands resting loosely on his knees. When he finally looked up, he wore a small smile that wasn't reflected in his eyes. Those eyes were black and depthless, giving away nothing.

Genevieve, on the other hand, was done being patient.

"What did you do to us?!" she snapped, her voice echoing through the trees. "What the hell is going on?!"

She shot to her feet. I stood too, more cautiously, brushing dirt and leaves off what had to be the least practical outfit I'd ever worn.

The man rose slowly, as though standing were an obligation rather than an effort. The way he moved suggested he could have done it faster but didn't feel the need to.

"Talk to us!" Genevieve demanded, stepping toward him, fists clenched.

He responded with a single, minimal gesture and lifted one arm, pointing behind him.

She kept going. "Answer me or I swear to god, I'll—"

She stopped.

Something moved in the trees. At first it was a ripple in the grass. Then it emerged.

The serpent slid into view, long, thick, gleaming, and easily thirty feet from head to tail. Its eyes locked onto us, unblinking, tongue tasting the air with deliberate flicks. It crossed the dirt road at an unhurried pace before disappearing into the trees opposite us.

Genevieve's hand shot out, gripping my arm hard enough to hurt.

The man smiled wider. "Welcome to Tir Na."

"We're outta here," Genevieve muttered. Grabbing my wrist, she started pulling me away.

"That would not be wise," he said calmly. "There is far worse out there than a Basilisk."

She shot me a look, like this were somehow my fault.

Her fury barely contained, she turned back on him. "Oh, so now you speak English?!"

"Wait." I raised a hand, trying to slow things down. "*Worse* than a Basilisk?"

"My world is full of terrors greater than you can imagine."

I caught onto his phrasing immediately. "Your *world*?"

Genevieve cut in. "Who are you?"

"I am Ramil." He inclined his head slightly.

"And why the fuck did you kidnap us, Ramil?!" She practically spat out his name.

I stepped between them before she could escalate further. "We just want to understand what's happening," I said. "Please."

Ramil looked annoyed because the conversation had already taken too long. Still, he drew a breath, visibly restraining himself.

"You are part of a plan," he said. "A necessary one. Tir Na is in danger, and you are here to help save it. I understand this is confusing, but we have far to travel before your training begins and—"

"That's not enough," I interrupted, my voice tighter than I'd intended. "You can't summon a giant snake, knock us unconscious, and expect us to follow you without explanation."

I stepped forward, meeting his gaze directly. "You can threaten us with monsters or whatever else is out there. But if you really need us, you're going to have to do better than vague details. We deserve that."

Something dark flickered behind his eyes—frustration, maybe anger—but he didn't strike.

"And if you want our help," I added more quietly, "then talk to us. Because otherwise, we're not going anywhere."

4

Snake Oil

Jonathan

Ramil gave a short nod, his voice low but firm. "We shall commence our journey as I explain."

It wasn't an invitation, exactly, but it was the closest thing to cooperation we'd gotten so far. Genevieve and I exchanged a look. She gave a cautious nod, and we started moving—one of us on each side of the man who towered over us with every stride. I kept a wary eye on the surrounding trees, half-expecting the Basilisk to make another appearance.

I tried to keep my tone measured. "Where exactly are we?"

Ramil shot me an annoyed look: asked and answered. "As I stated: Tir Na. More precisely, the kingdom of Cíbola."

"Tir Na isn't a country I've heard of. Are we... somewhere in Africa? South America?"

"You are not on Terra, my child," he said calmly, glancing up through the canopy. "I do not know the nature of the magic that brought you here. Only that it works. And works well."

My stomach flipped. The implications hit faster than I could organize them. Terra. Not Earth.

Genevieve caught the look on my face immediately, suspicion sharpening her expression.

"We're not on Earth," I repeated. The words felt unstable as I spoke them.

"What?!" she snapped. "You actually believe this crazy-ass shit?!"

I let Ramil walk a few paces ahead and leaned toward her. "Listen. Seriously. Have you noticed how light you feel? Gravity's off—not drastically, but enough to register. And the trees, the grass in those fields, the plant life. None of it matches any biome I know."

She planted hands on hips. "You're the science guy, and you're buying alien grass and funny gravity now?"

I hesitated. "You can't fake gravity, Genevieve. That's physics. Our bodies feel it."

Her expression shifted—defensive first, then uncertain. "Still sounds like high-level brainwashing bullshit."

"I only implanted a mindform to enable you to understand our language," Ramil called back, not breaking stride.

Genevieve surged forward, grabbing his sleeve. "So, you *did* mess with my brain?!"

He didn't flinch. "You must understand and speak the Queen's Language to survive in this realm."

"You're speaking English," she snapped.

"No," I said slowly, realization clicking into place. "He's not." I turned to her and spoke deliberately. "What I'm saying now—this is English. Listen to it."

I closed my eyes and focused, then spoke again in the other language: the one I shouldn't have known. "You hear this, right? You're translating it into English."

She stared at me. Something shifted as the realization landed.

"What the actual—"

I looked at Ramil. "Where is Tir Na? How far is it from Earth?"

"From the ancient texts, your world lies on the opposite side of Sol," he said. "We orbit Sol at the same speed, always missing one another. Many here believe Sol moves around us. This is incorrect."

"We know. Heliocentrism isn't exactly new. But we would've seen another planet. Satellites. Telescopes. Gravitational anomalies. It would have shown up."

"The gods did not allow it," he replied. "That is why they placed the World Serpent around us."

He pointed upward.

I followed his gesture and squinted. High above the atmosphere, barely visible, ran a thin, luminous white arc—too precise to be natural.

"That's what's hiding this planet?"

"It shields us from foreign gods... and likely from the eyes of your mages."

Mages. Scientists, maybe. Or something else entirely. Either way, my thoughts began to spiral.

"Who are these... gods?" I asked.

"That is a question for the scholars," Ramil said, a note of reverence in his voice. "The gods have long since turned from Tir Na."

My legs nearly gave out under the weight of it. Hypotheses collided, none of them stable. The air felt thinner... or maybe that was just me.

Genevieve bumped my shoulder. "You're buying this, aren't you?"

"I don't know," I said. "But parts of it fit."

We kept walking. Time slipped in a way I couldn't track. An hour. Maybe more. Ramil answered little, but I pieced together fragments—enough to form a working theory, however unstable.

We weren't on Earth. We were on a terrestrial planet with similar composition and orbit, synchronized on the opposite side of the sun. That alone explained invisibility, but not the lack of those anomalies or reflected light. Unless something advanced was actively masking it.

The World Serpent.

We had seen no technology, no infrastructure. If this world was hidden, someone else had done it. Someone far beyond their (or our) understanding.

My headache escalated from irritating to brutal.

"We'll rest here," Ramil announced.

He led us into a small clearing beside the road. Flattened earth, a charred ring of stones, a weathered log half-sunken into the ground. A regular stopping point.

"Seriously?" Genevieve muttered. "We're sleeping *here*? What if a bear wanders by?"

Ramil sat heavily against the log and closed his eyes. "The Basilisk will keep other creatures away."

Genevieve jabbed a thumb toward him and looked at me. I had nothing. I shrugged.

Everything hurt. My feet burned. My legs ached. I lowered myself to the ground and closed my eyes.

Genevieve stayed upright, perched on the far end of the log, scanning the dark. I doubted she'd sleep at all.

I tried but failed. Eventually, I stared up at the stars. When I blinked again, she was watching me. Her expression unreadable.

So, I got up and sat beside her.

When she was sure Ramil was asleep, she whispered, "What are we even doing here?"

"I wish I knew."

"You don't know anything," she said. "But you're acting like this is some kinda field trip."

"I'm not," I said quietly. "I'm trying to understand it. I'm fascinated. And terrified. None of this makes sense."

"I don't belong here," she said, crossing her arms.

"I don't either."

"If this is real," she whispered, "we're dead."

"I don't think we're going to die," I said. "We'll figure something out."

I reached toward her shoulder, to comfort her.

She was on her feet instantly. "Don't touch me!"

I backed off. "I'm sorry."

"I don't know you."

"I get it."

I returned to the ground. Eventually, sleep took me—heavy, uneasy.

We were far from home.

And despite everything I'd learned, I had never felt so lost.

5

A Hound of Flesh

Jonathan

I don't think either of us really slept. Maybe an hour, at most. When the first light cut through the trees, I sat up with a stiff neck and burning eyes. Ramil was already awake, crouched beside a small fire he'd built with unsettling efficiency. Thin strips of meat sizzled over the flames, greasy and unfamiliar, giving off a smell I couldn't place.

We didn't ask what it was. Or where it came from. We just ate it.

Genevieve was quiet at first, but after a few bites she looked up, chewing slowly. "Okay... where exactly are we supposed to go to the bathroom?"

Ramil didn't answer. He simply nodded toward the open field past a thicket of thorny brush.

She raised an eyebrow. "And what am I supposed to use for toilet paper?"

This time, he tilted his chin toward a neat stack of brittle, dry leaves arranged beside the log. They'd probably disintegrate under minimal pressure.

"Jesus Christ." Genevieve let out a short, humorless laugh, grabbed a handful of leaves, and stalked off toward the brush.

I waited until she was out of earshot, then leaned closer to Ramil. "Can you at least tell me where we're going? How far?"

Without looking up, he rotated the meat slowly over the fire. "We journey to Pandæmonia. To the Scholomance Academy. Far northeast of here. Many days by foot."

I opened my mouth to ask more, but Genevieve came crashing back into the clearing before I could form the question.

Her face was flushed, her voice tight with fury. "None of that matters! You need to take us back home. I don't care where we are—another country, another dimension—I want out!"

Ramil didn't flinch. His eyes stayed on the flames. "That is not possible."

"Yes, it is!" she shouted, throwing the remaining leaves at my feet. "You brought us here. You can take us back. Do it. Now."

He stood in one smooth motion. His expression twisted—not into rage, exactly, but something adjacent to it. He stepped toward her.

"I did not bring you here," he said. "I was given a task: deliver you to the school. That is all. Whether you arrive or not, I still receive my payment."

Then his gaze shifted to me. His finger followed. "He is the one they want. You were an added benefit."

Genevieve didn't move. I could see the shake in her hands, but she held her ground.

Ramil exhaled sharply and turned away, stopping at the edge of the road. He stood there, waiting.

"I'm not going," Genevieve said flatly, arms crossed.

"As you wish."

I hesitated, then stepped beside her. "Then I'm not either. We'll find our own way back."

Ramil glanced over his shoulder. His stare lingered just long enough to make my stomach drop. Instead of anger, something colder crossed his face.

"I see."

Genevieve took a step after him. "I don't care if your snake eats me. I'm done with you. With this place."

He lowered his head slightly. Then, without turning back, he spoke. "It is not the snake you should fear. Hellhounds roam this region. They do not ask questions. And they are always hungry."

And then he was gone.

We stood there in the silence he left behind, watching the road long after his footsteps faded.

Hellhounds? Did I hear that right?

The campfire crackled behind us, loud and startling. A massive white bird cut across the sky overhead, its shadow sweeping over us. An omen?

Nothing followed. No snapping branches. No howls.

Just stillness.

"Now what?" I whispered.

Genevieve stared at me, jaw tight.

I turned slowly, orienting myself. "If we want any chance of getting back, we need to return to that castle. Where we woke up. I saw something there—a metallic door. It didn't belong. It could've been a portal. Or part of a ship. Maybe?"

She nodded once.

"That's our only lead."

Without a word, she grabbed the leaves and headed south.

I jogged to catch up, realizing I didn't want to be on the wrong side of her or alone. "You're kind of a badass."

"No. I'm just not playing his game."

I tried to relate to her one more time. "So... what did you do back home?"

"You didn't ask."

"I'm not your enemy," I said, stopping.

She spun on me. "No. But you were ready to follow him without question! *That*... is messed up."

The words landed hard. "I'm sorry," I said finally. "I thought going along was safer. I'm not a fighter. But I'm with you now."

Her anger dimmed. "I'm pissed, Jonathan. I just signed a modeling contract. A real one. And now I'm gone from the goddamn planet, man!"

And it clicked. Even exhausted, filthy, and stripped of context, she still carried herself with unmistakable presence—the kind that didn't depend on lighting, makeup, or permission. The way she moved, the way her attention commanded space, it all tracked. Whatever this place had done to her, it hadn't erased that.

"You with me?" she snapped, waving a hand in front of my face.

We'd gone only a few hundred yards when we saw it.

The hellhound stood in the middle of the road.

At first glance, it registered as a dog. It was black and massive. Too tall at the shoulder. Too broad through the chest. Its eyes glowed red, steady and focused, not feral but deliberate. The beast held my gaze, unblinking, and I understood it wasn't reacting on instinct. It was assessing us.

Two more emerged from the undergrowth.

Whatever rational category I'd been reaching for collapsed under the weight of the word Ramil had used. Hellhounds.

So, of course, we took off running.

The ground blurred beneath us. They were gaining. And I was ready to stop.

Genevieve started sprinting well past me, but I saw a shape emerge from behind some trees.

Ramil.

"Genevieve!" I whisper-shouted.

He stepped out from behind a thick tree, motioning quickly for us to follow. I veered toward him. Genevieve glanced back and did the same.

He raised a hand and closed his eyes. Whispered something. His fingers traced circles in the air, the motion smooth and exact—like casting a spell in a language older than language itself.

The hounds were almost on us.

I saw shadows appear next to him. I swear I watched them *form* from the dirt and dust. At first, they were just silhouettes. But then... they were *us*. Ghostly copies of Genevieve and me, dressed exactly the same, down to the fraying cuffs and sweat-stained collars of our ridiculous Renaissance Fair outfits.

The shadows sprinted across the road in the opposite direction.

The hellhounds shifted, then shot off, snarling and barking as they chased the specters into the trees. We watched until their growls faded into nothing.

My breath came in ragged gasps. My heart thumping away.
Ramil lowered his hand. "I warned you," he said without turning.
And this time, when he began to walk, we followed.

6

Hey. It's Me. Finley.

Finley

I hate being queen. No, like, *actually* hate it. Being queen *sucks.*

It sounds good, in theory. You imagine lounging on some absurdly fluffy chaise while shirtless dudes with biceps for days fan you and hand-feed you grapes, right?

And maybe you order the execution of that one countess who always tries to out-dress you at the ball? But noooo. Apparently, that's "lazy" and "abuse of power" and, for some reason, "technically murder".

Phffft!

So here I am, Finley Maguire, Queen of Irkalla, stuck sitting on a rock-hard throne (they won't even let me use a butt pillow, by the way), suffering through hours of citizens whining about land disputes, welcoming sweaty diplomats, and making life-or-death appeal decisions based on laws I barely understood.

Long live the queen, I guess.

I tried to sneak off whenever I could, usually with all the subtlety of a drunk ratatoskr. I'd take swordplay over sitting in court any day, but Braylor and Pherric were basically royal babysitters, always dragging their wayward toddler back to the throne.

And then there was my real nemesis: Luchar. The chancellor, which is just a medieval way of saying "bossy know-it-all." He was an Irkallan who'd clearly memorized every rule, protocol, and etiquette scroll in existence. Basically, his full-time job was pointing out everything I was doing wrong... which, to be fair, was a lot.

And it wasn't just court stuff. I had to answer daily questions from my chamberlain, the treasurer, the steward of the keep, my constable, and a half dozen other people. I rarely had to time to spar with Braylor (or... *spar* with Braylor, *if* you get my meaning.) And never any chances came up to practice mindforms with Pherric.

I wanted to get out of the castle and run. I needed to wander, to explore Tir Na. I wanted to fight. But we were mired in a dull, bloodless peace. And even if we were waging war with some other kingdom, they wouldn't let me go out and play. Dickheads.

Instead, I got shit like this:

Some bejeweled land baron in twelve yards of curtain fabric shuffled in and bowed so low I thought his back would snap.

This is how he sounded. "Your majesty, if it please you to hear the humble words of your loyal servant..."

It never pleased me, but no one cared.

"A tragedy has visited my estate. The beasts belonging to one Lord Nemain have wandered into my pastures and tragically infected my herd. Many of my noble bicorns and majestic boars have perished!"

Cue the dramatic sigh. From me.

"I seek righteous justice, oh fair and just ruler, that I might find redress under your esteemed law."

I was halfway into a nap by then. And then, of course, my stomach betrayed me with a massive growl. Like, echo-across-the-hall *loud.* Luchar side-eyed me like I'd farted during a funeral.

"I dunno, make Nemain pay you back," I muttered.

"But your majesty, he has not the means for recompense!"

I leaned over to Braylor, who was crammed into a chair clearly made for a child.

"He means to say the man has no money," Braylor whispered.

"So *we* have to pay you?" I asked the landowner.

"If it pleases your majesty!"

"It doesn't, but fine. We'll pay then, I guess."

My treasurer cleared his throat.

"Umm. We'll pay seventy-five percent value per dead beast then?"

More throat clearing.

"Fifty percent! Final offer."

Mr. Fancy Robes looked crushed, but I had to pee and I was over it. "Great. Royal bathroom break. Be right back."

Everyone blinked as if I'd spoken in French again. Which I sometimes did to piss them off.

"I have to pee," I clarified. Gasps. Pearl clutching. You'd think I'd flashed them!

I ordered a snack from a servant and bailed to the courtyard. Sunlight! Fresh air! Slight chance of being hit with a rock from the angry mob gathered below the balcony. Ah, royalty.

As soon as I stepped near the edge, they spotted me.

"Usurper!"

"Dragonwitch!"

"Fire-haired demon!"

Lame. Only ten points for creativity.

Braylor came up behind me, wrapping his arms around my waist. "Ignore them. They do not know of what they speak."

"Neither do I," I muttered.

He brushed wind-tossed curly red hair from my eyes and said some encouraging thing, but I was already distracted by the smell of meat. The servant rushed in with melon slices and a literal *slab* of roasted bicorn.

Braylor gave me the eyebrow. "Hungry?"

"Not for me, you goof. I thought maybe Big Red might be lurking." I scanned the sky.

No sign of her.

But I heard more booing.

"I just... I wanna *do* something."

Braylor got philosophical. "Unless you raise taxes—"

"Nope." Spit out a melon seed. "Not robbing the already-broke."

"Kane's war cost Irkalla dearly. You have spent heavily. On rebuilding the army. On reparations to other kingdoms. The people may not be pleased by these acts, but they were necessary."

"But it's been over a year! And somehow everything is still bad."

"I have no answers."

I stepped toward the jeering masses. "They call me a *usurper*. I had to *look that up.* Apparently it means I took power I wasn't supposed to have. They don't want me here!"

"They hate the fact that you are not Irkallan," he offered.

"Well, *I* don't want me here either."

He reminded me that technically, legally, this was all valid. "You had no choice, according to their laws."

"Yeah. Doesn't make it suck less."

I heard a whoosh from above.

Wings.

Big. Red. Wings.

My mood flipped faster than a hot pancake.

I turned to the skies. The red dragon came soaring out of a cloud. She sailed below the level of our courtyard. I leaned back against the railing as she flapped her wings. The dragon flew low enough to the ground to scatter the Irkallan protesters who had gathered to scream at me. In a panic, they yelled and fled. I tried not to laugh as she swooped up and landed with a hard *thud* on the courtyard.

I grabbed the slab of meat and hurried toward her, slowing as I reached the edge of her shadow. Before her towering form, I bowed my head.

"My lady," I said softly.

I raised the roast above my head in offering. Her glowing orange eyes fixed on me, then the meat. She sniffed once, then nudged it gently with her nose. A huff of warm breath washed over me—approval.

I smiled, pressing my forehead against her cheek. Her scales were smooth, warm, and familiar. She opened her jaws, and I tossed the meat in. With a quick snap of her sharp teeth, it was gone. It would've taken me a week to eat that much...

She gave me a gentle nudge in return. A thank-you.

"Come say hi!" I called to Braylor.

He didn't move. His hand was death-gripping his sword. Big Red growled. I gave him *the look*.

He bowed instead and that was enough for Big Red.

"Scaredy-cat," I teased.

He retreated, muttering, probably adding "dragon-befriending menace" to my list of nicknames.

I turned back to her, stroking her scales.

"Just us again, huh?"

She snorted hot sulfur across my face. Nice.

"And you *have* to stop terrorizing my people," I scolded gently.

She raised her head and threw out a high-pitched roar. A dragon laugh, maybe?

I grinned. "You naughty girl."

But honestly? I was happy. Even if it only lasted a minute.

7

The Occasion of an Invasion

Finley

When Chancellor Luchar finally found me the next morning, I was in the Great Hall trying to get the court minstrels to play Ozzy Osbourne's "Crazy Train."

"No, faster," I told the poor fiddle player, who was already sweating through his tunic. "Play it like it owes you money!"

It was my dad's favorite song, and he played it all the time. Which made me hate it back in the day, but now I kind of missed it.

"Your majesty!"

That voice could chill soup.

I stopped, mid-air guitar riff, and considered whether I could dive behind the nearest tapestry fast enough to escape the looming cloud of responsibility. No such luck.

"Your majesty."

If a quill pen ever magically transformed into a person, it would be Chancellor Luchar: straight, stiff, and likely to stab you with a lecture about court protocols. He walked as though he was perpetually balancing a book on his head and spoke like every word must pass a royal inspection.

"Yes, Luchar?" I summoned the energy to face him before turning around.

He was wearing one of his robes that were always a perfect gradient of somber gray and deep navy, embroidered with the Irkallan seal in such precise symmetry it made your eye twitch.

I once heard him scold Braylor for sneezing too informally.

"At precisely the ninth bell, your majesty is expected to receive the delegation from Zerzura. Please refrain from your... informal greetings. They do not recognize *finger guns* as a diplomatic gesture. Following the council session, there is a brief audience with those from the Warehouse District. I have allocated twelve minutes, which should be sufficient for smiling, nodding, and appearing wise and benevolent. Lastly, there has been an invasion of Cíbola by the Atlanteans."

"Wait... what?!" The last part hit me. "Why would you save *that* for the post-credits scene, Luchar?!"

Luchar looked at my humor as a communicable disease. But I'll give him this—if I need something organized, categorized, or turned into a fifteen-page policy scroll (with footnotes), he's my guy.

"Because I knew you would ignore the rest, your majesty," he said, staring down his long nose at me. "They are waiting in your antechamber."

Cue me sprinting to my quarters like a late student realizing today *was* the final exam.

Inside, my team was assembled: Braylor, Pherric, Kasuma, and my knight commander Sandulf. He was Irkallan. Braylor hated him at first, because he's stupidly handsome, but Sandy managed to not lose his head when sword fighting against the big guy. And he refused to fight for King Malek and Kane before the war, choosing instead to hide out in Valhalla. So, he was also smart.

They bowed to me. Of course, Braylor always bowed slightly less than the others, with a smirk on his big, cute face.

"What have we got?!" I rubbed my hands together in excitement. "A war brewing? Big battles ahead? Where's my sword? I need to sharpen my sword."

My council leapt forward in unison with their outstretched arms, all shouting "No!" at once.

"What?"

Pherric gave me his best brotherly grin. "I do not know much at this time. So, we shall remain calm until we know all the details, your highness." By *we*, he meant *me*.

"And what we do know is this," Pherric continued. "My spy in the Scholomance discovered that the Atlanteans made an incursion into Cíbola and swarmed the Godsribbon Castle. The Scholomance warriors must have been overcome."

"How do you know?"

"Because it is believed that the magic of the gods was used."

The ring around Tir Na. The World Serpent. *Jörmungandr*. I remembered the sterile chill of the ring station. Waking up suspended in air, floating over a planet I thought I recognized. The elevator ride that lasted an eternity down to the surface. The day Pherric pulled me into this wild, terrifying world.

"Did they bring someone here?"

"That is not known."

I pondered the scenario. Why would Atlantis need someone from Earth? Or maybe they were planning an invasion of Earth? No. That made zero sense. "Are they still there? Occupying the castle?"

Braylor chimed in. "I have sent out a message to have our scouts in the area investigate."

"Okay," I paced the room. "How long will that take?"

"Several days, at a minimum. Perhaps a week."

"A week? We can't wait that long!"

"We can. And we will," Braylor said gently, already reading the look in my eyes—the *let's go right now and maybe die but it'll be epic* look. He knew I wanted to rush off to Cíbola, finger guns a blazin'.

But a really scary thought crossed my mind. I looked at everyone. "I need the room. Everyone out except Pherric."

Kasuma and Braylor glanced at each other, but the rest of them shuffled away.

"What bothers you?" Pherric leaned against the wooden desk, dropping down to my height.

"You have been to my world."

"Yes."

"And you've seen all the amazing technology there. All of their... magic."

"It was quite overwhelming, I admit. What are you thinking?"

I stopped pacing, pointing my finger at his chest. "What if that's why they went there? To steal that magic? Weapons that could destroy cities. End wars. *Win* wars."

Pherric didn't flinch. "It is unwise to leap to conclusions. And even if it were true, what could we do until we know more?"

"That's your answer?" I snapped. "Do nothing?"

"I know patience is not your strength—"

"There *is* something we could do! *We* could go. Ride out now, intercept them before they return. At least *try*!"

He straightened. "It would take days to simply prepare. Travel alone would take the better part of two weeks. They may already be gone."

...I mean, he had a point. But I didn't *have* to admit it.

"We simply must let our scouts learn more and report back."

"Braylor and I could easily slip outta here and be on the road before dark. We'd pack light and ride hard non-stop until we—"

"Your highness... Finley. No. We cannot risk you, out on the road, without your knights. And what would you two do upon arriving? Take on possibly the entire army of Atlantis? In a sufficient number that they were able to defeat the finest soldiers from the Scholomance?"

Well, when he said it all that way... But I crossed my arms and pouted. I hate it when I don't get my way. That should be one of the perks of being the goddamn queen.

8

I Am Genevieve.

Genevieve

I don't even know where to start.

For a hot minute, I thought all this was just some wild, messed-up nightmare. The kind that scares the shit out of you but you shake off and laugh about later. Nope. When that wore off, I figured maybe I'd lost my damn mind. Still, no way was I admitting that to Jonathan. Or anybody. That's how you get people looking at you like you're fragile. I am not fragile.

Thing is... it all felt too real. The air carried a smell I couldn't catalog—like rain and metal, and something almost sweet. And pain? Pain was pain here. You can't fake that. So yeah, after a while, I knew I wasn't imagining it and I wasn't crazy. But making sense of it? Good luck with that.

The simple truth was, we were on Tir Na. Another damn planet. And yeah... I was scared. Heart-in-my-throat scared. But that's not the part people get to see. Ever. My job was to keep moving, keep breathing, keep my chin up.

My plan was to do what Jonathan suggested: learn the lay of the land. Scope it out. Get some guns—or whatever passed for weapons here. Then storm that old castle, steal us a spaceship, and bounce right back to Earth.

Simple, right? (Lies. All lies.)

But walking through Cíbola with Ramil made pretending harder by the mile. From a distance, it tried to pass for Earth. Up close? No. Plants grew too tall. Strange colors were dialed all the way up. I heard new sounds that did not belong on my workout playlist. Fat bugs clicked, intense and rhythmic, talking their smack.

And then… the creatures.

That's when it hit me. This was real.

First, there was this bear. Or something shaped like one. Only bigger. Twice as big. No fur—just smooth, thick gray skin with the texture of old leather. It stood knee-deep in a river, scooping fish in paws the size of my head and snapping them hard enough to spray water across the bank. It never even glanced our way.

Thank God.

Then the fox. Three tails fanned out behind it, all gold and fire-bright, swishing in slow, controlled arcs. The fur trapped sunlight and refused to give it back. It moved liquid-smooth, silent, deliberate. Dark eyes sharp enough to cut. I swear it looked straight at me, as if it knew something I didn't.

We passed a field, and that's where we saw the Behemoths. Ramil called them that, like it was no big deal, but they were woolly mammoths built by someone with a gym obsession. Massive. Tusks curled like ivory spears. Shaggy coats rippled with each step. The ground thudded when they walked.

And their cows?

Oh no. Not cows. Bicorn, Ramil said. Two thick black horns. Faces that were… wrong. Too human—not in a cute way. In a *this thing is assessing my soul and remembers my breakfast* way. Gave me the creeps.

I didn't even realize my mouth was hanging open half the time until Jonathan nudged me. Meanwhile, he was losing his damn mind, peppering Ramil with questions. Me? I snapped my face back into neutral every time. No way I was letting either of them think I couldn't handle this.

I was going to survive Tir Na. I had no choice. I had a full-ass life waiting for me—fame, money, flashing lights. Runways. Commercials. I was going to be a supermodel. An actress.

And if this planet thought it could stop me?

Good luck, baby.

We finally saw something resembling civilization when we skirted a city. At first, I thought I heard a sound from a mighty river. Then I caught a glint of something bright between the trees and broke into a run.

Ramil was not happy.

"Stop!"

I ignored him, and broke through the last of the trees. And went still.

This giant city sat high on a mountain that split a river clean in two, its rooftops blazing gold in the sun. Not accents—entire towers, domes, walls. Gold everywhere, poured over the place and left to harden. Terraces carved into the mountainside held villages, orchards, neat fields stacked one atop another. The only way in or out was a narrow, guarded bridge stretching to the far valley wall.

Even from here, I could hear it—the hum of voices, the clang of metal, carts rumbling over stone. Tiny figures crossed the bridge in both directions, vanishing into gates or spilling into the valley beyond.

It was alive.

Jonathan finally caught up, wide-eyed and gasping. Ramil followed, looking like we'd dragged him through his personal hell.

"What is that?" Jonathan asked.

"The city of Quivira."

I tilted my head. "And all that gold? Real or just very committed paint?"

"The gold is real."

"What?!"

Ramil kicked at the dirt, sending up flecks of, you guessed it, gold. "Gold is plentiful here. Pretty, but too soft to be of real use."

Jonathan was too busy wheezing to pay attention.

"Come," Ramil ordered. "We have far to go before nightfall."

Part of me wanted to sprint down there, find the nearest cops, and get this guy arrested for kidnapping. But one look at Jonathan—still gasping, pale, barely standing—had me shelving that plan.

"Hey," I said, stepping in front of Ramil. He had the height advantage, but I squared my shoulders. "What exactly do these people you're taking us to want with Jonathan?"

"You will find out."

"No." I lifted my chin. "You will tell me now. Are we in danger?" I shot Jonathan a look. "Or do they just need him for a virgin sacrifice?"

"Hey," Jonathan protested.

"Relax, I'm kidding," I lied.

"You will be protected by, and in service to, the Scholomance," Ramil said evenly. "You both possess certain... gifts valuable to the protection of Tir Na."

"Yeah, that's nice and vague." I crossed my arms. "And no more 'all will be revealed' crap. Talk to us. You'd want the same."

He sighed. "You have seen what the mindforms can do. The Basilisk. The shadows I created that the hellhounds chased—"

Jonathan cut in. "Wait. The Basilisk isn't real?"

"Oh, it exists. But the one chasing you was created by my mind. Memory given form."

"And the hellhounds?"

"They were real. Otherwise, I'd have had no reason to save you with the—"

"Mindforms. Got it." I pointed at his head. "You can just... build things up here?"

"I can. And through our research of your world, we believe Jonathan may possess greater aptitude than many of our own."

Jonathan's eyes went wide, pride creeping in where fear should've lived. "Me?"

"So are you gonna explain?" He glanced at me. "What the hell are mindforms?"

Ramil did. And honestly? It sounded like something a therapist would sell you for two hundred bucks a session.

Every thought you've ever had—every memory, idea, or violent daydream—leaves behind a thread of energy. Invisible. Persistent. Those threads don't fade; they tangle through the world. Most people never notice. The trained ones feel the vibrations. Tug the right strand. Turn someone else's thought into their own.

Creepy, right?

Strong emotions make the threads hum. Anyone can stumble onto them by accident. Those gut feelings you've had? That's leftover thought-energy from someone who felt too much fifty years ago. And if you're trained? You don't just borrow memories. You project them. Full scenes. People. Living constructs pulled from the mind and let loose in reality.

"Not magic," he insisted.

Bullshit. But it worked. We'd seen it.

Jonathan was eating it up, firing questions nonstop. Me? I was scanning exits, angles, contingencies.

I cut Jonathan off. "Can your mindforms get us to the Scholomance? Because my feet are filing a formal complaint."

Ramil offered a rare half-smile. "No. But transportation has been arranged."

"When?"

"A few days."

I didn't love it. But it was more than his usual smoke and mirrors. Still, every step carried us deeper into someone else's plan—one we hadn't agreed to, weren't steering, and might not survive.

And if Ramil's "few days" meant what I thought it did, we were running out of time to figure out whose trap we were walking into—and how not to get crushed by it.

9

Our Final Destination

Genevieve

I did a photo shoot in Spain once, on the beach at Playa de Ses
Illetes in Formentera. The photographer was a total dirtbag, but
the place itself was gorgeous. Cíbola reminded me of that trip
almost immediately. Spain had this way of looking postcard-perfect but
overexposed, as the colors bled together from too much sun and time. Soft
around the edges. Still unfairly beautiful.

Cíbola was the same. Low, dusty hills leaned toward one another,
conspiring in silence. Scraggly trees clung to life in soil that looked ground
down to bone. The air tasted dry, but beneath it ran something green and
fierce—wild herbs tough enough to survive out here. Rosemary, maybe.
Or something meaner. Color flashed where it shouldn't: stubborn blooms
wedged into rock, thriving out of spite. And the light—slow, golden,
suspended—made it feel as though time had forgotten to keep moving.

I held onto those small details to stay sane.

Because walking for days on end without decent cross-trainers was
neither simple nor sane.

The farther we traveled, the landscape softened. The brittle crunch
beneath my boots gave way to springier ground, and this world finally
decided to show me mercy. Dust gave way to sweetness. There were

orchards, wildflowers, grass that remembered how to bend without cutting you. Hills rolled into pastures. Scrub became trees that cast real shade. Even the light shifted, trading gold bravado for something quieter and silvered. Most of Cíbola felt scorched and unforgiving. This place felt capable of holding you.

The way your momma used to do.

"We are now in the kingdom of Ogun," Ramil said, as if he were dropping the weather report.

"Okay?" I blinked at him. "And that means... what?"

"We are closer to our destination."

"In other news," I muttered, "water is wet."

That one landed. A bushy eyebrow rose, and for half a second, I thought I saw the faintest crack of a smirk across those perpetually dry lips.

"I have an ally in this land. One willing to make a great sacrifice," he added, all cryptic, because that should clear everything right up.

Jonathan was dragging by then. Honestly, so was I. Endless hills, no towns, no villages, not even a decent road. "This better be about the transportation you promised," I said.

He gave one of his single nods and led us off the trail into the trees. Eventually, we hit a small clearing. Ramil dropped to the ground, eyes closed because he was either meditating or beaming psychic nonsense to his mystery contact. Jonathan and I collapsed as we always did: fucking exhausted. My legs screamed, my feet were blistered, and my back was in open revolt. Ramil? Fresh from a day at the spa.

We shared water from his animal-skin bag. Jonathan gathered a few "safe" fruits Ramil pointed out. Think berries, if berries were salty and reminded you of licking a rock. But I was hungry enough to deal.

Then, we heard a rustling. Steps. My fight-or-flight was leaning hard toward flight when Ramil lifted a hand for me to stay put.

A woman emerged from the trees, dark-skinned like me, jet-black hair, green robe, tattoos climbing her skin. Fewer than Ramil's, but still enough to make me decide I wasn't getting any ink here. Not great for the modeling career.

They did some forearm-grab handshake, exchanged zero actual words, and she vanished back into the brush. Seconds later: crashing, branches snapping, grunts too deep to be human.

And then... yeah. What I saw shook me.

Two massive horse creatures lumbered into the clearing, roped together. Calling them "horses" was like calling a tank a big bicycle. Horns and all armor-hide and muscle, eyes glaring because you knew they'd stomp you just for standing wrong.

"These are karkadanns," Ramil said. "They will take us to Pandæmonia."

Jonathan stepped forward with the wide-eyed curiosity of a child at a petting zoo. I yanked him back. "You want us to *ride* those?"

They were saddled, if you could call a blanket and a few straps a saddle. Up close, they reminded me of a rhino, only taller, broader, and way less likely to ignore you.

Ramil thanked the tattooed woman, who vanished again, and vaulted onto one beast and motioned for us to follow. I touched its hide, expecting cold. Instead, heat radiated through my palm.

"You're gonna need my help," I told Jonathan.

"No, I've got it," he said, then attempted to mount it and failed spectacularly. The karkadann sidestepped in silent judgment.

He nodded sheepishly. I cupped my hands and launched him up.

"And now you," Ramil said.

"Nope." I grabbed the lead rope. "I'm good for now."

He didn't argue. Just kicked his mount forward, forcing me to follow, towing Jonathan and the walking tank behind me.

Half an hour later, Jonathan offered to switch. I refused. He called me stubborn. I gave him a look, then finally climbed up behind him, pretending I wasn't relieved.

Ramil glanced back, smug as hell. Whatever. I was too tired to care.

We saw more than a few ridiculously crazy things on the way to Pandæmonia—one of them being a herd of real, live dinosaurs, just chilling in the wild and grazing on leaves. They actually had them here on this planet! *Dinosaurs!* Ramil called them *torodans.* Which he said meant thunder lizards. No shit, Ramil. By that point, though? Even dinosaurs couldn't mess with my mind.

It took us a solid week of riding to make it to this new kingdom. The hills got steeper and the trees darker. Evergreens with silver-dusted needles caught the light. The grass had these weird blue lines, the streams ran clear, and every now and then something out there screamed. Beautiful.

Our journey near the academy led us to a huge body of water.

"Is that an ocean?" Jonathan asked.

"No," replied Ramil, weary of our endless questions. "That is the Lake Acherousia."

I'd heard people brag about how the Great Lakes were basically inland oceans, but hearing and seeing are two different things. This wasn't a lake. This was a whole personality. Small waves slapped the shore in lazy, smug little rolls. The water was this dark, sullen gray that swallowed the horizon, and there was something... unsettling about it. The kind of unsettling where your brain starts whispering, *you don't want to know what's under there.* And it was right. I really didn't.

We kept trotting our karks, their hooves crunching on the pebbled sand, until the shore started to twist into something out of a Gothy landscape painting. Massive stone rocks shot up—looking like long, scary fingers— and cast long shadows across the water.

Tucked in beside the water was a wall: a monster barricade of round gray stones, stacked so perfectly it screamed this is where you die in a very tasteful, architectural way. It didn't look built as much as conjured.

Peeking over the wall was a castle so dark it might've been carved straight out of midnight. Pointy spires soared upward and scratched holes in the gray clouds, and the stone sucked out what little light dared to touch it. Vines, thick and twisted things, had slithered over every surface, creeping into cracks and wrapping window frames.

Black towers loomed, joined by long, narrow halls lined with windows that reflected nothing but your own queasiness. The whole place gave off predator energy. It was all too still, too quiet, the kind that makes your skin itch.

If someone told me this was the set for *Vampire School: The Tuition's Higher Than Your Soul*, I wouldn't just believe them, I'd ask where craft services was. Because, you know, if I was about to get murdered by a bunch of immortal Goths, I'd at least want a sandwich first.

"And before you are able to ask, yes... this is the Scholomance Academy," explained Ramil as he dismounted his creature. "Our final destination."

"Welcome to Hell," murmured Jonathan.

Ramil seemed perplexed. "No... Hell is about two hundred axims to the east."

Naturally.

10

The Principal's Office

Jonathan

Calling the Scholomance Academy intimidating would have been a serious understatement.

I'm a scientist by training. Someone who prefers to build understanding from evidence, pattern recognition, and repeatable results. But the moment the academy came into view, logic became irrelevant. The unease was immediate and visceral, bypassing reason entirely. It was the kind of response you felt before you had language for it.

On the road, Genevieve had been unusually quiet. I, on the other hand, had been asking Ramil questions whenever he allowed it, which was rare and never with enthusiasm. Still, I couldn't stop myself. I was gathering data, however fragmented, trying to assemble the beginnings of a hypothesis about what awaited us. And about what awaited her.

What I kept circling back to were his *mindforms*. In theory, the persistence of energy made sense—energy could not be created or destroyed, only transformed. But the way Ramil manipulated it went far beyond anything I could map onto known models. It presented as magic, a category science has never been able to define in a useful way, let alone measure. From what he'd hinted, I was expected to learn this myself. The idea unsettled me. It also intrigued me, which bothered me more.

But I wasn't convinced this was the place where I wanted to learn it.

As we approached, a group of tall, sword-bearing soldiers stepped forward when a thick wooden gate creaked open. Their polished silver helmets flashed in the light, each crowned with a dark red plume. Over fine silver mesh armor, they wore fitted white smocks emblazoned with a bold red X—a combination that looked ceremonial until you noticed the reinforced joints and the condition of their weapons. Black trousers with a narrow red stripe completed the uniform, giving the group a precise, almost mathematical symmetry.

They formed two lines flanking the path inward. It might have been intended as a welcome. It read more as containment.

Ramil moved ahead without hesitation. Genevieve followed, her shoulders locked, her stride controlled, as if braced for an attack—or already planning an escape. I stayed close. Since leaving that distant golden city, Ramil had deliberately steered us away from villages, roads, and any sign of other people. These guards were the first we'd seen in days. And here, we were entirely dependent on his goodwill.

Inside, Ramil turned and extended his arms. "This is Scholomance. You are our guests here."

Genevieve made a sound that landed somewhere between a grunt and a scoff.

"Your training will begin in the morning," he continued. "But we have lived on berries and wild game for days. I suspect you are ready for a proper meal."

He dispatched several men in green robes to prepare something for us.

The foyer beyond was cool and dim, carrying the faint scent of smoke, old paper, and something sharper—crushed herbs or ground minerals. The floor was paved in massive slabs of black stone veined with silver, polished enough to reflect the light of iron sconces mounted along the walls. Between them hung tapestries in deep reds and golds, depicting scenes I assumed were historical, though none I recognized.

Ahead, a pale marble staircase split at a landing and vanished into shadowed corridors above. Beneath it, an arched passage hinted at additional rooms beyond.

"This way," Ramil said, suddenly more cordial than he'd been on the road.

We climbed. He followed a step behind us.

Halfway up, Genevieve turned. "If we're eating, I really want to clean up first. I smell like shit."

I winced. She had nerve. And I couldn't help admiring it.

"You will be shown to your quarters soon," Ramil replied. "But first, you must meet someone."

He surged past us and up the remaining steps, leaving Genevieve and me to exchange a look that communicated exactly how little we liked that phrasing.

He led us through towering double doors into a room that felt designed to enforce scale and permanence. The Scholomance had existed long before anyone entering it—and would remain long after.

"Preceptor," Ramil announced. "Our new guests have arrived."

Shadows pooled in the corners, broken only by thin light filtering through a high, arched window. Shelves of leather-bound tomes rose nearly to the vaulted ceiling, their spines stamped with unfamiliar symbols, interrupted by alcoves holding glass domes and sealed jars. At the far end, a massive desk of dark wood dominated the room, scattered with scrolls, ledgers, and delicate instruments that resembled relics more than tools.

Behind it stood the Preceptor.

His black hair, streaked with silver, framed a face, neck, and hands covered in intricate black tattoos that flowed across his skin in precise, interlocking patterns. They were even more elaborate than Ramil's. He wore a dark green robe and was bent over parchment, scratching methodical lines with a quill before dipping it into an inkwell shaped into a coiled serpent.

When he finally looked up, his gaze carried the same quality as the room itself—measured, evaluating, and utterly unconcerned with my comfort.

"Ah," he said, setting the quill aside with deliberate care. "The ones you spoke of so highly."

He came around the desk at an unhurried pace, examining us with the detachment of someone assessing resources rather than people. Up close, the tattoos caught the light in crisp lines, too structured to be decorative.

He was almost as tall as Ramil, which I was already filing away as a pattern on this planet. Gravity. The lessened gravity on this world meant taller people.

"Yes, Preceptor," Ramil said.

The man stopped in front of me. His eyes held mine a fraction too long. "The supposed prodigy?"

"That is my belief, sir."

Being called a prodigy didn't spark pride. It sparked dread. In my world, expectations came with mentorship and margin for failure. Here, the word sounded less like praise and more like a justification for whatever came next.

"Hmm." He stepped past me and turned his attention to Genevieve. "And this one?"

"We're right here," she said defiantly.

I closed my eyes for a moment. I was starving and increasingly convinced we were about to make a very poor impression.

The Preceptor ignored her, continuing his appraisal with the same clinical indifference. "Rather small, isn't she?"

"Again. Right here." She was going to get us killed.

"What she lacks in size, she makes up for in determination," Ramil replied, shifting subtly closer to her.

A faint chuckle escaped the Preceptor. "I can sense that."

He turned back to his desk. "I do not have high expectations, Ramil. But perhaps you will surprise me."

"That is my intent."

As we were led back out, my heart finally dropped from my throat. The encounter felt uncomfortably similar to being summoned to a principal's office—except here, I had no doubt the consequences could be permanent.

One thing was certain: I had no desire to be called back into that room anytime soon.

11

I'm Not a Killer

Jonathan

Our dinner at the Scholomance Academy was... well, different. Ramil led us into their Great Hall, a huge space lined with long wooden tables. A few workers moved quietly around us, stacking plates and wiping down surfaces. Leftovers from a meal we clearly had missed. We took seats at the far end, Ramil settling himself at the head in his throne.

"I am sure you have many questions, as you always do," he said with a tired glance. "But I am famished and would prefer to enjoy a proper repast."

The way he spoke always caught my attention. Not quite Shakespeare, but close. It was formal, old-fashioned, almost courtly. Paired with the medieval-style clothes and the swords hanging at people's belts, it was easy to imagine I'd stepped back in time. Still, I couldn't shake the feeling that this world should be further along. If Tir Na was as old as Earth, why had its advancement in technology stalled here? And yet... they had the means to transport us across worlds. They had a massive ring orbiting the planet that could hide it completely. That's not "stalled." That's something else entirely.

Then there was the moon. I hadn't thought much of it at first, but on the trip from Cíbola to the Academy, and it went full... I realized it might not be real. On closer inspection, it looked smooth, metallic, and bigger than ours back home. That would mean longer days here, stronger storms, wilder tides. If it was artificial... that would take an unimaginable amount of power and engineering.

Not from anyone I'd met here. No one on this "backwards" world could manage that. Which left me with one possibility—someone, or something, older and far more advanced had been here before. And they left their fingerprints in the sky.

"So, Jonathan," Genevieve said suddenly, breaking the silence. "Do you think I'd make a good warrior?"

Servants moved around us in silence, setting down plates with ritual precision. A small, seared portion of... something like meat, a mound of pale grains that resembled rice, and a handful of dark leafy greens. Nothing extravagant, but nothing familiar either.

I knew her well enough by now to catch the subtext: this was her way of asking questions without directly challenging Ramil.

"Well," I said carefully, "you might be on the small side for some of the people we've met here."

"Small, but... determined, remember?"

"True," I said, smiling despite the tension creeping into my chest. "True."

Ramil leaned back from his plate, exhaling to grant himself patience. "Ask your questions."

Genevieve didn't hesitate. "Why me? You made a special trip to New York to kidnap me. He's the prodigy," she jabbed a finger in my direction. "I'm just... extra baggage."

"As I have stated," Ramil said, his voice heavy, "you are both vital to our plan. A number of kingdoms are in grave danger. And we are—"

"Yeah, yeah," she cut in. "You keep saying the same thing. A danger from what? What is this plan? And how can we possibly help? Don't you already have warriors and... mind-formy people who already know what they're doing?"

His gaze cooled. "All of this will—"

"If you say, 'all will be revealed,' I swear to god…"

A small smirk tugged at his mouth, but he let the moment pass and returned to his meal. Genevieve leaned back, folding her arms tight, eyes on me like it was my turn to try.

I set my utensil down, heart thudding. "What she's asking, Ramil, is for more detail. We need to know what to expect."

He chewed slowly, then wiped his mouth with the back of his hand. "Why must everything be instantaneous with you? Have you no patience? Your questions will be answered, rest assured."

I leaned forward, locking eyes with him. "You kidnapped us. You took us from our world. We don't know anything about Tir Na, about this kingdom, about this school… and nothing about this plan. We've been with you for weeks. We're scared, Ramil."

He didn't look at me right away. Instead, he stared at the food in front of him before finally speaking. "You are to be trained as a mage. Only a small few can read mindforms. Fewer still can control them. And all of the senior mages here have determined you may be more capable than any of them."

"Me?" I asked. "Why? How could you know that?"

"Through mindforms, of course."

It sent a chill down my spine. "You mean you could read my mind from across the sun? Out of billions of people on Earth?"

"Using practices you do not yet understand," he said evenly, "and combining the abilities of the most gifted mages, after lengthy deliberations of several seasons, you were our optimal candidate."

I hated the way "optimal" sounded in his mouth.

Genevieve's voice cut in sharply. "What about me? Why me?"

Ramil's eyes flickered. "Ah, yes. I have been… misleading about your role in our plan."

"I knew it," she muttered.

"We believe you are perfect to train as an assassin."

The air seemed to thicken between us.

"And you will have the ability to do what no one else on this world can."

Genevieve gasped. "You want me to–to kill someone?!"

"In all likelihood, no. You are a meaningful contingency... in case Jonathan fails."

Despite her dark skin, Genevieve's face went pale. I could almost feel her pulse quicken from across the table.

Ramil stood, pushing his chair back with deliberate weight. "I will escort you to your quarters."

I shoveled a few bites into my mouth, but Genevieve didn't touch her food. She sat motionless, her lips parted, eyes fixed somewhere far away. "There's no way," she whispered. "No way in hell."

I went to her, resting a hand on her shoulders. She didn't move until I helped her stand. When she looked at me, there was no bravado in her voice, only fear. "I'm not a killer, Jonathan. I—I can't do that."

"I know," I told her quietly. "We'll figure this out. Together."

We followed Ramil from the hall, his stride brisk, purposeful. Shadows from the torchlight stretched long over the stone floor. After several turns and a climb up a narrow stairwell, he stopped at a heavy wooden door and opened it. I started to go in with her, but his strong hand held me back.

"This is her room," he said.

Genevieve turned to look at me, but the door swung shut between us. A key appeared in his hand and he locked her door. She called my name.

"I thought you said we were your guests?" I snapped.

"You are," he replied without looking at me. "But there are many... dangers in the Academy. I cannot have you wandering off and injuring yourself."

He opened the room farther down the hall for me. "Your training begins early in the morning."

The lock clicked before I could answer.

Our hospitable welcome at the Scholomance Academy was over. And in its place, the walls had begun to close in.

12

Bad News Gets Worse? (HINT: it always does)

Finley

It was late at night, and I was hanging out in the kitchen behind my keep. That was where all the important statecraft happened. I was parked cross-legged on one of the prep tables because the head cook wasn't there to give me that "get your royal butt off my workspace" glare. Perks of ruling the kingdom: strategic table-sitting.

I was dictating sandwich assembly to the undercook, a culinary general in full command, while swapping scandalous gossip updates with the servers and cupbearers.

"Wait, wait," I stopped mid-instruction, whirling on the baker. "She was with Siserich the whole time? And the brother, Berich, never caught on?!" I slapped my knees so hard it echoed. "Oh my god, that is hilarious!"

The undercook held up the cutting board, full of pride. It was her holy relic. "Meat is ready, your majesty."

"Perfect. Bread first. Now the meat. Good. Cheese next." I watched as she poured on her mystery sauce and made a dozen perfect little creations.

"All right, everybody try one."

They all stared at the plate like it was cursed, but hey, I was the queen.

They each took a bite. Eyebrows shot up. Nods all around. Success!

"They're good, right?" More nods. "They're called *sandwiches*."

The undercook lit up. "We shall name them after you, your highness!"

I immediately imagined bards singing about *The Sandwich Queen of Tir Na.*

She came, she saw, she sliced the loaf,
With humble hands and royal oath;
No blade, no crown did rule her reign—
But bread and fillings, stacked and plain.

I wanted to throw myself in the moat. "Absolutely not."

The pantler jumped in, holding up his treasure. "Yes, from here on this delight shall be known as *The Finley!*"

I leapt off the table as if it were on fire. "Stop. No! They are sandwiches. Not Finleys. Sandwiches, people!"

We were all laughing when Luchar stormed in, bellowing, "There you are!" And just like that—poof. Laughter dead. Luchar: the royal fun-slayer since year one.

"What did I do now?" I whined, because with Luchar it was always something.

He staggered into the doorway, bent over with his hands braced on his knees, breathing hard from his run across the length of the kingdom apparently. "I... have been..."

"Looking for me everywhere, yeah, I can tell."

He leaned back, inhaling deep. "Messenger... has returned... from Godsribbon Castle... your majesty."

"Messenger?!" My voice cracked up an octave. "There you go, burying the big story again!"

I was already sprinting for the door as he wheezed, "I have been trying... to tell you..."

Bursting into the night air, I tore across the courtyard toward the keep. The startled guards jumped aside, pulling the heavy doors open for me.

My boots skidded on the stone as I came to a halt in the Great Hall.

Inhale and exhale. Shoulders back. Queen-face on.

I strode to the far end where my inner circle was gathered around a makeshift planning table. Pherric, Braylor, Kasuma, and my knight commander Sandulf all looked up with that mix of amusement and curiosity that always made me suspicious.

Luchar stumbled in behind me, half-dead from his sprint.

There was a messenger, standing there next to them and nervously waiting. He was young, dark-haired, wide-eyed and clearly out of his depth. Maps lay sprawled across the table, one showing both Cíbola and the islands of Atlantis in detail.

"She was in the kitchen, wasn't she?" Braylor asked Luchar, who nodded between gasps. "I told you," Braylor mumbled with a smirk.

I started to reply, but he pressed a finger to my lips. "You hate me. I know."

I smacked his hand away and turned to the messenger. "What news?"

He glanced nervously at the others. Pherric gave him the nod.

"Yes, your majesty," he began, swallowing hard. "I have returned from Cíbola... with news."

We already knew the Atlanteans had taken Godsribbon Castle. A spy had confirmed it a week ago, but after that—nothing.

"Go on," I urged.

"The spy reports the Atlanteans used... the instrument in the castle. That is how he referred to it. I do not know what that is—"

"That's fine. Super top-secret, hush-hush stuff. What else?"

"They withdrew from the castle after two days."

Sandulf frowned. "Withdrew? Why?"

I already had a guess. "They retrieved someone," I told Pherric. He agreed.

Sandulf didn't know about the space elevator or the ring station above the planet.

"Retrieved someone... from where?"

"Need-to-know, Sandy," I whispered. He made that face I loved because he hated it when I called him that.

"But," the messenger added, "the Atlanteans have returned, your majesty. They are fortifying, patrolling, bringing in provisions. It appears they mean to stay at the castle."

That sent a ripple of unease across the room.

Braylor shrugged. He had no idea. Pherric shook his head as well. Nothing. But Kasuma's eyes met mine—focused, calculating.

"Kasuma?"

She drew me aside, away from the others. "What if they used the gods' magic to bring another from your world, and hid their soldiers so the person would not see them? Once the person was away, they returned to ensure no one could send them back."

"Or to keep the person from returning themselves..." I knew that's what I'd wanted when I first arrived on Tir Na.

"Yes."

"But why?"

"That is what we must find out."

I wanted to tell her to fly there herself: slip inside, overhear their plans, and vanish before they knew she was there. But her wing was still damaged from our final battle with Kane in Kunlun. Even with Pherric's best healers and his own magic, there'd been no fixing it.

I slid back to my spot at the war table, the map spread out before me, surgical and unforgiving. My eyes locked on Atlantis. Many axims off the coast of Cíbola. My guts twisted. Was this the start of an invasion? A test run to snag the southern tip of the continent? Or something worse... a full-on land grab?

"All right," I said to the wide-eyed kid. "What is the size of their occupying force?"

"I was told there are less than a hundred warriors maintaining a presence."

"Any news of additional troops amassing?" I asked, keeping my voice steady.

The messenger fidgeted, sweat beading on his brow. "No, sir... I mean, no, your majesty."

Not reassuring. At all.

I tapped the map. "What about Cíbola? Any word from them?"

He shook his head again. "We have not seen any response."

"Oh, what about the Scholomance? Their warriors were the ones guarding that damn place."

Pherric leaned over, lips pressed tight, finger tapping against his chin. "Not that I have heard."

Great. The big scary mage-school has their soldiers onsite, they get wrecked, and then—radio silence. Comforting.

"What are we supposed to do?"

Pherric started to speak to the boy, then turned to me. "We send word to our spy. Tell him to watch for additional troops. And any more coming from the sea as well. Ships may already be on the way."

Pherric had to remind himself he was no longer in charge. I was the one with the crown. Unfortunately.

I caught Braylor's eye. He winked, big as ever, while Sandulf gave a clipped nod. My stomach sank deeper.

"Fine. Let's do that," I said.

I grabbed the messenger by the shoulders, staring him down as if panic alone could glue my words into his brain. "Find out what they're doing—land, sea, everything. If our man down there needs backup, tell him to hire more eyes. People he trusts."

The boy bobbed his head so hard I worried it might roll right off.

"Luchar? Cash." I didn't bother hiding the irritation in my voice.

My chancellor grumbled but set coins into my hand. I pressed them into the messenger's palm. "This should cover it."

"Yes, your majesty!" He ran out like the room was on fire. Honestly, same.

Once he was gone, I turned back. "Kane's little war bled every kingdom dry. We're still limping. And Atlantis knows it. None of us are back at full strength. Not even close."

Braylor folded his massive arms, eyeing the map. "And you believe they will take advantage."

"Uh, yeah." I jabbed a finger at Quivira. "If the Cíbolans aren't lifting a finger to defend themselves, then—"

"Then they may already be allied," Pherric cut in smoothly, stealing the words from my mouth.

I scowled but nodded. "Exactly. And if Lord Diago's mixed up in this... and let's be real, that guy's due for a cosmic-level beatdown from me—then Cíbola's a staging ground. We have to take action, or they'll pour in from there, spread north, and before you know it—"

"No," Braylor said firmly.

I shot him my best stink-eye. "Excuse me?"

"Your majesty," he added, a bit too playfully for my liking.

"Quelle surprise?" Which is French for *Oh, really? Fuck you.* Well, not really, but...

Sandulf, the diplomat of the group, chimed in. "What Braylor means, your majesty, is we cannot march into another land uninvited. If the Atlanteans are welcome there, it is not our fight. If the Scholomance wants retribution, it is theirs to claim."

I crossed my arms, red flaring in my cheeks. "But from there they can march on Ogun. Elysium. Hell itself—though, honestly, who'd want it? Point is, they'll be at our door next!"

"And when that day comes," Sandulf said calmly, "we will meet them. At our border. Until then, our duty is here. To Irkalla."

"Aaagh!" The sound ripped out of me, half growl, half scream. I spun away, fists clenched.

Braylor stepped close, lowering his voice. "Your people need you here. That is your burden."

I wheeled back on him. "Don't you see? This is exactly what happened with Kane! Everyone gripping their borders until he nearly crushed us all. If we don't stop them now—"

Braylor's voice was maddeningly reasonable. "We do not know their plan. By the time word returns, they may already be gone from the castle."

I jabbed a finger at him. "Stop making sense!"

He had the nerve to smile and brush a stray curl out of my face. And dammit, it worked. It always worked.

I pulled Braylor close. "Hey. Can I get a bard?"

"A what?"

"You know. A bard. Someone to sing songs about my epic battles and *incredible* reign as queen."

"No," he said flatly. "He would drive you insane in under five minutes."

He had a point.

"Yeah," I sighed. "True. Also, he'd absolutely write a sandwich song."

That earned me a look I definitely earned.

He drifted back to the table, talking strategy and pushing little blocks around thinking that would save us.

I stared at the map, ice crawling down my spine. A storm was coming. I knew it. And none of this—*none* of this—was going to end well.

13

Quand Les Poules Auront Des Dents

Finley

After a night of tossing, turning, and mumbling curses into my pillow, I woke in the morning to find Braylor missing from our bed. I dragged myself up, pulling on a linen chemise and velvet pants—the only perk of having no meetings that day was getting to wear pants.

After pestering a few half-awake servants about the whereabouts of the big guy, I was pointed toward the lower courtyard.

It was a broad space ringed by high walls, sunlight just starting to warm the flagstones.

I'd made a vow in the dark hours of my restless night to *do something*. Atlantis wasn't going to stop at Godsribbon Castle—or Cíbola. No, I had that gnawing certainty in my bones. They were planning bigger, and I was going to stop waiting around for everyone else to catch on.

I found Braylor and Sandulf sparring. And not with blunted sticks either. They were using *real blades*. Steel flashed in the light as Sandulf, smaller but lightning quick, met Braylor's brute strength with careful technique. Braylor looked alive, practically gleeful, every swing reverberating through his huge frame.

When Sandulf spotted me, he stopped instantly and bowed. Braylor, the smug bastard, mopped his sweat with a towel.

"Oh, don't stop for me," I called. "Watching two hot guys beat the crap out of each other with swords is not a bad way to start my day."

Sandulf straightened, looking scandalized. "Your majesty."

"Eh, we are done here," Braylor said, stretching his handsome shoulders. "I needed a workout, and Sandulf is the only one who can keep up with me."

"Other than me," I said, lifting my chin.

He arched a meaty brow, his smirk threatening. "I would imagine your skills have diminished since your... rise to power."

"They have *not*!"

He held out his sword, wickedly heavy. "Then please. Demonstrate."

I grabbed it and instantly regretted every one of my life choices. "Nice try. You're not tricking me into dislocating my shoulder."

Braylor chuckled, then sauntered over to the weapons rack. He plucked a thinner sword free, swung it once to test the balance, and handed it to me pommel-first. "This should suit your weakness. I mean, your highness."

Oh, you know he got the one-finger salute.

I gave it a few test swings, the blade singing as it cut the air. *Much* better. A Kath blade—light, sharp, elegant. Perfect.

Sandulf gave a courteous bow.

"Give me your best, Sandy," I said, planting my feet.

"That is *not* my name," he growled, lunging for my head without warning.

I yelped, barely getting the sword up in time to parry. "Ooooh, struck a nerve, have I?"

Steel *shinged* as we circled each other. My arms burned within the first thirty seconds, and Braylor, ever helpful, decided to coach from the sidelines.

"Keep your feet balanced!"

"Stop lunging!"

"Raise your arm in defense!"

"Stop *talking!*" I shouted, blocking another swing.

At one point, Sandulf swung too wide, his momentum throwing him off balance. I darted in and placed my blade at his throat.

"Excellent, your majesty," he said politely.

But I backed off, shaking my head. "Nope. You let me win. Don't do that, Sandulf."

"I did not—"

"Yes, you did." I threw a finger at him. "I command you, as your queen, to try harder. No pulling punches."

He sighed like a man sentenced to the gallows.

"Come on... *Sandy*."

That did it. He lunged again, a bit more fury this time, and our blades rang out, echoing across the yard. He pressed the attack, eyes blazing, sweat dripping, and suddenly I was very aware that I was *woefully* out of practice. My arms shook, my lungs burned, and my legs were wet spaghetti noodles.

He didn't stop. Good. Because I didn't ask him to.

At last, with a grunt, he batted my blade aside and—before I could recover—slammed an elbow into my jaw. Stars appeared in my eyes, and I landed flat on the flagstones.

His eyes went wide. "By the gods, I apologize!"

I groaned, rubbing my jaw. "Ouch."

Braylor, of course, laughed so hard he nearly doubled over. Slinging his sweaty towel over his shoulder, he sauntered away. "I am famished." Translation: *I was right, you're out of shape.*

Sandulf hauled me back up, frantic. "Your majesty, forgive me! I should resign at once. I will accept any punishment—"

"Hey, relax," I cut in, wincing as I pretended to pop my jaw back into place. "I asked for it. Don't go all dramatic knight on me."

"But—"

"No buts. Oh, and from now on, you're going to train me. Daily. Until I can last more than three minutes without collapsing. And you are never, *ever* allowed to go easy on me again."

He gave a stiff nod, though the corners of his mouth twitched because he wanted to argue.

"Good. Now that I've got you all flustered and guilty, I need you to arrange a little trip. You, me, Braylor, and a handful of your best. We're going to Godsribbon Castle."

His jaw clenched. He knew me too well.

"No. This is not our concern. I will not meddle in another kingdom's affairs, your majesty."

"Yeah, yeah, official rules. But I'm not asking for an invasion. Just... a sneak peek. I need to see with my own eyes."

He lowered his head. "Then I resign. Find another Knight Commander willing to subvert the law. It will not be me."

I threw my hands up. "Sandulf, please! I can't sit here and wait for disaster. By the time we act, it'll be too late! Don't you *see*? I've lived this story before."

He turned away. "Everything will be fine."

I muttered, "*Quand les poules auront des dents.*"

Sandulf blinked. "What does that mean, your highness?"

I clenched my fists. "It means... where I'm from, it's something you say when you don't believe a thing will ever happen. *When chickens have teeth.*"

The word *chickens* clearly derailed him, so I tried again. "When Hell freezes over. When bicorn fly."

He smiled. "Ah, Hell would never freeze over. I understand."

Sandulf's voice dropped into that deep, lecturing tone he always used when he was trying to bash reality into my skull.

"We do not know a great deal about the Atlanteans, my queen. But make no mistake—they are ruthless. And power hungry. They have attempted incursions before. And do not be fooled by the word 'island.' Atlantis is vast. Their navy alone, with their black sails, could blot out the horizon if they chose. And their weapons..." He hesitated, eyes darkening. "Their weapons are said to be unlike anything forged here. Stronger. Deadlier. Entire fleets have been turned back or sent to the ocean floor."

I crossed my arms, heat prickling in my chest. "You're basically proving my point. They're dangerous, and we can't just sit here and twiddle our thumbs while they set up camp!"

He pressed on, ignoring my jab. "I am cautioning you against believing you could slip past such an enemy with a handful of friends and a few guards. Against Atlantis, even the boldest queen would be nothing more than a prize to be claimed."

"So, you won't help?"

He met my eyes, unshaken. "If I remain, I will only agree to send emissaries. In your name. This will provide a warning that we are watching. But I will not risk you."

My blood boiled. Everyone wanted to play by the damn rules. "Emissaries, huh?"

"I believe it the wiser course. If the Atlanteans are aware, our watchfulness may hasten their plan and may lead to a mistake. Then, we may act."

I exhaled, glaring at him. "I need more dumb people around me."

He blinked, confused. "You are accepting my resignation?"

"No! God, no. Just an expression. I'm not happy, that's all."

When Sandulf left me standing there, his words wouldn't let go. An island larger than some kingdoms. A navy that could blot out the horizon. Weapons deadlier than anything we had.

I could almost see it: black sails rising from the sea, and fire raining on Ogun, on Elysium, on us. And all of us too slow, too careful, too blind.

Maybe sneaking to Godsribbon was reckless. But waiting was worse. If Atlantis truly had that kind of power, then when they finally came, we wouldn't stand a chance.

And I couldn't—*wouldn't*—just sit here and let that happen.

14

Fresh Meat

Genevieve

The room Ramil had shoved me into wasn't much of a room at all. There was a sad excuse for a bed leaned crooked against the wall, its legs wobbling, threatening to collapse if I even breathed too hard. A tattered blanket lay crumpled on top, smelling faintly of mildew and dust. There was a window, sure, but the iron bars on the outside reminded me real quick that it wasn't meant for looking out. It was meant for keeping me in. Ramil locked the door behind me, and the sound of the bolt sliding home echoed with finality, a judge's gavel sealing my sentence.

So yeah, it was a prison cell. Let's not pretty it up.

Sleep? Please. Between the hard mattress, the chill creeping up through the floor, and the little detail of being told I was about to be trained as an assassin, my eyelids didn't get much rest. An *assassin*. What the hell did that even mean?

The next morning, the scrape of a key in the lock yanked me upright. My chest tightened, but I forced my back straight, lifted my head. They weren't about to see me fold. Scared or not, I wasn't giving them the satisfaction.

And then the door opened, and my bravado shattered.

An ape walked in. Yes, an ape. But he stood tall and straight, unmistakably man shaped. His face was rough, simian, the kind that makes your instincts scream *this is not normal.* Just like those gorillas at the zoo, his hands were thick and hairy and clutching a key ring. He loomed broader than me, wrapped in a leather tunic over chainmail armor. Black pants, heavy boots, and a jagged scar ran from cheekbone to jaw. Someone had once tried to carve him open and only half-succeeded.

"It is time," he said. His voice was gravel being dragged across stone, and the fact that he spoke at all almost knocked me out of my skin. He looked at me as if *I* were the odd one, because talking apes were just part of everyone's morning routine, right?

"What the fuck is going on? What are you?" My voice came out harsher than I intended. Part fear, part armor.

He grunted, unimpressed. "My name is Thagan. I am to be your instructor. If... you survive the day."

That shut me up. My back pressed hard into the wall, close to melting into it.

"Move," he snarled, menace oozing from every syllable. His patience was already gone. "Now."

I wanted to run, to scream, to fight. Instead, I pushed myself off that bed with all the swagger I could fake. My hands were shaking, but my head stayed high. If this was day one, I wasn't about to give them the satisfaction.

Without another word, Thagan jerked his head and I followed, my boots squeaking against stone as he led me down a hallway that smelled of sweat, mold, and something darker. Blood, maybe. My heart hammered, but I walked with purpose, projecting confidence I did not feel.

He swung open a door that led into a cavern of a room, ceiling so high they could've swallowed a church steeple, sunlight dripping through narrow windows far above. The whole setup screamed gladiator gym meets medieval nightmare. Four circles marked the dirt floor, outlined in white chalk. Every inch of the walls lined with weapons—spears, swords, axes, shields, things I didn't even have names for. Back home, the scariest thing I'd seen at the fitness studio was a guy grunting too loud at the squat rack.

Two giants, easily a head taller than me, were already circling each other, swinging massive hammers. Each clash rang out so hard I felt it in my teeth. Around the room, a half dozen more men—corded legs, arms thick as tree trunks—wrapped ankles, taped wrists, and limbered up, treating this like just another Tuesday.

"This is the training room," Thagan said, his voice carrying weight, pronouncing judgment.

"No shit," I muttered, quiet enough that he probably didn't hear. Or maybe he did and didn't care.

The place buzzed with testosterone, and then there was me. Correction— me and one other woman. But she wasn't company; she was a warning. A white girl with light brown hair, taller, broader, ripped, built of something closer to metal than flesh. She glanced at me once, eyes raking down my frame, then dismissed me with a flicker of contempt. The others did the same, sizing me up and returning to their routines.

Fresh meat. That's what they saw.

I squared my shoulders, biting down the knot of fear in my gut. Fine. Let them think that. They didn't know me yet.

Thagan's rough shove sent me stumbling into one of the chalked circles. My palms burned as I caught myself. "Hey! Watch it!" I snapped.

The ape-man didn't flinch. He plucked a sword from the wall with casual ease and tossed it at me. I jumped aside as it clanged to the ground. No way was I letting myself get skewered before I even started.

He grabbed another, heavier blade and eyed me the way a butcher sizes up a slab of beef. "I want to see what I am working with."

Reluctantly, I picked up the sword. Lighter than I expected, but foreign in my grip. He stepped closer, tapping the tip of his blade toward me.

"Defend yourself."

I lifted mine awkwardly, no clue what I was doing. Thagan jabbed forward. I yelped, dodging, but not fast enough—his blade flicked across my waist, slicing through my tunic, fire shooting up my side.

I clutched the wound, hot blood soaking through my fingers. "What the actual fuck, man!"

His brow furrowed in genuine confusion. "You have never held a sword? You are to train as a warrior and yet—"

"I just got here, dumbass!" I seethed, yanking up the fabric to check the damage. Shallow, but deep enough to sting like hell. Across the room, the woman smirked. *Dead meat*, her eyes said.

Thagan groaned, the sound a parent makes scolding a toddler. "Pick up the sword."

"What?"

"Pick it up," he growled, stalking closer.

"I'm injured!"

"That is but a scratch." His laugh rumbled low, mocking. "You will receive far worse today..."

He flicked my blade into the air with his own, forcing me to catch it. My hand shot out, smacking it straight back to the floor. "And if I refuse?"

His teeth bared in something between a grin and a snarl. "Then I will run you through and feed your body to the boars. You would be soft... a delicious snack."

That burned hotter than the cut. "Who you callin' soft, furball?"

I snatched the sword back up, fury crackling under my skin. No clue what I was doing, but hell if I'd let him see me quit. I kept moving, feet light, drawing on every half-assed sword fight I'd ever seen on TV.

Thagan circled, predatory, swiping lazy blows, testing me. When he pressed harder, I planted the sword against his strike. The grin that spread across his face held both approval and mockery. He feinted left, then right, and before I could track it, my weapon clattered from my hands. Cold steel pressed to my throat.

His breath reeked of raw meat and rot. "I am not sure you are even worthy to feed the boars."

Lovely.

He shoved me back. My body hit the wall, pain shooting through me as I slid down. Blood covered my hand where I clutched my side. My sword skittered under me as he kicked it forward.

"You will strike that post until I return," he ordered, tossing his thick head toward the scarred wooden column in the corner. "I must have a word with Ramil."

He stormed out, leaving me center stage in my own pity parade.

The others barely spared me a glance. Show's over. Back to business.

Except for her. The smirking woman still watched me, lips turned in satisfaction.

Grinding my teeth, I refused to give her the pleasure. I dragged myself up, sword clumsy in my grip, and staggered toward the post. The first strike rattled my arm so hard I nearly dropped it. I exhaled through clenched teeth. Reset. Tried again. Looser this time. Then again. And again.

The steel jarred me, pain throbbing down my side with every hit, but I kept swinging. Not for them. Not even for Thagan.

For me.

Because I'll be damned if I go down as a punk.

When Thagan lumbered back into the death dojo, the shock hit me all over again. Ape-man. Beast in a man's body. For a second, I wondered if the first sight of him had been some fever dream my brain cooked up to mess with me. Nope. He was real.

And he looked pissed.

Ramil must've whispered in his ear to "do his best with me." Cute. Thagan's version of his best turned out to be my worst imaginable.

I'll spare you the play-by-play bloodbath. Just know: he didn't stop. Not once. He beat down on me for hours—how to grip a sword without looking like a child clutching a broom, how to swing without slicing off my own ear, how to thrust with intent. He yanked my feet into stances until my legs shook, shoved my shoulders back, told me where to put my eyes, treating me like a blindfolded idiot stumbling through.

By the end, I wasn't just tired. I was exhausted. My arms hung useless at my sides, my body screamed, and I could barely lift the bowl of sludge they called food to my mouth that night.

Neck to ankle, I was a patchwork of cuts and bruises. But quitting? Not in my vocabulary. Every time he knocked me down, I dragged myself up again, swaying, bleeding, daring him to see I wasn't broken yet.

And then—nightmare on repeat—the sun rose the next day, and it all began again.

15

The Master Becomes the Student

Jonathan

My eyes flew open and my chest was heaving. Everything around me was black. Absolute, suffocating black. Not the familiar kind of dark, with faint edges of light seeping in from somewhere. This was deeper. Thicker. A darkness that pressed in, damp and heavy.

And it wasn't my room. The scent of wet stone and rot told me before my mind could even piece it together: a cave.

I tried to sit up, but something tightened around my chest and arms. Panic flooded me. My body jerked against invisible restraints, muscles straining, legs kicking uselessly against cold rock. My brain scrambled. Escape routes? A weapon? Anything! But there was nothing. Only the pounding in my chest.

Then I heard it.

A growl. Low, resonant, vibrating through the stone beneath me.

My eyes darted toward the sound, and from the darkness two pinpricks of color sharpened into being. Red. No, not just red—molten, ember-red slits. Fixed on me.

They blinked.

The sound came again, a guttural rumble that swallowed the silence,

74

growing louder, closer.

I thrashed against whatever bound me, desperation overtaking reason. My throat tore as I screamed, the word breaking free not in English, but in the Queen's Language. "Help! Please, someone! Help me!"

The answer came as a scrape. Metal on stone? No. Nails. Huge, hooked nails dragging across rock. Sulfur filled my nose, burning, choking me. Heat rolled through the cave as though the walls themselves were sweating.

And then, from the shadows, it emerged.

Scales the color of blood shimmered in the dimness. A monstrous head, horns shooting out in jagged spires. The dragon's eyes—orange-yellow with a dark abyss at their center—locked onto me. Its sheer size shattered logic: twenty, maybe thirty feet high, and still it kept unfolding from the dark, crawling closer.

My heart beat hard. The heat rose fast, sweat rolling into my eyes. My body shook so badly I couldn't tell if it was from the effort of struggling or the terror closing around me.

It drew back its massive head. For a single suspended breath, my world stopped. Then it roared. The sound didn't just fill the cave—it filled me. My skin crawled. My mind screamed with it.

And fire came. Red-hot, blinding, searing flame. I shrieked, flailing, the heat peeling at my skin—

And I sat straight up in my bed.

Air. Cool, real air rushed into my lungs. My small room at the Scholomance Academy swam into focus. My hands trembled against the sweat-soaked blanket. But the scent lingered. Acrid, sulfurous. My skin still burned with the memory of fire.

That was no dream. And no nightmare could leave me gasping with heat in my chest.

A rustle. I turned.

Ramil sat in the corner, shadowed, his posture easy. His eyes opened, catching the morning light from the window, and a grin on his lips.

"The gods have granted you the morrow, young Jonathan," he said softly.

"What?" I blinked, heart still racing. "No. I-I'm sorry. I must've been dreaming. A nightmare."

Ramil leaned forward, resting his chin on one hand. His gaze held me still, dark eyes fathomless. "That was no dream," he said. "That was a *mindform.*"

And that's how my first day of training to be a mage at the academy began.

However, my training did not begin with mindforms. My mentor chose to begin with something far more practical: alchemy.

I was escorted deep within the academy building to what could only be described as a medieval laboratory. The space was tucked away in a quiet corner, almost hidden. Inside, tall, narrow windows admitted streams of light that caught the dust drifting lazily through the air. Shelves climbed along the stone walls, crowded with ancient scrolls and weathered leather-bound volumes whose spines bore unfamiliar symbols.

In the center, several long oak tables stretched the length of the room. Upon them rested an array of apparatus—retorts, crucibles, glass flasks stained with residue, balances fashioned from brass—objects that felt at once archaic and oddly familiar to me.

For all their age and eccentricity, I recognized in them the same principles that had carried me through hours of chem labwork back at school.

The details, however, unsettled me. Along the benches and tucked into cabinets were jars filled with things no modern lab would ever permit: preserved creatures suspended in murky fluids, unidentifiable organs and body parts, powders in hues I'd never seen in nature, and liquids that glowed unnaturally as if alive.

It reminded me less of the sterile order of the labs I knew and more of a scene from some grainy old horror movie—except here, there was no director, no script. Just me, in a room where science and the arcane blurred into one strange and unnerving discipline.

"This will be where you work," Ramil announced, his tone flat and commanding as he gestured to the strange laboratory.

"And what work will I be doing?" I asked, though I wasn't sure I wanted to hear the answer.

"Learning our complex system of the elements, experimenting and maturing your knowledge of metals, and perfecting your ability to create diverse potions."

That last word made me pause. "Potions for what?"

"For treating wounds, prolonging life, curing diseases, and strategic purposes." His delivery was deliberate; he wanted me to pick up on the implication.

It didn't take long. "You mean poisons?"

"Any and all alchemic methods will be studied," Ramil said smoothly.

I straightened. "Just so you're aware, neither Genevieve nor I have any interest in killing people. That may be what happens on your world, but not mine."

His expression tightened—one eye narrowing, jaw rigid. "Let us see where your training takes us, shall we?"

I couldn't resist the urge to push back. "And you must be aware that I am a chemist. I already know a lot. And possibly quite a bit more than you."

"Is that a fact?" His voice had that dangerous calm; he was baiting me.

"I believe so," I said, though my confidence slipped as the words left my mouth.

"Then I would like you to create *gold*," he said simply, as a reasonable request.

My weight shifted awkwardly from one foot to the other. "Um... that's impossible."

"Is it?"

"Yes," I said, more firmly. "No combination of ingredients can be formed into gold. Elements are defined by their protons, completely different from each other. You'd need a nuclear reaction to change one into another."

Ramil's scoff echoed through the chamber. He circled the table with deliberate patience, selecting jars and canisters from the shelves. My eyes tracked every action, suspicious, certain he was preparing some sleight of hand.

He set down a stone mortar and pestle, its surface worn smooth with use. One by one, he measured and added ingredients with the precision of a seasoned chemist. A few drops of mercury first, handled with a care that told me he respected its volatility. Then sulfur, acute and acrid, its smell instantly transporting me back to the morning's nightmare of fire and scales. Lead, tin, copper—metals I recognized by their sheen—followed by a sprinkling of crystalline minerals. I thought I saw arsenic sulfide in the mix, along with ordinary salt.

As he worked, he said, "In my experience, those who claim to know the most usually know the least." He glanced up at me briefly, then returned to grinding the mixture. "And have the most to learn."

He ground the ingredients into a paste, added water, and ground again. A faint smoke curled upward, acrid and metallic. He angled his head away, careful not to inhale, while I instinctively stepped back.

"I truly expected more from you," he said, still grinding, his tone laced with disappointment.

When he was finished, he tilted the mortar toward me. I had been watching his hands the entire time; there was no chance he had slipped anything in unnoticed. If this was a magician's trick, he was world-class.

Inside the bowl, a dusting of black powder clung to the surface. But beneath it, as I shifted the mixture back and forth, I caught the gleam of metal. Small, solid chunks sat at the bottom—yellow, lustrous, unmistakable.

Gold.

I reached in and lifted one piece. It was dense, with that particular heaviness only a metal carries. My rational mind screamed at me to find the trick, to expose the mechanism behind it, but the scientist in me demanded verification. I grabbed a beaker of water, weighed it carefully on a set of scales, then dropped the gold inside. The scale shifted predictably.

Still not enough. I retrieved the piece, pressed it to my teeth, and felt the soft give of malleability.

"This is gold," I said, my voice cracking with disbelief.

"I know," Ramil replied.

"You can make gold?"

"I can do many things. And I will be teaching you as much as time will allow."

My mind spun. On Earth, alchemy had always been a failed promise, a dream that collapsed under the rigor of modern chemistry. But here... I was staring at the impossible, holding it in my hand.

In that moment, I realized the truth: if Ramil could do this, then I had to learn everything he knew.

And he knew it. The sinister slit of his smile made it clear.

I was his student now, and I no longer had a choice in the matter.

16

The Message

Finley

So apparently being a queen doesn't mean endless luxury, velvet gowns, and hours of uninterrupted sexy time with my man. No, that was never the case. Even at night, Braylor and I were lucky if we managed a shared cup of wine before collapsing into bed, two tired sacks of potatoes with one crown.

Late one day, when an ambassador from Svarga—apparently somewhere east of Pandæmonia, though whether that mattered was debatable—stepped forward to present me with a gift, I forced myself to pay attention. He held out a sleek silver drinking stein, its surface polished so smoothly it shimmered with moonlit sheen. Carvings along the rim depicted the gods, locked in an eternal dance of storm and flame. It wasn't just a cup, he explained, but a relic meant to honor them. A vessel believed to carry their blessing to whomever drank from it. Important. Sacred. The sort of thing kings and queens were expected to care deeply about.

I smiled, thanked him properly, even accepted it with both hands the way I'd been trained.

And yet my eyes betrayed me. They slid right past the gleam of silver and locked on Braylor's forearms as he steepled his long, thick fingers in thought—veins standing out as taut rope beneath his sun-browned skin.

I like forearms.

Anyway, by the time our final appointment canceled at the last minute, we gave each other the look. You know the one. Next thing I knew, we were racing down corridors like teenagers sneaking into the gym locker room after hours, ducking into the small private chapel behind the throne room. Braylor's sword belt clattered to the stone floor, and he tore his shirt off with a primal growl that should have melted me on the spot.

"Hurry," he barked.

Easy for him to say. I was fighting my way out of a gown, an under-gown, scratchy hose clinging to my skin, and finally got down to my sad little chemise when—boom. The door flew open.

Luchar froze, then slapped his hands over his eyes, a kid playing peekaboo. "Begging your pardon, your highness!" His whole face went crimson.

I laughed, because honestly? The chemise covered more than half the bathing suits back home. Meanwhile, Braylor looked one heartbeat away from murdering him with his glare alone.

"What is it?" I sighed, buttoning back up.

Luchar wouldn't even look at me. His voice cracked. "A... delegate from Atlantis has arrived."

I stopped mid-button. "Wait. What?"

"Your majesty, I—"

But I was already sprinting out the door, half-dressed, bare feet striking stone. Luchar yelped after me about propriety, but too late—I burst into the throne room where Pherric and my other advisors huddled, clustering like gossiping pigeons.

"Where is he?!"

Sandulf stumbled in, breathless. "He refuses to enter the keep, your majesty!"

The room went silent. Pherric leaned close, his tone cutting. "A deliberate insult. To stand outside the keep means contempt." His eyes flicked down to my state of dress and tightened disapprovingly, but whatever. Bigger problems.

I bolted again before anyone could stop me. Down the great staircase, past guards scrambling to open the heavy doors, out onto the keep's wide stone front steps.

And there he was.

The Atlantean.

He stood at the bottom with the confidence of someone who expected the world to bend—lean, bronzed skin glowing against a black cut-off blouse that showed off... gills. Actual freaking gills, fluttering faintly against his tight stomach. A sword hung at his side, and in his hand, he held a bulging linen sack.

Braylor appeared beside me, hand locked on his sword. "I do not like this," he whispered.

"Who are you?" I shouted, still panting.

A crowd of staff and visitors began to gather.

"My name is unimportant."

"Okay... Unimportant," I shot back. "What do you want?"

He smirked, the way adults smirk at children amusing themselves. Then he hurled the sack onto the steps.

It split open.

Heads rolled out.

My heart fell. Not just any heads. Our emissaries—a man and a woman. We had sent them to the Godsribbon Castle.

And then the boy. The sweet, jittery messenger kid who'd stumbled over his words the last time he'd spoken to me. His terrified eyes were locked open, staring at nothing.

The crowd behind me sucked in one collective breath. Faces went pale. Hands flew to mouths. Then the murmurs began—angry, swelling with menace.

Braylor's sword came free with a rasp. "I will end him now."

"No!" My voice cracked as I clamped onto his arm. I don't even know why I said it. A huge part of me wanted him dead. Desperately. Tears burned in my eyes, but I shook them off. I wasn't giving this bastard the satisfaction.

The crowd pressed closer. Archers lined the inner wall above, arrows drawn. People who'd just moments ago craned their necks for a better view now stared at me with wide, hungry eyes.

Kill him. Prove you're queen. Do something.

My body stalled before my thoughts caught up. Let him go and I look weak. Hesitate and I already am weak. And those expectant eyes? They knew it. They felt it. Awe curdled into restless doubt, a verdict forming before I ever spoke.

The Atlantean's smile widened, bright with amusement. "We found your citizens trespassing on our land," he said calmly.

Pherric stepped forward, trying to salvage the moment. "You are not a representative of Cíbola! You are clearly not Cíbolan! That is not your land to protect!"

"You have stolen from our seas and limited our resources," the Atlantean replied. "We intend to take back what is rightfully ours. The message has been delivered."

He turned and walked away.

Just like that.

The crowd hissed in outrage. "Coward!" someone shouted. Others spat curses—at him, at me. The archers begged me with their eyes to give the order. My pulse thundered in my throat.

I opened my mouth.

Nothing came out.

"Finley!" Braylor urged, ready to charge. "He must die for this treachery!"

Pherric hovered, eyes darting, head shaking just slightly. Even he didn't know what to do. The archer commander waited, desperate.

I panicked.

And the sky darkened.

Wind slammed into the area, heavy and violent. People cried out, pointing upward.

Big Red crashed down hard. Screams erupted as the dragon snapped the Atlantean up in her jaws, lifted him high, and swallowed him whole in two, awful gulps.

Silence.

Wide eyes turned toward me, my court staring as though I'd planned it all along.

"Did you command that?" Pherric asked, voice breaking. Pride or fear—I couldn't tell.

"I—I don't know," I stammered, every muscle shaking. "Maybe?"

Big Red roared, triumphant. Her wings shook the ground as she lifted off, her shadow dragging across the Black City below.

And as her shadow faded, one thought cut colder than the sight of those heads ever could.

We were at war.

With Atlantis.

17

Busy Making Plans

Finley

I paced the throne room like a caged animal, hand plastered to my forehead trying to maybe hold my brain together before it split in two. Headache incoming. And not the "oops, too much booze" kind—the "congratulations, you're responsible for a kingdom and might start a war" kind.

The others clustered in the middle, locked in yet another verbal brawl. Surprise, surprise.

"We cannot rush into anything at this point," said Pherric, ever the poster child for calm, rational doom.

Braylor practically exploded. "There he is! Ever the conciliator! Maybe we should beg for their forgiveness for killing our people!"

Oh boy. Here we go.

Pherric snarled back. "With our level of warriors depleted and the ones we have exhausted, I simply state we do not have what—"

"They killed the emissaries! The messenger, Pherric!" Braylor spat his name.

"Do my own eyes not function, Braylor? We are not ready for war with Atlantis! We are not ready for war with a herd of jackalopes!"

...Jackalopes. Right.

Braylor pivoted, a hovering WWE wrestler, on Sandulf. "Do you hear what he says about your warriors?!"

Sandulf clearly wanted nothing to do with that dumpster fire, so he redirected to me. "The army serves at your pleasure, my queen."

And cue another panic attack. Fantastic. My heart thumped, and for the thousandth time I wondered why my "I need adventure!" wish hadn't come with a warning label. Adventure is supposed to be fun: dragons, quests, treasure maps. Not... whatever the hell this was.

Naturally, Luchar hovered at my shoulder, carrying my gown as the world's most insistent wardrobe assistant. (I was still not putting it back on.)

Pherric dragged my treasurer into the fight. "Do we have the funds to mount a war?"

He fumbled. "Well, I... you see, it would certainly require a heavy tax on—"

"Pherric!" Braylor snapped, red-faced and nearly vibrating with fury. "We were attacked! Funding is not a barrier to our revenge, you fool!"

I dropped onto the throne and let it swallow me whole, rubbing my temples. "Guys, guys! This is not helping. At all."

That shut them up. For two whole seconds. Everyone bowed except Braylor, who stormed off to pout in the corner.

Luchar leaned in, whispering, "Your majesty," and still—still—offering the gown.

"What are our options?" I asked, praying someone had an answer that wasn't awful.

Pherric's mouth opened. I held up my hand. Nope. Not today.

"Anyone *except* Pherric?"

That actually got him. "I know the situation seems dire, your majesty. But as you recall from our campaign against Kane... we can do nothing alone. I will begin reaching out to other realms, including Cíbola, as to whether they would be willing to help."

Luchar, earnest as ever, handed me the gown. "They *have* offended the gods, your majesty."

Braylor swooped in, practically shouting, "Yes! You see! The gods are offended!"

I snorted. "Nice try! You don't even believe in them, you nutball."

Finally, Kasuma spoke up. Always the rational one. "I believe their hostile intent is clear."

I sat forward. "Give it to me, girl."

"In every kingdom, the killing of an envoy typically calls for retaliation. They know this to be true. And with this grave insult, they intend to draw Irkalla into a war."

Perfect. Just perfect.

I pondered her words. "Atlantis knows we are weak. Every nation is weak right now. They didn't come to our aid in the war against Kane…"

Kasuma finished smoothly. "And are prepared to reap the benefits."

"But what did he mean when he said we had *stolen from their seas* and… *limited their resources?*" I asked.

Pherric pondered that. "He may be referring to the time during Malek's rule. The king of Irkalla stole food from every realm, hoarded it. Many kingdoms had sold fruits, vegetables, and grains to Atlantis prior to his reign and there was nothing for anyone to sell in the latter years. As well as many fishermen may have plundered the seas for food, beyond an acceptable level to the Atlanteans."

"Well," I said. "They could have helped us defeat him, but they were no where to be found."

"The political damage may have been done by that point."

"So, we are to feel sorry for them? And do nothing?!" Braylor thundered, back in the fray.

My headache was now throwing a dance party inside my skull. "I need to think about this for a while." Which was code for: *I desperately need a drink.*

"But, your majesty…" Pherric, the disapproving professor, raised a hand.

Nope. I was done. I stood, nodded, endured the bows, and slipped from the throne room, every step heavier than the last. My head pounded, my guts rolled.

I so did not want to be queen. Not now. Not ever.

Lying down in my borrowed royal bedroom was a joke. The ceiling mocked me. The stone walls pressed in. I tried pacing, staring out the window, and even collapsing dramatically into a chair like some wilted Victorian heroine. None of it helped. My brain was running on a hamster wheel greased with panic.

Braylor, of course, waited just long enough for me to stew before knocking. He was a man who knew exactly how long my spiraling takes.

"Still feeling ill?" His head poked around the door.

"Obviously," I groaned, making sure to add enough whine that he'd believe I was suffering. (Which I was, but mostly from anxiety and crippling responsibility.)

He slipped in, clutching a bottle of wine. He poured me a goblet so full it was practically an Olympic event just to lift it.

"Oh, thank God," I muttered, gulping like hydration was a personality trait.

"I know," he said smoothly, and had probably choreographed this whole moment.

I pointed at my empty cup. "More."

He refilled it, his eyes gleaming. "And I know what you want to do."

"Do you?" I snapped. "Because I sure as hell don't."

"You want to go to the Godsribbon Castle."

...Well. I did. Back when it was just a castle and not a neon sign screaming *terrible idea, free death in the courtyard outside.*

"You want retribution," he pressed.

That word hammered me hard. Retribution. The image of the poor messenger's head—dropped like discarded trash on the steps—seared itself behind my eyelids. I *did* want revenge. God, I wanted it in my bones. But Pherric's constant sermons about caution and politics still rang in my ears, and damn it, he wasn't wrong either.

"They are poking you. Testing weakness. If you curl up, they will keep pressing. Why stop at the castle? Why not take the whole kingdom? And when no one stops them..." His voice softened, dangerous. "They will come for you."

I blinked. "So what, I just march an entire army down there? Hi, it's me, inexperienced queen, enjoy the bloodbath?"

"No." His smile curved into an edged knife. He leaned closer, his voice a whisper. "Just a show of force. Not all... but enough."

"What the hell does that mean?"

"The messenger reported fewer than a hundred Atlanteans guard the castle. We take a company, two hundred soldiers, quick and light. We travel by sea. A harsh smack on the snout, and they will back down."

"And if they don't?" My voice cracked just a little, traitorously.

His hand found mine, steady, warm. "To do nothing will be worse. Pherric's diplomacy will drag on. Even if he scrapes allies together, it'll be a season before we move. And by then—"

"It's too late."

"Exactly. Being queen means choosing the hard path."

I hated that he was right. Or at least sounded right. But wasn't that the trap? Everyone here sounded right until the consequences swallowed me whole.

"Sandulf is gathering his best men already. We could march for Hyperborea within a day."

"Relna Thune?" I asked, remembering that charming cesspit where I'd first boarded a ship to Kasuma's island. With Melcente.

"No. South. Where your Irkallan navy is moored." His grin widened. "Melcente commands them."

"Ha!" I barked, bitter laugh bubbling through the wine. "Ah, yes. The Commander of the Royal Irkallan Navy. Which I think is three ships and a dinghy. Some navy."

Still, the idea lit something inside me. Reckless? Absolutely. But better than paralysis. Better than waiting for the world to collapse around me.

My headache ebbed. The wine steadied me. A plan... our plan had taken shape. Pherric would hate it. The others would scold me. But for once, I didn't care.

Because dammit, we had a plan.

Braylor and I spent the next two days in a haze of preparation and excuses. I canceled meetings, dodged questions, and flat-out avoided Pherric and my other advisors. But avoidance only goes so far when your mage can slip into your thoughts like smoke through a keyhole. Pherric's presence pressed at the edges of my mind more than once, and I couldn't tell if it was because he sensed what I was hiding... or because he knew I was trying to shut him out. Either way, it left me raw and jittery.

We left under the cover of darkness, cloaks pulled tight, footsteps hushed against the stone corridors of the keep. The Black City never truly slept. There were always torches burning, shadows moving, but that night everything was too quiet. At the gates, a carriage waited, its karkadanns shifting restlessly in the lantern light.

Sandulf and Kasuma were already inside, jaws set, eyes watchful. His knights had departed in scattered pairs and singles over the past day, slipping into the countryside to build the illusion of nothing more than routine patrols. In truth, they were laying the bones of our escape—an encampment hidden beyond the city's reach.

I climbed into the carriage, the leather seat cold against my palms. The plan was to travel by night, conceal ourselves by day, and make for Hyperborea's shores where ships waited.

Weeks of travel stretched before me. Weeks in which everything could go wrong. The thought lodged hard, a stone in my chest.

The karkadanns snorted as we rolled through the gates. I turned for one last look at the keep. High above, lit by a wash of torchlight, Pherric stood at the top of the stairs. His gaze locked on mine, steady and unreadable, but I felt the heat of his disapproval all the same. He did not wave or call out. He only watched, as he weighed the fate of a kingdom in the silence between us.

Braylor's hand brushed mine in the dark, steadying me. "It is too late to turn back," he murmured.

I swallowed hard, dragging my eyes away from Pherric's silhouette. "I know," I whispered. "That's what terrifies me."

18

Polite Dinner Conversation

Genevieve

Her blade sliced air where my head had been a heartbeat before, but her fist didn't miss. It crashed into my cheekbone so hard the world popped in a glitter storm. My knees buckled, and I hit the dirt floor.

"Again!" Thagan's voice snapped.

I blinked hard, trying to right myself. Any other day, back on Earth, I would've been done. Thrown in the towel, iced my cheek, called it "self-care." But this wasn't Earth. And I wasn't about to let monkey boy grin down at me as just another soft outsider.

I shoved myself up, ignoring the swell ballooning under my eye, and raised my blade again in a sword-fighting stance.

My opponent? The only other woman training to fight at the Scholo-mance. We didn't speak, but I gathered her name was Kinnat. Half a head taller, twice the muscle, and mean as hell. If Thagan thought throwing me against her would be some kind of warm-up before the "big strong guys," the joke was on him. She _was_ the big strong guy.

But brute strength was her weakness. Her heavy feet thudded, solid and punishing, every time she rushed in. She fought to crush while I fought to slip. All those years of dance—spinning, leaping on sprung floors—had taught me something Kinnat had never learned: how to move without feeling tethered to the ground.

She lunged. I deflected. She swung. I spun. My blade nicked close enough to make her eyes widen before I dropped an elbow on her skull. She staggered, finally letting me taste victory... for half a second.

Then she roared, grabbed me with terrifying ease, and slammed me into the floor so hard the air blasted from my lungs. Panic. I couldn't breathe. Couldn't move. And then the tip of her blade pressed into the hollow of my throat.

"She yields," Thagan barked, exasperated.

I rolled, coughing hard, and jabbed a finger at her. "That's not sword-play! That's professional wrestling, dude. Totally not fair!"

Thagan stared at me, a blank look on his face. "There is nothing fair in a fight. However you win in battle is a win. Because the loser... is dead."

Yeah. Pep talk of the year.

He shoved a cup of water into my hand, then stalked off to lecture Kinnat about her mistakes. Me? Every inch of me begged to sprawl flat, to rest. But there was no way I was collapsing in front of these warriors, not when they lived and breathed training as naturally as oxygen. Back home, my friends thought two hours at the gym was obsessive. Here? I was barely staying afloat.

Thagan returned, eyes intense. "Go again."

Exhale. Fine. Let's go.

Except I didn't go. Kinnat wiped the floor with me. By the end, my body screamed, my forearm bled freely, and Thagan finally waved me off to the so-called healer. Which, for the record, is their version of a doctor—except their idea of medicine feels one step away from voodoo.

The healer wrapped me up, but one of my ribs was cracked. Nothing to do about that. I limped back to my room, every step pushing the pain home.

An attendant knocked a short while later.

I yanked open the door. Big mistake. My rib flared, severe and blinding.

"What?" I barked.

"Dinner."

I scanned the hall. No tray of gray slop waiting for me. "And?"

He gestured down the corridor. Great. Apparently, I'd earned parole from solitary and got to eat with the general population.

I followed, one hand pressed to my side, until the hallway opened into the dining hall. Calling it a "cafeteria" didn't do it justice. The space was massive. Wooden beams arched overhead, shadows clinging to the rafters. The ceiling belonged in a cathedral, not a prison-school hybrid. Dozens of candles lined the walls in iron sconces, throwing the room into a warm flicker that nearly passed for comfort.

I spotted a line for food and took my place at the end. They handed me a bowl of gray slop, but it actually smelled decent.

Four long rows of tables stretched across the stone floor, crowded with every kind of body: kids barely old enough to lift a spoon, gray-haired elders, and mostly those like Jonathan—young, bright-eyed mage hopefuls whispering over their meals.

Warriors clustered at one table; broad shoulders and scarred faces hunched over their food. I recognized a few from the sparring room. Kinnat sat among them, watching me as she shoveled the gray stuff into her mouth, eyes narrowing as she measured how broken I still looked.

"Genevieve!"

The whisper snapped my attention. Jonathan, trying not to draw notice, gave me a small wave from the end of a half-empty table. The new guy, sitting alone. Yeah. I knew that feeling.

I slid my tray down across from him with a thud, wincing. My ribs hated me, but at least I wasn't eating in silence.

"You okay?" he asked, eyes searching my face like he already knew the answer.

"As good as I'll ever be again," I muttered, stabbing at the stew. "Which is... not saying much."

"That bad?"

"Try worse. They're trying to kill me. Literally."

He glanced at the bandage on my arm. "I'm sorry."

"Not your fault," I said, chewing with the determination of someone who might not get another meal. "You seem to be holding up fine."

His mouth curved into something humorless. "Not all sunshine and lollipops."

I grunt-laughed, then winced. "What, do they slap your hand with a ruler when you mess up your homework?"

Instead, he tugged his collar down and showed the edge of a welt, purple and angry. "More of a whip."

The food stuck in my throat. "Jesus, Jonathan."

"He tells me something once. That's all I get. If I don't have it memorized... I pay for it."

I leaned in. "We've got to get the fuck out of here. Now."

"And go where?"

"Anywhere. Back to that castle. The Basilisk thing wasn't even real."

He shook his head. "You think he faked everything else we saw?"

"I don't know!" My voice cracked. "But we're going to die here. That much I *do* know."

His hand brushed mine, steadying. "We wouldn't last a day out there."

I clutched him tighter, staring into eyes that were far too calm for this nightmare. "Then we die trying. Because I'm not going out in this miserable hellhole."

He studied me, wanting to believe. "You learning to fight?"

"Trying," I said through clenched teeth, every bruise answering for me.

"And I'm learning a lot too. But we're not ready. Yet. We adapt, keep learning. Then we try to escape. With better odds."

The logic was solid. My heart hated it. "Yeah, but what if one of us gets killed first? You really think either of us makes it alone?"

He squeezed my hand. "Try not to die, okay?"

He winced at his own words. I laughed—ugly and real. "Wow. Stellar encouragement."

"Yeah," he admitted, a crooked smile breaking through. "I knew it as soon as I said it. That was awful."

"Yes, it was."

For a minute, we laughed. Quiet and cracked, but laughing. The first real light in weeks of darkness.

We traded gory details of our training—the pain, the bruises, the humiliations. The kind of things you're not supposed to laugh about. Somehow, it helped. Until a bell clanged and everyone rose, heading back toward their neat little cages.

I must've taken a wrong turn, because the next thing I knew, I was in a side hallway where every wall looked the same. That's when I heard voices. Low. Serious.

I locked up and finally peeked around the corner. Then ducked back.

Ramil. And Thagan.

"Is she improving?" Ramil asked.

Thagan snorted. "She is weak. Soft. You have handed me an impossible task."

"Is she improving?" Ramil repeated.

A pause. Then Thagan's grudging reply. "Aye. But it would take years—"

"I do not need perfection."

"That is very well," Thagan muttered. "Because the longer they are here, the greater the chance the Preceptor finds out what we are—"

He stopped.

I risked another look.

Ramil stood there in front of me. Not whispering. Staring straight at me. He'd known I was there all along.

"Uh..." I stammered. "Is there a bathroom nearby, or—"

He didn't answer. His hand clamped around my arm and fire tore through my cracked rib. I gasped. He hauled me back to my room, and shoved me into a chair that screeched in protest.

Then he crouched in front of me, iron fingers around my wrist. His eyes closed. Words spilled from him—low, vibrating sounds that crawled under my skin.

"What the hell are you doing?" I demanded.

"Making sure you forget what you heard."

Mindforms. He was going to wipe my brain clean.

Not today.

I shut my eyes and clung to every word, every syllable, every detail. I couldn't do his mental sorcery, but I could *hold on*. My life depended on it.

The chant grew louder. My skull burned. White flares exploded behind my eyelids. My heart slammed against my ribs as he held me upright, merciless, unrelenting.

Then—nothing.

Black.

When I woke, I was on the bed. My head throbbed, a deep, brutal ache. But I remembered. Every word.

Ramil and Thagan were hiding something from the Preceptor. Something dangerous. Something they were afraid would be discovered.

At the time, I thought I'd won. Thought my stubbornness had outlasted his spell.

What I didn't know then was that it was Ramil who had won.

19

High Seas and Wobbly Knees

Finley

Our journey across Irkalla and through Hyperborea went surprisingly smooth, even though we were traveling with two hundred soldiers. We slept during the days and marched at night. Kasuma was our stealthy spy, going out in advance, scouting for anyone watching, marking areas to avoid, and reporting back in the evening before we headed out.

It took us a week and a half to make it to the port of Caldrith, a few hundred axims south of Relna Thune.

Caldrith smelled nicer than Relna Thune. That was the first mercy. Instead of rotting nets and desperation, the air carried salt clean enough to sting and the faint sweetness of tarred ropes. The city rose in neat white-stone terraces above the harbor, roofs painted in shades of sea-green and copper that caught the morning light like polished coin. Even Tir Na's version of seagulls—the simurghs—seemed less vicious, wheeling politely instead of screaming bloody murder for scraps.

As we worked our way down to the docks, past merchants already shouting prices in four different languages, the whole place had the unnerving efficiency of somewhere that actually worked.

My three galleys were waiting, proud as swans at anchor. I grinned at the sight of the ships. Adventure was calling and, for a heartbeat, I almost forgot about all of my soldiers camped outside the city gates.

The galleys looked way too clean for anything I was supposed to be in charge of. Three of them, side by side, sails furled but still enormous. Three pale wings ready to shove a hundred men each across the Triton Sea. No oar banks, no sweaty rowers chained to benches... just wind and wood and more polished brass than I'd seen in months.

The decks gleamed. There was someone actually following through on a maintenance schedule. Standing there on the dock, I couldn't decide if they were warships or oversized toys built to make me look important. Either way, they were mine... or at least everyone seemed to think so.

"Permission to come aboard!" I hollered up the gangplank, every bit the owner. Which... I was. Braylor strode ahead, Sandulf behind him, tense and already twitching, and Kasuma bringing up the rear, glaring at the docks as if they'd personally insulted her.

A familiar head popped over the rail. Melcente, minus her pirate-queen getup. Instead of leather and menace, she wore a fitted jacket of navy and black, sleeves rolled to the elbow, hose tucked neat. She looked—well, respectable. It was unsettling.

"Everyone's welcome..." she bellowed. "'Ceptin' you!"

Braylor snorted a laugh. Sandulf stopped mid-step, head cocked, confused and his hand went straight to steel. "This is your queen!" he barked.

I touched his arm before he started chopping off heads. "Easy, Sandulf. If she kills me, you can have your turn then." I called up with a grin, "Refusing your queen, Melcente? Bold strategy."

She leaned on the railing, all mock-serious. "You bring bad fortune, firehair. Whole crew knows it."

"True," I said brightly. "But unfortunately for you, I'm still the one in charge. These beauties are mine."

Melcente dropped her forehead against the rail with a groan. "An' I just got 'em in perfect shape..."

I shouldered past Braylor and hauled myself onto the deck with a sailor's hand. Shiny planks under my boots, lines neat and coiled, sails crisp and white. Everything looked unnervingly… good.

"Relax. It's just a little sail down to Cíbola. Nice, easy trip."

She came down the steps, shaking her head. "Nothin's nice an easy wid you, princess. Death, destruction… den a sprinkle o' madness on top, jus' so the gods be entertained."

We collided in a hug that drew gasps from the watching crew. I whispered, "You doing all right?"

"I was, 'til you showed up, queeny," she shot back, smirk firmly in place.

I glanced around the deck again. The sailors actually bowed when I passed—which, yes, freaked me out.

"Tell me ya didn't bring dat Kraken along?" Melcente said, one eye squinted.

That whole Kraken thing was never going away. "Tried. I checked his calendar, but he's booked solid this season."

Her grin turned wolfish. She swept an arm wide. "Then welcome aboard, yer royalness. Dis is da *Aegiros*. And yonder—*Thalyra* and da *Skathis*."

"They're magnificent," I admitted. "And now I know where several thousand talmar disappear every year."

"That's good coin well spent, my highness!" she protested.

Sandulf rumbled, "It is *your highness*."

Melcente gave him a slow up-and-down, unimpressed. "Dat's what I said."

I hooked her arm and tugged her toward the command deck. "Come on. Let's figure out how to cram two hundred soldiers aboard our ships without sinking them."

She shot Sandulf another sideways look as we climbed. I had the sneaking suspicion she was deciding whether to gut him, seduce him, or both.

I wasn't surprised when I saw Big Red flying out over the Triton Sea. She flapped her wings once, twice, then vanished into the clouds before anyone else caught a glimpse. My heart leapt into my throat. She'd followed me. My guardian angel.

By nightfall we'd managed the impossible. Two hundred soldiers funneled aboard the ships without so much as a riot, along with all the food and supplies we'd need. Darkness was our friend; it hid the chaos of men stumbling up gangplanks, armor clanking and gear rattling.

Melcente barked orders, sailors ran lines with practiced ease, and I... pretended I had any control over the whole thing.

The sails went up with the sound of thunder, cream fabric snapping open under the strange blue glow of the false moon. It felt unreal—three giants stirring awake, pulling us from the safety of Caldrith's harbor and shoving us into open water. The city lights dwindled behind us, a warm cluster of jewels, while ahead stretched only black sea and the promise of Cíbola.

I leaned on the rail, trying to look like a queen admiring her fleet, chin up, cloak snapping dramatically in the wind.

In truth, my gut twisted hard. This was the adventure I'd wanted, wasn't it? High seas, a mission, mystery at the other end.

Only now, every scrap of it sat on my shoulders. Braylor, Kasuma, Sandulf... they all looked at me because I held the map, the plan, and the certainty to carry us through (not really!) Two hundred men crammed below deck trusted me with their lives, though most had never even heard my voice.

I'd had so many adventures on Tir Na... but usually on my own. Now I was responsible for one.

My mouth smiled, practiced and confident. My heart clenched into a fist. If fear was going to eat me alive, fine. I'd let it gnaw quietly—while I kept moving forward, as though the gods themselves had my back.

20

A Tiny Tin Cup

Jonathan

After weeks of training, my brain felt scorched. Elixirs, mindforms, endless drills—ten, twelve hours at a time until I could hardly think straight. I'd made progress, I knew that. Mistakes still happened, but the punishments had slowed.

From what I overheard between my teachers and Ramil, I was further along than most at Scholomance. Not that it mattered. Every success was picked apart. If I managed to brush against another person's thoughts or summon the shadow of someone long gone, it was never enough. The thoughts weren't perfectly clear, the shadows weren't real-looking enough.

Nights weren't any easier. I was given ancient texts to grind through, then tested on them at dawn. Some lessons stuck—fragments of Tir Na history, religious practices, conflicting theories about whether or not spells actually worked. The books also described other intelligent species in Tir Na. One of my instructors was a Prominan, a towering, ape-like being who spoke and reasoned like any Hominan—what humans are called here.

Our potions master was Fomorian, and standing next to him always made me feel small. Eight feet tall, with the look of some Neanderthal giant, yet he deftly handled powders and glassware that should easily shatter in his huge hands. Strange to see such size bent over delicate measures. Then I read about the Bànshēn rén, short and feral with hair across their bodies. The merfolk of Atlantis, too—yes, Atlantis exists here. But the ones that caught my imagination, even through the haze of fatigue, were the Tengu. Winged, capable of flight. I kept thinking of watching the world from above, instead of buried under books and bruises.

I had a breakthrough one afternoon. At least, it *seemed* to be one. Ramil might say otherwise.

The day started with him looming over me, an executioner waiting to drop his axe. The task was simple. On the surface. A tin cup sat on a scarred wooden desk.

All I had to do was move it. Not with my hands. With my mind.

Easy, right? Except it wasn't. I believed it to be a massive waste of time. And energy.

I stared at that cup until my eyes ached. I pressed until the veins in my forehead stood out. Sweat trickled down my back. Still, the damn thing just sat there, mocking me. I knew it would.

"Focus," Ramil said for what had to be the thousandth time. "Focus." His voice was brittle. Glass ready to shatter.

I closed my eyes, exhaled slowly. I *saw* the cup, not with my eyes but with something deeper. I could *feel* its weight, its cold tin surface, the echo of all the times someone had gripped it. But sliding it across the desk? Lifting it? That was beyond me.

The only variable I could control in a situation was myself—and somehow, it was always the last thing I would try to correct.

"Move the cup," he snapped. I was simply a disobedient child refusing to obey.

I tried. My head throbbed. My cheeks flushed with heat. Nothing.

"Move the cup," he repeated.

"I'm trying!"

Then the crack came—his hand against my face. I reeled back, hit the floor. My cheek burned.

That's when the anger erupted. A spark, then an inferno. "You asshole!" I snarled, my voice raw, and as the words left my mouth... the cup flew.

Not slid, not tipped. It *launched.* Clattered against the stone wall. Ramil actually ducked. For once, he looked alive. Eyes blazing, like he'd just seen fire born from flint.

But instead of praising me, or even helping me off the ground, all I got was:

"Do it again."

I gaped at him. "Do it again? Wait. No! That was *telekinesis*! Mindforms are about energy, not throwing objects. That shouldn't even be possible!"

My heart pounded. Folklore. Science fiction. A magician's tricks. Yet I had just hurled a cup across the room with nothing but my fury.

Ramil bent, picked up the cup as if it were holy. "At some point in history, someone has thrown a cup across a room. Likely a cup was thrown in this very workshop. You were able to take into that energy and reenact the motion. Physically. Using that energy. You gave it form."

"But how? Can *you* do that?"

A pause. Too long. Unsure if he wanted to expose his limitations. "I cannot."

That floored me. I, a novice, had just done something the master himself couldn't replicate. "Then how could...? I just started training!"

His gaze lingered on the cup, not me. "You are unique, Jonathan." But he stopped there.

"And?"

"Those on this world who are well-adapted to become mages are *strorgrir.*"

For some reason, that word did not translate over into the Queen's Language. "What does that mean?"

"Strorgrir. The person lacks an emotional responsiveness. They may not have concern for others. The best ones are indifferent, and usually are detached and withdrawn from society."

"Apathetic. They lack empathy."

"Well, that is not a word known to me. But great mages are not emotional.

They are impartial. And—"

"Well, that's not me," I said, shaking my head. "I care. I *feel*. And I can still throw cups, apparently."

"As I said, you are unique. Very few, if any on Tir Na, possess the mental fortitude to read and perform mindforms... and at the same time be able to understand and share their emotions and care for others. None that we have been able to find. On your world? There may be many similar to you, but you were the first we found in our collective conclave during the search process. That fact that you were also well-studied in alchemy made our choice abundantly clear."

My knees practically let me down. My heart raced. I was... special? I was filled with pride, I'm not going to lie. But also a sense of foreboding. What was I meant for? He had mentioned that Genevieve was to be trained as an assassin.

"Back to work now. You must be able to move the cup without the incitement of violence. An emotional reaction, by the way."

"So... why am I here?"

His expression hardened. "Because your abilities are required here. That is all you need to know."

"No." I planted my feet, chin up. "You can beat me until I bleed, but I won't do another damn thing until you give me real answers."

That earned me his wrath. He lunged, slammed me against the wall. Glass cracked, vials shattered at our feet. His face was a mask of anger.

"There is a usurper on the Irkallan throne!" His fiery words shot out. "She slaughtered the Bànshēn rén. That *firehair* razed the Irkallan city of Ker-Is, killing the entire population. She hunted down and killed off a large portion of the Prominans. She butchered our king and his knight commander, and with the aid of an exiled mage, she made herself immortal! Her name is Finley Maguire, and it is my destiny to end her evil reign!"

The force of his grief hit me harder than his shove. I saw the slaughter in my mind's eye—mountains of corpses outside cavern mouths, cities drowned in dead bodies. His fire ignited mine.

"What do you need me to do?" I asked, before I could think better of it.

"I need you to poison Queen Finley of Irkalla."

My mouth went dry. "Poison her? How? With what?"

He held up the cup.

I didn't know what he meant. But my gut told me whatever path he was setting me on, it was already too late to turn back.

21

What's Her Name?

Week after week, I told myself I could handle this. Swords. Axes. Shields. Bruises stacked on bruises. A new scar every damn day. My body was screaming at me—bones aching, muscles burning, skin split open so many times I was a patchwork quilt stitched with blood. But the scars? Those were the killers. They stared back at me in every reflection. No filter, no foundation, no concealer would erase what was done. That version of me—the girl who could've made it in front of cameras, runway lights in her eyes? She was gone.

I was damaged goods.

One afternoon, Thagan was on his usual kick of grinding my patience to dust. Kinnat and I had swords and shields, circling, jabbing, both of us dragging from exhaustion. My arms were wet sandbags.

"Given up, have you?" Thagan leaned against the wall, lazy and focused all at once. "Female Hominans. Absolutely worthless."

God, his voice grated. I wanted to shove those words back down his throat. But all I could do was raise my shield again as Kinnat snarled and bashed at it.

"Females," he sneered again. "I would throw you to the boars for feed, but they would spit you back at me. Not worth the effort."

I tried to step forward, tried to go on the offensive, but she caught me with a slash across my shoulder. The cut lit up my nerves, and I almost dropped my weapon right there. Almost.

"Rearing younglings is all you females are worth. That and cooking my meals," he continued. "Not fighting."

I snapped. Red filled my vision. Anger was the only thing keeping me upright, the only spark I had left. I spun and swung at him, reckless and raw. For one heartbeat I thought maybe, just maybe, I'd land it. But of course not. He ducked and my blade screeched against the stone as it missed, sparks flying uselessly.

With a kick, he knocked me flat on my back, his sword at my throat. The fight was gone from me in that instant, replaced by a sting of fear. For a moment, I maybe wanted him to finish it. Just end me, and I wouldn't have to keep pretending I could survive this.

"I should run you through, whelping," he growled.

"Then do it!" I screamed back, voice shaking even as I tried to make it sound like fire. "I'm sick of this. Sick of you."

My hands trembled as I shoved away the paw he offered, forcing myself to stand on my own. Anger kept me upright, but fear curled low in my gut.

"If you want to live, you must improve," he said.

I brushed straw from my sweaty arms, pressed my hand hard against the cut on my shoulder, and forced my voice steady: "What do you think I've been doing here?"

"All I had to do was provoke you," he said, calm as ever. "You fight with anger. You'll never win that way."

"Anger... and my hatred for you, is the only thing keeping me going."

"Then you will die. Every soldier uses fear or anger to motivate himself to fight. And every one of them, at the end of the battle, is burned on the funeral pyre. Fight with the skills I have taught you, not with emotion."

I didn't need his knockoff kung-fu movie philosophy. Please. My fingers clenched the hilt tighter, knuckles aching, daring him to keep talking. But of course, Thagan caught it—the tension, the tell—like he always did. With one casual flick, his blade sent mine spinning out of my grip, dancing across the stone.

Humiliation burned hotter than the cut on my shoulder. I shoved past him before he could see my eyes sting, snatched up my water skin, and dropped into the corner. My back hit the wall, my chest heaving, and I wished the floor would just swallow me whole. But I took a long drink of water instead, letting the cool remind me I was still here. Still breathing. Still pretending I wasn't two steps away from breaking.

Kinnat sat on the bench nearby. Her piercing voice chimed in: "He is correct."

"Shut the fuck up," I snapped, because if I didn't bark back, I'd collapse. I stared across the hall at him, my enemy, my teacher, my tormentor. He smirked because he knew how this story would end. He already saw me dead on the pyre.

And maybe, beneath all the bravado, I was starting to believe it too.

For weeks they'd forced me to sit with the warriors-in-training at dinner, all grunts and gristle and chest-beating jokes I barely understood.

But one night, in the cafeteria, Tattoo-Neck in the green robe, that usually shoved me to the warrior table, straight-up acted as though I didn't exist. Honestly? Fine by me. I wasn't in the mood to fight for table scraps of respect. So I drifted toward the table where Jonathan usually sat, always by himself, the awkward nerd.

He set down his bowl of his sludge, beaming like a kid on Christmas morning. "I've had an amazing breakthrough!"

Oh boy. Here we go. Dude looked acted he'd just invented the wheel.

"Jonathan, listen to me," I cut in, because I had bombshell news.

But he steamrolled right past me. "Have you heard of telekinesis?!"

I blinked at him. "Yeah, but you need to hear this—"

"It's moving an object with your mind! I can do that! Wait—why are they letting you sit with me?"

I wanted to shake him. Here I was, about to drop the kind of news that could change our whole survival game, and he was buzzing about magic tricks. His breakthrough was cool and all, but... priorities, babe.

I grabbed his hand, squeezed it tight. My voice dropped quiet, but urgent.

"Please. Listen to me."

The smile slid off his face. "What?"

Rip off the bandage. "I found out something. And it's *fuckin' huge*. Ramil bringing us here? Not approved. At all. That Preceptor dude we met—he's the one in charge—and guess what? He knows *nothing* about us. No clue we were kidnapped from Earth. Ramil and the furball training me? They're pulling some shady-ass shit here, babe. We can report them. We can get sent back. We can go *home*."

Jonathan just leaned back, still smiling. Like I'd told him something obvious. Like the punchline hadn't landed.

"It's okay, Genevieve. Ramil has already told me why we're here."

What? My stomach flipped. He wasn't hearing me. "Jonathan, you don't understand. We can go home! I just don't know how we can get to the Preceptor-dude."

He leaned in close, checking around as if he was suddenly part of some spy thriller. "We are here to help. There's an evil queen out there, and she has killed so many. But he has a plan. And after what we discovered that I can do... you won't have to play any part in it."

My brain short-circuited. Did he not hear me? "Jonathan. We were taken here against our will. *Illegally* or some shit. We can go home!"

Too loud. Heads turned. Spoons paused mid-bite. I felt my cheeks heat but glared back until they turned away. Whatever. Let them stare.

Jonathan leaned forward, glowing with purpose. "But don't you see? If I can make this happen, we can do something really good here."

"You're serious? You're really buying into this?" My voice dropped back into a hiss. "You're talking about assassinating someone. Using this stupid new power?"

He shook his head, frustrated. "You don't understand. She's bad. *Really bad.* She's killed thousands. She wiped out an entire species of people—the Bànshēn rén. And she's—"

I cut him off before he got carried away with his hero monologue. "And what? What exactly are you gonna do, huh? Stab her *remotely*? Push a knife into her chest with your mind?"

His face hardened. "No. Not stab. Poison."

Poison. My stomach turned. I looked at him and didn't recognize him. "Look, I don't care what she's done, you can't just... murder somebody, bro. She should go to prison, face trial, or *something*."

"She's the usurper of a kingdom," he snapped, voice low but fierce. "There's no one to arrest her. She *is* the authority."

The walls started closing in on me. I could barely hear the clatter of dishes, the warriors laughing a few tables over. It was all too much. Unreal and overwhelming.

"Okay... okay, let's just say you actually poison this woman. This queen, um..." My voice cracked but I forced it steady. "What was her name?"

Jonathan's eyes locked on mine. Dead serious.

"Finley Maguire."

22

She's Alive...

Genevieve

Finley. Maguire.

My whole body went cold. Every nerve just short-circuited. I damn near slid out of my chair.

"What... did you say?" My voice cracked so low it was almost a whisper. My eyes were bigger than the bowl of stew in front of me.

He looked spooked, fumbling, his face going pale. "Um, what's wrong?"

"Her name! Say it again," My hand slammed the table before I even realized it, drawing more stares.

"Uh, it's, um... Finley. Finley Maguire. She's the fire-haired usurper in—"

"Stop."

I leaned back in my chair, my arms crossing over to hold myself together. Guilt washed over me. My friend... one of my best friends. Finley. She'd been dead—well, missing—for years. We'd gone out to a club, then hit up a party. She was entirely too wasted. We were up on the terrace of this apartment, and I went to get her a water. When I came back, she was gone. I thought for sure she fell off the roof, but there was no body. We searched everywhere, called the cops... but we only found her shoes and her phone. Her dad went crazy, offering a big reward for her. But nothing.

She had simply vanished. And it was all my fault. I made her go out that night. Forced her to. And she was gone. They tried to say she had run away, because her dad was always putting too much pressure on her. After a while, everyone stopped looking. But I knew she had been kidnapped. And I never forgot about her. Never forgave myself.

And then her name came out of his mouth.

"Genevieve?"

But then I thought about how we ended up on Tir Na. We both got kidnapped. Taken here against our will. And if that could happen to us, then... maybe.

I leaned forward, gripping his hands hard. "What did you say about her?"

"Th-that she's the usurper, and she's—"

"No. Not that." I tried to focus on his words. "Fire-something."

"Oh, Ramil called her a firehair."

"Finley has... red hair." My throat closed up. Finley's hair—wild, curly, fire-red. Gorgeous. Jealousy-inducing. And she was alive. Here.

"Wait, you know her?"

"Yes, I do! It's gotta be her. She was taken... just like we were!"

"How can that be?"

"Oh my god. She's alive. She's..."

Jonathan was trying to figure it all out in his head. "That doesn't make sense. The woman Ramil is talking about is a tyrant. A mad queen who has been invading and killing people."

"No, it has to be her. How many *normal* names have you heard on this world?"

"So, your friend came here and they made her queen? As simple as that? And now she's murdering—?"

"No. Never. Not her. There is no way any of that is true, Jonathan. Finley couldn't kill a spider without crying. She's smart, introverted, but not a murderer. She's kind... well, she's funny. But in no way is she a killer."

"Then it can't be her."

"Or... what you heard were straight-up lies. Ramil could be lying to you, sweetheart. I just told you that he's lying to the Preceptor! Yeah." I thought it all through. "Yeah, he's telling you shit so that you'll assassinate her. That's gotta be it!"

"Why?"

"Well, if I know Finley... she's pissed off more than a few people with that smart mouth of hers. But becoming queen? Damn, girl."

Jonathan rubbed his forehead, lost. "I'm so confused."

I carefully placed a hand on his cheek. "Listen to me. We have to get out of here. Okay? Ramil is using us."

But the thrill of her being alive curdled into fear. If she was here, she was in danger. So were we. And Ramil? If he knew we were onto him, we'd be dead. We needed to get out before the whole twisted game swallowed us whole.

Jonathan reluctantly agreed we would try to escape.

The next few weeks turned into reconnaissance disguised as routine. I made a show of "accidentally" wandering into places I shouldn't— hallways that curved into dead ends, staircases that twisted down into damp corridors, labs, libraries, and scary rooms with locked doors that buzzed against my fingertips. I figured exactly out how far Jonathan's room was from mine. I mapped the routes in my head, scribbled half-coded notes that looked like bad poetry, and asked endless questions under the excuse of being "the clueless new one." The problem? The place was a prison wearing a school's skin. No weak spots.

Which meant we'd need a distraction so big no one would care about us.

Jonathan promised he could handle that part. Something about using his new talent. I didn't press—I just trusted him to cook up some chaos while I handled the rest.

Meanwhile, I went digging into Finley. Or, as the whispers had it: Finley the Evil Bitch. Opinions split down the middle. Some painted her as ruthless, power-hungry, cold. Someone even called her an immortal witch! As if. Others swore she ended a war and toppled a crazy king. Honestly? That part sounded more believable. Still... picturing her in armor, sword flying, blood on her hands? Couldn't do it.

My training doubled down, because Thagan must've known I was planning something. Sparring left me bruised, gasping, flirting with collapse. Kinnat, my favorite sparring partner slash accidental executioner, broke me down more than once.

After one especially brutal session, I decided to probe her about Finley.

"So, have you ever heard of Queen Finley in Irkalla?" I asked between gasps.

Kinnat grunted. That was actually progress.

"So, you have?"

Her glare could've cut glass. "Why?"

"Curiosity. You know. Just wonderin'."

She downed her water. "Perhaps focus on staying alive."

"That's fair," I said, wiping sweat from my eyes. "But seriously—what have you heard? Is she evil like everyone says? Is she invading other kingdoms and wiping out whole species?"

Her shoulders tensed, then loosened, just slightly. "She may be doing bad things. I do not know. But she must be better than the king before her. His men stripped my land bare—took our food, our young fighters from the village. My brother. She must have killed the king. And they made her queen after." She tossed the last word. "My mother was forced to sell me to the Scholomance so my sisters could eat. So they could survive."

I'd thought she was older than me, hardened beyond recognition. But listening to her, I realized she was likely younger. The academy had stolen her years, carved them out and replaced them with muscle and scars.

For a moment, I wanted to tell her everything—my plan, the escape, the slim chance of freedom. But trust was a luxury I couldn't afford. So I swallowed the words. And let the silence stretch between us be a secret pact neither of us wanted to break.

23

No Coils. No Teeth. No Fire.

Finley

I was floating. Just me, in this rickety excuse for a boat, bobbing like a cork in the middle of a gray, endless sea. The fog wrapped around me so thick it felt alive. The water lapped lazily against the wood, each sound too loud in the silence, the sea reminding me how very small I was.

Then came the splash. Off in the dark somewhere. Too big to be a fish. But very close. I squinted through the mist, straining for shapes, for movement, anything. My chest should've been tight with panic, but for some messed-up reason, I felt almost calm. Numb. The part of my brain meant to scream *run* had already checked out.

The first thing I saw—the eyes. Glowing, bloody red. Twin fires cutting through the fog, unblinking, drawing closer. The water surged as the beast surfaced, and then I knew: *dragon* was too small a word. This thing made dragons look harmless. Its body was a wall of scales, each one the size of a dinner plate, woven tighter than chainmail. Its neck rose from the sea, a living tower of muscle shifting beneath slick, ocean-blue armor.

The forked tongue darted out, tasting the air... tasting me. I scrambled back, pressing myself into the farthest corner of the boat, pretending distance meant safety. The sea serpent's head reared high, red eyes burning straight through me. Then its jaw opened—wide enough to swallow me and my sad little boat whole. Fire erupted from its throat. Heat slammed into me so hard I flinched, throwing an arm up. The world burned orange, the serpent painted in sapphire. The scales caught the firelight like gemstones dragged straight from hell.

Smoke curled from its nostrils as it lowered, inch by inch, until its massive head hovered level with mine. I screamed—loud, raw—but the sound vanished into the fog. The serpent exhaled, sulfur scorching my nose, tearing at my throat. Then it slid its jaw across the bow, close enough for me to see the ridges of its teeth. Its lips curled into something that might've been a smile. Or maybe I was already losing it, because I swore it looked amused. A predator savoring the moment before eating.

I turned, desperate, searching for land, another boat, a miracle—anything but endless ocean. That's when I heard it.

"Finley," the voice hissed.

I whipped my head back—and the serpent was gone. Just... gone. In its place, perched neatly on the bow, sat a woman. Young. Beautiful. Very pale, bluish skin. Long dark hair spilling down bare shoulders, because she was naked. No idea why. Her hand reached toward me, delicate, perfect—except her eyes still burned with that same red glow.

Her smile deepened. Fingers close to brushing my cheek when—

I woke up. Gasping. Drenched in sweat. Heart pounding. I was in a bed. In the captain's quarters. On the ship. Braylor snored beside me, blissfully unaware.

Dream. It had to be a dream. Except I could still feel it—the furnace heat of that breath, the acrid sting of sulfur clawing the back of my nostrils. My hands shook as I grabbed a silk robe and splashed water on my face.

That wasn't just a dream. It felt like a warning.

I slipped onto the deck, the night air cool against my burning skin. Melcente stood at the helm, steering us through the real sea, while I tried to convince myself I hadn't just locked eyes with something that belonged only in nightmares.

"Da seas be calm," she rasped, her voice rough with the night air. "Why you not sleepin', girl…? Oh. Sorry. Queeny."

The word landed heavy. A joke, a jab, a reminder. I leaned on the railing, squinting at the waves, half-expecting some massive silhouette to break the surface. My pulse hadn't slowed since I woke. Those glowing eyes were branded into me.

"Oh." The word rattled out. I shivered. "Had a bad dream."

"Dat so?" she asked, already unconvinced.

I told her—about the sea serpent, the blue scales, the deep, dark red eyes. Saying it out loud made it worse, tempting the water to answer back.

"Bygods, no!" Melcente's hands flew off the wheel. She staggered forward, dread breaking over her. "You saw the Leviathan?!"

"The what?"

Her eyes went wide under the lantern light. "Leviathan! Most fearsome creature in all da Triton Sea!" She rushed to the rail, head whipping side to side, waiting for it to rise.

"It's real?" I asked, though I already knew. Things were always real here.

Her eyes flashed at the water. "Real as me and you, girlie. And you brought it here?!"

I stumbled after her, heart thudding. "No! It was a dream!"

Her gaze snapped back. "Dreams be doors, aye? And you always openin' 'em for da wrong things. To ma ship! To ma crew! Every cursed time!"

Her words hit hard. The Kraken had sunk the *Jaculus*. Nerus had pulled death from the deep—true—and Melcente wasn't wrong that trouble clung to me. I hated that part of me wondered if she was right.

"I don't think this was a mindform vision," I muttered. My throat was dry. "I haven't had one since we defeated Kane."

"Well, you havin' 'em now, dontcha?"

My chest tightened. The weight of the dream. The silence. The certainty pressed down on me. Warning or terror dressed in scales? I couldn't tell anymore. I was too tired. Too wrung out.

Melcente barked orders to the lookout, but he called back saying nothing stirred. She didn't relax. Even with her dark skin, her knuckles were white on the rail. Eyes wild.

"What is a Leviathan?" I asked.

"Evil sea serpent, love. Twice da size of a Kraken. Armor no blade nor harpoon can pierce."

"And they breathe fire? Dragons do that."

"That's what they be sayin'."

"So... you've never seen one?"

Her stare burned hotter than a torch. "Offnot. Dose who see her don't live long enough ta tell da tale."

"So... it might not exist?" I reached for hope, clinging to it.

Melcente shook her head hard. "Oh, she be real. You were in Relna Thune, aye? Saw Castle Leviathan due south? Da blackened fortress on dat beach?"

I nodded, remembering the scorched ruins crumbling into the tide.

"They told me dragons did that."

"Dey didna wanna scare ya, love. Castle Nightveil, dey called it, long before Leviathan burned it black."

"So... is there more than one?"

Her lips pressed thin. "No one know. If she be alone, she ancient as da tides. Older dan songs. Whisperin' tru sailors' tales for hundreds of years."

The sea stretched out before us—empty, cruelly calm. No coils. No teeth. No fire. Not even sirens calling us to drown.

But I couldn't shake it. Melcente feared monsters from old stories. My dread pointed somewhere else entirely. Toward Cíbola. Toward the Godsribbon. Toward whatever waited for me there.

And I didn't know which terrified me more.

24

Go!

Genevieve

I lay rigid in the dark, every nerve alive. The sweat from my sparring clothes clung sour against my skin—I hadn't changed into any night clothes.

I was ready to run.

Beyond the thin wood of my door, the lamps in the stone corridor had been put out long ago. Silence pressed in. The patrol that checked our door locks had gone by. We were sealed up.

All of us—except Jonathan and me. We had no roommates to watch us. No whispers to betray us. Everyone else bunked with several others. But Ramil had arranged it so that we were kept alone, I was sure. Isolated and hidden away. A secret within his secret.

The faintest *click* tore through the quiet. Jonathan. He had used his telekinesis, after practicing this for weeks. My pulse slammed. I bolted from the bed, turned the handle. The door opened.

Shadows stretched long in the hall. Empty. Waiting.

I crept forward, boots grazing stone. I held my breath for fear of making too much noise.

I heard voices. Shouting. Far off... but getting louder. My body locked. They knew. They *knew*! Did I have time to run back to my room?

"Fire!"

The word detonated through the school.

Jonathan's distraction! He had started a fire. Far enough away, I hoped.

The academy roared alive. Boots pounded away down below. Orders were barked, buckets were dropped, water sloshed. More running. Shouting.

I sprinted through the corridor that smelled of smoke. I rapped hard, desperately. "Jonathan!"

"I'm here!" His voice muffled, urgent.

"Come on!"

The handle jerked under his grip but held tight.

"What are you doing?" My whisper broke, panic snapping at my throat.

"It's Ramil," Jonathan said, voice strangled. "He's locked it with a mindform. I can't. I can't break it."

I kicked the handle. Pounded on the door. Useless. The wood didn't give.

"Run," he hissed. "There's a fire burning in a lab, at the back of the school. But you don't have much time!"

"No!" My heel slammed again, pain jolting up my leg. "I'm not leaving you!"

"You still have a chance," he gasped. "He never thought I would open *your* door. Only mine."

Seconds dripped away like blood from a wound. The storm of boots and shouts grew louder.

"I'll come back," I said, forehead pressed against the door, the wood cold against my skin. "I swear it."

Part of me didn't believe him. Something in the back of my head said that he really wanted to stay. Why? I'm not sure. But there was no way I could stand there and argue with him.

"Then *go*!"

The word ripped through me. My chest split with it. But I turned and ran.

Hallway rushing. Heart pounding. The floor groaning beneath my weight.

I heard a voice from behind a door.

"Genevieve?"

The sound stopped me mid-stride. It was faint. Female.

"Genevieve."

I spun, pulse pounding in my skull, eyes dragging over doors in the dark.

"Yes?" My whisper barely audible.

"Are you escaping?" It was Kinnat. Her voice from behind a door.

My gut twisted. Was this a trap? Or the truth?

"I am."

A pause. Too long. "Take me with you."

My skin prickled. I looked up and down the hall. Nothing but darkness and the echo of chaos from below. No time. No trust. Only the beating clock of survival.

I yelled down the hall. "Jonathan! Can you hear me?"

A muffled voice called back. "Yes. But—"

"Listen to the sound of my voice. I'm standing in front of another door. I need you to unlock it for me. On the opposite side of the hall from your room." I quickly counted the doors. "Five doors down from yours."

Silence. My chest crushed under it.

I heard a *click*.

The door swung wide. Kinnat burst into the corridor, eyes wild, tunic half-pulled on. No deceit there. Just fear. Real fear.

"Let's move," I whispered, already pulling her forward.

We sprinted away. Feet pounding, smoke curling along the ceilings, shouts echoing everywhere. Others rushed by us—mages, guards, servants—too consumed by the chaos to notice two girls moving against the current. I trusted the map I'd made in my head, prayed I hadn't missed anything. One wrong turn, but I corrected fast, and kept us cutting through the building.

The main doors came into view. We were almost out.

Then I saw the two men planted between us, swords drawn. They weren't moving for anyone. The bearded one stepped forward, blocking us.

"Back to your rooms."

Kinnat stiffened beside me, ready to go for him barehanded. Brave, but stupid. I caught her arm.

"Our room's filling with smoke!" I cried, pointing back, letting panic coat my voice. "Please! You've got to help us!"

He frowned, scanning the haze down the hall. "There are no rooms in that wing."

I stepped closer, touching his arm. "We're in special rooms. Near the workshops. Look—smoke's already down there—"

Kinnat caught on, sliding nearer the other guard, nodding fast.

"Please."

And then we struck.

I kicked, hard, but it wasn't clean—his knee gave but he turned on me. He was heavier, stronger, only I didn't let myself think. Instead of trying to topple him over, I dragged him down with me. My fingers clawed at his face, went for the soft parts. His eyes. His scream filled the air, and his sword slipped free.

Kinnat was faster. Her opponent already out cold, her elbow strike to his jaw brutal and precise. She rose with a blade in hand.

I climbed off the guy, shaking, and grabbed his sword. My guard pushed onto his elbows, his eye bleeding, rage twisting his face.

I went to cut him but I couldn't move.

Her sword sliced down, clean and tight. Kinnat's steel ripped through his neck.

The sound was worse than the sight. Wet, choking. Final. Blood poured out *so* fast.

I froze. The sword nearly dropped from my hands. My chest heaved and my eyes stung, and I hated that I couldn't stop it. I always talked tough, but watching someone die inches away? That hit different. My body knew it before my brain did—bile already burning my throat, tears breaking loose.

Kinnat didn't blink. She grabbed my hand, pulled me forward, and shoved open the doors.

The night air slapped us. Cold and real. My lungs seized, then dragged in a breath so deep it hurt. Smoke clung to my hair, my skin, my clothes, but out here, it was cleaner.

We stumbled across the bridge and onto the grass. The Scholomance loomed behind us, black against torchlight, a dark twisted creature watching us race away.

I looked back once. But all I could hear was the guard's scream in my ears, sticky as the blood on my hands.

But I couldn't stop. If I stopped, I'd break.

I forced my legs on, running.

Shock pulsed through me, hot and cold at the same time. I was shaking, fighting tears, bile still rising, but beneath it all—beneath the horror— was something I hadn't expected. A spark. The first taste of being free. Of knowing we'd actually done it.

We got out.

The night opened up around us. Tall grass, rocky hills, silence. Anything could be waiting out there. Maybe worse than what we'd just left.

But there was no going back.

I gripped the sword tighter, swallowed the fear creeping up inside me, and ran with her into the dark.

25

Let's Go for a Ride

Finley

We docked at Canela, a city many axims east of Godsribbon Castle. Melcente looked positively thrilled to have me—and only me—off her ship. Couldn't blame her. I had a knack for drawing trouble like moths to a bonfire (that I probably started. On accident.)

Similar to Quivira, Canela gleamed as though it had been hammered straight from the sun's own anvil: rooftops shining gold, walls plated in gilt, domes flashing as miniature suns above the red-brick maze of streets. Overhead, aqueducts crisscrossed the skyline, pushing water into plazas where fountains burbled beside statues polished within an inch of their marble lives. The air smelled like a spice rack had exploded—cinnamon, citrus, and something so sweet it made my gut ache.

Melcente didn't waste time. As soon as my little army of two hundred disembarked, she hauled anchor and scurried her fleet off to loiter somewhere offshore.

Sandulf marched the troops far from the city and set up camp. Braylor bolted off into town on a mission to wrangle up karkadanns for Kasuma, himself, and, most importantly... me. We needed mounts to scout ahead. Sandulf hated that idea.

By sunset, Kasuma and I watched soldiers wrangle poles and canvas to erect my tent. Sandulf, in full overprotective-dad mode, pleaded: "Your majesty, you cannot ride off unattended."

I gave him my best queenly side-eye. "I'll be fine. I've got Kasuma, who could stab you three times before you blink, and Braylor who is... well, Braylor."

Sandulf puffed up, a proud pigeon. "He is as fierce as they come, your majesty. But he cannot fend off a hundred soldiers."

"It's just reconnaissance, Commander. Quick in, quick out."

He whined about spies, that they were perfectly capable of scouting for me. I shut him down. But then, in my infinite genius, I joked: "In reality, the best thing would be if Kasuma here could fly over the castle and check things out."

But her damaged wing prevented that.

Kasuma dropped her gaze. "I am sorry to have let you down, your majesty—"

Panic mode. "No, no, no! That's not what I meant at all!"

Her lips slipped into a grin, but she wasn't looking at me. Her eyes were focused past my shoulder.

"You have your own wings, majesty."

I spun. And there she was. Big Red. My dragon.

She loomed behind the trees, snorting like a forge bellows, her claws ripping little furrows into the dirt. Soldiers gasped.

I took off running. Sandulf shouted for me to stop. Something about needing to put on ten layers of armor. I ignored him. Because it had been *forever* since I'd ridden a dragon, and you don't keep a girl from her dragon.

Approaching slow, I bowed my head, empty hands raised. Big Red's eyes were twin suns, and her growl vibrated in my bones. Our ritual. Always the same: I kneel, she huffs, stomps, and pretends she's the boss. (She is, but don't tell her that.) Finally, she nudged me hard enough to nearly topple me, then purred low in her throat as I pressed my cheek against her scales.

"Okay, girl," I whispered reverently. "We're going on a trip."

She crouched low enough for me to clamber aboard. When I vaulted onto her back, she roared in mock protest before flaring her wings wide. Three massive beats later and we were airborne. The camp below gawked, mouths hanging straight down.

"Head east!" I shouted. "To the Godsribbon Castle!"

Now, flying a dragon is simultaneously the most exhilarating and most miserable experience known to anyone. My hair whipped into a disaster zone, my eyes watered nonstop, and yep... I'm pretty sure I swallowed a bug. Note to self: keep mouth shut next time. But honestly? Who cares? Because riding a dragon is *fucking awesome.*

We soared along the moonlit coast, diving low and hovering over the sea, then rocketing skyward into wisps of dark cloud. I'd been told queens shouldn't ride dragons, that it wasn't "proper." Proper could shove it. I'd missed this.

Half an hour later, Big Red circled high above the Godsribbon Castle. From the air, the place was less a fortress and more of a corpse dressed in borrowed finery. It was a bit worse than I remembered. Its towers were cracked and covered with ivy. Whole stretches of wall were strangled by moss, their stones dark with age and rain. Trees had crept up to the outer battlements, roots splitting stone where no roots should ever be.

And yet, the Atlanteans had plastered their claim all over it. Blue and green banners whipped in the wind, snapped defiantly over crumbling ramparts as if fabric could erase fifty years of rot. Fresh torchlight outlined the walls, their glow mocking the dark, skeletal ruins within. Petty. Defiant.

In the fields beyond, thirty or so canvas tents sprawled in uneven clusters. I could see soldiers hunched at their fires, armor catching the orange glow, their voices faint on the night air. With those inside and camped in the field, the count fit our spies' numbers—about a hundred troops total. Enough to be trouble, but not enough to be invincible.

I pushed Big Red toward the sea, trying to peer past the black horizon. "Out there," I told her. She resisted hard, neck straining, wings fighting me with every beat. I pressed her again, even kicked my heels—but no. The great beast would not budge. And it wasn't just stubbornness. Her growl wasn't her usual "Finley, you're an idiot" rumble. This one was low, wary, almost fearful.

Dragons do not spook easy. Which meant something out there was off. I couldn't see it, but the air itself felt heavier the closer we angled toward the sea. We pressed against invisible hands. My ears popped once. Then again. I forced a laugh and shook it off. Just nerves. Just me overthinking. (Yeah, right.)

Instead, I steered her further east over the shadowed forest Pherric once dragged me through when we escaped from Malek's troops. From above, the trees were an endless black sea, branches shifting in the faint wind. No glint of steel, no fires glowing in the clearings. Just silence and dark. No armies waiting in ambush. That, at least, was something.

I patted her thick neck. "Take me home, girl. You've done well."

With a deep rumble, she banked wide, her wings slicing the clouds as we turned westward.

The campfires of our own forces soon blinked into view.

And I couldn't help grinning. Sandulf had wanted to rely on spies and their whispers. But I'd needed to see it with my own eyes. And now I had. The Atlanteans weren't invincible. They were foreigners waving flags from broken towers, hoping no one looked too closely at the cracks.

We could take them if it came to that. But it didn't have to. Sometimes a little show of strength was enough to rattle the cages of men clinging to ruins. And if we were lucky, they'd slink back to sea before blood was spilled.

26

Loose Ends

Jonathan

The potion lab smelled of crushed roots and chemicals, the kind of scent that clung to skin and never quite left the lungs. I measured out powders with careful fingers, grinding bone to dust, but even as I stirred, my mind was elsewhere.

I kept circling back to Genevieve. She had managed to escape, and better yet, she wasn't alone. One of the warrior women had gone with her. Knowing Genevieve, she would throw every ounce of strength and stubbornness into surviving. She was tough in ways that had nothing to do with weapons. Still, this world had teeth, and even someone like her could be swallowed by it. That thought gnawed at me.

If anyone could carve a path out of this place on nothing but sheer will and raw fury, it was her. I almost smiled, imagining her face set in that determined glare, pressing forward simply to spite everyone who had ever doubted her.

But then the guilt returned, heavy as a stone pressing on my chest. I could have gone with her. I had lied when I told her otherwise. I had the power to open the lock on my room door. Freedom was there for me. And still, I stayed.

The truth was as selfish as it was simple: I wanted more. I was learning things here that no book in my world could have offered me. And I was getting rather good at it. Ramil didn't praise me, but I didn't need him to. I could feel it in the way my mind reached further, grasping at every concept. I was becoming something sharper, more effective, and I couldn't bring myself to turn away from it.

That hunger to learn was at war with my conscience. Ramil's task was simple: assassinate the evil queen. But Genevieve swore she knew her, that she wasn't the monster he claimed. And I wanted to believe her. I truly did. But how could I be certain?

This realm changes people. I only had to look at myself to know that. Tir Na bends you, remakes you. What if the woman Genevieve remembered wasn't the one who ruled now? And then there were the visions Ramil had shown me. They were too real, too visceral to dismiss.

The city of Ker-Is reduced to ash, the dead piled like refuse, banners torn down and replaced by the usurper's flag. I still saw the burned streets in my mind; the heads mounted on pikes outside the city. And then there were the tens of thousands of Bànshēn rén corpses rotting outside their caves. Those horrors weren't lies. They felt etched into the fabric of truth itself.

Ramil watched me work from the corner of the room.

Jonus' massive shadow fell across my table, pulling me back to the present. The Fomorian instructor was as patient as stone, though even stone could crack.

Under his watchful eye, I tipped two grams of this world's monkshood into twenty grams of powdered wyvern bone, ground the mixture into a gray slurry, and diluted it with more water. When I offered it up to him, he sniffed, his lips tightening.

"Drink it."

The words stopped me cold. "What? No. That's not... No way."

His thick arms folded over his chest, immovable. "Drink."

My throat went dry. "I got it wrong, didn't I?" The steam curled between us.

"Drink your potion."

I shut my eyes, inhaled deeply, and tipped the cup back before the smell could turn me away. The taste was foul, clinging to my tongue. My stomach clenched immediately.

"Am I going to die?"

Jonus glanced out the window, measuring time by the sun's arc. "This evening you will sit above the privy, praying for death, but death will not answer. Drink this." He pushed a massive jar of water into my hands.

As I gulped it, he flipped open a yellowed tome and tapped the brittle page. "Nineteen pols monkshood, one pol wyvern bone. That was the balance. Instead, you have crafted a most efficient purgative."

Already my stomach shifted uneasily. My second real achievement in the Scholomance: a laxative. Perfect.

The door creaked, and Thagan entered with heavy steps, his eyes darting from me to Ramil. The ape-man's presence filled the room with unease. He bowed slightly but wasted no time.

"Leave us," Ramil commanded.

Jonus and I started toward the door, but Ramil's hand caught my sleeve, tugging me back.

Thagan's brow furrowed. "This is a delicate message, Ramil."

"He has earned the right to hear it," Ramil said. "He has demonstrated his loyalty."

The ape-man studied me for a long moment, as if weighing my soul. At last, he grunted. "As you wish."

He delivered his news carefully, each word deliberate. "My spies confirm the Atlanteans still hold Godsribbon Castle."

Ramil's jaw flexed. "Why are they still there?"

"I do not know. It was not part of the agreement. And... there is more." His hesitation shifted the tension in the room.

Ramil's head snapped around. "What is it now?"

"The queen has left Irkalla. She travels with a company of soldiers."

Ramil staggered against a table, hand pressed to his temple. "Headed where?"

"West. Toward Hyperborea."

Ramil's fury boiled over. He swept his hand across the workshop table, glass and stone breaking on the floor.

"To where her ships are moored! From there, she will sail them to Cíbola! Greedy, treacherous Atlantis! You cannot trust them with so much as a handshake. They betray for the pleasure of betrayal!"

Thagan's expression didn't change. "We expected risk."

"And yet we played their game," Ramil growled, voice raw. "Damn the gods!"

I stood there, locked in place, the burn of the potion still smoldering in my gut while the weight of Thagan's report pressed against my thoughts.

They spoke in fragments about their next move, intense words passing on what they would do next, but all I could hear was the echo of failure. Their plan to kill the Irkallan queen had faltered. Maybe that meant I wouldn't need to bloody my own hands with her death. The thought should have been a relief, but then I realized something darker: I might no longer be useful. And loose ends... well, men like Ramil didn't leave them dangling.

Thagan slipped out the door, leaving the workshop cloaked in simmering silence, I forced myself to speak.

"So, not good news, I take it?"

The words left my mouth before I could stop them, and I knew instantly it was a mistake.

Ramil's eyes fired at me, cold as winter. He let the silence draw out until it bit, then began pacing, the hem of his cloak whispering across the stone floor.

"The queen of Atlantis lured Finley out. Clever, and for her own ambitions. But Thalassa does not know who she truly is, nor the breadth of her power. My design is in ruins... but perhaps not beyond repair."

Hope. A dangerous, fragile word. Hope meant I might live.

I needed to include myself in there somehow. "What should we do?"

"You will continue your training," he said, his tone concise, "but adjustments may be required."

A chill threaded through me. Adjustments could mean anything in this place.

Anything.

27

A Capalu? Yes, a Capalu

Genevieve

We ran past the rocky hills and across the tundra of Pandæmonia long into the night, two fugitives sprinting away from the prison. My lungs felt shredded. Each inhale scraped like broken glass, but I didn't dare slow down. Not when every shadow behind us might be the Scholomance guards ready to drag us back.

No one came. There was no shouting. No armor or shiny helmets sparkled under the moonlight.

Maybe the fire was still keeping them busy. Maybe they hadn't even realized we were gone. But that was doubtful.

Eventually, the adrenaline burned out, and our legs gave up on pretending to be steel. I collapsed into a narrow and dried creek bed, too tired to care that it reeked of dead fish. My chest heaved. My arms trembled.

Kinnat stayed upright, scanning the darkness that was seemingly coming to get her.

"I think... we... did it," I wheezed between gasps.

"We did," she answered, but her tone was suspicious. "But it was easy... too easy."

I squinted at her from the ground. "What do you mean 'too easy'? We've been running for hours. And we're not exactly slow."

She didn't even look at me. "No, I mean our escape. Your plan. Getting out of the academy was... unexpectedly convenient."

I propped myself up on my elbows, stubborn. "I don't think so! We had a good plan. A big distraction. You had to... kill those guys. They never saw it coming!"

Kinnat gave me one of those cool glances, the kind that makes you feel dumb even if you're not. "Two seasons ago, there was an uprising in the great hall, during a meal. Three students tried to escape. But as the fight broke out, many soldiers immediately guarded every exit. They did not do that this time."

Her words pricked under my skin. Maybe she was right. It *had* been too easy.

No. No, I couldn't think about that.

"There was a fire! All-hands-on-deck kinda thing..." I forced a grin that I didn't feel. "They weren't expecting Jonathan to throw a little arson into their nighttime schedule."

But deep down, my stomach tightened.

Jonathan.

"I just wish he could have made it out," I muttered, and the guilt hit me. He'd risked everything for me, and now...

"What will they do to him?" I asked quietly.

"Your friend?" Kinnat tilted her head. "Depends on how valuable he is to them."

"Well, that Ramil guy said that Jonathan was the headliner and I was just an opening act." My voice cracked. Her brow furrowed at the reference. "They wanted him, basically. I was an added bonus. The backup plan."

"Then he will be tortured for his actions. But they will keep him alive."

My heart sank. I already knew that and hearing it out loud made it worse.

Silence stretched between us until the cold finally got loud enough to notice. The wind slashed across the plains, needling my skin. I rubbed my arms.

"Can we start a fire or something? You know how to do that shit, right?"

Kinnat sat across from me, unsheathing her sword and laying it across her lap. "I do know how, but this is all I have."

I snorted softly. "Same."

We had nothing. Two swords, ragged clothes, and a lot of questionable life choices.

She studied me, unimpressed. "I assume you brought no food or water? You smuggled out no flint?"

I gestured to my blade. "This is all I have."

Her exhale was half sigh, half judgment. "You were even less prepared than I imagined."

"Hey!" I jabbed a finger at her. "You can always go back! You asked to come along with me, girl!"

"I am not ungrateful. I am merely worried," she said calmly. Worry was something she carried in her pocket and forgot about.

She didn't seem scared. Just... annoyed.

"At least we have weapons," she added. "What is your plan?"

"Plan was to get out of that damn place. That's the plan," I shot back, maybe too fast.

"Where will you go now?"

Her question struck me. *You.* Not *we.* Like she was already halfway out of this mess.

I stared across the dark tundra. The bushes swayed at me, whispering threats I couldn't hear.

"Um," I stammered, then forced my voice into something steadier. "Well... the only place I can, I guess." I lifted my chin, faking bravado. "My friend. Finley. Apparently, she's some kinda queen or something. I've got to find her. And let her know she's in trouble."

"Then you head for Irkalla?"

"Yeah," I said, praying she'd say she was going that way too. "Wh-what about you?"

She leaned back on her arms, eyes tracing the constellations above. "I am free now. I can go anywhere."

"Where are you from?"

A shadow crossed her face. "I hail from Hyperborea. But I cannot return to my village, on the outskirts of Nirvana."

"Why not? Nirvana sounds... nice. Where I come from that means heaven."

"It is anything but nice. I have shamed my family by escaping the Scholomance. However, I may find work in the kingdom. Some rich merchant might need a guard. Or I could join a band of mercenaries for a lord. My academy training, even though it was not complete, is not without merit."

"So," I said, cautious, "is Hyperborea on the way to Irkalla?"

She sighed. "Yes, I can take you there if you do not know the way."

Relief whooshed out of me. "Girl, I have no fucking idea where I'm at right now. I don't even belong on this world."

Confusion flickered over her face. "Everyone has a right to a life in this world. You do belong and—"

"No! No, you misunderstand. I'm not from here. This planet. Tir Na, or whatever it's called."

Her eyes narrowed. "I do not understand. All people are from Tir Na."

"Oh, girl. Not at all." My laugh came out brittle. It hadn't even hit me until now—these people didn't know Earth existed. And I hadn't known this place existed until I was dragged here, kicking and screaming.

I almost told her. About the skyscrapers, taxis, streaming shows, pizza slices at midnight. About New York. But the wild look in her eyes stopped me cold.

"What I mean is that I'm from a faraway land. Really far. Whole other continent kinda thing. To the, uh, far west. You know what I mean?"

"You are from Mu?"

"Yes, Mu. That's it. Me from Mu." Totally nailed that lie.

"That makes a great deal of sense now. Your language and mannerisms. Your inability to fight..." I arched an eyebrow at her. "...at the beginning of your training. Mu must be a strange place to be raised."

"Oh, it's very strange. Very different," I said lightly, and it was killing me to pretend.

She rose fluidly, scanning the horizon. "We must be on the move again.

We will head northwest, toward Irkalla."

"And how do we know how to do that?"

She seemed confused and pointed at the stars like they were a damn GPS.

So I stood, brushed the dirt off my legs, and ran after her into the darkness.

We jogged on and off for most of the day, our shadows stretching long across this strange world. Tir Na seemed like it was a redesign of Earth, but built from reflections in a mirror—the shapes were familiar with no detail quite correct. The grass glowed faintly under the sun, silver-green and slick.

We managed to find a thin, winding river and drank until our stomachs ached. The water was icy and sweet, kind of fizzy, and for a terrifying second, I wondered if it was even safe—but thirst didn't give me the luxury of caution. Kinnat found clusters of berries that bled blue juice down our fingers. She tried spearing fish in the river, then went sprinting after two squirrel-looking creatures with too many joints in their legs but came back empty-handed. Even that bland slop from the Scholomance mess hall sounded good by the end of the day.

With no one chasing us, we decided it was safe to walk by nightfall.

"There are too many terrors in the night, waiting for us, to be running into their traps," Kinnat warned in the same calm tone she used for everyday observations.

And it didn't help that we had wandered off the open plains into a thick forest that seemed to swallow light. The canopy blotted out the bluish moon, plunging us into a living shadow. Every sound felt magnified: the distant hoot of something with too many lungs, the click-chatter of odd little insects. Breezes slithered through the branches and made them scrape against each other. Leaves rustled with unseen things.

Every noise, every blur of motion between the trees made my skin crawl. And every time I jumped, I told myself I wasn't scared. Not yet.

"Yeah, too many damn terrors," I muttered, voice cracking halfway through.

But Kinnat marched through the forest like it was a Sunday stroll down

Park Avenue. She moved with this calm, predatory grace, eyes forward, shoulders loose. Unbothered. Either she was immune to the dangers—or she just knew exactly which ones were worth fearing.

Me? I tried to mimic her breathing, her stride, her stillness. Anything to stop my pulse from beating out a battle drum inside my skull. The deeper we went, the more the trees pressed in. Their trunks were warped and bending, their bark slick and black as oil. Shadows curled at the edges of my vision.

We heard a snap of branches off the path. Far, but not far enough.

Kinnat's arm shot out across my chest, halting me.

"What?"

"Quiet," she whispered, voice clipped. She sniffed the air, eyes narrowing. "Do not move."

Everything in me went tight. The forest waited with me.

I stole a quick look behind us. Two glowing yellow slits hanging in the dark, eight or nine feet off the ground. Unblinking.

"Um," I stammered, tugging on Kinnat's sleeve. "There."

She spun, her sword flashing in the dim light. I fumbled for mine, nearly dropping it as she backed silently away from the path.

The creature sank lower, melting out of the black, those eyes drilling straight through me. It was crouching. Waiting. My sword shook in my grip. My whole body did.

"Capalu!" Kinnat barked. "Run!"

I didn't need to know what that meant. My survival instinct understood just fine.

I sprinted hard. Branches tore at my clothes. Heavy thuds pounded the ground behind me, as if boulders were slamming into the dirt. I almost lost my footing and caught myself on the trunk. I slid around the tree.

Something massive lunged past—a blur of bluish-black fur slicing through the moonlight.

Panic hijacked my body. I staggered further off the path, sword trembling out in front of me.

The creature returned to me and stalked into view, padding through the trees and no longer trying to be silent. Each step was deliberate, crushing dry branches. It growled, a rumble that vibrated the air, and hissed all around.

And then it stepped into the light.

The capalu was a giant cat—but not any kind that belonged on a cute calendar. Ten feet tall, shoulders rippling with muscle under patchy blue fur streaked with old scars. Tall, pointed ears crowned its head, and a long wisp of a white beard swung from its chin. Two yellow slit-eyes glared. From its forehead rose a pair of twisted horns, black as night.

It snarled, lips peeling back to show thick, blood-stained jagged fangs.

I was locked in place. Couldn't pull in any air.

It reared back, coiling to pounce.

And I... did nothing. My sword was up, but my eyes squeezed shut. I was a child hiding under the covers. This was it.

A whoosh cut the air.

The capalu shrieked—a raw, bone-splitting sound. I opened my eyes.

Kinnat's blade cut across its cheek, her whole body a blur. She ducked under its clawed swipe and drove her sword up into its chin, blood spraying everywhere. She spun, trying to strike again, but the beast fell back, staggering.

She shouted, brandishing her sword, arms out wide to make herself bigger. The capalu hissed, ears flat, and then turned, crashing away into the trees with a final enraged snarl.

Kinnat grabbed my arm in an iron grip and yanked me to the path.

"Run."

We ran. Fast. Branches lashed our arms and faces. The forest was a haze of thorns and shadows and teeth I imagined chasing us. We didn't stop until the trees thinned, and open sky finally returned above us.

I bent over, choking on air. "Thank you."

"You nearly got us killed!" she screamed, voice cracking as she tried to catch her breath.

"What? I... I didn't know how to—"

"You paused. The way you did at the entrance to the academy! That guard would have killed you. And so would the capalu!"

"What was I supposed to do?! I've never seen anything like that before!"

"When you are faced with death, you must fight or run. That creature is slow, but if you simply stand there, you die!"

"Fuck that! I was scared to death!"

"And to death you will go. You run, jump to the side, slash at a beast that large. You hurt it any way you can, if you want to live. Together, we would have killed it... and had food to eat!"

I wanted to scream that this wasn't fair. That I didn't grow up here, that this world didn't come with a goddamn instruction manual. That no one back in New York ever taught me how to stab a demon-cat with horns.

But she was raised here. This kind of terror was her alphabet, and I hadn't even learned the letters.

I swallowed my excuses.

"I'm sorry."

She sheathed her sword with an elegant motion. "Save your apologies for when you stand at my funeral pyre because you have gotten me killed. If you outlive me."

She marched ahead without looking back.

I stood there shaking, staring at the black mouth of the forest behind us. Hoping we'd hurt the thing enough that it wouldn't follow.

But those glowing eyes were burned into my brain.

I shuddered and forced my legs to move.

28

A Lesson in Truth

Jonathan

As I made my way to the workshop the next day, the hallway felt too quiet. The stone walls seemed to be listening. Anticipating.

I rounded a corner and almost collided with Thagan. I tried to slip past, but he stepped into my path with the subtlety of a large rock, his broad shoulders swallowing the torchlight. The ape-man wasn't prone to wasted words, which made the ones he spoke land with more weight.

"You need to know something," he rumbled.

"Okay," I said carefully. Part of me braced for some scandalous revelation about Ramil, a man I still wasn't sure I trusted. I glanced past him, then behind me. No one else was around.

"Whatever Ramil has told you about Queen Finley," he said, eyes narrowing, "it was not enough."

"Um... what?"

His jaw tightened. "About what she has done."

"He's told me. And he's even shown me with his spells. I have a pretty good idea of what she's—"

"You do not." The snarl in his voice vibrated through the air. "You were not there."

"Look, you really don't need to convince me. If you all say she's bad, I-I believe you."

He stared me up and down, weighing my worth. "I doubt your conviction, acolyte. If you have not seen her deeds with your own eyes, it will be difficult for you to make her pay for her crimes. And she must pay. But when the time comes, I fear you will hesitate."

The look in his eyes said more than his words. "She did something to you," I said quietly. "Personally."

He lowered his head—shame, or something close to it.

"I was away from my home, fighting beside the Prominan military in the mountains of Kunlun. When her overwhelming force broke our ranks, I retreated. I returned to my village to regroup before the battle of Shangri-La."

Real tears welled in his eyes.

"She and her knight commanders had already been there," he said. "When I arrived, the village was razed. Only one survived—my daughter. She crawled out from beneath a mountain of smoldering corpses, half her face cut away. Delirious. Dying. She spoke of the fire-haired queen who ordered the slaughter. Of children torn from huts. Elders beheaded for refusing to kneel. A night when smoke blotted out the stars."

He swallowed hard. "I carried my child to the river crossing and held her to keep her warm. She died before sunrise. But the look in her eyes—the fear, the anguish—I will never forget. Nor will I forgive."

He met my gaze, and for the first time since I'd met him, I sensed something brittle beneath the unbending steel of him.

"If you think Ramil lies," he said, voice low and ragged, "know what I saw with my own eyes. Bodies. The dead stacked high. Unarmed females and children gutted. Blood running in the dirt. And among it all, my daughter's voice. She feared only one name."

Finley.

He left me with that—a single, haunting testimony echoing in my brain long after he disappeared down the corridor.

The workshop felt quieter than normal after my encounter with Thagan.

The alchemy room was filled with everything one would expect: glass vials, a brass alembic, bundles of dried herbs, and a mortar and pestle.

But only one object mattered that day: a squat metal calibration weight, no bigger than my hand, sitting dead center on the table.

I inhaled and slowly let it out. Settling my mind.

Without anger or any emotion. I needed to lift the weight.

Easier said than done.

I extended my hand... not physically reaching, but letting the energy unfurl, thin and invisible, a vapor tracing toward the weight. I placed my mental fingers around the object, feeling the smooth metal without really touching it.

The metal quivered. A faint tremor, barely perceptible. My pulse jumped, hope surging a hair too fast.

The tremor died. My mental fingers passed through and disappeared in my mind.

I exhaled. "Okay. Cool. This is going well."

I tried again, slower this time. Shoulders relaxed. No clenching. Anger made the power spike. Calm made it slippery, evasive. The trick was holding on without squeezing too hard.

"C'mon," I whispered. "Float. Levitate. Do literally anything except lie there like a smug little paperweight."

The chunk of metal scraped the table. Lifted maybe a millimeter. Then thunked back with the sad decisiveness of a falling teaspoon.

The power warmed in my chest. Not hot, but present. A thread being pulled.

I focused. Narrowed everything down to that stubborn piece of metal. Gently, gently—

It rose.

Barely. A hair off the table. But it was *up.* Suspended on nothing but intent, my heartbeat, and the hope that I wasn't about to faceplant onto the counter.

I held it. Held it. My vision blurred slightly at the edges, but I didn't dare blink. The weight hovered in a shaky ellipse before I guided it down, slow as drifting snow—

It touched the table with a whisper.

"That," said a voice behind me, "is progress."

I spun. Ramil stood in the doorway, expression unreadable.

"Oh," I said, heartbeat still hammering. "I, uh... didn't hear you."

Ramil stepped into the room with the quiet authority of someone who'd never once questioned whether he belonged somewhere. His eyes switched from the calibration weight to me. "How long have you been at it?"

"No idea," I admitted. "Time got weird."

"That is a good sign." He circled the table, hands clasped behind him. "You draw from emotion, but not only from it. You discipline it. That is rare."

"Thanks," I said, still gasping. "I'll, uh... and hey. I just want you to know that I'll be ready for Finley."

His eyes narrowed to slits as he stared at the metal weight. "Why do you bring this up?"

"Oh, well, Thagan really convinced me earlier today."

It was the wrong thing to say.

Ramil's head snapped toward me so fast I flinched. "Thagan spoke to you?"

"Yes? I mean... Yeah, he caught me in the hallway and—"

Ramil was already sweeping toward the door, robes flaring in a violent storm front. "Stay here."

His footsteps vanished down the corridor. Then came raised voices—muffled, echoing, unmistakably angry.

A moment later Ramil strode back in, dragging Thagan by the wrist. The ape-man yanked free the instant they crossed the threshold, snarling low in his throat.

"You presume too much," Ramil snapped at the ape, jabbing a finger at me. "You do not approach him without my sanction."

Thagan squared his shoulders, unafraid. "He is untested. He has not seen the queen's crimes. I fear he will falter."

"That is *not* your concern!"

Thagan's jaw tightened. "If he hesitates, even a moment, all we have worked for will crumble."

"And if you interfere again," Ramil said, voice dropping to a cold near-whisper, "I will cut out your tongue and feed it to the mountain wyrms. You are not to meddle with my acolyte."

For a heartbeat, no one moved. Then Thagan dipped his head, barely, and stalked out, his heavy footfalls shaking the glassware.

Ramil smoothed his robe, collecting himself. "Do not concern yourself with Thagan's theatrics. He is loyal, but... rigid."

I nodded, throat dry. "Right."

Ramil studied me for a long, searching time. "Tell me, Jonathan. What did he share? I do not want him to have distracted you in any way."

The memory of Thagan's story, his daughter crawling from the ashes, danced behind my eyes.

"He told me of the destruction of his village," I said quietly. "And the loss of his daughter."

Ramil's expression shuttered. "Ah, yes. That is when I found him, shortly thereafter."

He started to walk off but paused, considering everything.

"If he sees doubt," he said without looking away from the floor. "then perhaps I should give you access to... the memories."

I blinked. Memories?

He turned on his heel. "Come. I believe you are ready for this. Your mindform abilities are extraordinary for someone with your limited training." That bit of praise should have given me cause for concern. But it didn't.

I followed him out of the workshop and into the spine of the academy. The deeper we walked, the colder the air became, as though the stone remembered every sorrow etched into it. Lanterns shone warily as we passed.

"Where are we going?" I asked, unable to shake off the chill invading me.

"To truth."

We descended a spiral staircase carved so narrowly it forced us single file. The air grew ancient—heavy with dust and something foul that clung to the tongue.

At the bottom, the corridor widened into an archway framed by black iron. Beyond it lay a circular chamber unlike anything I'd seen. Blue fire burned in sconces without consuming fuel, casting a cold glow that made shadows ripple unnaturally. The stone floor was etched with concentric rings of runes, each one pulsing faintly to its own heartbeat.

Ramil stepped inside. "The Historium."

He said it with reverence, but also something else. Dread, maybe.

Along the far wall, half lost in the wavering blue light, stood a huge ornate cabinet. Ten doors were lined up etched with more symbols. Ramil approached, pulling one door open. Inside, shelves held an assortment of relics and instruments—obsidian phials, folded scraps of parchment, crystal shards sitting on dark cloth, and small metal implements arranged with ritual precision. Nothing was dusty. Nothing looked unused. Each object rested in its own cataloged niche.

"What is this place?" I whispered.

"Memory. Proof. I collected items from the destruction of Ker-Is. To preserve what was done so none may deny it."

At the center of the room stood a stone pedestal. He pulled three items from the collection and laid them on the surface.

Ramil motioned me forward. "Approach."

My feet moved even when my doubts told me to turn back. The air shifted as I neared the pedestal—charged, expectant, a thunderstorm in waiting.

He set down a blackened dagger, a child's blood-soaked wool shirt, and a dented soldier's helmet still streaked with ash.

Ramil took my wrist. His grip was cool, precise. "These contain the echoes of Ker-Is. The night the queen obliterated the last defenders. When you touch them, you will see what was seen."

"See," I repeated. "Like an illusion?"

"Like truth."

A tremor shivered down my spine.

Ramil guided my hand toward the child's shirt and placed my other hand on the helmet. "Do not fear. Let it speak."

My fingers brushed the surface.

The world didn't just fade—it was torn away.

Heat slammed into me first. A wet, suffocating, and breathing heat came through the blood-soaked cloth. The sky above wasn't a sky anymore but a veil of smoke ripping open to reveal a burning red wound. Screams echoed from nowhere and everywhere at once. My knees faltered.

I was standing—no, *dragged*—into the ruins of Ker-Is.

Bodies lay in heaps, twisted into angles no living thing should ever make. The stone streets ran slick with a dark, steaming slurry. Square towers belched fire into a sky that looked ready to collapse.

I looked down and I was holding the limp body of a small boy, his blond hair matted with crimson.

Women huddled together nearby, shielding children with whatever remained of their strength. An Irkallan soldier, wearing the same battered helmet I had touched, staggered past me, armor half-melted, his face locked in a mask of horror.

And there—at the heart of the inferno in the city square—

A silhouette crowned in red.

Here hair was a living flame.

A blade rose high, dripping dark blood.

Her voice cut through the carnage and it was metal shearing bone. I couldn't understand the words, but I felt the fury in them—the power, the unrelenting certainty—as they crawled beneath my skin and hooked into my ribs.

The queen.

Finley.

She turned.

Her eyes, burning with rage, locked onto me.

And the world shattered.

I crashed back into my body with a strangled gasp, hitting the stone floor hard enough that dust rained down around me. My lungs convulsed, dragging in air that felt too thin to fill me. Cold sweat raced down my spine, chilling so fast it left my skin prickling.

But nothing could cool the heat of the memory still seared behind my eyes.

The smell of burning flesh clung to the back of my throat. The boy's limp weight still ghosted in my arms. The soldier's hollow stare was etched into my eyes, carving it there with a hot knife.

I squeezed my eyes shut, but the images didn't vanish—they sharpened.

A wave of disbelief surged up... followed immediately by something heavier, denser, impossible to escape.

Acceptance.

Not the quiet kind. Not peaceful. The kind that slams into you when you fall from a great height.

Ramil hadn't lied. Thagan hadn't embellished. The Historium wasn't a trick. All those horrors, they were real, and I had felt them.

My stomach fell. And for the first time since arriving in Irkalla, I felt something break open inside me.

Ramil watched me, hands folded, expression unreadable. "That was only one atrocity."

I shook my head violently. "It felt real."

"It *was* real."

"I..." My voice cracked. "Maybe Genevieve knew another version of her. Maybe she changed. Maybe—"

"Enough." Ramil's tone cut cleanly. "If you needed any more proof, you have it now. Irkalla has given it. Is there any remaining doubt?"

I stared at the items on the pedestal.

I didn't answer but shook my head.

Ramil stepped closer. "Good. You now understand what we are up against."

Later, back in the workshop, my head still ringing, I stood before him. "I want to help. I need to help. To end her reign. What was your plan?"

His head snapped towards me. "You need not concern yourself."

But I could see it now, the pieces arranging themselves in my mind.

"Here's what I think I've figured out. You were going to bring me to Irkalla. Close, not too close. Somewhere near Finley but not within her sight. You've already smuggled the poison in, or you have a way to. And then... you were going to have me to move the poison unseen with a mindform. Into her food, her wine. A simple swallow, and the queen falls. Clean. Silent. No one the wiser."

His eyes narrowed, suspicion surfacing.

"But Thagan has told you that she's left Irkalla. What if the game isn't over?"

"How do you mean?" he asked, arms folded.

"Find out where she is now. We only need to follow her there. Your plan can still work."

Abruptly, he surged forward. I flinched back, heart hammering, but he caught my face in his hands before I could retreat. His grip was iron.

And then he smiled. Wide. Devilish.

"I have underestimated you," he whispered.

I forced myself to square my shoulders, standing taller though his touch chilled my skin.

"Maybe we will have easier access to her," I said. "We can bring the poison to her."

For a moment, he said nothing. Then his hand patted my cheek. Too hard. It was a mockery of affection. His nod was curt, measured. Approval or calculation, I couldn't tell. But I'd given him a sliver of strategy to chew on.

29

Thalassa

Finley

Sandulf marched our troops east over scrub-choked slopes and harsh ridgelines, each rise sucking the air from their lungs and every descent sending loose stones clattering under their boots. Kasuma scouted ahead, a silent wraith against the hills, occasionally slipping back to report that there was still no sign of Atlantean patrols. Which was odd.

Braylor and I rode at the rear of the company, our karkadanns plodding side by side in cold silence. Well—*his* silence. I was still persona non grata for taking Big Red and scouting the castle alone. Honestly, fair. As a leader, I kind of suck. I'm not a delegator, I'm a doer. It's hard enough to trust the words of others, and even harder to ask them to risk their lives based on my instincts.

Naturally, he had to make it worse.

Without looking at me, Braylor finally spoke, voice clipped and cold. "When we arrive at Godsribbon, Sandulf will array the company in the field as a show of force. You will not be an active participant. Sandulf will address whoever is in charge."

I blinked at him. "Oh, so you're going to forbid me? We *both* know how well that works."

"No, I—"

"I am queen, dammit!"

"You saw what they did to our messengers," he snapped, the words were whip cracking hard. "One crossbow bolt from those walls and—"

"I will not be left behind like some fragile whelpling!"

"I did not say you would."

"...What?"

"You will be present. Among the soldiers, dressed as they are. You will listen. But you will not speak, nor reveal yourself as Queen of Irkalla."

Okay. Annoyingly... that actually made sense. The whole *not speaking* part? Asking a lot.

His voice softened. "You must understand. I fear for you. Despite your immortality, flawed as it is, I do not wish to see you harmed."

"You and me both, big guy. But I need to be there. To see this through."

"I know. That is why I will not try to stop you. I am simply... trying to make you as safe as possible."

"Just say you love me and get it over with," I teased, because humor is cheaper than therapy.

"I do..." he mumbled.

"You do... what?"

"Love you."

I slapped his arm as I laughed. "See? That wasn't hard."

He shot me a mean stare—but it cracked, and when I blew him a kiss, he finally broke into a reluctant grin.

Sandulf did exactly as Braylor predicted. When we reached Godsribbon Castle, he lined our company in crisp formation across the grassy field before its looming stone walls.

And just like that, I was back in that moment when I first arrived on Tir Na—standing with Pherric, peeking through the gate as King Malek and his Irkallan soldiers stood in terrifying formation. Funny how the tables turn. The irony was not lost on me. (If that's irony. Is it? I really need someone to explain irony to me. Later.)

One poor soldier was drafted to strip off his chainmail, black tunic with royal blue trim, and the shiny helmet crowned with a black-and-blue plume. I threw on the outfit, tugged the helmet low, and rode out to take my place in the kark line, like just another sword in Sandulf's company.

Sandy and Braylor rode their karkadanns to the fore, all full of badassery.

Atlanteans watched from the battlements. Their troops who'd camped outside had vanished inside—hard to blame them. Two hundred armed Irkallans approaching doesn't exactly whisper "friendly visit."

Finally, after making us stew in silence, a figure appeared atop the barbican.

Not tall like most Tirnians. Lean build, skin baked golden brown from sun and salt. Short dark hair. Bare-chested, with gills slitted along his sides. I could just make out the webbing between each finger. Hence, the merman bit, I guess. A silver circlet with a single green gem rested on his brow. He planted a trident on the stone and propped one foot on a broken battlement, gray eyes flaring with disdain.

"What do you want?!" he called down, voice full of cocky derision.

Sandulf straightened in his saddle. "I am Sandulf, Knight Commander of the Royal Irkallan Army and—"

"I do not care." The man began picking his teeth. We were an annoying interruption to lunch.

"You are trespassing on Cíbolan land."

"I could say the same of your Irkallan incursion," he spat. He gestured at Braylor. "And who are you?"

"I am your worst nightmare," Braylor growled.

Sandulf cleared his throat. "He is the Royal Consort to the Queen of Irkalla."

"Ah, the queen's whore," the man sneered.

Braylor's hand went to his sword. His kark stamped the ground.

Sandulf's arm shot out. "Braylor... stand down."

"I want his head."

"And you may have it. Later. Not now."

Braylor sheathed his blade, knuckles still white on the pommel.

"We will not be leaving. This castle is ours. And I will speak only with the one in charge!" the man shouted.

"I am in charge," said Sandulf.

The man laughed, slow and disbelieving. "No. I will speak with your queen."

Sandulf glanced at Braylor. Braylor shook his head.

He raised his voice. "You will speak with me... or with my sword."

"I am Goran, First Sea-lord of Atlantis," the man declared. "Be a good little messenger and tell her I await her presence. We know she travels with you."

Sandulf began. "Do not assume these crumbling walls will protect you."

"And do not assume we need them," Goran cut in.

While the men postured, I nudged my karkadann forward.

"Your highness," Sandulf hissed.

"Finley!" Braylor barked. "What are you—"

"I got this," I said, flashing them a grin. I looked up at Goran. "Yo, Sea-lord guy! Goran, right? It's me. Finley Maguire."

Goran eyed me, then shook his head. His gaze slid to Sandulf as he pointed at me. "You expect me to believe this waif is your queen? Have you no shame, boy?"

"Hey! Limp-dick! Down here. Eyes on me!" I yanked off the helmet, letting my red hair spill.

That made him pause. Really *look* at me.

I tossed the helmet into the grass. "Now. Be a good little errand boy and fetch your queen. Because I'm betting she's here, too."

His mouth opened.

"Ah-ah!" I cut him off. "Off you go—or this magnificent specimen..." I thumbed at Braylor, "... will climb your wall and cut your tongue out before you can even cry for your mommy."

Sandulf leaned closer and murmured, "I am quite sure he believes you now, your majesty."

I winked as Goran's face tightened. He turned on his heel and stalked off the barbican, his arrogance cracking just enough to make me feel like

I'd won that round.

We waited. And waited.

The hot sun pressed down, sweat tracing slow rivers down my spine beneath the black tunic and suffocating chainmail. The metal had been roasting in the sun for hours, turning me into a human baked potato.

"Fuck this," I muttered, shifting in the saddle. "We're done waiting."

I was about to kick my karkadann into a dramatic charge when Sandulf raised a hand, eyes fixed on the barbican.

"Wait," he whispered.

Several Atlantean mermen strode out onto the barbican in perfect unison. Each wore light gold armor chased with sea-green enamel and gold capes. In their hands... harps. Not normal harps, either. Strange crescent-shaped things strung with shimmering silver wire.

They fanned into a line and began plucking in eerie harmony.

A haunting melody poured over the field, fluid and otherworldly. The silky notes slid through the air, reverberating off stone and bone.

When the final chord shivered away, every single Atlantean on the walls dropped to one knee, heads bowed low in synchronized reverence. The sudden silence throbbed.

"Oh, boy," I whispered. "This oughta be good."

A herald stepped forward from behind the harpists, posture straight as a spear, head lifted. His voice boomed out, amplified by the walls.

"Make way and bow low! Behold Her Sublime Majesty... Thalassa," he bellowed. "Sovereign of the Nine Currents, Keeper of the Abyssal Crown, First Voice of the Trident, She-Who-Binds-the-Tides, Queen of Atlantis Eternal and All the Sunken Realms, Warden of the Twilight Gates, Scourge of Tempests, Breaker of Storms, Mother to the Drowned, and The Radiant Pearl of the Deep."

We did *not* bow.

But I did try really, really hard not to laugh.

I leaned toward Braylor and whispered, "I need a better title. Similar to hers."

He ignored me, eyes forward and jaw clenched. Typical.

Okay, yes—I made fun.

But then she appeared.

She glided out and the world was hers. The rest of us just got to play along.

Her thick liquid obsidian hair spilled down her back, moving in slow waves as though the wind itself knew better than to muss it. Her tanned skin caught the sunlight and *glowed*. Not sparkled. Not shimmered. Glowed.

Her bright gray eyes—so pale they were nearly translucent—swept across the field. She was cataloging which of us would die first.

Her clothes (if you could call them that) clung and fluttered, conspiring to make everyone stare: a white split-thigh skirt with fine gold cords hugging her hips, and white silk straps crossing her torso that somehow managed to highlight every curve while revealing just enough of her gills to remind you she wasn't exactly Hominan.

She walked with the kind of easy, devastating grace that made every step look choreographed, hips swaying, chin high. This was her stage and we were lucky to watch.

And god help me... I am not into women. But she could have made me switch sides on the spot.

Easily.

Even Sandulf and Braylor sat locked in place on their karkadanns, two slack-jawed and drooling idiots.

"Braylor," I hissed.

He didn't blink. "What?"

Men. All the same.

Thalassa stopped at the center of the barbican, hands on her hips, a goddess surveying her lesser creations. Seriously. She stared down at us. We were ants to her; ants she could crush between two lazy fingers.

"I am Thalassa," she said.

And her voice? Oh, god. Low. Gravelly. Sultry. Dark honey poured over jagged stone.

"I am Thalassa," she repeated. "What would you like?"

Well, to punch you in your stupid perfect face.
Or kiss you.
I couldn't be sure which at the time.

30

Zeranthyl

Finley

Thalassa's words flooded my brain.

Her question.

"What would you like?"

Most people say *What do you want?* or *What can I do for you?*

Her phrasing was something spoken by a god, not a mortal queen. As if she weren't offering negotiation… but granting boons. *Gifts from on high.*

And that—that—bothered me.

I had no idea why I did what I did next, only that I ran with the impulse. Old me never would have. Maybe it was the weight of my invisible crown. Maybe I just couldn't stand sitting on my karkadann, mouth agape like Braylor and Sandulf, while she loomed over us, as a mother scolding her wayward children.

So I ignored her. And I channeled my inner Genevieve (man, I *really* missed her.) I kicked my kark's flank and circled out in front of my army, turning my back on the queen of Atlantis.

My heart thundered. I hoped they couldn't see the way my hands trembled on the reins.

"Soldiers of Irkalla!" I shouted. My voice carried, stronger than I felt. "Today we face the might of Atlantis—but be not afraid!"

Braylor hissed, "Fin, what are you—?"

"Relax," I muttered from the corner of my mouth. "I got this."

I let the kark pace as I raised my sword skyward. "The Atlanteans are trespassers! They have invaded Cíbola and slain the brave soldiers of the Scholomance!"

Thalassa's voice cut in, cold and edged. "What is happening here?"

I drowned her out.

"They occupy this ancient castle and misuse a forbidden magic reserved only for the gods themselves!"

Gasps rippled through my ranks. I darted my eyes up—Thalassa had crossed her arms, smiling as though watching a child perform a magician's trick.

"Today," I roared, "we will drive them back to the sea and return this castle to its rightful guardians!"

The Irkallan soldiers erupted, slamming shields and raising swords, their cheers echoing. My throat was dry as sand. I spun my kark to face her again.

"Is this how you negotiate, Queen Finley?" she purred.

"Well, your sea lord dude said you weren't leaving."

"Goran does not speak for me."

"Then put someone in charge who does." My voice held steady; my stomach lurched. Sweat slid down my spine. I tasted bile.

She tilted her head, eyes twinkling. "I see why you were victorious at the Battle of Shangri-La. Despite your fear, you stand tall against your enemy... even without the right to interfere."

There it was again—that condescension emanating off her words.

"Cíbola is a nation of city-states," I managed. "I speak on their behalf. And the Scholomance."

"Did they summon you?" she asked, striding along and vanishing, then reappearing between each battlement. "Did they specifically ask for your help?"

My mind scrambled. "No."

"I see..."

"But what's in that castle is off limits. To everyone. That's law."

"That is *your* law."

"Oh, sorry—are you above the law? How nice."

"We do not recognize it," she said with a feline smirk.

"Convenient." I nudged closer. Sandulf's warning throat-clear vibrated behind me. "But I know what's inside. And what it does. I was a victim of it. And I will not let you use it. Not one more second. Understand me?"

Her gaze sharpened. I couldn't tell if she suspected I wasn't from this world—or just admired my defiance. I channeled Genevieve and prayed it showed.

"Such a violent little Hominan," she stated. "You are bold to ask me to leave. But boldness has always been a surface trait, has it not? Charging ahead, trusting the land beneath your feet to stay still."

Her gaze drifted to the bay behind the castle. "The sea... is less forgiving. It remembers every wound. Every neglect."

A slow smile. "And one day, it remembers back."

"I have no idea what that means," I shouted. Because I didn't.

"What if I refuse to leave?"

Braylor and Sandulf edged closer, blades half-drawn.

"Then we remove you," I said. "By force. We outnumber you. And that would be a mistake."

Her laugh was a bell. "Oh, I never make a mistake."

A nod from her, and Goran vanished.

Then came the whoosh.

Low at first, a distant wind rushing through the field, then louder—a roar of air that grew until it drowned out everything else.

The harpists scattered. Atlantean guards fled the battlements.

A shadow blotted out the sun.

A massive purple dragon surged up behind the castle, wings stretched wider than the barbican itself. Each downbeat sent hot gusts whipping my hair into my eyes, snapping banners and swirling clothing.

It banked, circling, and then slammed down onto the roof with the weight of a collapsing mountain. The ground lurched under us. Dust geysered from cracked stone.

The beast reared back and bellowed.

The sound punched straight through my chest.

All around me, my soldiers faltered. Boots scraped on grass as lines broke. Gasps rose. Someone screamed. At least three took off outright, throwing down their shields as they fled.

I kept my eyes locked on her. My body screamed to run.

The dragon prowled forward, layers of violet sliding over one another as he shifted. His great head dipped, nuzzling her shoulder with careful restraint. She smiled, calm as still water, and stroked his jaw with long, perfect fingers.

Shit. Now I knew why Big Red had refused to cross the sea. She'd sensed this monster. And it was likely flying around out there in the dark.

"Let me introduce... Zeranthyl," she stated. "Do you still think you outnumber us?"

My brain spun. I needed focus. Needed clarity. I made the call. *Mindform time...*

I waited, hoping to time it right, and snapped my fingers. But nothing happened. Because naturally. Embarrassing.

A few awkward seconds later, a new rustle split the air.

It started low, more thunder and even more rage, the wingbeats shoving warm air down.

My big red dragon dove from the western sky, sunlight blazing off her dark scales. She skimmed the treetops, tearing them open with her slipstream, and then dropped. My very own shooting star.

She hit the field with an earth-shaking boom. Clods of dirt and crushed grass shot in all directions. My troops staggered back, raising arms against the blast of heat from her wings.

But none of them ran. Not this time. They stared, wide-eyed, giving her a wide berth as she folded her wings with a leathery snap. When I heard no one cry out or run, I imagined them standing there, eyes wide but emboldened by having a dragon on their side.

I didn't look back at Big Red. My gaze stayed on Thalassa.

The dragon threw her head up and unleashed a screech fierce enough to rattle my chainmail—a challenge, raw and primal.

A smirk cracked my face. *My girl.*

"Yes," I said. "Yes, I do."

The purple dragon Zeranthyl snarled. Big Red growled back, deep and murderous.

But one spark in that moment from either one and it was fire and death for everyone.

Thalassa only smiled, stroking her beast.

"Ah, the tales are true," she mused. "You are a dragonwitch."

"They are," I said, bluffing confidence I didn't feel.

"How delightful!" she squealed. "And now... what are we to do?"

She tossed it to me, wanting to see how I'd react as a leader. I wanted to cry *attack*—but we would all die. And we were the ones picking the fight.

"That's up to you," I said.

Her smile widened. She knew I wouldn't.

"Then... we are at an impasse. I am famished. I shall retire to my new chambers and dine. If you attack, we will be ready."

She swept away. At least fifty Atlantean soldiers suddenly appeared along the walls of the castle. Each was armed with spears, tridents, and traditional bows. What scared the hell out of me were the ones with crossbows.

The Atlanteans were said to have superior weapons, and the crossbow was not something I expected. From everything I remembered, they were more accurate and way more powerful than bows. Even though they were slow to load, they could have several rows of shooters lined up behind the one firing. They would do a lot of damage to us if we rushed the battered castle walls.

Oh, and the dragon was still leering down at me.

"Your majesty?" Sandulf asked.

The Irish in me screamed to say *fuck it* and fight. But I wanted my people alive.

"Back up. Nice and slow," I said. "We're leaving..."

"Finley!" snarled Braylor.

I shot him a pained, pitiful look. And he quickly realized what I was going through. He lowered his eyes, probably in disappointment. I was certainly disappointed in myself.

We turned our karkadanns. The purple dragon prowled forward but held his fire. Big Red stood guard as we retreated, her tail lashing.

We had been outplayed. It burned.

But my soldiers were alive.

And I had no idea what to do next.

No plan. No hope of reinforcements for weeks. Just shame chewing through my chest.

And Thalassa knew it.

God, I hated her.

31

All in a Day's Work

Genevieve

After my whole humiliating debacle with the Capalu, I stuffed my pride in a mental lockbox and decided maybe—just maybe—I should start asking questions instead of winging it. Kinnat made that a joy, of course. She had the warm personality of a wet boot: mostly grumpy, sometimes angry, and always acting as though words cost her money.

But here's the thing—I *hate* screwing up. I want precision. Flawlessness. Or at least something close enough that no one can tell the difference. And I definitely didn't plan on dying in this world before I figured out how to escape it. Somewhere in the back of my mind, I kept this fragile, glowing hope that Finley might be able to send me home. But then... she was still here. Which was its own question mark.

We were trudging down a hill through pine needles when Kinnat suddenly veered off, as she spotted a treasure. She stopped at this thin tree with flaming red leaves, eyeing it carefully.

"Ah. Here it is," she said. "You always ask what I know that is useful. This is useful."

She bent the whole tree down.

"It's a tree," I offered, because apparently my mouth works faster than my brain.

"Aye. A valuable one. Especially for weary travelers on foot."

Two sword swings later, it was timber. She stripped the bark, shaved thin slices of tan wood, and strapped them to her feet as ankle braces.

"That's awesome! Can you make me some?"

"Make your own," she said, smacking my shoulder hard enough to rattle my teeth before stalking off.

I'd never made anything in my life except a lopsided pottery bowl in a class as a kid, but she waited patiently while I hacked and cursed my way through it. By my second brace, I was weirdly proud. So much so that I wanted to redo the first set. But her patience was gone by then.

And the braces worked. Walking on the hills, over the rocks and uneven terrain, was easier. My feet still hated me, but at least they were quietly resentful instead of screaming bloody murder.

With our ankles set, we needed to tackle our biggest priority: finding food. And fast. With only swords, catching wild animals was a joke. We'd occasionally snag a fish—well, Kinnat would—and we found enough berries and leaves to keep from starving. But we needed real protein.

By the next evening, after climbing a vertical wall of stone masquerading as a mountain, we finally saw it: a cluster of farmhouses nestled in the valley below. Crop fields fanned out in neat rows around them, a silver river slicing beside the land. Pens lined the banks, holding bizarre, three-legged chicken-things that strutted like they owned the place, and hulking bicorns.

My stomach actually growled. "Hey," I whispered, tugging on her tunic. "What do you say we wait until dark, sneak down there, and grab a chicken-thing to roast?"

She turned on me. "Are you asking me to steal from them?"

"Yes," I said, hunger beating down my shame. "I'm starving. And we haven't got money to buy one."

"That may be how you live in the land of Mu, but not here. That is not what I do. Those are hard-working people down there. Those birds belong to them. We would be taking food from their mouths."

Guilt stabbed me. "Fine. Sorry. Just trying not to die, that's all."

She glanced around the slope. "We will camp here tonight."

This part of Tir Na was trapped in a stubborn spring: hot days, bone-cold nights. Sleeping on the bare ground with no blankets was its own form of torture.

"Could we at least make a fire? Rub some sticks together or something?"

"No." She piled pine needles by a fallen log. "This is their land. I do not want to be killed for trespassing."

"But it's so damn cold."

I copied her, laying down my own sorry bed of needles, curling up as tight as I could. It didn't help. The cold bit through my clothes, gnawed at my bones. Soon I was shivering hard enough to rattle my teeth.

After a while, Kinnat muttered a curse, sat up, and began piling more pine needles on me—my legs, my hips, even behind my back. Then she lay down behind me, looping an arm over my middle and pulling me in.

"Whoa! What's going on?!" I squeaked.

"Be quiet," she hissed in my ear. "I can no longer bear your rattling teeth."

I wanted to protest. But... shit, she was warm. I was asleep in minutes.

I woke to a bright sunrise and empty arms. Kinnat stood at the tree line, staring down at the farm.

"Come," she called when she saw me stir. "We are going to earn our keep."

"Earn it?" I rubbed my eyes.

"You said you are hungry. As am I. So, we will ask for work."

"Work? We're trying to get to Irkalla. We don't have time—"

"To finish our journey, we will need supplies. If we do not do this, you will not reach Irkalla."

I grumbled all the way down the hill. "Still think stealing a chicken would've been faster."

"When I was younger, before my mother sold me, I worked our farm," she said flatly. "There is nothing dishonest about hard labor."

She approached a lean farmer tossing dried grass to his bicorns. He gripped his pitchfork, not threatened but wary.

"Yes?" he said, sun-creased face and callused hands marking a lifetime of toil.

"Begging your pardon, good sir," said Kinnat, head bowed. I cowardly stayed half-hidden behind her.

"What do you seek?"

"My friend and I are weary travelers. We have only our swords. I humbly ask if we may earn a meal for a day's hard labor in your fields."

The farmer's eyes narrowed. He opened his mouth.

"And we are very hard workers. With experience," Kinnat added quickly. "If you are not pleased, you need not feed us."

Hey! Speak for yourself, overachiever.

He sighed. "I do need weeds cleared from the embergrain. And it is time to start the bloodfern harvest."

Bloodfern? What the hell was she getting me into?

Work. That's what. All-day, hot, sweaty, back-breaking work.

We started in the embergrain fields, yanking barbed weeds from around stalks of rust-red grain that glowed faintly in the shade. The stalks hissed in the breeze. My arms ached long before we were done.

Then came the bloodfern.

Its fronds were sheets of translucent crimson, veined with glowing orange light, slick and edged with tiny teeth that tore at my gloves. It wasn't just a plant—it was half predator, half miracle cure. Kinnat said the resin inside could seal wounds shut in seconds, heal broken bones, and the dried fronds were ground into a spice that fetched more than silver in the mountain markets. But cutting it loose was hell. The fronds clamped down with tiny jaws, and if you weren't fast, they spat a red metallic mist that burned your skin and made your tongue go numb through a mask.

By dusk, my hands trembled, my forearms screamed, and my pride was just barely holding me upright.

The farmer's mate and daughter invited us into their home and brought out a feast: slabs of tough meat in some smoky gray sauce, a red starchy thing similar to a potato, and vegetables still warm from the sun in their field. It might as well have been five-star cuisine. I devoured it like a starved animal. Probably the best meal I've ever eaten.

Kinnat, though... she was different. She sat at the table, perfectly straight-backed, chewing each bite with careful precision, her eyes fixed on the table as the family bustled around us. When the farmer's youngest darted past to grab more plates, she flinched ever so slightly, then smoothed her expression into that same impassive mask she always wore.

And yet—when the farmer's mate laughed at something her daughter said, Kinnat's gaze flickered up, just for a heartbeat, softening in a way I'd never seen before. It was gone the moment she noticed me watching. She dropped her eyes, focusing on her food again, jaw tight.

I didn't say anything. I just kept eating, letting the silence stretch between us.

When we left, the whole family came out to see us off.

"We thank you for your hard work today," said the farmer.

"I have a favor to ask," said Kinnat, bowing her head. "We are in need of a waterskin for our journey."

He motioned, and his mate handed him one. Full of water.

"I noticed you did not have one when you arrived," he stated.

Then the woman rushed forward and handed it to me. She also gave a small leather sack to Kinnat.

"For your journey," she said, smiling.

Kinnat showed me the satchel contents: fruit, dried meat, a small knife, and *flint*. Fire. We could finally have a real fire!

"Thank you," I said, smiling.

"We are forever in your debt for your kindness," said Kinnat, bowing deeply. I tried to bow too, but fruit tumbled out. I scrambled to collect it, grinning like an idiot.

We followed the river out of the valley, our packs a little heavier, our bellies full.

I waited for her to say I told you so. She didn't. She didn't need to.

I was wrong. Again.

I almost mentioned what I'd seen back there—the way she'd gone quiet when the little girl laughed, how her face had softened as if she were remembering something she didn't want to—but the words caught in my throat. It felt... private. Fragile. Touching it might make her pull away.

I said nothing.

I was sore from the work. Looking forward to setting up camp. And finally getting some rest.

32

My Rock Bottom Has a Trapdoor

Finley

We marched for an entire day, putting as much space as possible between us, Thalassa, and her soldiers. And her dragon. Especially her dragon. No one spoke much. Braylor tried once, some muttered attempt to vent his frustration, but I shot him an icy glare that could've frozen boiling water. I wasn't ready to talk. Not yet.

When we finally set up camp in a wide clearing, the tension was palpable. We huddled around the fire outside my tent, drowning in wine and mutual misery. I stalked the perimeter like an overcaffeinated raccoon.

Out beyond the trees, Big Red's eyes partially glowed—half-asleep but always watching. I wished I had half her control.

"How could I be so stupid?" I blurted. "Rushing in there without an actual plan."

Braylor shifted on his log; it groaned in protest. "We would have won that battle," he offered.

I stopped pacing. Stared. He immediately found the ground fascinating. "We would have," he mumbled, less sure.

Sandulf cleared his throat. "If only I had employed more spies, developed more intelligence on the situation, instead of allowing you to go in blind."

"This is on me." The headache that had been stalking me all day pounced.

"I wanted revenge. For our messenger. For our emissaries. You did your best. I did not."

Braylor snorted. "What now, then? Skulk home like a sigbin with its head between its hind legs?"

I didn't know what a sigbin was but, on this world, I imagined that it was barely able to tuck its head between its hind legs.

I spun—and nearly jumped out of my skin. Kasuma stood there, silent as moonlight. "Shit!"

"You have forgotten your senses," she said lightly. "You should have heard me coming. My steps on the branch at the edge of camp? My foul scent from running all day? Your—"

"I know, I know," I cut her off, grabbing her shoulder. Thank the gods she was back. "I'm a little busy orchestrating my public humiliation. What did you find?"

She settled near the fire, declining Braylor's wine with a look that could curdle milk. Sandulf passed her his waterskin. She drank nearly all of it.

"While you were engaged with the Atlanteans, I managed to sneak into the castle—"

"How?"

A smirk. No answer. Typical.

"They have indeed occupied the castle, but it does not seem as though they are planning to stay for an extended period of time. There has been no activity in the hall with the Godsribbon carriage that travels up to the sky. A fine layer of dust has formed on the floor in that room. I searched but found no maps or written plans on any further invasion of the continent."

"Then why are they here?" I asked, holding out my cup. Braylor refilled it; bless him.

Pherric would've known what they were up to. Pherric would also have told me this whole thing was idiotic.

"I found no explanation," Kasuma said.

"Sandulf?"

"Perhaps a trap," he said slowly. "I can only think they were laying a sort of trap for you. They hoped to draw a company of troops here, as you did, with the plan of destroying them with their dragon. Thus, compelling you to start a full-scale war. Or they were trying to draw you here, but did not plan on your dragon."

I glanced at Big Red, who was finally asleep. "She did surprise them," I muttered. "Though they'd heard the rumors. But I will say, they are pissed about something."

Kasuma cocked her head. "Yes?"

I tried to form a sentence. "There's... something. It's vague. Their messenger said we had taken from their seas and limited their resources, right? And Thalassa said something about... *the sea remembers every wound and every neglect.* And that one day *it remembers back.* We've, meaning all of us on land, hurt them in some way. And they want payback."

Everyone let that sink in, but no one had any clue. Especially me.

"Your majesty," Sandulf said gently, "what are our next steps? Do we hold here? Call reinforcements?"

"Or," I sighed, "do we slink home..." I shot Braylor a look, "*tails* between our legs?" He squinted, clearly lost on the metaphor.

The fire popped, startling me. My head swam with wine and worry.

"Can I have the night to think?" I muttered, rubbing my temples.

"Of course," Sandulf said. "Your majesty."

I slipped into my tent while they immediately began arguing, starting off in whispers and then their voices rising.

Inside, it was still. Too still. Only the flap of the canvas in the breeze. My chainmail sat draped over a chair, judging me. My sword leaned nearby, silent and useless. The air was warm from the day but cooling fast, carrying that strange edge that makes my skin crawl.

I curled under a blanket and stared at the tent roof. I wanted to run. Disappear. Let someone else wear this crown that was really a collar tightening around my throat.

I hated that I'd failed. And that everyone still looked at me to fix this.

I was twenty-three. I didn't know what the hell I was doing.

I fell off a cliff into sleep fast. My last coherent thought was that the canvas above my head looked smug about how worthless I was.

"Dragon!"

The distant scream sliced through the night. Outside, feet pounded the ground, voices barked orders.

I jerked upright—

—and a hand slammed over my mouth.

Another hand pinned my arm down as I thrashed, tangled in my blanket.

"Shhh," a voice rasped at my ear. Smooth. Measured. And cold.

I went still. Not calm—never calm—but still. My eyes darted toward the flap of the tent, where shadows danced from the firelight beyond.

No one was coming.

All my soldiers were stampeding toward the other side of camp, chasing the phantom of a dragon.

"Come quietly, dragonwitch," the voice whispered. "Or watch your company burn."

My captor's face slid into view: sea-dark hair, eyes polished gray onyx. Goran. Sea-Lord of Atlantis. And next to him, another soldier—dark hair, gills exposed, thin lips, knife wet with blood.

Rage flared, hot and stupid. My Irish said *never go easy.*

I snapped my head backward and cracked Goran square in the nose. He grunted but didn't loosen his grip. The other soldier hissed and lunged; I kicked, catching him in the thigh.

They slammed me back onto the cot, my head hitting the wood support. Stars burst in my eyes.

"You might take some of us with you, but we have the advantage of surprise. Fight and they all die," Goran murmured. "Your soldiers. Your royal consort. Your friends."

Braylor. Sandulf. Kasuma.

I went still again. This time it wasn't defiance. It was surrender, bitter as it was.

They bound my hands. My sword lay three feet away, might as well have been on the moon.

Outside, shouts faded deeper into the clearing.

Goran pulled up the back of the tent wall and dragged me under.

And there—on the ground just outside—two of my soldiers lay sprawled in the dirt. Eyes open. Throats open wider.

They pushed me among the trees. Every step had me walking off the edge of the world.

Somewhere behind us, an enormous *thrum* split the air. That magical whooshing sound.

Wings.

Big Red.

For a heartbeat, hope clawed up my throat... and vanished. She wasn't coming for me. She was chasing something else.

Maybe the real dragon. Zeranthyl. The decoy.

I stumbled as they dragged me, the forest swallowing campfire light behind us.

I had thought I'd reached rock bottom earlier tonight.

Apparently, rock bottom had a trapdoor.

And the Sea Lord was hauling me straight through it.

33

To Be Reckless and Stupid and Free

Genevieve

"J ump!"

Kinnat fended off the giant beetle with her sword as its front legs reached for her—hooked, thorny things that clicked against the blade. The creature was as big as a horse and twice as mean, its shell a slab of black glass. Seams in between the shell pulsed wetly, and the air around it stank of something acidic, like vinegar.

Mandibles scissored—long, serrated, and pitted from whatever it had chewed through before finding us—while two threadlike antennae tasted the night, twitching toward our sweat and panic.

"Now!"

She wanted me to launch myself onto its smooth, hard back and stab it.

The beetle started to charge her, faking left with its shell and snapping right, trying to sweep Kinnat's legs with the armored ridge of its head. A rope of spit hissed from its mouth.

But I hesitated. Again. By the time I leapt, sword in hand, the beetle reared—front end tilting like a pried-up manhole cover. I slid right off its shell.

It slammed back down, the impact thudding through my chest, and came for me this time: antennae flared, mandibles opening wide enough to frame my whole thigh. Its legs pistoned, hooks snatching for my boot, trying to drag me under where its weight could do the rest.

"Cover your face!"

I managed to scream. "What?!"

"It wants to lay its eggs in you!"

Oh, hell no.

Kinnat tried to jump on it but slid off the same way I did.

"Do not let it in your mouth!"

"Wasn't... planning... on it!" I shoved with both heels as the body spun over me. The beetle squatted on my hips to pin me while it squared to Kinnat, wanting to fight her and finish me in the same breath. My sword arm was trapped, shoulder screaming.

Kinnat roared a raw, human sound that cut through the insect clicking. And I heard the whistle of her sword, then the crack of it biting shell. Another hiss as she shaved a chunk from a mandible. Something heavy hit dirt; she rolled and came up cursing. The sound that followed—deep and torn—told me she'd found meat.

The beetle answered by trying to lay eggs. A wet tube flexed; a jet of black goo shot at my face. I jerked my head aside, eyes and mouth clamped shut, thrashing my neck like a dog trying to fling off a collar. The slap of eggs on my cheek was obscene—warm, pasty, alive.

But Kinnat didn't quit. She carved and stabbed until the clicking stuttered. The weight slid off my legs, thumped beside me, and she was on me in the next heartbeat, hauling. Her fingers dug into the slime on my face and ripped it away in gobs, disgust be damned. She grabbed a fistful of brush and scrubbed, brisk and gentle all at once.

We knelt there, both of us sucking in air.

She leveled a look at me over her knees. I could already hear it, the lecture I deserved.

"Don't say it," I gasped. "I know. I hesitated again. I'm sorry."

"This was not entirely your fault," she said between gulps. "I tried while the chepri was prone and still slid down. She is a formidable foe. But I must ask... did any get inside you?"

"What?! No. No way." My mind ran the replay on fast-forward and slow-motion at the same time. "So... it was trying to lay eggs?! In me?"

"The larvae grow in you and consume you from the inside for food."

Wait. Hold on. My brain did not compute any of that. The worst thing that usually happened to me in a day was a barista butchering my iced latte order. Not... parasitic nursery school in my intestines.

Something broke loose. Not a clean snap—but threads parting one by one until the whole net failed. I shook. Teeth chattered. Vision tunneled. Heat rushed my face while my hands went pins-and-needles cold. (Oh cool, panic bingo—got the full card.)

I pushed to my feet on autopilot, because distance would fix the biology of horror, and made it three steps before my knees quit. I folded into my hands, sobbing, and then the sob snapped into gagging and I puked on my fingers. Classy. Ten out of ten.

Breathe. Just breathe. In—two—three—four—

Nope. Air got stuck halfway down as my throat narrowed to a straw. The taste of beetle glop was still on my lips. I could feel the smear on my cheek even though it was gone, the ghost of it, my skin convinced there were eggs in every pore. *Not in me. Not in me. Not in me.* The words looped so fast they tangled.

I did not belong here. I did not want to die here. It felt guaranteed. And that certainty, more than the gore and the fight, sank its claws in and pulled. I was tired of being brave for the camera of my own pride. And pretending every new terror was just a level to beat with sarcasm and a sharper sword.

And the embarrassment—God—because I'd failed some test Kinnat was grading. I could *feel* her smirk, her head shaking, the quiet, disappointment sitting on her tongue.

Arms wrapped me. Not beetle legs. Human. Strong. She pulled me back into her chest and I stiffened out of reflex, ready to shove her away and go finish humiliating myself in private. But I didn't have the energy. Or maybe the will. If I let go, I might keep falling, and there was no bottom in sight.

"You are safe," she said, low and firm. "Do not argue."

"I'm not—" I choked. "I'm just—"

"I know," she cut in. "Be quiet."

It wasn't comforting. It was commanding. And somehow, that helped.

I clung. God help me, I clung like the child I swore I wasn't, when my grandma used to say—*holding on for dear life*, as though life were a rope and my palms weren't wet with beetle shit and vomit and fear.

My thoughts kept trying to spin out. Larvae gnawing my hollowed-out stomach. But her breath was steady against my hair, a metronome I could borrow. In. Out. I matched it. Once. Twice. Ten times. The world widened an inch. I heard leaves fluttering in the breeze. The shakes dialed down from earthquake to tremor.

Her grip stayed steady. Impersonal. Grounded. Like she was anchoring a flailing thing until it stopped thrashing. I focused on that—on the fact that she wasn't judging me, wasn't lecturing, wasn't *leaving*.

The shaking ebbed.

"I hesitated," I whispered, the confession leaking out. "I keep hesitating and you keep paying for it."

"You are alive," she said simply. "So am I. That is the only measure that matters."

A wet laugh cracked out of me, ridiculous and human. I wiped my face with the back of my sleeve again, spat until the taste was mostly gone, and stood. My legs rattled but held. The beetle lay a a few feet away, shell split, green guts cooling in the night air. It looked smaller now that it was dead. Monsters usually do.

I met Kinnat's eyes. "Thank you," I said, and meant it. "For the save."

She snorted.

She looked me up and down and then down at the slime streaked across her own clothes. "We must get this filth cleaned off us."

"Ya think?" My voice cracked on the words. I still hadn't recovered. The world wavered at the edges of a heat haze, but I tried to put on that brave face. Once more.

She stared at me for a long moment. "Let us find nearby water," she said at last.

We walked far too long with our boots squishing on every step. The smell didn't help my nausea, but the silence between us was strangely gentle. Eventually, we came to a broad, slow river snaking through a group of trees. Moonlight silvered the surface.

Without hesitating, Kinnat threw off her boots and leapt into the river. The splash broke the quiet. She vanished under, then surfaced with a toss of her head, flinging arcs of water.

Scrubbing furiously, she pointed at a thick stalk along the bank. "Sapon. Cut it."

I hacked one free. When I tossed it to her, she cracked the stalk and squeezed out a glistening smear of reddish sap into her fingers.

"Use it," she ordered.

I waded in, gasping at the cold. It felt brutal and incredible all at once.

She worked methodically, scrubbing clothes and straps like this was a drill she'd practiced a thousand times. I tried to copy her and failed spectacularly.

"You are doing it wrong."

"Shockingly," I said. "I was not raised feral."

As I rinsed off, I found myself watching her. For the first time, I noticed a small black tattoo on her arm. A mark from the Scholomance. They loved their black tattoos. She had finished scrubbing and now sank low until only her nose broke the surface. She blew a stream of bubbles, then waved her hand gently through the water to make ripples, eyes following them as they spread. She giggled. I was watching a child at play. The contrast struck deep—this was the same girl who had just flung herself at a monster without hesitation, and now she was marveling at how moonlight danced on the water.

For a moment, I could almost see her as she might have been, before this world took away her innocence.

She caught me staring. "What is the matter?"

I startled a bit, tore my gaze away, and started scrubbing at my hair again. "Nothing. Nothing at all."

Kinnat paddled over and gently took the sapon stalk from my hand. "Turn around," she said, and when I hesitated, she added, "Hold still."

Awkward at first, I let her soap up my hair. Her fingers were firm, working through my curls, through the tangles.

"I take it you've done this before?" I asked, hoping to peek behind the armor.

"Oh, yes," she said easily. "I used to wash my sisters' hair. They were not very good at it either."

A slow realization crept in. I bet she was the oldest. I think on a farm, the oldest becomes another parent. Kinnat probably never had a chance to be... a kid. She never got to play. To be reckless and stupid and free. She had been holding her world up for so long she didn't know how to put it down.

And yet here she was, washing my hair as if tasting a forgotten piece of her own childhood. I glanced back. Moonlight rippled across her face. I saw the girl she might have been if no one had turned her into a soldier.

I let her wash my hair. For a few sweet seconds in time, I was at peace.

34

I Love This for Me

Finley

So, I've been kidnapped. Again. Yay me.

At this point, I should really get a punch card: "Survive nine kidnappings, your tenth one's free!"

Goran and his beef-slab sidekick easily dragged me along the coast because I weighed nothing to them. I kicked, twisted, dead-weighted my body, even tried the limp-like-a-drama-queen trick. Nothing worked. They hauled me as if they were sick of the chore, and the worst part was, they didn't even look winded.

I was trying to slow them down, any way I could. I wanted to give Braylor and the others a chance to catch up. But they never did. We were moving too quickly.

At first, we headed east toward Godsribbon Castle, which nearly made me choke on my own heartbeat. If Braylor thought I'd been dragged there, he would've stormed the place without a second thought. And then? Slaughter. I could practically see him: teeth gritted, sword out, blind rage blazing while Kasuma and Sandulf tried—and failed—to rein him in. The thought made me sick. If he died charging headlong into the castle because of me... I blinked hard, but the tears still came. Queens weren't supposed to cry. Heroes weren't supposed to feel small. But here I was, small and scared.

Eventually, we veered toward the sea. Which, cool. Because nothing says "future murder victim" like kidnappers who take you out on a boat.

Through a cleft in two hills, we scrambled down the beach looking out on the Triton Sea. A little vessel waited, the front of it bobbing about because it hadn't yet decided whether it was seaworthy.

Two Atlanteans stood at the ready, oars in hand. They searched the area, wanting to crack skulls, until Goran made some creepy low dolphin-death squeak that calmed them right down. But they kept their eyes glued to the cliffs overhead, watching for enemies.

They bound my ankles, tossed me into the boat, and, because the humiliation wasn't complete yet, pulled a black hood over my head. Darkness. Salt air. The sound of shifting wood.

"Really? A bag? How original," I snarled.

The men climbed in the boat with me, but their oars didn't hit the water. Instead, I heard the splash of bodies, as two of them leapt in and pulled on our boat. We surged forward unnaturally fast, dragged along by mermen swimming beside us. The wood creaked with each yank of current. I pictured their hands gripping the hull, towing me toward gods-knew-what, and shivered.

Time stretched. Every splash was another reminder of how powerless I was. While we traveled, I tried to rest, gather strength and steel myself, but my mind ran in cruel circles.

I knew the castle would be empty. Their whole goal was to get me. But why? What did they want with me? Ransom? Joke's on them. The Irkallan coffers were emptier than my stomach after Kane's little folly. Was I part of some prophecy? Or... a blood ritual? If this ended with my body dumped into the ocean, would anyone even know? Would Braylor search forever, never finding me? The thought hollowed me out.

I pictured him, sword drawn, tearing apart the forest looking for me, fury and fear tangled together on his face. And the others, forced to follow him into madness because of me. I hated that image more than the bag over my head, more than the rope cutting my wrists. Because it was true:

I wasn't scared of dying. Been there and done that. I was scared of what my absence would do to the people who loved me.

By dawn, I was stiff, nauseous, and close to screaming to hear my own voice. Hunger gnawed, my bladder protested, and still... I kept quiet. No way was I giving Goran an excuse to dump me overboard.

The boat slowed. Something heavy sloshed as a swimmer hauled himself up beside me. My hood was ripped back, sunlight knifing into my eyes, and Goran's wet face came into focus. He was smiling insanely.

"We have arrived at Atlantis."

I blinked at the horizon.

All I saw was an island the size of a forgettable fishing village—sun-bleached rock, a handful of white structures, and a lonely watchtower barely tall enough to spot incoming boats.

If this was Atlantis, it looked... underfunded.

"That?" I asked. "You're kidding, right?"

Goran's grin deepened, all bright teeth and pride. "Patience."

As we drifted closer, the water shimmered—not the normal reflection of sun on waves, but something tighter. The light was straining against its own shape. The tiny island wavered; its edges were wet paint smearing. Buildings doubled in my vision, then overlapped again. My eyes couldn't decide where they belonged.

The island seemed to shift again—not moving, not growing, but *reorganizing.* Pieces of a puzzle clicked into a different arrangement while I blinked. Bridges that didn't exist a moment before, shadows hinting at courtyards that couldn't possibly fit behind the visible walls.

A depth that shouldn't be there.

Then the distortion slipped out of alignment, and the island shrank back to its modest facade, still just an outpost on a rock.

I grabbed the rail. "What was that?"

Goran watched me with the smug satisfaction of a king unveiling his crown jewel. "Reality," he said. "Or rather... the part you are capable of seeing."

Pride rolled off him in waves. He wanted me to understand—not the geography, but the glory. The superiority.

And for the first time since they'd thrown the bag over my head, my panic softened. I wasn't planning escape. I was wondering what it meant that they'd brought me here—to this place that bent the world.

The oarsmen dipped their paddles again, though the water ahead of us still looked empty except for the modest shoreline and a few scattered domes. Goran and his companion slipped into the surf and swam ahead; they were knives cutting through the waves. The boat rocked in their wake, nudging me toward an island that seemed far too simple to carry the weight of a legend.

We rounded a cluster of smooth rocks and the horizon warped again—just a ripple. The modest domes doubled in my vision, then stretched, gaining impossible height. A line of columns appeared where smooth cliff face had been a blink before. From one angle, the island was a handful of buildings; from another, a skyline unfurled as if a banner had caught the wind.

As we stayed in alignment, and the city expanded—avenues unfurling, terraces stacking upon terraces, white marble glaring. Structures I'd taken for huts now towered high enough to scrape the sky. Gold tracery glimmered along balconies I'd swear hadn't existed moments earlier.

They had been blessed by the gods. Similar to the floating city that the Tenguans had in Oceantis. And our own cloak of invisibility surrounding The Black City. But this seemed to be a miracle that put every other miracle to shame.

No walls. No battlements. Nothing to defend.

Of course. Why need fortifications when the island itself refused to present the same shape to anyone twice? Why build an army when invaders couldn't even *find* you unless you wanted them to?

The shoreline curved in a sweeping crescent, embracing a second island nestled in the center of the bay—smaller at first glance, but surrounded by a massive circular wall far higher than anything around it. It radiated importance. Mystery. The kind of place people whispered about and never returned from.

My stomach sank. Naturally, that's where I assumed we were going.

But the oarsmen angled toward a stretch of sand on the main island instead—white grains speckled with gemstone-bright stones. A perfect landing. Private. Unassuming.

My relief evaporated the moment I noticed the steps rising from the shore: broad, bright, meticulously carved. Way too pristine for kidnappers smuggling a prisoner. Each tier was flanked by statues of gods with faces chiseled in contempt, their stone gazes following me because I was unworthy to be there.

At the top, a crown perched on a ledge that should not have physically fit on the island's exterior, stood a fortress-palace: sprawling arches, a hundred columns, a facade far larger than the land beneath it could logically support. We were approaching the mouth of something ancient, patient, and hungry.

The oarsmen grounded the boat, dragged me out, and forced me up the steps. Every rise made me feel smaller, while the palace seemed to grow. The doorway loomed high enough to welcome giants. Marble glittered with a cold inner light.

"This has to be it," I muttered, every nerve ending screaming. "Queen Thalassa's lair. Awesome. Fantastic. Love this for me."

We reached the threshold—an archway yawning wide, shadows thick beyond it, a darkness that felt too deep for any building of this size to contain.

And then they shoved me forward, bound and breathless, straight into the mouth of the beast.

35

As If I'd Tell You

Finley

My cheery oarsmen dumped me in what had to be Thalassa's throne room. And wow… this wasn't just better than mine. It was Mount-Olympus-meets-interior-design-magazine, "your whole life looks shabby now" better.

Columns ringed the circular chamber, tall enough that my neck popped trying to see the tops. Not simply stone but *coral-marble hybrids,* smooth in some places, textured reef walls in others, shot through with veins of iridescent blue light that pulsed with the palace itself. They rose into a domed ceiling so vast I wasn't entirely sure it obeyed the same dimensions as the floor beneath it.

The dome was a living mural: merfolk with blade-fins and jeweled tails, sea serpents twisting through kelp forests, ancient queens riding chariots pulled by sharks. The brushstrokes shimmered, scales catching sunlight underwater, giving the illusion that everything above me was moving… just slowly enough that I couldn't be sure I imagined it.

The room was a perfect circle. Two massive pools flanked a narrow walkway, their waters impossibly clear, lit from below by soft golden light. Schools of silver fish flickered past. Even the sound was hushed as the water lapped without splashing.

186

At the end of the walkway, a wide staircase unfurled upward in shallow steps, each one carved seamlessly from the same dark stone. And at the top: the throne. Not a chair but *a geological event.* Pointed and regal, there were shaped scales and fins and sweeping arcs of carved coral, as though some ancient sea creature had grown a skeleton and decided to accessorize.

Just behind the throne, elevated on its own block of stone, stood something that did *not* match the rest of the room. A smooth, seamless, matte black pedestal held a sphere the size of a human skull. It didn't glow or pulse or hum, but it *felt* loud somehow. Its surface was pitch-dark but mirrored the room in warped reflections, bending columns and statues into impossible curves. I couldn't tell if it was ancient or brand-new, only that it didn't belong. Not to the throne or to this palace. Not to *anyone.*

The floor gleamed, polished smooth enough to see my own sad reflection. In parts of the room, water flowed across it in thin, controlled sheets that fed back into the pools—intentional, ritualistic, and the whole room was part of a living tide.

Between columns stood statues: kings and queens crowned in coral, warriors with tridents raised, guardians caught mid-strike. Their expressions weren't proud. They were judging, and they already knew where I ranked... and it wasn't high.

It was stunning. Intimidating.

And really made me wish I wasn't dressed in damp trauma chic.

What came next? Well, more of her pomp and circumstantial bullshit.

Harp players drifted forward, music syrup-thick and smug. A herald appeared, lungs full of self-importance, announcing Thalassa's forty-seven exalted titles: each one was another dagger aimed at me. Soldiers emerged from behind columns with predatory grace, uniforms dark against the gray stone. Sharks in human form.

Then Her Holiness Queen Thalassa swept onto the dais, and everyone bowed deeply. The oarsmen, subtle as always, shoved me to my knees. I snarled and forced myself back up.

"I bow to no one!"

Yeah, not exactly thunder-god material, but it was the best I had.

They slammed me down again with casual efficiency.

She was wearing next to nothing again—different straps, somehow more insulting. She descended the steps with the smooth precision of someone walking a runway suspended over an ocean, hips that owned rhythm itself swaying back and forth. The pools mirrored her perfectly; no ripples, no distortion.

"Queen Finley Maguire," she purred. "We meet again."

"Yeah, but not by choice." My voice was higher than I wanted.

Goran appeared, bad timing made flesh, at the foot of the stairs. An old Atlantean—thin as driftwood, robe whispering silk—emerged from behind the throne. Her mage, I guessed.

"I do hope my mermen were not overly harsh with you. I only asked that they bring you here alive."

Goran straightened, chest puffed with the pride of a man who delivers on orders.

"And here I am. Now... what the fuck do you want?" I kept my jaw level, though every muscle buzzed.

Thalassa took a step closer. "Such defiance, even though you are my captive. You impress me more and more." She smiled at her new, interesting toy.

I fixed her with my best stare. Hard, steady, don't-look-away. Inside, my guts were on a roller coaster. I could feel my pulse in my teeth. One small pleasure... seeing her up close, she was a bit older than I surmised. Crow's feet sketched at her eyes; she'd powdered them away with makeup and arrogance. She was vain. A bit self-conscious. I made a mental note of that.

"As I said... what do you want with me?"

She signaled, and the goons hauled me up. She was barely taller than I was; living on Tir Na had taught me to look up a lot.

Her fingers threaded through my hair with the intimacy of someone cataloguing a specimen. "What a lovely shade of orange. I have never seen hair this color before."

I sniffed at her. "And you... stink like a fish." The words felt juvenile, but they were out there.

Her lips curved. "Thank you." She took it as a compliment. But she didn't smell like fish. She smelled of sunshine caught in linen, and citrus and jasmine on a summer breeze. It was infuriating.

Her hand stroked my cheek. I flinched and turned away. My eyes burned and for the first time I bared my teeth. "Well, now that the *Finley Appreciation Moment* has passed... let's get down to business."

"Leave us."

The court melted away, bowing and disappearing behind the columns—everyone but the old man with the gray beard. He stayed, hourglass face folded in patience. They had planned this. He was there for a reason...

"So, is this the part where you give me the tour of Atlantis and show off your space-bending island?" I tried for light. It came out thin.

"Perhaps another time," she said, voice low and silk-sweet. She pivoted and strolled to the old man.

He descended the stairs carefully and handed her something.

I felt the panic hollowing me. Heart hammering, breath shallow, sweat slick down my neck. I was small on the floor and the whole room was a trap closing in.

Thalassa loomed over me. "I have a question for you."

I swallowed hard. "Shoot. I mean... go ahead."

"How does it feel to die?"

The words snagged. I swallowed hard. "What?"

"It is a simple question. I am merely wondering... tell me how it feels to die?"

Heat flushed my face. Did she—did they—know? The immortality thing wasn't gossip to trade; it was mine and Pherric's and the bloody thing that kept me awake at night. I tried to sound casual. "I have no idea what you're talking about." Liar, liar, my pants reminded.

"Do not play a children's game with me, my child."

"Sorry, but... uh, this is me. Here in the flesh. Not dead. So..." I trailed, buying time. Behind her back something gleamed.

Her hand shifted back there, and I braced for a weapon. Instead, her fingers unfurled to reveal... a goblet. Jewel-crusted, golden, the kind of thing you'd see in a cathedral or a museum exhibit labeled *"Please Don't Touch."* She wagged it at me.

"I know of the rumors, Finley."

"Um, rumors?"

She laughed, a cold thing that scraped the marble. "Come now. You and I know they are more than wild fables whispered by tide-mothers while weaving nets in the shallows."

"I—I really don't know what you mean, Thalassa. Seriously."

Her shoulders dropped with a practiced sigh. "You wish to make it difficult. I see. Fine, then. But the *grimwise* I know say you are... immortal. You were given a potion by your mage while awaiting death. It has been said you have died several times and come back to life. Therefore, you are *immortal.*"

The words settled deep. "Well, that's not exactly true, is it? If you die, then you're not really immortal, are you?"

"Byfire, girl! Now we play silly word games? The truth is that when you are killed, you do not stay dead. And that is the heart of the matter."

"Potato, potahto." Yep. I said that. And I got the look you'd expect. Hey, I was nervous.

"So, I'll ask again. What is it like... to die?"

I should have shut up. It was too late. "It fucking hurts really bad," I said. "Usually, I've been hacked up by a sword... and then, well, you know... you die."

"You simply cease to exist?" She sounded genuinely perplexed.

"Are you asking if there's a light at the end of a tunnel? Or if I'm talking to Saint Peter at the Pearly Gates?" I tried to make a joke. "No, nothing happens. You're dead. It's not dark. It's not light. No time passes. You're not waiting or anything. You're just... gone."

"And how soon before you return? Alive?"

"Oh, that's complicated."

"Explain."

The answers wanted to come out; nerves unspooled me. "It takes longer each time. The first time I died, it was a few minutes. And it seems to just about double every time after. I was dead for almost a month last time."

Her other hand came forward, saving it for the big finish, and yeah—I knew before I saw it. Not a scroll. Not another pretty trinket. No, of course it was a dagger. Slim and mean-looking—exactly the kind of party favor she would keep handy for moments like this.

"If everything you say is true, then we shall talk very soon for *you*. But... two months for me." Her voice hardened into an order.

The dagger sank into my belly. Pain exploded—hot, immediate, a brand searing into muscle and tendons. I gasped, a sound that felt too big in that ornate hall. My knees folded. The world narrowed to a hot, pulsing point. I felt hands catch me, rough and certain, and the old man's robe in my line of sight as I doubled over.

"Drink from her," the old man said, his dried paper voice crackling.

Thalassa looked at him. "You are sure?"

"This is the only way," he answered, calm as a clock.

She lifted the jeweled goblet. Blood welled from my wound and ran warm down my legs. The cup tipped until full. She pursed her lips and drank. For a moment, the room stilled and some part of me hated the sound of it.

"That's not how it works, you fucking idiot," I croaked, blood in my mouth and rage tangling. My voice was thin. I was a little proud I could still spit profanity. "There's no secret serum in my blood!"

Thalassa's eyes slitted as she stared at the old man.

"Then how does it work?!" she snapped, panic sharpening her pretty features.

"As if I'd tell you."

She lowered herself and drove the dagger again, deeper this time. Pain unreeled in a long, cruel line. I screamed, a raw animal sound, and my hands—bound, useless—couldn't do anything to stop the blood. It went warm and slick across the floor, pooling at my knees.

"I can make this very painful for you. A wound to the abdomen can keep you alive for quite a while." Her tone was clinical. Her threat had taste.

The knife pressed at me again, but she didn't stab me. And my world broke. White light edged my vision; sound retreated into a distant, underwater pop.

"Okay, okay. You've got to... drink the potion." My voice was sand. I didn't know if I believed it. "It's all from a book... a Scholomance one. That's all I know."

She stabbed again. The pain was a hot coal dropped into my gut, and someone stomped on it. My breath came in shards; the floor blurred into a strange, soft focus.

"Stop stabbing me, bitch!" I yelled.

I could feel the blood leaving, and an odd, traitorous chill that I remembered trailed down my limbs. Color bled out of everything.

"What book?!" Again, the knife tip moved close to my open wounds.

"The... *Arcanum Libellum*, I think."

Her mouth was next to my ear. "Where is it?"

I wanted to lie; I wanted to spit; I wanted to live. "Irkalla."

"In the possession of your mage?!"

"I don't know," I lied. Pherric had it, but I would not put him in danger.

"Who has the book?"

"Fuck you," I said. It was the last clear thing I could manage. The rest unraveled—murmurs, a word from the old man that might have been *Pherric*, and a strange, sudden light that had nothing to do with heaven and everything to do with the last flare of the world before it goes out.

I was at *neardeath.* Pain hollowed into a cold blank. The hall receded from me like the tide pulling back. My hands and legs went numb. My lungs refused to work. I thought about stupid things—the color of my hair, the smell of the ocean, a joke I'd never get to tell—and the thought of those small, useless things made me clench my jaw.

The throne room slipped out of focus. Someone had yanked the plug on reality. Just the cheap trick of nothingness.

And then I died.

36

The Black City

Genevieve

Kinnat and I cut through Irkalla like we belonged there. The landscape was stunning. Forests so thick the sun had to fight its way through. Hills were a rolling green ocean. Mountains in the distance flexing, because they knew they were hot. Streams clear enough you could see every pebble, and nature had its own high-def setting.

If Finley really did snatch up a kingdom, the girl knew how to pick prime real estate.

After weeks of walking, we finally made it to Ker-Is. I'd pictured some haunted, burned-out husk from the horror stories, people whispering about how Finley had rolled through with her army and left nothing but ash.

But instead? Damn. This city was alive. Sitting on a big plain, there were gray walls that went up forever, and half a dozen major roads feeding in that were clogged with caravans. Tents and huts were scattered outside city. Farmers worked the fields that were spread out across the region. Wagons creaked under loads, carriages rattled, with those ugly pissed-off karkadanns dragging them along.

People waved at us, nodded, and kept moving. Nobody cared who we were or where we came from. No questions about being escapees from a cruel school to the east. After weeks of being hunted and hushed, it felt... good. Too good.

Walking through the gates, the bass drop of noise hit me. Vendors yelling prices, wagon wheels banging over stone, kids screaming with joy. Color everywhere. Banners strung between windows, market stalls stacked with food I couldn't name but desperately wanted.

My stomach was ready to flip the table over the smell of meat sizzling on open fire, vegetables hissing in oil, spices drifting through the air thick enough to taste. After silence and shadows, this was music. I couldn't stop grinning.

Kinnat noticed, of course. "You seem happy."

"Girl, I'm in my element," I shot back. "The city. The people. The smells. This is home."

"Too noisy," Kinnat muttered. The market offended her ears.

I rolled my eyes. "That's the point, sis. Noise means life. People are moving, working, arguing over the price of onions. Noise means nobody's dead in the streets."

Still, I couldn't shake the whispers I'd heard about Finley, about her supposedly torching this place. Part of me wanted to write it all off as propaganda. Another part, the soft one I usually shove in a box, worried that maybe I'd been wrong about her.

Reading me carefully, Kinnat pointed to all the new buildings and then to the second story wall of an apartment. There were black scorch marks licking across stone, several small holes in the stucco... from arrow fire. I noticed fairly recent circle paint marks on other walls, like someone had tried to cover over graffiti. But they were probably covering blood stains. My grin faltered. Yeah, this wasn't just fairy-tale perfection. Somebody had left their fingerprints here in fire and death.

I veered off before I could overthink it, stopping a woman balancing a basket while her kid tugged at her sleeve. She gave me the once-over, cautious, until I hit her with my best smile: the one that says, *trust me, I know things even when I don't.*

"Excuse me," I said, keeping it soft. "I'm not from here. I heard this city was destroyed a while back. Is that true?"

Her shoulders tensed, as if she was waiting for a trick. "Yes."

"I also heard that it was your queen. Finley, I think her name is?"

Then, after a beat, she sighed. "No. Not by our queen. That was Malek. He killed our people to make it seem as though the Bànshēn rén had done it. To stir hate for them. To build support for more killing." Her face tightened. "*Yetstill*, the queen has not done much for us. This city used to be twice as full as you see now. But people have no coin to buy. It is heartbreaking."

That landed hard. Relief, sharper than I expected, cut right through me. I reached out, touched her arm. "Thank you."

Turning back to Kinnat, I couldn't help the smirk tugging at my lips. "See? I told you. Finley didn't do it."

Kinnat's gaze swept the crowd, unimpressed. "And I could find another here who swears she did."

Maybe. But my gut knew. The Finley I knew was stubborn, shy, sarcastic enough to peel paint... but she was never cruel. Not mass-murderer cruel. Or burn-a-city cruel. She was the kind of girl who'd rather hole up in her room with a book than march an army through anyone's front door. And if anyone tried to tell me otherwise? They'd have to go through me first.

We didn't linger in Ker-Is. Kinnat caught sight of some soldier guarding a puffed-up merchant and walked right up to him. My heart nearly stopped—*hello, are we trying to get arrested today?*—but then I saw the familiar black markings twisting down his forearm. She flashed her Scholomance tattoo, her VIP pass, and as easy as that, the guy slipped her a few coins. Instant solidarity. Great, secret Scholomance tattoo club. Good for us. Enough to buy food, though not the kind that smelled heavenly from street vendors. No, we got the peasant special.

And then we were heading on, toward Biringan. The Black City. Capital of Irkalla. Just the name made my skin prickle. "Black City" sounded less like a place you want to visit and more like a streaming horror special. My brain was already queuing up the jump scares.

The walk was brutal. Days on end. My body hated me. Every joint ached, and my feet felt were raw meat jammed into boots. What I needed was a week's rest, an ice bath, a hot shower, and—hell—a massage. But all I had was grit.

Kinnat pushed us forward, a relentless damned metronome. I kept going. Because Finley was waiting. My best friend. My reason. And okay, she was a queen now. Queens had to have palace-sized bathtubs or something, right? Maybe my loyalty would score me a spa day.

The road cut through a forest of monster pines that were two hundred feet tall, trunks as wide as a city bus. Spring was already tipping into summer, the air heavy and hot.

We sparred whenever we stopped, sword against sword, sweat dripping into my eyes. And without Thagan breathing down my neck, I was improving. I even managed to beat Kinnat one out of four times. Okay, five. But... progress.

The day we bathed in a pond beneath a waterfall, I thought I'd died and gone to a very cold heaven. The water froze me straight through but stripped away days of grime. We swam naked because neither of us wanted to hike the rest of the way in soaked clothes.

I tried not to notice her shoulders. The cut of her waist. The way light slid across her skin. I told myself I wasn't looking.

I was absolutely looking.

I redirected. Finley. Always Finley. My mission. My anchor. The problem was that the idea of Kinnat dropping me at Biringan and disappearing afterward sat in my gut like a bad stone. Heavy. Unsettling. Completely unwelcome.

Kinnat hadn't really softened since I pulled her away from the academy. Maybe here and there. I noticed it gradually, the way you do when something important is changing and you don't want to give it a name yet. I told myself my pull toward her was practical. She protected me, kept me alive. My brain was still wired to confuse safety with attachment. Trauma math.

That explanation worked right up until it didn't.

On our long walks, she talked about the world she knew—the soil, the plants, the crops she'd raised on her farm. She had always been silent, but now she would talk forever if I didn't interrupt her. I usually filled silence out of habit, but with her I didn't want to. Listening felt... easy.

When she realized how long she'd been talking, she'd look away, embarrassed at her weakness. As if she hadn't just handed me something rare and unguarded. I saw her smile when she cared about a subject, the light in her eyes when she forgot herself.

I softened. Quietly. Stupidly.

But none of it was for me.

That was the part I had to keep reminding myself of. Her attention never lingered. Her touches never strayed. Whatever gentleness she offered was the same she gave the land, the work, the people she felt responsible for. I was just another thing under her care.

By the time the forest thinned and spilled us onto a wide plain, the mountains rising black and scary ahead of us, I'd settled it in my mind. Whatever this was, between her and me—it lived entirely on my side of the line.

"We are here," Kinnat said.

She didn't look at me when she said it.

I squinted. Ahead were some farm fields. There were a few wagons on a road ahead. And more than a few sad-looking houses. "Uh, where exactly? Because unless the capital city is farming turnips, I'm not impressed."

A corner of her mouth lifted. Not a smile. A trap.

"Biringan."

I laughed outright. "Oh, come on. Stop screwing with me."

She finally turned to face me, eyes bright with something dangerously close to delight. "I am not joking."

I stopped walking. "Okay, if this is some academy hazing ritual you forgot to warn me about—"

"You cannot see it," she said, flatly.

I looked harder. Empty. Just mountains and farmland. "Girl, seriously. My feet hurt too much for jokes."

She sighed. Loudly. "You are *exhausting*."

"Wow. Bold talk from the person hallucinating cities."

She stepped closer and pointed down the road. "Watch."

In the distance, a pair of karkadanns pulled a flat wagon filled with boxes down the dirt road. I stared as, one by one, the beasts vanished. Then the riders. Then the whole damn cart. Poof. Gone. I gawked, my jaw hitting the dirt. And right on cue, another group of men walking along appeared out of thin air, headed in the opposite direction as though nothing happened. Reality had just glitched.

I turned slowly to Kinnat. "Nope."

"There is a veil around the Black City," she said, clearly enjoying this. "Dark magic. Old. Precise."

Dark magic. Right. Exactly what I needed in my life.

We kept walking, until our boots were crunching on the dirt road. Ahead, nothing but the black mountains rising up, daring us to come closer. No shimmer. No ripple in the air. Just... normal. I tightened, waiting for some gut-drop, some electric jolt to announce we were crossing into sorcery.

But nothing happened.

Step after step, the road stretched empty before us. The air was heavy, quiet. And subtle at first, I caught something at the edges of my vision. A blur. A wrongness. Shimmers rose off ground. Shapes I couldn't name shifted in and out, dissolving when I blinked.

I rubbed my eyes, but with every step, the haze thickened, the mountains wavering and melting. Lines formed where there had been only shadow. Angles. Towers. Bridges. My breath stopped in my throat.

And then, the curtain yanked open... clarity.

White stone walls towered over us, massive gates flung wide. Beyond them, a city stretched in every direction, bigger than Ker-Is by miles. Round and square towers stabbed the sky, connected by dizzying bridges. Green vines and flowers spilled from balconies, softening all that stone.

The streets glittered with clean cobblestones, each line between catching the lamplight. Men with tall poles were walking along the street, lighting torches one by one, creating strings of fire waking across the city. The air vibrated with life: laughter, shouting, music tumbling from fiddles and drums. Perfumes of spice, roasting meat, and blooming flowers tangled together, throwing me off.

In the distance, an arena like the Coliseum in Rome loomed, tiered and immense, promising spectacle. And above it all, what must be Finley's keep. Massive, radiant white, and perched on a hill. Its towers seemed endless, reaching for the sky, glaring down at the city it owned.

The sun melted into the horizon, painting everything gold and orange. Ker-Is had impressed me, sure. But this? This made Ker-Is a back-alley street fair in comparison.

Kinnat's eyes glowed, reflecting the firelit display.

"Welcome to the Black City."

I had several comments lined up.

None of them survived the view.

37

Time to Meet Finley

Genevieve

I wanted to storm the city, march straight up to her damn gates, and make a big entrance. But Kinnat dragged me back to reality.

"Pounding on the castle doors after dark," she said flatly, "is how you get skewered."

"Wow. You really know how to crush a girl's dreams."

She didn't even look at me. "I am trying to keep you alive. You should be grateful."

"I am grateful," I said. "I'm just also annoyed."

"Good," she replied. "Hold on to that feeling. It keeps you moving."

Fair.

Instead, we wandered the streets. The Black City was... loud, alive, and seemed to say it knew things about me it wasn't sharing yet. Every alley smelled of incense and hearth fires, every window spilling secrets if you stared too long.

Eventually, we slipped into a karkadann stable. Big, horned nightmares snorting in their pens. The perfect place to "blend in," according to Kinnat.

I stared at the busted wagon stuffed with bright orange hay. Traffic-cone orange. "You're kidding."

"Get in," she said.

"I will never emotionally recover from this."

She climbed in without comment.

Sleep didn't happen. My brain was too busy running laps. What was I gonna say to Finley? "Hey, surprise, I crossed worlds and practically died about fifty times, but... hi again!" Yeah, that'd be real smooth. Every time I shut my eyes, I saw her face... and then promptly imagined about twelve ways it would go bad.

When the workers arrived in the morning, Kinnat hauled me out by the collar before I could embarrass us further.

"Quiet," she hissed.

"I'm wheezing." The hay had given me the lung capacity of a seventy-year-old smoker.

"Yes. Do it quietly."

We wasted precious time picking hay out of our clothes and hair, flicking away orange bits of guilty confetti.

"This was your plan," I muttered.

"It worked," she said. "You are still breathing. Barely."

We finally started our journey.

The closer we got to the castle, the fancier everything looked. Streets cleaned up, houses similar to brownstones in New York lined the way. Double doors, iron fences, guards who didn't even blink when you passed. And the people? A whole damn spectrum. Prominans, Fomorian giants, humans of every shade. Even a few faces that looked like me.

And that's when it hit me. For a place literally called the Black City, it was... actually diverse. Unexpected. I was almost back home. Almost.

When we arrived at the main gates to Finley's castle, the walls were cliffs of white stone and dark iron. My heart was vibrating, but I pulled my chin up and threw on my best "I run this place" face, waving at the guards to open up, as if I had a whole army at my back.

Spears slid out of the shadows, shields gleamed in the cold light. The hiss of metal leaving scabbards scraped at my nerves. They were having none of my bullshit.

"Go away," one barked, his deep voice echoing off the gate.

Huge men in chainmail glared down at us, eyes raking over me and Kinnat. We must've looked wild... two mud-streaked, travel-worn stray cats trying to waltz into a palace.

Kinnat didn't flinch. She never does. She stepped forward, voice low and steady, explaining that we were messengers carrying vital information on the queen's fate from the Scholomance Academy. She rolled up her sleeve and showed the tattoo burned into her skin. Just saying "Scholomance" made the guards stiffen; they shot nervous glances at one another.

For a moment, I thought it was working. They let us through the first gate. But when we reached the main entrance gate, they locked up again. Crossed spears, no smiles.

Kinnat tried reasoning with the men. But I was done. My shoulders ached, my throat was dry, and my patience was gone. I pushed Kinnat aside. She glared at me, but I didn't care.

"Look," I said to the nearest guard. He loomed over me, a stone tower, and bent down as I leaned in. "I'm a friend of Finley's. The queen? You know her, right? We, uh, grew up together. On the mean streets of Manhattan. We go way back."

He leaned in closer, eyes flat as slate. "So?"

Hands went to hips. "You know how everyone makes that one big mistake? The one you regret for a *lifetime*? This is yours."

I think he blinked once.

"She is a friend," I continued, quieter but harder. "All you have to do is say that Genevieve from New York is here to see her. Send someone up and tell her that. Or, I promise, she'll be seriously pissed off at you. Do you understand?"

This time he blinked a lot. But still nothing. No words.

"We escaped the *Scholomance*, just like she tried to tell you. And someone is trying to kill Finley. I have details. Send someone. Now. Because I'm not going anywhere."

I glanced at a patch of grass near the wall, then pointed at it. "I'm gonna camp out right here."

He rolled his eyes, huffed, but finally nodded to one of his men. After a quick whisper, the soldier disappeared toward the keep.

Twenty minutes later, the quiet cracked open. The heavy doors of the keep burst wide, spilling out a rush of people. Fifteen, maybe more. The soldier at the top pointed at us. They came clattering down the grand staircase. Armor, boots, robes, all of it moving at once.

The man leading them was tall and lean, skin an olive brown, jet-black hair brushing his shoulders. He wore the same plain green robe as the mage instructors back at the academy. Black tattoos curled over his hands and up his neck. He gripped the bars of the gate, wide-eyed.

"I recognize you," he said.

I grabbed Kinnat's tunic. "Shit! They're Scholomance!"

She already had her hand on her sword hilt, face frozen with fear.

"Run!" I yelled, spinning, but guards had already closed in, weapons drawn.

Too late.

"Please!" the dark-haired man called, voice breaking with urgency. "You are from... New York? Yes?"

Heart pounding, I nodded.

He turned to the guards, arms spread. "Weapons down. Now. These are friends."

Swords and spears lowered all around us, but Kinnat and I stayed on edge.

The man in the green robe stepped forward slowly, hands still raised, a calming look on his face. "You are among friends."

I pointed my sword at him. "You're from the Scholomance! We are *not* going back!"

His eyes dropped to his robe, then to the tattoos on his hands. He took a step back. "I am a mage. But I also escaped. Many years ago."

His head lowered, eyes locked to mine, and he tried to convince me without words.

"You for real?" I asked.

"I am Queen Finley's mage and confidant. If she trusts me...?"

Only problem was... I didn't know if I could trust Finley. What if she'd turned into some power-drunk monster? Wiping out whole species for sport? But something about this guy hit different. Some gut-deep reason told me I could trust him. No idea why.

I exhaled and lowered my sword.

"Good. My name is Pherric," he said, shoulders finally relaxing. "Please come with us. We have much to discuss."

Kinnat and I exchanged a look. *Are you sure?* her eyes asked. *Yes,* mine said back. She eased a little but kept her sword ready.

I started forward, then stopped dead.

A woman standing behind him was watching me, still as stone. She was unlike anyone I'd ever seen—tall as me and slim, wrapped in a white suit that shimmered faintly. She looked slightly Asian. Her skin glowed faint blue, her hair blinding white, and her black eyes pinned me in place.

I tensed, every nerve ready to fight. Then I saw them—wings. One perfect and flawless, the other bent and unable to rise. For a heartbeat, my facade cracked, replaced by sheer disbelief.

Pherric caught my reaction. He knew I'd never seen her species. "This is Kasuma. And, yes, her people can fly. But she is... injured."

Kasuma gave a small nod, but her gaze stayed hard. Distrust radiated off her.

They led us up the grand steps and into the palace. Overwhelming didn't even begin to cover it. Massive white walls stretched upward, every surface polished clean. Tapestries and portraits stared from above. Every king and queen who'd ever ruled here claiming not just the palace, but me along with it. Workers scurried past, heads down, eyes averted, trained into blindness. Light poured everywhere, through windows and off flickering torches. Too bright. Too perfect. Beautiful, sure, but built as a reminder of how small you are.

One painting snagged me mid-step. A young woman with a crown stood beside a throne. Red hair. A smile that didn't quite fit. Finley. My Finley. It really was her! Well, in a painting.

They brought us into what I can only call their war room: a narrow chamber with two windows at the far end, chairs lining the walls, a long table buried under maps, books, and papers. Tiny wooden pieces dotted the maps, pawns in a game I didn't know the rules to.

I introduced Kinnat, but Pherric barely looked at her. His focus was locked on me. He ordered food and drinks, then came close, his hands settling heavy on my shoulders.

"Before your meals arrive, tell me everything."

And I did. I told him about falling asleep in my New York apartment and waking up in Tir Na. About Ramil. About Jonathan. He knew of Ramil, but Jonathan made his brows knit tight.

"And you did not know this Jonathan before meeting him on this world?"

"No," I said. Was he suspicious of Jonathan? Was Jonathan not even from Earth? My mind spun conspiracies. "But from everything I could tell, he was from my world. Wait... you said you... recognize me?"

His arms crossed, head cocked. "I am sorry?"

"You said, out in front of the gate, that you recognized me. How is that possible... if you're not really with the Scholomance?"

He gave me a sheepish grin. "Well, I was the one who brought Finley to Tir Na."

"What?!"

"I used the Godsribbon to travel the vast black ocean. I chose your city because of the dense population. And I—"

"You kidnapped her?!"

"Yes. But for a good reason—"

"No. There is no goddamn good reason to snatch someone away from their friends, their family!"

"I am entirely at fault, and it was my decision to make. To be honest with you, *you* were my first choice. I noticed you at the event on the rooftop, when you were comforting Finley. You were lively, fit, and obviously intelligent."

"But you went with the drunk girl puking in the corner. Because she was an easier target? Why did you take her?"

"I am assuming you have heard of mindforms?" I nodded. "Good. I was able to trace back Finley's lineage. She comes from a line of warriors, even though she was not one herself. But she became one in time. And I would make the same decision a thousand times over. She saved our world…"

He let it all sink in. And… all right. That kind of shut me up. But I was still mad. Mad at what he'd done to her. Mad at what had been done to me. Just plain fucking mad.

When food and drinks came in, Pherric pulled up chairs for Kinnat and me. I ate because I was starving, but my eyes kept drifting.

"Where is… when can I see Finley?"

Pherric and Kasuma exchanged a look.

"What's going on? What's wrong?"

He pulled a chair close, sat down. "Eat." He waited until I took a tentative bite. "Finley has been kidnapped by the Atlanteans."

"Atlanteans… As in Atlantis?"

"Yes," he said, watching my face. "Atlantis, from your folklore, exists here. For reasons beyond our imagination, they have taken her. They had occupied the Godsribbon Castle, where you woke up. And I am assuming they are the ones who brought you and this Jonathan to Tir Na, just as I brought Finley here. Kasuma and her mate Braylor were with her. He still searches for her in Cíbola and she returned with the news. I believe the Atlanteans were plotting with Ramil, for some reason."

"Yeah, they were! To kill her!"

"How do you know this?" He edged closer, hungry for anything I could give him.

"In a short amount of time, Jonathan advanced enough in his training that he could move objects with his mind. He's some kind of magician." Pherric nodded, biting back more questions. "Ramil told him they were going to use his powers to poison Finley. And that I was the backup plan. That's why they trained me to be a warrior. But we escaped before they had time to set their little plan in motion."

"We? Jonathan is with you?" Pherric's eyes swept the room as if he failed to see him there.

"No," I admitted. "He couldn't unlock his own door. Only mine. But she and I made it out. Ramil must've used his magic on his door to keep his door locked or something."

"Or something," he repeated.

Pherric sat back, taking it all in.

I pushed up from the table. "Then we have to go get her! I'll help. Kinnat, will you help?"

She exhaled through her nose, clearly unimpressed. Then her hand when to the hilt of her sword. "Do not make this a habit."

Pherric leaned in. "It is not that easy. Please sit. Eat."

"No. We have to do something. Get her back!"

"Genevieve, please," he begged. "We have done everything. Kasuma and Braylor searched everywhere for her. We scoured the coast. Our ships sailed the Triton Sea for weeks. They could not even find the island. She is missing until someone wants us to find her."

I dropped back into the chair, defeated. "But why don't you use your mind trick to find her?!"

He sighed. "I can tell you that she was alive when she was captured. But Finley's mind is no longer connected with mine."

"What does that mean?"

"Finley is dead."

38

Hope is a Dangerous Word

Genevieve

Finley was dead.

The words didn't just land—they exploded inside me. The air left my lungs so violently it felt as though my body caved in. I leaned back in my chair, blinking hard against the tears threatening to spill. My jaw locked until it ached, each tooth grinding hard to chew through the grief.

"I am very sorry to be the one to tell you this news," Pherric said softly. His hand reached for mine, but I snapped it away because his touch might shatter me.

"But there is something you should know," he added.

I couldn't hold it anymore. The sob broke free, jagged and raw. My body folded over, chest caving, forehead nearly striking the table. I had lost her again. The universe had already stolen her once—and somehow, miraculously, given her back. Now it had torn her from me all over again.

My cries tore through me until my throat burned. She was gone.

"Genevieve—" Pherric started.

"If only I'd escaped earlier. If only I'd reached her," I choked out. "She woulda known I was here. That she wasn't alone."

"The blame lies with her captors, not you," Kinnat mumbled, voice firm.

"There was nothing you could have done."

Her words didn't soothe. They just slid off the walls of my grief. My body was bone-heavy, screaming for sleep. My stomach still hollow with hunger, but it was drowned out by the fatigue of too many battles, too many losses.

Pherric let me cry until my body emptied itself. No more tears left, just the dull ache of absence.

"I want to offer you a small amount of hope," he said.

"Hope? How the fuck are you gonna give me hope?!" My grief snapped into fury, hot and wild.

He looked around, signaled. The others left until only Kasuma remained.

"What is it?" I rasped, straightening with shaky hands.

"I am an alchemist. Trained at Scholomance. Before I escaped, I stole an ancient text. And when Finley was wounded in battle, I used a forbidden potion on her."

"Okay..." My heart tripped, suspicious, desperate.

"There was, however, a page missing from the ingredients. She is not immortal, but she does not remain dead."

My face twisted through confusion, disbelief, fury, and the wild flicker of a smile before I could control it. I felt ridiculous, almost hysterical.

Pherric looked deeply uncomfortable. "It is what Finley would call *'some crazy shit.'*"

A laugh tore out of me—loud, unsteady, but real. God, that was *exactly* what Finley would say.

"But when she does die," he pressed, "she remains dead for longer and longer periods."

"She has... died more than once?!"

"She has. Several times. On her last death, she was gone for a full lunar cycle."

"Finley stayed dead for a month? Get the fuck outta here!" My voice pitched up, equal parts disbelief and terror.

Pherric lifted a goblet, draining it to steady his hands.

"And if she has been killed by the Atlanteans, there is a chance she may return."

Hope pricked inside me. I shoved it back into its cage before it could bloom and betray me.

"And... there's a 'but' coming?"

He stood, pacing. His face was carved with restraint—he wanted to believe but wouldn't let himself.

"We are not sure..." he said at last. "...but if Finley is burned to ash, or if her head is removed, we do not believe she would return to life."

The fragile spark of hope extinguished, leaving me hollow.

"And how long has she been dead?" My voice was flat, mechanical.

Pherric turned. "One month and twenty-one days."

The numbers looped through my brain.

"So if... if she comes back within the next few days or something, you'll know?"

"If she returns in her right state of mind, I should be able to detect her vibrations."

"And if after two months... nothing?"

His silence was enough. Then, softly: "You already know the answer."

The weight of it pressed me into my chair. Pherric shifted, his tone suddenly gentler, all but parental. "Now, you must eat. You need your strength."

A doting mother hen, he nudged my chair closer to the table and poured water into a cup.

"Could I get some of that wine?"

"After you've finished your meal and drank plenty of water." Thanks, mom.

I stared at the cup of water. My throat was raw, swollen from crying, but I forced myself to take a sip.

Pherric's words rattled around in my skull—one month and twenty-one days. It sounded too exact, some sort of countdown clock that had been ticking before I even knew it existed.

"You really think she might come back?" I asked, voice barely above a whisper. It wasn't for him. It was for me.

"I do not think. I only hope. And... listen."

Hope. The word burned. A knife in my guts. Because hope was dangerous. Hope was cruel. Hope had teeth, and every time I let it bite, it never let go clean.

Kinnat shoved the food closer. "Eat," she urged. Her tone was steady, grounding. "You cannot fight if you collapse."

Fight. Yeah. That was all that was left for me now. Fight, wait, and pray Finley clawed her way back from whatever abyss she'd been dragged into.

I tore a piece of bread from the loaf, stuffed it into my mouth just to prove I could. My body obeyed, even when my heart didn't want to.

I looked at Pherric. "When she comes back," I said slowly, "you tell me first. Before anyone else. You understand?"

"I understand," he said simply.

And there it was. I let the smallest, sharpest shard of hope pierce me.

Pherric led us down a long corridor lit by flickering sconces, shadows stretching and breaking across the stone walls. My body protested every step, but I kept pace. Kinnat walked beside me, close enough to block anyone from getting between us, far enough not to touch.

Pherric stopped before a heavy oak door inlaid with iron and pushed it open. The hinges groaned. Inside, a fire burned low in the hearth, amber light spilling across a wide canopy bed draped in velvet. It was the kind of room designed to impress, to reassure.

"This room is yours, Genevieve," Pherric said, gesturing inside. He nodded across the hall to a second door. "And this one is yours, Kinnat. Hot baths have been prepared for both of you."

"She is safe here? Free to do as she pleases?" Kinnat asked.

Pherric studied her for a long moment, then inclined his head. "She is." He looked at me. "She will be right there."

Right there.

The phrase lodged somewhere uncomfortable. Right there had never meant much to me before.

When Pherric left us, the room felt suddenly too large. Too quiet. The fire, the bed, the bath—being placed somewhere meant to feel safe tugged loose an old memory. Stone walls. A narrow cot. Long nights at the Scholomance where silence pressed harder than fear ever had.

Kinnat noticed.

"This is your room," she said, practical, as if assigning a post. "No one will enter without your permission."

She checked the door. The lock. The windows. Drew the curtains with a soldier's efficiency.

"As he said, you are free to leave," she added, almost as an afterthought.

Then she turned back to me. "Come."

She helped me out of my ruined clothes without lingering, without apology. Guided me into the bath. When she washed my hair, her hands were steady and familiar, the motions practiced.

I closed my eyes.

Not because she asked me to. Because my body needed the care, even if my heart knew better than to read into it.

When she wrapped me in clean linen and led me back to the bed, I felt unarmored. Exposed.

She tucked the blankets around me, precise and efficient. Then she stepped back.

The space between us felt deliberate.

"Kinnat," I said quietly. "You'll come back?"

Her expression didn't change. "I am across the hall."

I hesitated. I wanted to ask her to stay. To say something reckless. To name the warmth we'd shared on cold nights in the woods, when survival had blurred lines and made honesty feel simpler.

But I said nothing.

She seemed to sense the pause and cut in before I could make a mistake.

"Things are different now," she said, not unkindly. "You are safe. You are among allies." A faint, distant smile touched her mouth. "You do not need guarding."

The words were meant to reassure.

They landed like distance.

"You should rest," she added.

She turned to leave.

The fear slipped out before I could stop it. "You're leaving Irkalla, though. As soon as you can?"

She paused in the doorway and looked back at me, her face unreadable.

"Yes," she said. "That would be for the best."

Then she was gone.

The door closed softly behind her.

I lay staring up at the canopy, listening to the fire settle, and wondered if what I'd felt in the woods had been born of closeness and danger—and if, now that we were safe, it belonged only to me.

39

I Felt Suddenly Very Small

Finley

As I've said, being dead is a whole lot of nothing. Blank. No thoughts, no dreams, no light. My brain finally shut up for once. But coming back from it? Coming back is hell. (No, not Hell the kingdom, but... you know that already.)

It starts with having the wind knocked out of you, but worse. My body had been sucker-punched by the universe. I clawed at the air, trying to drag it into my lungs, but it kept slipping out of reach. My chest spasmed because I'd seemingly been holding my breath for ten minutes. My heart screamed: _breathe, breathe, breathe!_ and my brain was like, _calm down, I'm trying!_

Then the pain hit. Oh god, the pain. Fire in my veins that burned through muscles and tendons. There was molten metal in my bones. Instinctively, my hands roamed over my body, expecting scorched skin, open wounds, something—anything—to explain why I was burning alive. But there was nothing. No stab wounds or scars.

I don't think you'll ever actually know your own death. I do. I have. Several times.

For most people, the brain lets you get right up to the edge and then pulls the plug. You feel it closing in—the pain, the narrowing, that heavy

214

sense of *this is it*—and then you're out. No final moment. No awareness of the actual death. The world doesn't fade to black. It just... cuts.

Everyone else gets the aftermath. They buy flowers. They cry. They tell stories and turn you into something they can carry with them. You never know you've become a memory. From your side of things, the thread snaps mid-thought.

Me? I don't get that mercy. I get the full experience. I see it. I feel it. It still drops into nothingness in the end, but I'm conscious for the fall.

And yeah. It really, really blows.

Then I remembered where I was. Atlantis. That bitch queen. The way her blade slid into me again and again. Like she was trying to carve out my soul. Two months. It had to be almost two months since she killed me. Two. Fucking. Months. My blood was already boiling just picturing her stupid face when I drive a sword right back through her.

Every movement was agony. My joints were rusty, muscles stiff and foreign, bones hummed with anger. My body's screamed at me to stay down, to rest for a few days, but rage wouldn't let me.

I tilted my head, my neck protested with a harsh bark, and took in the room. Sleek black tiles. Smaller columns circled the chamber. I was sprawled on a flat stone table that explained the ache in my back. Well, besides the whole "death recovery" thing. Above me, a domed ceiling with a translucent circle leaked sunlight onto my face. Daytime.

Two months.

The thought alone made me sit up, even as pain clawed at my spine. Thalassa must've let a herd of karkadanns trample me just for fun after I died. My lungs dragged in one more gasp of air.

I was back.

An Atlantean servant walked in carrying a tray of towels, soap, and a steaming pitcher of water. Apparently, they had some guy bathing my corpse. Ew! Gross.

The moment his eyes landed on me, the tray exploded from his hands and hot water arced across the floor. His face went white in pure panic, and he raced from the room shouting something in Atlantean.

Good call, mate. Run.

My head throbbed; I rubbed at my temple, trying to scrape the headache away. Someone had clearly left the pain dial on cruel.

Thalassa swept in, a storm in sandals, with that proud grin already carved on her face. I snarled and pushed off the stone table, intent on ending her in that very moment. My legs, however, had different plans. I fell face-first and slid across the smooth tile with all the grace of a dropped sack of grain.

She laughed. A clean, cold sound that polished the room.

"Careful, child. I do not think you are quite ready to tear me limb from limb just yet."

I crawled toward her on my elbows, cheeks burning with fury and humiliation, fingers clawing at her ankles. She set a sandal on my skull and pressed. Bone met tile; pain flared hot. Reason #13 on my growing list of why she needed to die.

"We shall feed and water you," she purred, sweet and lethal. "Let you rest from your... ordeal. And then I shall take you on a tour to 'show off my *space-bending* island,' as you requested."

She glided out, sandals slapping in perfect time with my rage. I rolled onto my back, my nose picking up the slightly Thalassa-scented air. My lungs ached, my pride lay in shards on the floor, and the world stubbornly continued to exist.

I had a long day ahead of me.

Thalassa thought it was cute to send me a bunch of raw fish and some water. I downed it like someone who hadn't eaten in two months, because—well...

I curled into a tight ball in the far corner of the chamber, which oddly seemed to be my mausoleum, and let my body do what it needed. I must have dozed off, because every time I blinked the bruise of sleep receded a little more. Eventually I forced myself upright, stretching joints that had not wanted to cooperate, testing tendons and ligaments.

When Thalassa and two of her bulging minions returned, I could walk. My knees still trembled, and my temper still seethed; I wanted to scratch her eyes out. The guards with their glittering swords made that impractical.

"Let us walk," she purred. "I have much to show you."

"You know, to be perfectly honest, I really don't need to see your little slice of perfection. Now, that you've seen me die, I want to know... what's next?"

"At the proper moment, child."

I started to protest, demand answers, but my mouth wouldn't form the words. She spun, assuming I would follow. I did. Her bodyguards stayed on my heels.

Thalassa led us through a long corridor lined with pearl-white columns and rippling tapestries that seemed to shift when I wasn't looking. The floor sloped gently upward, guiding us toward daylight and a growing breeze.

We passed through a final archway and the corridor opened onto a massive balcony. The air hit me first, but without the roar of waves I expected at this height. The island stretched wide before me.

Atlantis finally made sense.

From up here, the city wasn't a cluster of huts or a trick of the horizon—it sprawled across the crescent-shaped island in sweeping terraces of white stone, each tier broader than the one above it. Sunlight shone off rooftops tiled in pearl and gold. Broad areas cut through the city in open courtyards of polished marble. Canals wound between them, shallow and clear, reflecting the sky.

Buildings weren't crammed together. Wide colonnades, gardens carved into terraces, open grass fields, amphitheaters, and public baths shimmered beneath us. The scale was monumental, but not confusing.

Something caught my eye.

In one of the largest plazas, a flat expanse of polished stone the size of a stadium, a regiment of Atlantean soldiers trained in perfect formation. Dozens of them, maybe more, moving as a single organism. Their armor flickering in the sun, scaled and pale gold, and every one of them wielded a trident. They thrust and pivoted in synchronized rows while a commander stalked the front line, barking orders.

A show for my benefit? Probably. But the ground trembled with each coordinated slam of weapon butts against marble.

To the south was a harbor so vast I couldn't understand how I'd missed it on the way in. Black-sailed warships lined the docks in tight formation—sleek, angular, built for speed and fear. Dozens, maybe more. Their hulls gleamed, trimmed in blue and gold sigils that caught the light.

As I stared, the ships were still, but I could feel the potential in them. The waiting force. The kind of fleet that didn't defend an island but might conquer an ocean.

I gripped the balcony rail, cold stone biting into my hands. "We sailed right up to this island," I murmured. "How did I not see any of that?"

I tore my eyes away and rounded on her. "I'm here because you want to be immortal."

"You are here, my child," she said, voice soft enough to cut, "because you are a means to an end."

I threw up my hands. "God, I am so sick of people speaking in riddles. Just say it. It's not that hard. Use. Your. Words."

The guards moved in, hands brushing their weapons, and I suddenly remembered my body had been wrung out and left to dry.

Thalassa drifted closer, voice silky. "The city you see before you is glorious, yes. But we have been wronged by those on the mainland. Exploited. Used. Forgotten."

"Hey! Newsflash—*everyone* got screwed," I snapped. "King Malek... okay, Kane, burned half the continent to the ground. You're not special because you ran low on food or tributes or whatever—"

She pressed a finger to my lips, a gesture that made my blood boil.

"We are Atlantis. We do not suffer," she whispered. "But we do avenge. What was taken from us will be reclaimed. And what was denied us will be ours."

Her eyes burned, not with grief but hunger.

I opened my mouth to demand details, but I didn't get the chance. Her soldiers seized my arms, dragging me backward as she turned away with the calm of someone who already owned the ending.

We moved downstairs. The shift was immediate. Sunlight dropped away, and our footsteps echoed off stone that felt too old for torchlight. Each step took us deeper, past polished marble into rough-cut walls meant for containment, not beauty. The air thickened, stale and damp, washed in a silence that didn't belong in palaces.

The stairs groaned, shadows stretched long, and the world narrowed into a corridor that could only lead one place.

A dungeon.

Welcome to my new home, I thought.

"This way," she motioned with one of her long, exquisite fingers.

Rows of iron-clad cells lined the corridor. A few held Atlanteans; one fossil of an old man sat with his stare fixed at nothing. At the last cell Thalassa hesitated, turned on a heel as if revealing a trophy.

"May I present my latest prize catch," she stated.

I peered around the bars. In the far corner, bruised and bloodied and folded into himself, was someone I'd prayed for in my nightmares.

Braylor.

My love. My everything.

The sound I made was not a sound so much as a torn rag of a scream. I launched myself against the bars. One eye was swollen shut, the other a raw, red gutter. A scar split his cheek; dried blood crusted on his skin. He'd been here a day, maybe more.

When he recognized me, he growled; getting to his feet nearly toppled him. His huge fists braced against the wall; he pushed himself up with a noise of effort that made my heart ache. He reached the bars and gripped my hands with grimy, bloody fingers.

"Finley." That took a lot of energy to say. "You... live."

"Well, now I do," I said. The tears came, hot and uncontrollable. "I do."

He pulled in ragged breaths, each one a small violence. He bent forward with pain, and I died a little bit. Braylor was a mountain of a man in every other life; to see him humbled was a personal wound.

"You did this!" I lunged at her, anger a living thing in my head. Swords flashed to my throat and a dagger pricked my side.

"It was not an easy task," she said, admiring him the way one admires the curve of a blade. "He took five of my finest to their deaths in capturing him."

"Good!" I spat, hatred tasting sweet. I saw only red.

Thalassa barely glanced at me, still appraising him. Somehow, I bet she ached to own such a fierce warrior. "But, as it turns out, he is not quite as an effective fighter when he is in the water."

I turned back, frantic. "Are you okay? How bad is it?!"

He rested his forehead on the iron. Fresh blood trickled from his nose; a lip split and bled again. "I will live."

A list of reasons—#14 through #47—why she should not be allowed to exist flashed through my buzzed mind. She would pay for every cut, every bruise. My hands flew out at Thalassa, impelled by a rage I barely recognized.

The swords bit lightly into my flesh and the world narrowed to steel and heat.

Even the Queen's finely poised stance faltered under the force of my fury, and she took a step back. Then her smile returned, calm and cruel. She was in control.

Braylor's rough hand caught mine, anchoring me. "No. Do not."

I was torn between killing the thing that had wrecked us and staying to hold him while he mended. I ended up stuck in the terrible middle, heart trying to pull itself in two directions.

I pressed my forehead to his across the bars and exhaled. "What do you want?"

Her answer was a chill that slid between my ribs. "I want your mage. I want his secret. You will write a letter. One that could only be from you... and we shall seal it with your signet."

My eyes shot to the ring on my finger, the gift from Pherric.

I felt suddenly very small.

"He is to come here, with the tome containing the mixture for this magic immortality elixir. If you do not, your royal consort dies. If he does not come, we burn you until there is nothing left but bone. Of which, we will crush up and feed to the sea."

"Fuck you."

"I shall take that as an affirmative response."

The smile never left her face as she glided away, feet whispering on stone. My legs trembled. The guards hauled me back roughly; my hands slipped from Braylor's.

"No! Braylor! No!" I screamed until the corridor swallowed my voice and he was out of sight, and the sound that came from me was not just grief but the terrible promise of a thing that would not rest.

40

Kelthar's Wake

Jonathan

Ramil and I rode through a bustling coastal village in southern Cíbola, just off a wide blue stretch of the Triton Sea. The chatter of merchants and sailors spilled into the narrow streets. Painted shutters hung crookedly on squat houses, and strings of drying clothes dangled from balconies, offerings to the sea breeze.

The cobblestones were uneven, worn smooth from centuries of footsteps, and I had to keep my eyes down or risk twisting an ankle.

Ramil stopped to ask directions to a tavern from a tiny old woman with skin dried thin by the sun; she muttered in a dialect thick as smoke and pointed a knotted finger toward the building crouched at the far end of town.

I had thought we were headed to Godsribbon Castle to confront the Atlantean queen, to finally demand why she still remained as an occupying force. But Ramil had heard news instead. She had captured Queen Finley of Irkalla, taken her alive, and returned to Atlantis. That wasn't part of the plan.

We traveled for weeks by karkadann from the academy, their thunderous steps eating up miles faster than our legs ever could. The beasts carried us through jungled lowlands, across bare ridges, and into a harsh desert until we reached the water. This journey was easier. Ramil had secured rides, better food, and proper tents. Still, every stretch of road stirred memories of my last passage through this land.

With Genevieve.

Her face surfaced in the quiet moments more often than I cared to admit. Every day. I prayed she had found her way to safety, and the knowledge that she had escaped alongside another initiate steadied me, even if that hope felt dangerously thin.

The tavern he was looking for was straight out the movies: crooked beams, a roof patched with driftwood, lanterns casting honey-colored light across the front.

Music burst through the doorway in uneven waves: fiddle strings, clapping hands, someone shouting at a dice table. The sign swinging overhead bore a chipped painting of a massive, coiled serpent wrapped around a cup of frothy ale, its fangs glinting through faded paint.

"The Leviathan's Mug," Ramil said, scanning the street. "The contact will meet us here."

My pulse took off. In places like this, unpredictability ruled.

Inside, the tavern burned with sound and smoke. Heat pressed in from bodies crowded around tables. Filled by sailors with darkened skin, villagers dusted in flour or fish scales. The smell was piercing—spilled ale, brine-soaked clothes, sweat—yet comforting in its own way. This was the sort of chaos where no one cared who you were, provided you kept your head down.

We slipped through the crush until we found a shadowed corner booth, one suited for quiet words. Ramil ordered drinks. A serving girl set two mugs before us.

"Drink," he said. It was a command, not a suggestion.

I wasn't much of a drinker. The ale was warm and sour and strong, but I swallowed a mouthful to appease him.

The man Ramil waited for appeared soon after. He was wiry, hunched, with eyes that darted constantly, as if danger might erupt from any corner. His beard grew in patches, and his hands shook as he set a satchel on the table.

"You have the coin?" he asked, his voice thin and fragile.

Ramil placed the pouch down with deliberate calm. The clink of metal cut through the din, and the man's fingers twitched before he touched it. From the satchel, he pulled a folded sheet of treated vellum, edges stained, corners worn. He spread it on the table and weighted it down with my mug.

I leaned forward. The map showed the southern coast of Cíbola, the reefs of the Triton Sea, and beyond them a series of markings descending into the deep. There, drawn in careful ink, was the island of Atlantis, curved into the shape of a C, with a smaller island nestled inside it.

The man licked his lips. "This," he said, tapping the map, "is the true location. I've arranged passage on a fishing boat at dawn. The captain won't ask questions, and you should offer no answers. She will land you there and not return." He glanced over his shoulder and lowered his voice. "Take it, and may the sea favor you."

Ramil nodded once, gathered the map, and pushed the coin pouch across the table. The man snatched it up and vanished into the press of bodies and noise.

I stared at the map, tracing the ink with my eyes, trying to quiet the storm in my head. Atlantis. The word itself carried weight.

Ramil folded the parchment and stuffed it into his bag. "We go to finish what I started," he said quietly, his voice smooth but unyielding.

He didn't elaborate. I didn't ask.

By the time we reached the docks in the early morning, there was the chill that clings to everything before sunrise. Fishermen moved with mechanical precision. Their ropes coiled, sails unfurled, nets prepared. Voices called back and forth. Their movements carried the ease of long habit. Mine did not.

At the far end of the pier waited our vessel.

Kelthar's Wake.

The name was painted in chipped blue across the stern. I couldn't decide whether *wake* referred to the trail a ship leaves behind or a funeral. I hoped for the former.

The captain was a Prominan woman shaped by sun and seawater. Thick-browed, broad-jawed, her eyes measured you before you spoke. She sat on the edge of the boat, fingers working a net with slow certainty, hands fluent in knots.

She glanced up without lifting her head. "You ready?"

Ramil straightened, chest puffing briefly in a way that recalled a boy showing off a prize. "We are."

There was no bravado in his voice, only resolve.

She rose, untied the lines, and as we climbed aboard, the dock drifted away beneath our feet.

We sat at the stern. Before untying a rope and releasing the sail, she turned to Ramil. He produced a small sack of coins with a steady hand. She inspected it, counted with a grunt. Trust here was measured in metal. Satisfied, she nodded, and the sail caught wind as the boat slipped into the bay.

Out on open water, the waves grew heavier, rocking us hard. Nausea followed, and I fixed my gaze on the horizon, the only thing that stayed still.

Ramil leaned over the captain at the wheel, finger pressed to the map in determination. She pointed out shoals and currents, muttering warnings about kelpies and a school of plesiosaurs known to favor both wood and men. I listened, pretending the names meant something to me, but they were simply another reminder of how many ways this world would kill you.

As Atlantis began to exist not in sight but in thought, a slow unease settled in my gut that had nothing to do with the sea.

Ramil would expect me to kill the queen of Irkalla.

Training at the academy with the polished mindform techniques, the elegant blending of potions? That felt like art. Precise. Detached. Turning those lessons into a hand that ends a life felt obscene and brutally practical all at once. There was romance in learning to bend the world; there was something colder in the doing. Real lives. Real consequences.

And we were sailing straight toward a place that devoured plans.

The queen would not welcome us killing her prisoner. We had no escape route waiting if things unraveled. That truth settled between Ramil and me, an unspoken third presence.

And the weight of what we were doing pressed down on me, tide-heavy and inevitable.

After a time, the captain pointed ahead to a tiny island. Just bare rock and scrubs, a lone watchtower slumped against the sea. I almost laughed. *This* was Atlantis? An outpost, perhaps. A decoy.

The captain didn't slow.

I watched as we approached, waiting for details to come into focus. Nothing changed... until the tower's outline wavered, as the rules that seemed to govern shape were being quietly revised. Lines thickened into walls. Shadows resolved into archways. Features appeared all at once, as if they had always existed and my mind had simply failed to register them.

I blinked. The barren rock became terraces of white stone. Blinked again, and columns stood where open sky had been. The city assembled itself, the way a puzzle locks together once you recognize the image.

A slow nausea rolled through me. Not seasickness.

Atlantis hadn't been hidden or distant. It had been compressed into a smaller conceptual frame until we crossed whatever boundary allowed it to be perceived correctly. Space here wasn't deceptive, it merely refused observation from an imprecise angle.

Another swell carried us forward, and scale snapped into place. What had been a speck became a vast crescent-shaped island crowned with a city. Wide avenues, marble plazas, canals cut through stone. At the harbor's edge, dark sails lined the water. Rows of warships, that had not existed moments earlier, appeared at the docks.

I swallowed.

This wasn't spectacle magic. It was engineering. Dimensional editing. Evidence of construction by tools we barely understood.

Behind me, Ramil murmured, "Magnificent, is it not?"

It wasn't magnificent.

It was a thought too large for the human mind.

Atlantis didn't reveal itself.
It allowed me to notice it.

41

Like a Fish in an Aquarium

Finley

Thalassa's guards dragged me forward and dropped me hard at the base of her throne. My knees slammed against stone, and the echo of it filled the chamber. A servant appeared with parchment, quill, and ink.

Thalassa reclined in her towering chair because she had all the time in the world. Behind her, that strange black sphere perched on its pedestal again: silent, reflective, impossible to ignore.

Her gaze found mine, determined and unblinking. They locked on my hand when I picked up the quill like it was a weapon.

Because it was.

"Wipe the thought from your mind, Finley," she said, voice calm but edged with warning.

I felt the steel of swords press against my back in an instant.

And here's the thing: every cell in my body screamed at me to tell her to shove it. But Braylor—sweet, stupid, too-brave Braylor—was still bleeding in that cage below us. And apparently, I had no survival instincts, because instead of quietly obeying, I slammed the quill down so hard ink spattered.

I forced myself up, lifting my chin. She nodded and the guards let me stand.

"I'll write your damn letter," I said, pointing my finger. "But only if you bring him a healer. Now. He's in bad shape and needs help. I will not let him suffer. If you want to kill him and me, fine. But you take care of him? I sign. Those are my terms. Take it or leave it."

For a long, terrible moment, she only studied me. I thought I'd gone too far. But at last, she sighed, lips tightening.

"I will provide him a healer," she said finally, each word dipped in venom. And when she stepped down from her throne, closing the distance between us, I couldn't stop the fear curling in my chest. "Now write."

"No," I said. I swallowed hard as I watched rage build within her.

"What?"

"One more term."

"No."

I stepped away until my back found the cold steel sword I knew was waiting for me. The tip met my spine. I forced myself to lean in until the blade bit, watching her face for any slip. Blood welled along the line where steel sliced skin.

"You promise to let me and him go. When this is over. Your word must mean something. Promise me."

She held me with a look that could have frozen fire. For a long, impossible beat nothing moved but my pulse and the slow, steady drip of heat down my back. The soldier's blade trembled under his hand; I pushed against it until it found purchase and cut deeper, and the world narrowed to the sound of my own breathing.

A flash of fear crossed her eyes. "Yes," she said.

"Yes, what?" I pushed back harder still, more blood dripped down.

"I shall release you and your consort when I have the potion. And it has proven effective."

I sank to the floor with the parchment, knees unsteady, the room tilting as my hands shook while I bent to write.

I wanted to slip in some secret message, some code only Pherric and I would understand... but we had no code. No plan. All I could do was write the words plainly: that it was me, that he had to come, that he needed to bring the book. I tried to make it sound regal, convincing.

When I finished, Thalassa hovered close, reading each word and weighing them for treachery. Then she seized my hand and dragged me behind the throne.

A woman glided out from behind the curtains with a dark red candle, dripping wax onto the folded letter. That part was normal. The next part wasn't.

Thalassa shoved my hand into the firelight of a torch until the ring on my finger burned hot enough to blister. I clenched my teeth, tasting blood. I'd survived *dragonfire*. I wasn't going to scream over this.

She pressed the hot metal into the wax. My skin sizzled; the seal held.

It was official.

"You still feel pain?" Thalassa's voice was smooth, curious. She was observing an insect under glass.

"Fuck yes," I snapped through my teeth. "Pherric's potion brings you back from the dead; it doesn't make you impervious to pain."

Her lips turned. "Pity."

"You're doing all this so you can live forever?" I asked, rubbing at my crispy fingers.

She didn't look at me but watched the woman carrying away the sealed letter. "No."

"Then... why?"

"I need a select group of warriors," she said. "Ones who will not die."

Soldiers? An immortal army? Shit. What had I done...

She turned toward a set of curtains, her skin catching the light as her thugs shoved me forward. My boots dragged over cool marble as we left the throne room for an antechamber glowing with lamplight.

I walked into the world's most obscene museum. Gold coins spilled across the floor. Bejeweled boxes and filigreed daggers lay scattered beside statues of creatures I couldn't name. Everything glowed, desperate to be touched. Gifts? Spoils? No. Loot. Shiny things she'd demanded or stole simply because she could.

"This isn't grief," I said, voice low. "This is preparation. For something."

Thalassa kept walking, gazing forward.

"People don't stockpile wealth and make immortal soldiers because they're sad they missed out on some food shipments during a war." My eyes narrowed. "It feels like you're gearing up for something bigger."

Still no answer.

And that was the answer.

"Allow me to show you to your... quarters," she said.

We passed a massive glass tank brimming with water. Inside were eggs—nine, maybe ten, each larger than my head. My steps faltered.

"What are those?"

She turned with slow annoyance. "Those are dragon eggs."

My heart thumped. "Wha—?"

But she was already moving.

"Wait. Why? Why do you have dragon eggs? In an aquarium?"

Her sigh was heavy, as she fielded another of a child's endless questioning. "When the eggs are submerged in water, they do not hatch. They need heat to hatch."

"Okay... but why have them at all?" I demanded. Zeranthyl, her purple dragon, was male. These couldn't be his.

"I am a collector of valuable artifacts."

I stared at the shimmering shells. "Dragon eggs aren't artifacts! They belong with... dragons! You've stolen these from them?"

"Zeranthyl has been quite effective in gathering them for me."

"And what—y-you just hatch a new one when Zeranthyl gets too old?" My insides knotted. The audacity.

"As I said, I am a collector. Now," she swirled away, arms out wide. "On to your quarters!"

Something in me snapped.

"You cold-hearted... evil... nasty... greedy... little bitch." The words tore out of me before I could stop them.

Thalassa stilled at my words. Her webbed fingers splayed, then curled into fists.

"A dragon isn't a toy! It's not a tool or a weapon! You can't take the eggs away from mothers, from fathers! They're endangered! You don't get to control dragons!"

Her fury was a tidal wave. She stormed towards me, and I held my ground. Her hand lashed across my face, fierce and stinging. I stumbled, tasting blood.

"Dragons have terrorized all people, for generations!" she hissed. "Do not tell me, Terran, what I can and cannot do to enact my revenge!"

"They're not evil killing machines!" I shot back. "They're sentient. They're scared. They're disappearing!"

"Good riddance! You know the damage they can do!"

"So wiping them out is the answer? No! You know it isn't. Because you have a goddamn dragon! You, of all people, should understand!"

Her gills fluttered as she fought to steady herself. Closing her eyes, she inhaled, the movement oddly graceful. "What I understand," she said softly, "is that I am protecting my people. Those eggs are mine. I will do with them as I see fit. By preventing them from hatching, I have saved thousands upon thousands of lives. At sea and on the accursed land! And no one will ever give me credit for my courage."

"If you're so protective, why not destroy them?" I demanded. "Why keep them at all?"

Her eyes snapped open. "I do not answer to you. The only reason you yet live is because I need you here when your mage arrives. Do not test me further."

She waved her hand. The guards' grips tightened.

I began to see her more clearly. Most rulers would do anything to protect their people. I'd never harm a dragon, but I hadn't lived their history. Tir Na was a death world. There were so many ways to die here.

Yet to keep the eggs, hoard them. That wasn't about survival. Or about power. Kane wanted power. No, it was vanity. Ego. Thalassa wanted to be immortal. To be a god. To command an army of gods.

She floated up a wooden staircase. We stepped onto a deck lined with dozens of trapdoors. A servant opened one. Below glimmered another glass tank of water.

"No," I stated.

"Yes," she murmured.

The guards shoved me. I fell, plunging into the saltwater. Cool, but not freezing. My lungs seized as I gasped and kicked, searching for a floor that wasn't there.

"What?" I coughed, spitting brine. "You can't leave me in here!"

"This is where I keep my prisoners," she said coolly. "I am sorry you cannot breathe underwater. That is a flaw of your species, not my concern. However, I am showing you a kindness. I have placed a bar at the top, for when your legs get tired."

I reached up and gripped the iron bar anchored to the cage ceiling, my legs still kicking. "How long do I have to stay in here?"

"Until your mage arrives," she replied.

"This is cruel, Thalassa! And you know it!"

"Goran says you will not last the night," she said, voice almost bored. "But you are a determined, angry young woman. I expect to see you alive in the morning."

The trapdoor slammed shut.

The rest of that day and into the night became a war of inches and pain. My arms burned from clinging to the bar. I alternated hands to save strength, swam slow circles to relieve the ache, kicked at the glass even though I knew it wouldn't break. Each time I drifted toward sleep, water filled my mouth or nose and yanked me awake.

Hours passed. My muscles trembled. My lungs felt smaller, tighter, as if the cage itself were squeezing me. Somewhere in the dark I realized how long it would take—a message crawling across the seas and through several kingdoms before arriving in Irkalla, Pherric weeks away, and then more time for him to even reach Atlantis.

I would be nothing but bones by then. The thought slid in, dark and treacherous—*what if I just sink and let it be over?*

For a heartbeat, I just about did.

But the panic yanked me back. I forced air into my lungs, forced my eyes open against the sting. I learned to float, stealing micro-naps between sinking and gasping. Saltwater burned my eyes, my lips. My rage, once a hot pulse, curdled into something harder—grim, deliberate, unkillable.

If Thalassa wanted me to drown, she'd be disappointed.

And the night dragged on.

42

Breakfast Interrupted

Genevieve

With the morning sun rising, Kinnat and I ate breakfast on a massive terrace that overlooked the city. It was Finley's favorite spot, I was told. Warm bread in my hands, spiced fruit on my tongue... I was finally well-rested. The sun poured over my skin, loosening the knots in my shoulders. For a moment, it almost felt normal.

Almost.

Kinnat sat across from me, posture relaxed but attention sharp, and my heart immediately decided to make this harder than it needed to be. I'd managed, somehow, to convince her not to leave. Not because she'd wanted to stay, but because she'd agreed we needed answers first. Maybe she wanted to know if Finley would return from the dead. Maybe it was because she worried about me. But I doubted it.

Oddly enough, she was still carrying around the satchel given to us by the farmer's wife. It seemed to mean something to her now.

Below us, the city stretched out in a thousand colors and sounds. Far below, black and blue banners shivered in the breeze, and the streets teemed with activity. I heard workers clanging about, carriage wheels rattling, voices drifting faint but alive. For the first time in days, maybe

235

weeks, I was me again.

Except *me* was still a bit of a mess.

Now that the danger wasn't actively trying to eat us, the quieter questions crept in. Was I falling for Kinnat? Yes. Uncomfortably so. And every once in a while, when she wasn't looking, I let myself wonder if maybe, just maybe, she felt something too.

Then doubt would crash in and drown the thought.

But she could have left that next morning. I knew that. Instead, she sat across from me, eating slowly, as if she'd decided, at least for now, that this was where she belonged. She was still there.

I've always been into girls and guys. Finley was my proof of that—a crush I wore like a secret badge until it fizzled into a great friendship. She never felt the same, but her quiet snark, the way she could level a room with a look. Her sense of humor. That was enough to keep me orbiting her.

With Kinnat, I wanted more. If I accidentally touched her, it wasn't just comforting. It was nuclear, sparking down my nerves, grounding me and burning me alive all at once. I longed to kiss her, to strip away the what–ifs and simply tell her.

The problem? Well, one... she didn't seem to like me very much. And, two, I didn't know the rules here. In this world, in her world. If I confessed, she would laugh me off. Or worse... hack me to pieces for daring suggest anything was possible.

Kinnat reached for another piece of bread, then paused. After a moment, she slid it across the table toward me without comment and took one of the smaller pieces for herself.

But then again, she might scoop me up and carry me straight to bed.

And wasn't that the most dangerous thought of all?

Pherric pulled me out of my daydreaming funk when he came rushing onto the terrace.

"Finley is alive!"

My plate of food went flying as I launched to my feet. "What?!"

He carried a devilish smile, but his joy was tempered. "She is alive."

"How do you know?"

He placed his hands on my shoulders and sat me back down. Kinnat was caught halfway through chewing her food, eyes wide.

Pherric pulled up a wood chair, the feet scraping across the smooth stone tiles.

"I have been searching for her, for her energy, across the void. And I finally felt her. Hard, thick strings. Heavy vibrations. Nothing specific, but I can tell she is in distress. So anger, but also fear. Desperation. And worry."

"You can tell all of that? With your mind?" Kinnat asked.

Yeah, I nodded along with what she said. None of it made sense but from what Jonathan had told me, some sort of sense. Ish?

Pherric nodded. "I can. But these are merely raw emotions. I cannot read her thoughts. Tell you where she is. Nothing like that."

"So what do we do?!" I shouted, palm slapping my thigh. "Can we go find her? She needs our help."

His hands went up. "I do not know what more we could accomplish. We still do not know where the island is located. And we have heard no news from Braylor."

"How can a whole damn island be missing?"

"This world is a very isolated one, as you will learn. Many different species have stayed apart from others. Kasuma is from an island to the west and, up until Finley intervened, most had never been there. Atlantis is no different. Some realms even have laws against intermingling with other species."

"You mean no 'man-on-monkey' love?"

That made him chuckle. "Yes. I can see why you and Finley were friends."

And if they had laws against different species being together, what did that mean for two people of the same sex? I stole a glance at Kinnat.

"Can we at least go down there? Closer to where she is? Just in case this Braylor guy finds the island? I hate being so far away, unable to do anything."

He pondered the idea. "That is not a terrible idea. But we have left our ships down there, with the troops. And Braylor is in the area. My worry would be that we would also be targets."

"Wait. So... they killed her. And she's back, right? How do we know they're not gonna kill her again?"

"We do not."

"That's not good enough, Pherric. We have to do something!"

"I understand your frustration. I feel it as well."

I looked at Kinnat. "Maybe we should go?"

She nodded.

"I do not think that wise, Genevieve. There is much you do not know of this world."

"Well, at least I'm not sitting around here on my ass doin' fuck all."

"Oh, it is amazing how similar you two are," he said.

Kinnat bristled at that. Her head went back a little as she stiffened up. Was she... jealous? God, I hoped so.

"Let me talk with the queen's council. With Kasuma. We shall see what our options are. Will that suffice?"

I started to complain again, but we all heard shouting. In the distance. And then more shouts. Some screams even.

That is when we heard loud whooshing noises. Like a flapping bird, but a really big one.

Pherric backed away from the terrace, closer to the keep. We both followed along.

"Dragon!" we heard someone yell. A guard or someone.

Huge wings came into view. Then the frightening head. Finally, we saw a whole dragon fly around the terrace, swoop up in the air, and land with a heavy thud on the stones. A real live dragon!

My back hit the wall as I screamed out. Pherric held his arm up, protecting me. Kinnat was instantly by my side. I was in a full-on panic, hyperventilating. But those two were scared, yet... not surprised. They had seen such a creature before.

The purple dragon roared at us, growled at the sky. Letting us know who was in charge.

You grow up reading about cute magical dragons in children's books.

You see them on TV shows. Maybe in a movie. But you don't ever expect to see one... in real life. No way, no day.

The dragon landed on the edge of the terrace.

Pherric looked away, convinced we were about to be sprayed with fire.

"Oh, my god! Oh, my god!" I whispered.

But no fire came. The huge, winged creature, its front legs fused with its wings, pawed forward a few steps, head down, orange slits for eyes glaring at us. Fangs bared.

When Pherric realized we weren't going to get barbecued, he straightened up. His eyes scanned the beast.

"Wh-what does it want?" I asked, scared shitless.

"It is not here to kill us," he said, though his voice carried no certainty. "I do not think. Or we would be dead."

"Okay..." I muttered. "So, now what?"

His finger pointed to a chain wrapped around its neck. A small gold tube hung between the links in the center.

Pherric took a step forward. The dragon lowered its head even more, growling. But did not attack.

Another step, his hand held out.

Without taking his eyes off the dragon, he whispered to Kinnat. "Stop any soldier who comes through those doors."

She stood up straighter. "I will." She slid over to the double doors that led onto the terrace.

Slowly, Pherric made his way to the dragon. He kept his head lowered, hands out. Step by step until he was near enough to touch it.

The beast rumbled, shifting its weight, but remained calm.

Carefully, he flipped open the gold tube around the dragon's neck. He pulled out a piece of folded paper.

Pherric then backed away, very slowly. He didn't turn but just kept retreating, head still bowed, as if paying homage.

When he returned to us, I inspected the letter. His face froze. There was a red splotch of wax sealing it up, pressed with a marking.

"What is it?"

He examined it closely. "That is Finley's signet."

"Huh?"

"A marking, in wax, was made using the ring on her finger. This was to let me know it was from her. From her captors."

"A ransom note?"

He shot a look at me before tearing open the letter. He read it, then scanned it again.

Several soldiers came rushing up to the doors, shoving them halfway open. They were armed to the teeth, ready to charge. Kinnat braced herself, throwing her shoulder into the wood to keep them back.

The dragon snarled, its whole body coiling. It pawed and snapped, wings spreading wide as its throat glowed faint with fire. The roar that followed shook the terrace, the soldiers stumbling back.

Pherric spun, hands high. "Stop! Stop. We are fine! Wait there!"

The men hesitated, terrified, but obeyed. The doors slammed shut again, leaving us alone with the beast.

I couldn't tear my eyes from it. My chest rose and fell in panicked bursts.

"What does it say?" I whispered sideways.

"This letter was written by Finley. She asks me to come to Atlantis," he said carefully. "And I am to bring... one of my alchemy books," he lied.

"And?" I felt the weight of it coming.

"And I am to return," he gulped, eyes on the creature, "...on the dragon."

It was then that I saw the saddle—dark leather strapped to its spiky back. Empty. Waiting.

"You gotta be kidding me."

He gave me a look laced with fear. "I am not."

"Wait!" I yelled out. "What about the book?"

Pherric patted the ever-present leather satchel that he carried around— he already had the magic book.

I had never seen a man look so scared. But he didn't falter. He released the letter, letting it float to the terrace floor.

He approached again, slower this time. The dragon roared, wings shoving air against the walls, nearly lifting the chairs from the terrace.

Its head snapped, jaws cracking inches from his body. It was testing him, daring him.

Pherric ducked low, pressing close against its scaled hide, and forced his way to the saddle. With shaking hands, he seized the straps and locked himself in, so close to the pointy spines that one slip would impale him.

The beast reared, shrieking, wind battering us in a windstorm. Plates and cups shattered against the stone. Kinnat and I clung to the wall. Soldiers inside cursed and fumbled as the doors rattled under the gale.

Pherric's knuckles turned white on the reins. He looked back once, voice carrying through the chaos: "Tell the council where I have gone!"

And then the dragon leapt.

The tiles shook with the impact. The air exploded as its wings beat down, launching man and beast skyward in a blur of purple and shadow.

I screamed as the wind tore at me, hair whipping my face, chest burning with fear.

Kinnat dragged me to the railing, and together we watched, clutching the cold railing, as Pherric and the dragon climbed higher, higher, until they were nothing more than a speck burning against the clouds.

43

A Drop in the Ocean

Jonathan

The captain of the fishing boat left us at the steps of Atlantis without a backward glance. She turned the main sail, steered away, and in seconds we could no longer hear the sound from the slap of waves against her hull.

Atlantean soldiers converged almost immediately, swords and tridents glinting in the dim light. They ran down the steps with that coordinated calm you see in well-trained teams. Their faces were unreadable.

Ramil, by contrast, remained composed. He stood there, shoulders back, jaw steady. The world simply owed him an explanation, and he was waiting politely for it.

At the top of the palace steps a figure detached himself from the shadows: lean, sun-darkened skin, actual *gills* fluttering faintly along his stomach. The webbing between his fingers threw little prisms of light as he flexed, and a silver ring sat on his forehead.

He descended with slow, careful steps. Ramil didn't bow. He turned, quiet and formal. "This is Goran, First Sea-Lord of Atlantis." Then he introduced me: "May I present Jonathan. My acolyte mage."

Goran acknowledged me with a bare nod. He asked, cool as water, "What do you want, Ramil?"

Ramil's mouth tightened; I saw the twitch of anger in his eye, but he kept his voice steady. "I want what was promised to me. Take me to Thalassa."

Ramil tried to push past. The Sea Lord's hand reached out and held him by the chest with a grip that was firm and unnervingly gentle.

"She deals with another concern," Goran said.

Ramil shoved his hand off. "I am the only one who matters, boy," he snapped, and then marched up the steps as if consequences were an abstraction he found tiresome. Goran watched him go and, for the first time since we'd arrived, smiled. Not cruelly. He was amused by a predictable reaction in an experiment. When his attention turned back to me, the smile fell and his face registered pity. I hated that look. I followed Ramil because it was the safest option.

Ramil threw the palace doors wide. We entered a vast chamber: a grand staircase ascending to a throne, a narrow walkway flanked by two dark pools of seawater. The water gurgled and a woman's head broke the surface. She pushed damp hair from her face and turned to us with a smile.

"Ramil. An... unexpected pleasure," she said, the words silky but precise.

"I am quite sure it is... unexpected," he replied, equal parts apology and accusation. He bowed the barest degree. "Queen Thalassa."

A servant rushed from between two tall columns with a silk robe. With the poise of someone who knew the world bent to her, the queen climbed the steps—unclothed, unhurried, and entirely unbothered that we were watching. Heat crawled up the back of my neck, and I turned my head when the servant draped the robe across her shoulders.

Thalassa smiled the whole time. She enjoyed watching me squirm. She stood before us then, water trailing from her skin, the robe clinging to her. The light caught her golden-brown frame, every motion radiating an elegance so natural it felt rehearsed. And when her pale gray eyes met mine, cool and cutting, I understood this wasn't beauty alone I was staring at—it was authority, absolute and undeniable.

She approached us, trailing a webbed finger along my cheek without malice. "And who is this charming young man?"

"My acolyte," Ramil said. "Jonathan. But I am here to discuss—"

"A pleasure, Jonathan," she purred, circling Ramil.

I said "Ma'am" out of reflex. It sounded absurd in the echoing hall.

"Thalassa," she corrected, then drifted up to her throne as if an invisible current carried her. Ramil and I followed, both of us playing our parts.

Once she was seated, Ramil crossed his arms and cut to the point. "We had an agreement, your highness."

She feigned hurt with theatrical poise. "Yes. In return for a mighty sum, I occupied Godsribbon Castle and extracted two people from Terra for you, using the magic of your gods. I accomplished what you asked."

"You remained in the castle. You have taken the woman who was to be—" Ramil began.

"Your what? Quarry?" she said with a mocking tilt. "Your prey?"

"That is not of your concern."

She slid from the throne. "Oh, but it is. She has something I want. Something you might have offered, had I known." Her eyes flicked toward me with the sort of calculation I'd seen before in grant reviewers deciding which proposal was worth funding.

Ramil's confusion turned to frustration. "That secret is no longer in our possession."

She tapped his chin, amused. "No, it is not. But Finley's mage does have the book in question. He is on his way to me as we speak."

"Pherric... is coming to Atlantis?"

"Yes. I shall have what I want."

"Then you will release the Irkallan queen to me."

Thalassa considered him, almost bored. "No. I will not."

Ramil flushed. "What use could you have for her? You will have her mage and she is not part of your plan!"

"She will be released once I am satisfied," Thalassa said, casual as tide. "I have given her my solemn oath."

"Your... your oath?" Ramil barked. "Why would you be bound to anything? You have the morals of a ratatoskr—"

The queen rushed at him, slamming a finger into his chest. "Watch your tongue, sorcerer, or I will have it removed," she hissed, then settled back onto her throne with deliberate boredom.

Ramil tried bargaining. "I will pay handsomely if you hand her over."

"Why are you so eager to kill this young woman, Ramil?" she asked. "What harm has she done?"

"She is the usurper of Irkalla. She invaded my homeland. She is an outsider. A *Terran* on our throne." He growled the word.

"No. There is more to it than that." She smiled with curiosity. "This seems personal."

Ramil inhaled, measuring whether to reveal the wound underneath his fury. "She is responsible for my younger brother's death. She took him from me in the Battle of Shangri-La."

"And what was his name?"

"Nerus. Mage to the Kings of Irkalla, Malek and Kane."

I had no idea what they were talking about, but that news reframed everything. This wasn't a political squabble for Ramil; it was a wound that had calcified into resolve. I understood, in that instant, why he had gone around the Preceptor's back. He wanted revenge more than anything.

Thalassa shrugged lightly. "When we return her to where we found her, what you do afterwards is between you and the queen."

Ramil scanned the guards, signaling to me with a raised eyebrow. Then, lower and quieter: "I wish to see her. Confirm she is alive."

"She is. But why would that matter to you? You want her dead."

"If she is to die, I prefer it be by my hand."

Thalassa gave a slow nod. "Follow me."

She rose, walking through a curtain behind the throne.

Thalassa guided us across a room filled with treasures. We climbed some stairs and stepped onto a deck lined with dozens of square trapdoors, each one framed in brass. She stepped to one without hesitation, nodded to a servant, and the panel swung open on hidden hinges.

I leaned forward and saw water below, refracting the torchlight into a wavering, distorted lattice. It took me a moment to understand what I was looking at. Then my stomach dropped.

Inside the glass tank, barely visible beneath the surface, a woman clung to an iron bar fixed at the roof of her prison. Her red hair streamed around her. Her arms trembled as she hung there, chest rising and falling. Then she shifted and I saw her face, ghostly white under the water's sheen, lips cracked from salt.

"Finley," I whispered, not even realizing I'd said her name aloud.

She had been in there for at least two days. I could see the toll it had taken. Her skin was ghost-white where it had soaked, soft and swollen to the point of tearing. The pads of her fingers were practically translucent, her nails rimmed in red where the water had split them. Each breath cost her effort, yet her eyes, when they met mine, were steady. Defiant.

A knot formed in my chest. Part of me wanted to reach for the nearest lever or mechanism, to drag her out and wrap her in something warm.

But then I remembered Ramil's voice: the stories of how she'd led the slaughter of the Bànshēn rén, leveled the city of Ker-Is, how whole communities of Prominans had vanished under her command. And the images of death and destruction he had shared. The memories of those who had died at her hand.

I clung to that as an anchor, forcing myself to see more than just a body in a tank. She wasn't helpless. She was captured.

I straightened, gripping the edge of the trapdoor until my knuckles hurt. The shock still sat in me, but it hardened into something more deliberate. Not pity, but focus.

Whatever she had done to end up here, whoever she had been before this, Finley was not innocent. And if she survived this, she would be dangerous again.

Below, she adjusted her grip on the iron bar, muscles shaking, lips parted as she drew in air. The water closed around her shoulders.

"She will likely die in there," Ramil said at last, his voice low.

"Is that a problem?" Thalassa asked, puzzled by the statement. "She acted supremely defiant."

"We are different from you," he replied.

"You most certainly are," she answered, amused.

"Hominans submerged for too long lose their skin," Ramil said, clinical and blunt. "Protective oils are stripped, tissues macerate. She will develop open sores, necrosis if you push it. It will be quite a mess for you to keep clean."

Thalassa's smile didn't change, only the tilt of it. "Oh, I am quite aware, Ramil. This was but a test."

He looked down at Finley, at the way the water clung to her shoulders and the ragged set of her jaw. For a moment his face was unreadable. Data waiting for interpretation. Then something in him eased—not relief, exactly, but a recognition.

"She survived the ordeal," he said, softer. "A test she seems to have passed."

44

What Did I Do?

Jonathan

I started to speak out about her conditions, the words clawing up my throat. No matter how much hatred I felt for this woman—no matter how often I'd heard her name—no one deserved that level of torture. Not even her.

I opened my mouth, felt the first syllable form, and then the Atlantean queen waved a hand in verdict. The two guards who'd accompanied us shoved Ramil and I out of their path and reached down for Finley.

She didn't go quietly. She moaned as they hauled her out of the water, the motion violent enough to wrench a sound from her that was half protest, half surrender. When they tossed her onto the wood platform she rolled, coughing, hunched against the sudden weight of the world.

Water clung to her hair and sleeves, and it slid off in slow, reluctant beads that pooled around her on the planks, blackening the grain. The stench of the sea and the sourness of old fish hit me full in the face.

Thalassa put a sandal against Finley's shoulder and rolled her onto her back with a casual authority that made my teeth ache.

The queen's voice, calm and flat, carried across the throne room. "A reprieve for you," she said. "But if you act out, back to the water you go."

Finley's eyes snapped open. She was a wild animal—teeth bared, muscles knotted. She launched herself at Thalassa, fingers clawing for the queen's leg with that terrible, animal desperation. I had to admire the impulse; it was pure and ugly and brave all at once.

Thalassa stepped aside. The motion was effortless. Finley's attack misted into exhaustion. She collapsed to the floor, lungs heaving. In that moment—flat, raw, exposed—I saw something I hadn't wanted to admit: the absolute, incandescent hatred in her face. It was sharp enough to cut me.

For a horrifying second, I realized the stories about her cruelty were true; the thought sickened me.

"Fine," Thalassa said, voice bored. She turned to her guards. "Return her to the water."

They reached to pick her up. My mouth moved before my brain caught up. "No."

Every head turned. For a heartbeat I felt naked under those eyes—Thalassa's curious, Ramil's tight with anger, the guards' scowls.

The queen leaned toward Ramil, all silk and shadow. "Why is your acolyte speaking to me?"

Ramil's glare was hard enough to bruise. "I have no idea," he said, but he didn't step forward to drag me back. I wanted to shout, that this is what we're here for, and there was more at stake than my moral outrage. I could feel the lie trembling at the edges of what I wanted to say to Ramil: you can't poison a woman floating in the water. It would dissolve and go nowhere.

"At least give a day out of the water. You can punish her tomorrow," I said.

The queen moved in close to me, scent of sea and citrus wreathing her.

"I can punish her whenever I choose, young man." Her voice had no malice, only the immutable certainty of someone who could rewrite consequence simply by existing.

I flashed a look at Ramil. He met it with the narrowed eyes of agreement: do it, for the plan, for the work. His look steadied me.

"The boy is correct, your highness," he said aloud. "And a day away from this... torture will make it much worse when she must return to it."

Thalassa's expression softened into amusement, a slit of a smile that reflected in her eyes.

She nodded to the guards. "Pick her up."

They dragged Finley out of the treasure room and through the throne room. She tried to walk but her legs refused, slick with seawater and trembling with fatigue. Her movements left a dark, snaking trail across the polished tiles.

We descended stairs into the palace's belly, the air cooling and smelling of stone and stagnant water. The torches threw yellow rings of light across walls where mold hung in the corners.

We stopped at a cell near the end of a damp corridor. The guards flung her into the small room, and she landed in a brittle, ragged heap.

I backed away to give them room. The iron door slammed shut with a groan that echoed down the corridor.

Finley stirred, coughing as the damp air wrapped around her.

The torchlight flickered off shiny walls, revealing shadows that weren't only her own. I inspected the other two remaining cells.

An old merman was crumpled in the corner, his limbs twisted awkwardly beneath a threadbare cloak. At first, I thought he was dead, until his fingers twitched.

In the far cell was a huge Fomorian. He didn't look so hot, wedged in the back of his cell, his skin dull and gray from confinement. But his eyes burned with life. Fierce, intelligent, and utterly unbroken. He glared at me, wanting to peel the flesh from me with a look.

"That is the queen's consort," I heard Thalassa yell out.

The Fomorian's mouth turned down.

Ramil leaned close, voice a scarcely audible rasp. "Remember this place."

I understood. I ignored the others and let my eyes scan the corridor, counting, measuring, my brain mapping the area as if there were equations. The cell was small, two by three meters, maybe. Iron bars sealed the entrance; the walls were roughly hewn rock, no windows, no mercy. Water seeped through hairline cracks.

Thalassa came close. Her finger traced my chin with the kind of domesticity that was a reminder of power. "Will this be satisfactory?"

"Yes," I said. "Your highness."

She turned away, and one of the guards locked the iron door with a clang that echoed down the corridor.

Ramil, when he thought no one watched, palmed the ring on his finger. He twisted the top, and a fine powder spilled onto the cell floor—the only evidence, a tiny heap of light blue piled near the corner by the bars. He glanced at me with an imperative look—notice, *remember*—and I offered the smallest nod I could manage.

We walked back up to the throne room, and Thalassa, satisfied, shrugged off her robe and slid into one of the pools. A goddess returned to the sea.

She sank and surfaced with an almost purring delight, arms folded at the edge, watching us with eyes that saw everything but felt nothing for us.

"They will show you to your quarters. You may rest here but we will return you to the land tomorrow morning."

Ramil bowed. "We thank you for your hospitality, your highness." His face held a politeness that did not match the lines in his jaw. Thalassa gave him a puzzled look and then sank into the water, the ripples swallowing her figure.

The palace outside of the throne room spoke in curves and currents—walls flowing in gentle arcs instead of angles, pillars etched with spirals that mimicked tides and whirlpools. Light refracted off polished stone in ripples. It wasn't decorated in the traditional sense; the structure *was* the art.

They led us to a wide chamber that opened onto a balcony, and the view made the room feel small. The city swept outward in precise tiers of marble and polished stone. The island curved far beyond what I remembered approaching—roads, canals, terraces—too vast to have fit inside the footprint my eyes had insisted on from the water.

I glanced at the horizon, at the sheer *distance* between the palace and the far curve of the harbor. The size still bothered me.

"When we arrived... the island looked small. Barely inhabited."

Ramil nodded once, because it was obvious. "Atlantis hides its fullness from outsiders. The earliest stories say their ancestors rose from the sea and found this place waiting already shaped. Land that chose them, not the other way around. They simply built a city upon it."

"Meaning what? Illusion? Telepathic camouflage? Folded geometry?"

He lifted a hand to stop me. "Meaning a gift from the gods. The how does not matter."

Of course it mattered. If the island wasn't shrinking or expanding but *editing what the mind could process*, then this was more than architecture— it was technology. Or something older than technology. The kind of trick that could only exist if someone had designed this world on purpose.

Maybe these gods, these ancient aliens, hadn't just seeded life here.

Maybe they were still running the experiment.

We used to have a variety of humans on Earth, but now only one remains. Most of us carry a trace of Neanderthal DNA; those from Australia and South Asia, some Denisovan. But on Tir Na, the differences stayed distinct—isolated branches that never blended. It was as if someone had locked the evolutionary doors on purpose. Protecting them.

Ramil's voice pulled me back into the immediate. "Tell me you saw what I did in the cell of the usurper?"

"Yes. I did." My voice came out flat; my hands were still damp with someone else's courage.

"I will attempt to track the servants providing food in the dungeon," he said. "They are usually hungry themselves and do not eat until after they have distributed the meals. That hunger creates a powerful, emotional string."

I was not yet a master of mindforms. But Ramil's craft of reading minds and conjuring creatures was a different species of talent. I trusted the logic: hungry people are predictable, and predictable hearts make good handles for a mind-reader.

"Your task will be to act as quickly as possible," he continued.

"I'll be ready."

"You will. Your focus will be on the pile of poison. It does not require much, but it will need to either be in her food or her drink. I saw no cups in the cell. They will likely be bringing that along with a tray."

Simple. My telekinesis would be enough. It was small, precise, clinical. This was how we'd do it: steal the grains and tuck them into a bowl with a sleight of hand. Or... mind.

"What if she sees the poison... floating across her cell?" The thought sounded ridiculous out loud, but I couldn't unknot the image.

Ramil looked toward the balcony, assessing the light. "We are almost at dusk. They will begin delivering food soon. The usurper was overly tired and strained from her ordeal in the water. It is likely she is either asleep or still in the process of recovery. I doubt she will be staring at the tray of food. While she may be hungry, they will not provide a quality meal, so she will be in no hurry."

"Okay," I said. My voice had the brittle steadiness of someone pretending this was not an abyss. "So... I'll begin preparations."

"Do so. We have one chance at taking her down for good."

"And you don't think we could maybe wait for her? On land? When the queen releases her?"

"If she releases her. And no. Finley's troops may still be in Cíbola. If they are, she will be swept away and lost to us. We might still try once she returns home." Ramil cataloged contingencies the way some people catalog recipes. It was both comforting and terrifying to be that planned out.

"Wait, how were you going to do that?"

"I had an ambassador from Svarga gift her a silver drinking stein," he said suddenly. "The bottom was painted to look empty, but once filled with liquid, it would dissolve and provide the dose of poison."

He had thought this out, every minute detail lined up. I tried not to resent the efficiency. "I see."

"Prepare yourself."

We took opposite ends of the room and sat like two sentinels. I breathed slow. Cleared everything out. I let Finley's cell bloom in my mind: iron bars knitting shadow lines; a narrow cot bound with metal straps and no mattress; rough stone walls pocked with chisel marks; the constant, faint drip of water. I fixed on Finley—half-draped over the cot, head between her knees, hair draped down. Arms wrapped around her knees, trembling, the remnants of composure gone from her posture. In the corner, the blue mound of powder gleamed in my mind. Death waiting in a neat pile.

"There is the servant," Ramil murmured.

I narrowed my focus until the world reduced to the cell and the powder and my hands. The servant descended the stairs. The smell of fish hit me, and my stomach turned in sympathy for someone who would hand out someone else's only scraps. She carried two bowls—soup, fish. The cloying steam curled up my throat in my mind. I was there.

"She stops at the cell beyond Queen Finley's, sets the bowl down for that occupant."

The servant paused at the neighboring cell, set a bowl down, then stepped toward Finley.

"She turns. Now, she stops before Finley. She watches. No movement. It is safe."

The servant hesitated, listening to the room.

"She sets down the bowl, her arm rubbing slightly against one of the bars."

Seeing no movement from the other prisoner, she placed the bowl down for Finley, her forearm sliding on the iron bar as she withdrew.

"And she walks away, down the corridor."

I could feel the rhythm of her steps recede, the scrape of leather. This was the window.

I extended my hand in the mind-space. I cupped the grains with my mind, scooping them up. Most of it pooled into my imaginary fingers; tiny bits sifted away but made no sound. I guided the poison up, along the bars, along the cold stone, toward the bowl. It felt absurd and intimate to move it. My skin prickled with the strain; edges of the mindroom blurred.

Now.

I eased the grains. The world narrowed again to a thread of blue and a bowl. I imagined the bowl's lip, the murky surface of the soup. The powder slid like a whisper over the bowl. I let it fall, not with a splash but a soft settling—tiny weightless motes sinking into broth. I felt them dissolve under my mental fingertips, saw them be swallowed by the murky water.

My chest hollowed. I released the control and let the image fold away.

"It's done," I said, my voice thin.

Ramil moved toward me, his face bright with a terrible satisfaction. My temples pounded; my eyes felt raw. I blinked, trying to bring the edges back into focus.

"Are you sure?"

"Yes." I wasn't sure how I could be sure about anything anymore, but I told the truth. "I do not know if she saw anything, but the poison is in the bowl. Nothing spilled on the floor around it."

Ramil's hands were unexpectedly warm and rough as he gripped my shoulders. "Excellent work, boy!" he said, and I wanted to tell him that excellent is not the word I would choose, but it all lodged in the back of my throat.

He closed his eyes and invoked a mindform—he reached into the room we'd both just left and read the emptiness there.

"She is not restless. No thoughts of fear, or even worry. She is tired, but that is all I see. She did not bear witness to the poisoning."

I felt as though someone had unhooded me. A nausea rose—part adrenaline, part shame—and suddenly perspective came. I had helped seed death into someone else's meal.

My hands, those neat, controlled hands, had been instruments. I tried to catalog the reasons we'd done it: tyrant, usurper, threat. I tried to measure the weight of lives saved in some abstract ledger, but the math failed me. The only thing that registered was the image of those blue grains dissolving, quiet as a secret.

And in that impossible quiet, I realized the truth: the line between right and wrong had not blurred as I feared; it had been erased, and we had walked across it.

I just helped to murder someone.

45

Hungry Like a Hellhound

Finley

I sat in my cell beneath Thalassa's palace, shivering so hard my teeth knocked together. The damp stones pressed against my back, leeching what little warmth I had left. I should've been lying down, letting my body recover, but every time I tried to rest, a tremor rolled through me. I drew my knees to my chest, wrapping my arms around them to trap the heat before it fled.

Somewhere down the corridor, a door clanged. Footsteps. Then a bowl scraped across the floor. The reek of fish drifted up before I even saw it. My stomach growled in protest, though I felt too nauseous to eat. I wasn't sure if it was the hunger or the guilt that made me sick.

My mind replayed what I'd seen when they threw me down here—those mages in their green cloaks. Not Pherric. Different faces, colder eyes. One of them had wanted me pulled from the glass tank. I was some strange creature worth studying instead of saving apparently. I tried to remember his voice, the edge of it, but the memory slid away before I could catch it.

"Finley."

The voice was low and familiar, echoing off the wet stone. I scrambled to my feet, pressed my face against the bars. "Braylor!"

In my misery, I'd forgotten he was here too. Another cage separated us,

256

but I reached my arm between the bars.

"Are you well?" His voice was rough, the words clipped with effort.

"I am. How are you?"

"Better," he whispered, though I heard the pain beneath it.

"Really? Don't lie to me."

"A healer came by—bandages, a potion or two. I'm on the mend. I have you to thank for that?"

"Yes," I said, though the word came out thin, shaky. Guilt again, heavy as a stone.

"What did you give in return?" he chided softly.

"Oh, just Pherric," I muttered, "and the magic potion of immortality."

"Finley..."

"I know. You don't have to tell me. I made her promise she'd release us once it's done."

He tried to laugh, but it came out a strangled grunt. "Doubtful."

My heart cracked a little. Braylor was proud, unbreakable. Hearing pain in his voice—seeing him reduced to this—made something in me harden.

"I'll get you out," I whispered fiercely. "That's a promise."

"Did they feed you?" he asked.

I glanced at the bowl. "If you can call this food."

He nudged his own bowl with his foot, metal scraping stone. "Eat what there is. You'll need your strength."

I forced a laugh. "You sound like me. Rest," I told him, scooting back from the bars. "Sleep if you can."

"I will," he murmured.

The silence stretched between us, filled only by the steady drip of water somewhere down the hall. I cupped the bowl in my hands, the chill seeping in until they ached. The smell of the fish stew was rank, but hunger had a way of erasing disgust.

I lifted it to my lips, the rim brushing my mouth. A drop on my lip. Just a sip, I thought. Anything to quiet the emptiness gnawing inside me.

Click.

I halted mid-sip. The sound was precise, mechanical. Close.

I lowered the bowl an inch, eyes darting toward the cell door.

Creeeak.

The iron door began to move. Slowly. On its own.

I blinked, uncertain if I was seeing right. The heavy door protested in a drawn-out groan.

For a moment I sat there, the bowl still in my hands, steam—or maybe just the cold—rising between my fingers. Then instinct took over.

The corridor was empty. Still.

I stepped closer, watching the door inch wider as though something unseen had brushed past.

I stepped out, every muscle tight, waiting for the shout of guards. None came.

"Braylor," I whispered, hurrying to his cell. He was already standing, his hand meeting mine through the bars.

"What is happening?"

"I don't know," I hissed. "But we're leaving."

I yanked at his door. It didn't budge. My eyes swept the corridor, searching for keys, a mechanism, anything. But there was nothing.

Then—*click.*

His lock released.

Magic? No. But this was familiar. A *mindform*? Perhaps the mages from before. Someone wanted us out.

"Can you walk?" I asked, already slipping an arm around his waist before he could lie.

He grunted but nodded. "We must go."

His grip on my hand was iron, but I felt the tremor in his body.

"You look tired," he said.

"No. I just haven't slept much..."

Together we started for the stairs, our footsteps soft on the cold stone. Every step was a bet, hoping whoever freed us still meant us no harm.

46

There is Always a Secret Door

Jonathan

"**S**omething is not... right." Ramil's words were a knife through the quiet.

I kept my head down, pretending to study the fire burning low in the brazier between us. My pulse was a steady roar in my ears. *He knows. He knows I opened the cells.*

Ramil stood at the window, half-lit by moonlight. "Her spirit," he said, voice taut. "It has altered."

I blinked. He must've sensed her vitals: pulse, breathing. Maybe I had done it in time.

My throat closed. "That could mean a lot of things," I said, trying for even. "Pain. Fever. Fear. It could be the... poison."

"No." Ramil pressed two fingers to his jaw. The blue moonlight reflected in his eyes. "This isn't distress. It's movement. She's alive. Alive and... running."

I felt every muscle in my body tense. My hands curled against my knees. *She is alive.*

Luckily, he didn't seem to be monitoring me. He made no note of my unlocking the doors to those cells in the dungeon.

But he was focused on her.

259

He turned toward the door, testing the handle. It didn't move. He slammed his fist against it. "Locked?"

Ramil's temper flared. "Guard!"

Leather sandals scuffed outside. "Sire?"

"Open it!"

The latch clicked. The door swung wide, flooding the chamber with torchlight.

"I have every reason to believe she has escaped," Ramil said, his tone razor-sharp.

"Who?" asked the guard.

"The Hominan prisoner! Red hair! The usurper!"

The guard hesitated, uncertain, but Ramil didn't wait. He stormed into the corridor, shouting orders, his green robe flaring behind.

I stayed still until the echo of his voice disappeared down the hall. Then I exhaled, slow, shaky.

You did this.

The thought lingered, accusing.

I rose, pulling on my own robe and adjusting it, to try to feel composed. The corridor beyond was empty. The guards had pulled away, chaos beginning to ripple through the palace.

I slipped out, following the shadows. Down the marble stairs, through the cold archways that led toward the throne hall.

The air grew heavier the closer I got. A few Atlanteans scrambled about, but they paid no attention to me. I rushed along a hallway until it opened to a foyer.

I saw activity at the far end of the hall.

Two figures climbing the stairs. One limping. One pressing a hand to his chest.

Finley.

Her eyes found mine, wild, wary, burning.

For a heartbeat, everything went still.

The world narrowed to that look.

"Who is he?" Braylor's voice broke the silence.

Without looking away from me, she said, "I don't know."

I swallowed hard. My voice came out low. "You need to go. Now. They know."

Finley didn't answer. She stared, trying to see through me.

"Did you release us?"

I closed my eyes. "Yes."

"Then you have to come with us. They'll figure out what you did and they will kill you."

My heart sank. She was right. I had messed up. Big time.

Boots. Shouting. They were coming for us.

I turned toward the stairwell. "We have to go! Head back down!"

Finley grabbed my sleeve before I could take a step. "No." Her voice was urgent. "Never go up or down. Because then there's no way out."

I stared at her, thrown off by the certainty in her tone. "What does that even—"

She turned us toward the direction of the main entrance. But we heard boots on those tiles. The clashing of armor. Swords being drawn. Coming from the main corridor leading to the front doors.

"We can't go that way," I said.

"Down," Braylor said, already half-limping toward the stairs.

Finley exhaled through her nose. "Fine. But we're not getting caught again."

We raced down the spiral stone stairs, the air once again growing colder, thicker. Back to the dungeon.

Finley slowed, scanning both directions. "Left?" she asked, unsure of herself.

"No," Braylor said. "The cells lie that way."

She didn't hesitate. "Then right."

We ran. Past rows of empty cells. Without even slowing down, Finley grabbed one of the torches from the wall to light our way. The air smelled of mildew and rust and something older beneath it, a rot that had never quite died.

At the end of the passage, Finley stopped short. "Through there," she said, nodding toward a closed wooden door.

We slipped inside. Crates. Dust. Empty wine or ale kegs. Iron boxes. No one had been here in years.

Finley's eyes darted all around the dark room, until she stared at the far wall. "There."

I followed her gaze. Faint lines in the stone: a rectangular outline, half-hidden behind a stack of boxes.

Without speaking, we started shoving them out of the way. My hands stung from the splinters. The boxes thudded softly as we slid them aside. Beneath, a seam. Then a hinge.

Finley grinned, breathless and wild. "I knew it. There's always a secret door. Has to be."

Her confidence was almost absurd. Almost. But when she pressed the side of the wall, it gave with a soft groan and swung inward.

Behind it: a small, dark chamber.

We slipped inside, closing the door behind us. The air was still, stale, but not dead. The room was circular, carved with faded reliefs of Atlantean script and a god I didn't recognize. A figure with too many eyes, its face worn smooth by time. Candles long extinguished sat before a broken altar.

Braylor whispered, "What is this place?"

"An old temple," I said quietly. "Well before Thalassa's time, I'd imagine."

Finley's flashlight eyes scanned the carvings. "Okay. Spooky temple room. No other exits. There has to be another—"

"Secret door?" Braylor frowned.

"Yes," she said. "Help me look." Her hands swept across the nearest wall.

I joined her, hands flat against the stone. The surface wasn't smooth: it was alive with texture. Rows of carved symbols wound across the walls, their grooves filled with black dust. The faint outlines of figures I almost recognized, fragments of an old tongue.

The room wasn't empty, either. Little alcoves punctuated the circular chamber, each holding some relic: a cracked statuette of an Atlantean god with six limbs, a copper bowl flaking green with corrosion, a stone dagger carved into the top of a pedestal.

Finley brushed past me, eyes darting from one carving to another. "There's got to be something—"

Her voice trembled just slightly, but her hands never stopped roaming. She traced lines of script, pressed at seams in the wall, tugged at the broken altar. One statue shifted beneath her touch. It was a tiny thing, its face worn smooth, its arms outstretched toward the ceiling.

Behind us, faint footsteps echoed in the hall beyond. Fast. Purposeful.

"They're coming," I warned.

"I know!" she snarled back, pressing harder on the stone. "There's something. There *has* to be."

The statues seemed to watch us in the flicker of our light. Rows of eyeless faces, silent witnesses. My fingers caught on a small indentation between two runes. Smooth, different than the rest.

"Finley—"

"Wait—" Her fingers landed just above mine, on the shoulder of the statue she'd been examining. She pushed hard.

A soft *click* sounded deep within the wall.

She stopped and held her breath.

The stone wall parted inward.

We heaved the slab wider, muscles straining. A thin stream of seawater slipped through the gap and pooled at our feet. Beyond the ancient stone door stood... metal. A seamless wall, slick and gleaming. No hinges. No handle. No window. It didn't belong here.

Finley's excitement faltered. "That's not possible," she whispered.

I pressed my palms to it. The surface was cold, damp, alive somehow. When I pushed, the air snapped with a loud suctioned pop. A vacuumed seal had broken. The wall became a door and slid inward, revealing a tunnel beyond. Long and black, stretching into nothing.

Braylor took a step back. "No. I'm not going in there."

Finley turned to him, fierce and unyielding. "You're not doing this again." She shoved him lightly toward the opening. "We don't have a choice."

The echo of boots was closer now, just outside the storage room door.

Braylor hesitated, then ducked into the tunnel, muttering something about hating small spaces.

Finley followed, glancing once over her shoulder at me.

I lingered a heartbeat longer, hand pressed against the doorframe.

"You better be one of the good guys..." she said, concern covering her face.

Me? What about *her*?

I pulled the stone door closed behind us and then slammed the metallic door home. There was another solid suction, separating the tunnel from the island.

As I turned, Finley's sad torch was the only thing I could see. And she was walking away.

I didn't know where the tunnel led. But staying behind would mean facing what I'd done—and that scared me more than the dark.

47

The Tunnel of Love Had a Dead End

Finley

Ever heard the phrase *"out of the frying pan and into the fire"*? My dad used to say it meant you could always make your situation worse. And I wasn't sure if that's exactly what I'd just done.

Sure, maybe Thalassa would've let us go after she got Pherric's magic elixir. But I never believed she'd live up to her word. The bitch was cruel for the sake of it. If we'd stayed, Braylor, Pherric, and I would've been chopped up and tossed to the fishies before dawn. So, when that cell door creaked open, I didn't think twice.

Still, the tunnel we'd raced into had my nerves crawling. It wasn't rough stone or ancient earth—it was metal, slick and cold similar to the door we came through. Not mortal work. This was built by gods. Which meant I had no idea what kind of fire we were running into next.

So, I decided to test it out.

"Stop!" I said.

"Why would we stop?" Braylor rumbled behind me.

"They're right behind us!" cried the new guy.

I held up the torch to see him better. Thin, wiry. A little taller than me. Sandy blond hair, bloodshot eyes, and the kind of exhaustion that looked permanent. The world had been pressing its thumb into him for days.

265

"Are they?" I asked.

We waited. The tunnel filled with the steady drip of water off the metallic frame. No shouts. No boots. No suction pop from that door.

Nothing.

They either couldn't find the secret passage, or... they were afraid to follow.

"Maybe whatever's out there"—I pointed into the dark ahead—"will kill us off so they don't have to."

The mage swallowed hard, eyes shooting past me. He expected monsters to materialize.

A few more silent minutes. Still nothing.

"Then we should stay here," he whispered. Fear had him by the throat.

"We cannot," Braylor said, pushing ahead. His shoulders brushed the low ceiling. He hated confined spaces. His whole body hunched, looking miserable.

I patted his arm. "Easy there, big guy. You'll be fine."

"No, I will not," he muttered, a pouting sulky mountain.

I raised the torch again, turning to the mage. "What's your story? Who are you? Why'd you unlock our cell doors?"

A flicker of realization crossed his face. He leaned forward, voice suddenly crisp. "First, I must ask you. Did you eat the food they gave you?"

"Huh?"

"The bowl of food. The fish stew. Did you eat it?!"

"I—I, um—"

He stepped toward me, panic edging his tone. Braylor moved instantly, one massive hand shoving him back.

"Did you take even a sip? Of the broth?"

"No," I said. "Nothing. I never got a chance. Maybe a drop touched my lip. The cell opened before I—wait. Why?"

"The food was poisoned."

My hand flew to my throat, my finger touching my lower lip where the broth had dripped. "I was her captive. Why would Thalassa poison me?"

"She didn't. I did."

Braylor snarled. His fists balled into the mage's robes before I could blink, hoisting him off the ground. The man's feet kicked helplessly as Braylor's teeth bared in a sound halfway between a growl and thunder.

"Wait! Stop!" the mage screamed. "I changed my mind!"

Braylor pressed him higher until his head thudded against the ceiling.

"That's why I opened the cell doors!"

I shoved Braylor aside—well, he let me—and the man dropped, gasping.

"Explain yourself," I demanded.

"Look, my name is—"

"I don't care. Why did you try to poison me?!"

"I'm Jonathan," he said quickly. "I'm not from here. I'm from Earth. I was brought here against my will."

I shot a look at Braylor. The Atlanteans. The Godsribbon. Their abductee.

"Prove it."

"You're from New York, right? Yankees or Mets?"

"Well, Boston originally. So... Sox. And that proves nothing. Someone could've told you that."

"I'm a graduate assistant working on my doctorate. At Brown. Well... I was."

I reached out with a mindform, testing the edges of his truth. Fear, guilt, confusion. But no deceit. "Degree?"

"Chemistry."

A chem major from Earth, turned alchemist here. It fit. But it didn't explain *why* they'd used him to kill me.

"How'd you poison the food?"

"You see, there are these mindforms that—"

"Yeah, yeah, I know about those. *How* did you do it?"

"Ramil at the Scholomance thought I had special abilities," Jonathan said. "That's why he brought me here. To learn how to move things with my mind. Including the poison from the floor of your cell and into the food."

"With your mind? You can move shit with your mind? Get outta here."

"I can," he said, voice trembling. "I don't know how or why, but that's what he trained me for. We were supposed to poison you at your castle, but... you left. Came here."

I grabbed his robe again. "Why did you change your mind?"

"I'm not a murderer," he said, eyes shining in the torchlight. "No matter how... awful some of the things you've done are, I couldn't kill you."

I turned to Braylor. He shrugged.

"Wha—no! I haven't done *shit*! I'm not *awful*. Like, at all."

"He told me what you did to the Bànshēn rén. That you killed the citizens of Ker-Is. Attacked the Prominans—"

"No! Wait. No." I forced my thoughts into the open, flooding him with truth.

I told him how Malek had stolen resources from every kingdom to build his army, then wiped out an entire race just to prove his power. How he'd slaughtered the people of Ker-Is to frame that same race and justify his war. I told him how he'd known about our plan to kill him from the start—how he'd rounded up my friends and killed half of them in front of me. How I tried to stop him and succeeded, only to learn Kane had been behind it all along. That I was the one who united the kingdoms, led the underdogs, and ended the war. That I wasn't the villain he thought I was—I was the reason anyone was still alive.

Braylor leaned against the wall, arms crossed, eye-roll included. He'd been there. He didn't need the recap.

"But he showed me," Jonathan said weakly. "Ramil gave me a vision in the Historium. With artifacts from Ker-Is."

"He lied. Those were more mindforms. Did he ever create shadows? People or things that weren't real?"

"Yes. A Basilisk."

"Then he did the same thing with those visions. He made them so real you could probably smell the blood, right? Yes, the Bànshēn rén were wiped out. Yes, Ker-Is fell. I was there after it happened. And we found Irkallan arrows left behind. They did it, not the Bànshēn rén. But he made *me* the villain in your mind. He probably showed me doing all that. But

I didn't do any of it. Look, he's never met me. Did you ever see my face, perfectly clear, doing those things?"

He shook his head. "No."

Jonathan's expression fractured. One realization after another hit, until he stood frozen, mouth open, horror dawning.

"Oh my god," he whispered. "I'm sorry. I should've known. I could've—"

"It's fine," I said softly. "Sounds like this Ramil guy's a real pro at mental manipulation. So... I'm Finley. This is Braylor. Don't let him fool you; he's basically a big teddy bear."

Braylor grunted. Which, for him, meant "yes."

While we talked, I kept my eyes on both ends of the tunnel. No Atlanteans. No monsters rushing us from the other side. Just the echo of dripping water and our uneven breathing.

But we couldn't stay here forever. We needed to find a way out. Get off the island. But I had no plan. I didn't even know if that little boat was still out there in front of the palace.

"All right," I said finally. "Let's go see what we're up against."

No weapons. No food. No water. Just one flickering torch and a lot of bad luck.

We were *royally* screwed.

Still, I started walking.

The tunnel stretched forever, until another metal door blocked our way. I gestured to Jonathan. "Your turn, mage."

He pushed. Nothing. He shot me a look before trying to pull at the edges. There was another *pop* and the door swung inward.

We both exhaled. Braylor, impatient, shoved past.

In this new area, the space returned to carved stone—rough, cold, smelling of damp and decay. A single wooden staircase led upward, long and steep, vanishing into darkness.

We climbed. Braylor had to rest a few times, pain etched into his face. He'd been through hell, and every step showed it.

At the top was a set of slanted double doors, chained and locked—from the inside.

"To keep something *out*," Braylor stated.

"Shit," I said aloud.

Braylor gripped the rusted lock. With one twist, it crumbled in his hand. He yanked the chain free and shoved the doors open.

Light hit us. We squinted, blinking into it—only to see giant concrete walls encircling us, four stories high, smooth as glass. The sun had nearly set, and it would be dark soon.

Braylor strode to a corner, disappeared briefly, then reappeared looking grim.

"We are in a labyrinth," he said.

"A labyrinth? What are you talking about?" I followed him, heart thudding.

He met my eyes, all trace of humor gone.

"This is the Minotaur's Labyrinth."

48

Let Them Play with Their Blocks

Genevieve

Pherric's silhouette was already shrinking against the clouds, a streak of light flashing from the dragon's scales as it vanished beyond the horizon. The sound of its wings still pulsed in my bones.

He was gone. Just like that.

I stood motionless, mouth slightly open, looking a fool.

I turned to Kinnat, throat dry.

She was the first to speak. "What should we do?"

Several soldiers burst onto the terrace, their armor clattering as their eyes combed the skies for more danger. The youngest one aimed his spear at the clouds. Great. That'd be useful.

My fingers trembled around nothing—I hadn't realized I was gripping the air, as if that would somehow hold the moment together.

"I guess we should tell someone," she stammered, trying to sound like a person who wasn't on the verge of hyperventilating.

A glint caught my eye. The folded letter tumbling near the terrace wall. Pherric's. He dropped it in his rush. I lunged forward, snatching it before the wind could carry it away. My heart was still beating crazy hard.

Kinnat came closer. "Are you well?"

I looked up at the blue sky. "Yeah. I think so. But... that was—"

"A dragon. Yes."

"You've seen one before?!" I couldn't keep the disbelief out of my voice.

"When I was younger. It flew over our farm looking for prey, but our livestock were in the barn," she said, eyes scanning the clouds nervously. Her voice was steady, but her hand gripped her sword hilt hard. "Byfire, we were fortunate. Most do not live after seeing one so close."

I rubbed my arms, still cold despite the heat rising off the terrace stones. "So, who do we tell? Pherric's gone and... wait." My brain caught up. "The woman with the broken wing!"

"Kasuma. Yes," said Kinnat.

We both turned—and there she was. Standing not two feet behind us.

"Jesus!" I yelped.

Kasuma's mouth slid into the faintest smile. "Finley uses that word as well, when I sneak up on her."

This goddamn world was going to give me a heart attack.

Kasuma's wings—well, *wing*—shifted slightly, the broken one trailing behind. "Come with me," she said simply.

No arguing with that tone.

We followed. I quickly realized how she kept appearing out of nowhere. The woman didn't make a sound. Her footsteps were air moving over silk, not a single creak or shift. Chasing after her was eerie. She was the shadow of a whisper.

The great hall opened before us, full of torchlight and tension. The Queen's council was already gathered, maps sprawled across the table, wooden pieces marking armies and borders. Maybe that's how they made decisions here—one little carved block at a time. I had no idea.

One of the advisors stepped forward, chin tilted in disapproval. "What happened?"

The way he said it, like I was personally responsible for the dragon problem, made me grit my teeth.

But I told them. The dragon, Pherric, the letter. Every frantic detail. All but how my guts were still doing somersaults.

"And he said to tell you where he'd gone. That's all," I finished, trying not to sound guilty.

Kasuma's gaze went to the folded paper still clutched in my hand. "Did Pherric leave this behind?"

"Oh, yeah." I passed it over, my lungs still catching up.

She unfolded it carefully and frowned.

"It's a letter from Finley," I offered, trying to help. "She said Pherric has to come and bring a magic book. The dragon would fly him to Atlantis."

Kasuma's brows furrowed. "This appears to be her handwriting."

"Pherric was sure it was from her." I said.

Kasuma's expression didn't change, but her wings shifted slightly— nervous tell, maybe. "And he took the book with him?" she asked. "The *Arcanum Libellum*?"

"Okay, I'm gonna need subtitles. What's that?"

"The most dangerous book ever written," she said softly.

That got my attention.

"Do you recall when Pherric told you how Finley came back to life?"

"Yeah."

"He used a potion from that book to revive her."

"Wait, you mean the thing that makes her... immortal?"

"Yes. And he took it with him."

"Why?"

Kasuma's expression darkened. "Because the Queen of Atlantis knows of Finley's immortality. She wants it for herself. She captured Finley to extract it. And when she failed, she summoned him."

I stared at the letter in her hands. "Will he give it to her?"

"If it is the only way to save Finley," Kasuma said. "Perhaps. But whether he does or does not, she will likely kill them both."

"Shit."

"Yes," she said calmly. "Shit."

My pulse roared again. "Then we have to go after him!"

Kasuma shook her head. "A journey to Atlantis will take a long time. Pherric left on a dragon. Even if we had one, we would not make it in time.

Finley's would not bear us anyway; she obeys only her."

I crossed my arms, anger prickling through the fear. "So what, you're just gonna stand here with your war table and your fancy blocks while they both die?"

Kasuma blinked. Then, to my absolute shock, she smiled. It was small, dangerous, and full of secrets.

"No," she said quietly. She leaned in close enough that her breath brushed my cheek. "The three of us are leaving today."

"Wait, what?" I glanced between her and Kinnat. "Where are we going?"

She didn't even flinch. "To Atlantis."

"But you just said it would take a long time."

"We will not be able to help them in the short term. But we need to be there in the event they need us. Finley has a way of... surviving. Pack quickly," she ordered. "We leave before sunset."

Kinnat blinked, stunned. "But what of the council?"

Kasuma didn't stop walking. "They will keep playing with their little blocks."

And then she was gone.

The hall buzzed with whispers, but I could barely hear them. My brain was spinning. Dragons, potions, immortality, Atlantis.

I looked down at my hands. They were still shaking.

I whispered, "What the hell are we walking into?"

Kinnat glanced at me, her expression caught somewhere between awe and terror. "Into history, perhaps."

"Yeah," I said, exhaling. "Or a very stupid obituary."

49

The Maze That Preys

Finley

"The Minotaur's Labyrinth? Are you kidding me right now?"

Braylor angled his head, all calm composure and ancient confidence. "No."

"Of course you're not," I muttered. Why did I still get shocked by this stuff? You'd think after dragons, hellhounds, and giant spiders, my internal disbelief would've packed up and gone home. But nope. Still hanging on like a tick. "You mean from Greek mythology? Half-man, half-bull, trapped in a maze?"

"I do not know of Greeks," he said evenly, "but yes."

Jonathan blinked, his jaw slack. "He's serious?"

"Oh, completely," I said. "This is just a Thursday for him. Did I tell you he once took me to Hell?"

"Hell?"

"Yes, Hell. There's literally a kingdom here called Hell. Guess what it has? Fire, brimstone, pain, despair. You know, the greatest hits. Just... very on brand."

Braylor gave a casual shrug. "It is a dry heat."

I glared. "Oh, well then. My mistake. That makes it *much better.*"

He didn't flinch. "You survived."

"Barely." I sighed. "Anyway, I've got a theory. Hear me out. I think aliens used to be here—on this planet—and maybe they were the reason stories from *our* world exist. Maybe they ferried people between Tir Na and Earth, and this is how our myths started. Because half the stuff I've seen here? We'd call it fairy tales and mythology. My friend who can fly, well... she used to be able to fly... anyway, you'd easily mistake her for an angel. Or cupid. And dragons? They're here!"

"There are dragons?!" he asked, like a kid who just found out Santa was real *and* carried a sword.

"Yes," I said.

Braylor smirked, shoving me lightly. "She *is* the dragonwitch."

"Stop it," I said, swatting him. "Point is, someone on Earth probably saw this labyrinth. Or heard about it. And that's how we got the myth."

Jonathan looked almost giddy. "I've been thinking something similar. It's... fascinating."

Braylor's tone cut the wonder short. "Fascinating, yes. But none of this changes the fact: we are now in *his* Labyrinth. I have heard tales of this place. I thought they were just that. Stories to scare frightened children. And I did not know the maze was close to Atlantis."

The words hit harder than I wanted to admit. I glanced up at the towering stone walls, too smooth to climb, way too high to jump, and realized where we were. The smaller island. The one inside the crescent of Atlantis. The one surrounded by a single, unbroken wall.

I turned on Jonathan. "Okay, genius. What do you know about the myth?"

He blinked. "Uh... a lot?"

"I don't want a TED Talk, I want to know what keeps me from being eaten."

The wheels in his mind started turning. He looked to Braylor. "Tell me if any of this... tracks with your version here."

Braylor nodded once, impatient but listening.

Jonathan exhaled. "So, the Minotaur, half bull and half man, was born after King Minos' wife, uh, had relations with a bull sent by Poseidon."

I grimaced. "Gross."

"He became a monster, bloodthirsty for human flesh. Minos built a maze to keep him contained. Every nine years, they'd feed him sacrifices: seven maidens and seven youths."

Braylor frowned. "I know nothing of any maidens or youths being thrown in here."

Jonathan pressed on. "Eventually, a hero named Theseus volunteered to go in. He had a magic sword and used it to kill the Minotaur."

"All right," I said. "I think I've got the picture. And, of course, we don't have a special sword."

"We have no swords," Braylor confirmed.

I threw up my hands. "No shit, Braylor."

The torchlight flickered as I scanned the endless stone corridors ahead. "You said 'nearly impossible,' right? Which means it's not *completely* impossible. Otherwise, why build a maze? Why not just... a pit? Or a stone cage? So, there has to be an exit."

Jonathan shrugged. "You're asking the wrong guy."

"Then we better start walking," I said.

He stopped me with a raised hand. "Wait. King Minos' daughter... Ariadne. She gave him a spool of thread to use to find his way back."

He motioned for my torch. I handed it over, and he used the charred end to smudge a dark mark on the wall.

Old Jonathan might actually help us survive this after all.

We hadn't been walking long before the light started to fade.

The sky shifted from gold to bruised purple, then to black. The air grew colder as the maze exhaled around us. My torch sputtered, throwing uneven light across the curved stone walls.

Curved. The corners weren't really corners at all. They bent. Subtle at first, but gentle turns continually pulled us in the same direction. The longer we walked, the more I realized it: this maze wasn't built as a grid. It was a circle.

"Tell me you're seeing this," I said. My voice bounced back at me, warped and distant.

Jonathan turned, eyes reflecting firelight. "Yeah. Every time we turn, we angle inward."

"Meaning what exactly?" asked Braylor.

"Meaning we're being funneled somewhere."

"Great," I said.

As we walked, at every turn, I'd mark the wall with the black edges of the torch.

Braylor mostly kept quiet, his expression unreadable in the dim light. He walked with purpose, but even he couldn't hide the tension in his shoulders. The man who'd faced off against an entire army was... cautious. To be honest, it didn't make me feel better.

The torch gave a final spit of flame and dropped to a sulking glow. Shadows stretched out, long and liquid, merging into something seemingly alive.

"Hold up." I crouched. My boot had nudged something. A *clinking* sound. I crouched down to pick it up.

Bone.

Not fresh, thank god. But not ancient either. The remains were slumped near the wall, scraps of torn cloth still clinging to it—gray, sun-bleached, Hominan. The skull had a dent the size of a grapefruit.

Jonathan swallowed audibly. "So... he eats people. Confirmed."

I forced a laugh. And it belonged to someone else. "Guess we're not the first idiots to take the tour."

A little farther ahead, we found another skeleton. Smaller. Curled in on itself, like they'd known what was coming and tried to make themselves smaller than fear.

I tightened my grip on the torch. It was barely more than an ember now. The dim light painted the walls in orange heartbeat flashes.

Every sound began to matter. The shuffle of our boots. The distant drip of water. The faint hiss of wind slipping along the walls.

And then... something else.

Low at first, it was the growl of thunder buried beneath the ground. Then it came again, rising, breaking, echoing through the maze in waves, making the ground hum.

Jonathan froze. "Um, what was—"

"Definitely a roar," I said.

No one spoke.

We just stood there, surrounded by the bones of the ones who didn't make it out, with nothing but a dying flame and the sound of something enormous—hungry—moving somewhere ahead.

The Minotaur was awake.

50

The Labyrinth

Jonathan

The night pressed close around us, still and sharp as glass.

Our torch threw out a weak circle of light, barely enough to see the next turn.

At first it was faint, a dull rhythm underfoot. Then a scraping, the heavy thud of something moving. And it was too big, too steady, too sure of its steps.

Braylor stopped mid-stride, eyes narrowing toward the dark behind us. "Keep walking," he murmured.

No one argued.

The maze stretched endlessly ahead of us, just turn after turn. The smooth walls were wet with dew, the scent of old moss and something fouler buried beneath. The air carried little breeze, no hint of direction. Only the sound of our boots and the whisper of something following. Sweat trickled down my back.

I glanced over my shoulder. But the way the walls curved, I only saw a few feet until they veered into darkness. And the lingering shadows shifted with weight.

The sound came again. Closer this time.

Finley turned to Braylor. "I think it's right behind us."

He nodded once. "Run."

We ran.

The maze turned and folded on itself, each wall high enough to block out the stars. My lungs burned, the torch sputtering in Finley's hand. She'd stopped marking the walls. There was no time. Every second mattered now.

The ground tilted slightly, throwing off my balance as we turned corner after corner. I could feel it trailing behind us; there were vibrations through the soles of my feet. Heavy, rhythmic. Getting closer.

"Which way?" I called.

"Keep going!" Braylor barked.

We did. Until a sound broke the night, freezing us in place.

It wasn't a roar. Not yet. It was a deep, grinding exhale, almost a voice, rising and falling in some awful rhythm—half-human, half-animal, no where near normal.

Finley stumbled. "It's close—"

Then it spoke. Not in words, but sound: a guttural rumble rolling through the maze, bouncing off the walls.

I didn't think. I ran harder.

We came to a three-way split. The left path turned slightly downhill, swallowed by dark. The right barely curved upward. The middle was straight, wide, empty.

Braylor's arm wavered. "Middle. Keep it simple."

The air shifted again, and suddenly the sound came from *ahead*. Along with the same heavy drag, the scrape of claws on stone, impossibly fast and impossibly near.

"How—" I started.

"He's herding us," Finley said. "He knows where we're gonna go."

We spun left instead. The new path was narrow, hemmed in by twisting walls brushing my shoulders as I ran.

The ground began to slope down again, and I heard the sound move with us—ahead, behind, both at once. A trap.

"Can it—" I gasped. "Is it... throwing these sounds? Creating them to fool us? It can't be everywhere at once!"

Finley didn't answer. Her face was pale in the sad torchlight.

Behind us, a loud snarl split the night.

It came into view, torn straight out of nightmare.

A shape too large to be real rounded the corner, horns catching the faint glow of moonlight filtering from above. Its hide gleamed, body shifting beneath it in heavy, deliberate waves, each step flexing power meant for breaking walls and bodies alike. Its torso was unmistakably human, shoulders broad and arms long, only scaled up and wrapped in muscle that no human frame should have been able to carry. The head was unmistakably bovine, but wrong—elongated, scarred, the muzzle split by a mouth full of blunt, crushing teeth made for grinding bone, not grazing grass.

Eyes the color of molten gold fixed on us.

The Minotaur.

I'd seen dozens of drawings and renderings. None of them had captured this thing. The intelligence in those eyes. The patience. This wasn't a beast driven by rage. It was calculating distance, angles, timing. Hunting.

Braylor's hand went for a weapon he didn't have. He whispered, "Do not stop."

Finley broke into a sprint in the opposite direction. The sound of the creature's hooves pounded after us, shaking dust loose from the walls.

We turned. And turned again. Every corner felt the same. My chest ached, my legs were numb. Behind us, the sound grew louder.

Eventually, we rounded a turn and burst into an open space... wider than any corridor before. For a heartbeat, I thought it was a clearing. Then I saw what filled it.

Bones.

Thousands of them, scattered across the stone floor. Some fresh, some so old they'd seemingly fused into the stone.

A stone chair loomed in the center, massive and crude, carved with shapes that looked disturbingly like faces. The Minotaur's seat.

Finley slid to a stop, voice trembling. "Oh, fuck."

Braylor's face was unreadable. "This is where he rests. Where he feeds."

The torch was only a weak, guttering glow. The air was vile.

A harsh noise rose from somewhere deeper in the maze. Behind us? A low, rolling, wheeze and it almost sounded like laughter.

"He's not coming?" I asked quietly.

Braylor shook his head. "He does not have to hurry. We are where he wants us."

The words had barely left his mouth when the opening ahead of us shuddered. There were two ways into this round room. The Minotaur burst through the gap, his shoulders forcing their way through the narrow space.

Finley actually growled. "We face him here. Not in the narrow maze."

"Face him?!" I was ready to run.

The creature moved with a strange precision, each swing of its arm wide but purposeful. Braylor darted toward it, drawing its attention. His body hit the beast's shoulder, but it didn't move. It caught him by the chest and hurled him across the clearing. He struck the ground and didn't rise right away.

"Braylor!" Finley shouted.

The Minotaur turned toward her voice. I grabbed a shard of bone from the ground and hurled it. It struck its back with a dull crack. The thing barely noticed, but its head turned. Just enough.

"Run!" Finley yelled.

I sprinted toward the far side of the chamber, weaving between bones. The creature bellowed and charged, hooves striking sparks.

Finley grabbed my arm, pulling me along. "Go!"

We raced into the other hallway. The Minotaur stomped after us. My head spun. The maze circled us around, guiding us back toward the heart.

Braylor stumbled into view from the chamber, blood streaking his temple.

The stone chair loomed again. The Minotaur's domain.

Finley looked all around. "We've gone in a circle."

There was truly only one exit. The one we came in. And the Minotaur blocked our escape.

Something in me gave way. I turned, searching wildly for any way, any hint of escape. Nothing but walls, bones, and darkness.

The creature stomped toward us. Its breath steamed in the night air, nostrils flaring.

And Finley—trembling, exhausted—dropped down behind the great chair. Braylor squatted beside me. She raised her hand, eyes half-shut, and the air itself seemed to bend.

Three shadows peeled away from us. They were tall, hazy, perfect silhouettes.

They ran from around the chair, sprinting across the room. No bones crunched, no boots slapping stone. They made no sound.

For one heart-stopping moment, even I believed they were us. She was using a *mindform*. I managed a smile. She knew the art of mindforms... they were crude, but effective.

The Minotaur lunged after them, his roar shaking the air. The ground trembled as it gave chase, and the creature disappeared into the dark of the lone corridor.

Finley sagged against the wall. "It won't fool him for long."

"If he goes far enough," Braylor said, limping back toward us. "It may not need to fool him."

We started toward the only exit, following after him. But we didn't make it far.

Ahead of us, the sound returned. Heavy steps. Deep grunts. Closer.

Finley's voice was thin. "He's back."

"We shall truly make our stand," Braylor said simply.

The Minotaur appeared again, blocking our way. His eyes locked on us. It didn't charge right away this time. It stood there *studying* us.

Braylor took a step forward, bare hands curling into fists. "Stay behind me."

We backed into the circular chamber yet again.

When the Minotaur emerged, Braylor lunged, aiming low. His shoulder drove into its midsection, forcing it back a step—one, then two. It slammed both fists down, cracking the ground where he'd been. He ducked, grabbed a bone the length of my thigh, and swung it. The bone shattered against the creature's strong midsection.

Finley shot ahead with her torch pointing out. She drove it into the Minotaur's leg. It bellowed, snatched her up by the arm, and tossed her aside like a doll. She hit the wall hard, the sound tearing through me.

"Finley!" I ran to her, but Braylor's shout stopped me.

"Jonathan!"

The Minotaur flung out his arm, striking me in the chest. The air blew from my lungs, and I sailed back to a far wall.

My shoulder hit stone and I slid to the floor, trying to exhale but I could only take short inhalations.

Braylor rushed the beast again, leaping to its back. His huge fists pounded at the thick hide. Flailing about, the Minotaur grabbed hold of him. He was tossed across the room, hitting the floor hard and tumbling into the wall.

Finley launched herself and tried scratching at its eyes, but it shoved her away. She rolled backwards, striking her head on the base of the stairs leading up to the chair.

I uselessly threw another bone to distract it from her.

When it turned to me, I pushed myself against the wall. My lips trembling, hands shaking. Afraid to stand up.

As it started toward me, I slid along the wall.

I inched away as the creature took one step, then another. And I fell backwards.

I looked up. I was lying in a small, round tunnel. When I stared down at my feet, my lower half was still in the chamber.

The air on the other side was cooler, silent. When I reached out my hand, the wall shimmered like water where I'd fallen through. Beyond it, I saw Braylor, bloodied and staggering, still fighting.

"Finley!" I screamed. "Here! There's a way! Through the wall!"

She pushed herself upright and then wobbled to her feet, dazed. When she saw me reach through the shimmering surface, her eyes widened. She sprinted toward me, limping slightly.

The Minotaur saw her too.

"Hurry!" Braylor shouted, blocking its charge. Its horns clipped his shoulder, spinning him sideways, but he didn't fall. He threw out his leg and the Minotaur tripped, sliding through a pile of bones.

Finley grabbed my outstretched hand, and I yanked her through. She stumbled, half falling onto me.

Braylor turned, saw the opening, and started toward it.

"Come on!" I yelled.

I sat up and yanked Finley all the way into the narrow tunnel.

Braylor reached the entrance, pressing his hands against the shimmer. His head passed through—but his shoulders caught on the rim.

"It is too small!" he grunted. "Go!"

"No!" Finley reached out for him, clutching his face with both hands through the barrier. "You're coming with us! Do you hear me?!"

He smiled faintly, eyes soft despite the blood. "You found the way. This is enough."

The Minotaur's shadow fell over him.

Braylor turned, drew one last breath, and drove a jagged bone straight at the beast's throat. It didn't pierce the hide but partially closed the windpipe. It tried to roar, grabbed him, and slid him away from the opening.

Finley screamed as his hands slipped from hers. "No! Braylor!"

He growled as his body was dragged toward the darkness beyond.

His eyes locked on to hers, one last time. "Goodbye, my love..."

He was gone.

Finley lunged out after him. But the shimmer of the tunnel opening was gone, replaced by a thick, solid metal wall. She slammed hard into the surface. More alien tech at work.

She pounded on the surface. "No!"

I reached out, but there was nothing I could do.

"No! No, no, no, no... no..."

She fell to the floor hard, sobbing. I caught her before she collapsed completely, holding her as she shook.

"He's gone," she choked. "He's gone—"

Her tears fell hard.

"I know," I whispered. My throat burned, but I didn't know what else to say.

The space we were in was narrow, claustrophobic. The walls pulsed faintly, light ebbing and flowing.

Finley lashed out again, striking the new thick wall with her fists, screaming his name again and again until her voice broke. I held her as she crumpled, as if she might shatter if I let go.

There were no sounds from the chamber. No footsteps. Just silence.

When she finally went still, she whispered against my shoulder, "He was everything."

"I know."

For a long time, we just stayed there.

Then, finally, she pulled away. Her face was streaked with tears and blood, but her eyes burned with something fierce beneath the grief.

"Let's go," she said quietly.

We crawled forward on hands and knees through the tunnel, the sound of our movement echoing in the stillness.

I didn't say anything. There was nothing to say. I just kept close enough, so she knew she wasn't alone.

51

Through a Forest Darkly

Genevieve

We rode away from the Black City at breakneck speed on the fastest karkadanns in Queen Finley's possession. And yes—saying *Queen Finley* would always crack me up. My best friend turned royal. It was the punchline to a joke I never agreed to tell.

Kasuma wanted us to travel light and quick, so it was just me, her, and Kinnat. No soldiers. No entourage. Just food, water, weapons, and a change of clothes I'd probably ruin before sunrise. Minimalist living, warrior edition.

The karkadanns were massive—thick-muscled, thick hides glowing when the light hit just right. Their strides swallowed the ground, and the lighter gravity here made me feel as though I were bouncing through a fever dream. Still, running them this hard through Irkalla's wild terrain—slate valleys, lush plains, thick forests—wasn't exactly relaxing. Every jolt of the saddle sent a new complaint up my spine, and by the second day, I was convinced my ass had achieved enlightenment through pain.

Kasuma had arranged for fresh karkadanns along the route. In quiet villages, bustling towns, even lonely farms the people bowed low but didn't meet her eyes. Power followed her.

I tried not to think too hard about what was to come. The way she moved—urgent but composed—and our rushed race toward Atlantis made me feel like whatever was coming, we were chasing its tail.

By the second night, the world felt smaller. The stars leaned closer, the trees taller, the quiet heavier.

I kept glancing over my shoulder, swearing I saw something. Eyes in the dark. Maybe paranoia, maybe instinct. But I've learned to trust my gut. It's kept me alive longer than any sword has so far.

The forest grew quieter the farther we rode. All the weird birds and insects were silent. No wind through the trees. Even the karkadanns had gone tense, their ears darting at sounds only they could hear. I kept my eyes on the shadows just beyond the moonlight. Every so often, something would catch the corner of my vision: something large, fluid, and silent.

"Something is out there," Kasuma said without looking back. Her tone was calm, but her jaw wasn't.

"You feel it, too?" I asked, adjusting my grip on the reins. "Thought it was just me."

Kinnat gave a quick nod.

We heard the crack of a branch in the distance. A sound too deliberate to be wind, too heavy to be human.

We pushed the karkadanns harder. Their hooves pounded through the dark until the trees finally broke open into a clearing, wide and silver under the bright moonlight. For a moment, I thought maybe we'd lost whatever had been tailing us. Then the ground trembled.

It wasn't subtle. The rumble shook us and made my heart stutter.

The karkadanns screamed in pure fear and reared back. My hands clenched the reins, nails digging into my hands, as I tried not to fall. The tremor rolled again. And then I *heard* it.

A heavy, thrumming growl, coming from the earth itself.

"Kasuma..." I said, my voice low.

"I know."

She dismounted slowly.

"Why are you getting off?! We need to go," I whispered. She shook her head.

Kinnat's eyes were wide, too. Mine were fixed on the treeline, where something massive exhaled.

Behind several trees, two red eyes opened.

I inhaled deeply.

Every childhood story I'd ever heard about dragons came flooding back at once. I'd seen the purple one before in the Black City, while Pherric rode it away. Which was terrifying, sure... but there'd been control in it. Purpose.

This wasn't the same.

The creature before us seemed wild and untamed, its scales the color of blood and fire. Smoke rippled from powerful jaws, coiling through the clearing.

The karkadanns went rigid. Kinnat didn't move a muscle. The instinct in my legs screamed *run*.

For one awful second, I thought this was how we'd die, burned into the dirt of some nameless forest, eaten by something older than history.

Then Kasuma whispered, barely loud enough for me to hear:

"Big Red."

The dragon's eyes shifted toward her at the sound of it—slow, deliberate. Had it recognized the name?

And I realized with a kind of dizzy relief: Kasuma wasn't afraid. Not really. She stood there calm and certain.

Big Red.

The name rolled through me.

The dragon didn't roar or lunge. It *watched* us, her eyes full of some ancient, intelligent calculation.

Kinnat whispered, "We should go around. Far around."

Kasuma lifted a hand, silencing her. "No sudden movements. She is not attacking."

"It is *breathing smoke* at us," I hissed.

Kasuma gave me a small, infuriating smile. "She is thinking. Which is far better than attacking."

We started to edge along the outer rim of the clearing, giving the dragon as wide a berth as possible. My pulse beat so hard it hurt. The karkadanns snorted and stamped, desperate to flee. But the dragon only tracked us with those burning eyes.

Then she moved. Well, I guessed it was a *she* from what Kasuma said.

A single step forward. Strong, smooth, and deliberate. The ground sank beneath her.

Kasuma stopped. "She will not let us pass."

The dragon lowered her head slightly, huffing steam. Her gaze went from me to Kasuma to Kinnat, as if deciding which of us was worth her time.

"She waits," Kasuma murmured. "This one is a true ally to Finley. And.... she recognizes me."

I swallowed hard. "Recognizes you as in *not food*?"

Kasuma ignored me. "Finley always lowers her head when she approaches. Dragons believe they are superior to us. They are not wrong."

Kinnat stared. "You have seen her ride one?"

"Many times."

Kasuma stepped forward slowly, hands open, head low. The dragon's nostrils flared as she leaned close, so close the heat washed over us. Kasuma pressed her fingers to Big Red's snout, whispering something I couldn't catch. The dragon's eyes softened, just a fraction.

Then Kasuma turned back to us. "I believe... she wants riders. Two of us. She can take us to Atlantis faster than anything else alive."

"Two?" Kinnat said. "You mean you and—"

Before she could finish, another sound rolled from the shadows behind us.

A deeper growl, a bit meaner somehow.

I spun, hand on my sword hilt, as a second dragon trudged out of the dark. This green one was smaller but still built tough, scales shining forest jade, and its eyes shattered emeralds.

Kasuma exhaled through her nose. "Of course. Big Red has brought... a friend."

Big Red gave a low, rumbling snort. It sounded suspiciously like approval.

Kasuma smiled faintly. "The gods are not finished being dramatic tonight."

She approached the green dragon just as she had before—head lowered, hands out, voice steady. The dragon snarled, backing up. It lifted its head and roared.

"Kasuma," I said, heart racing, "you sure about this?"

"No. But Big Red is used to a rider. Finley. You and Kinnat will ride with her. But the green one is unsure. I ride with him."

"Wait, what?"

The red dragon stepped closer to me, wings half-folded, her head dipping low. Her heat was a furnace. Her eyes, brilliant and knowing, met mine. And suddenly I understood. She *wasn't* asking.

"Fine," I murmured, trying to sound braver than I felt. "But if I die, I'm haunting all of you."

Kinnat stood behind me, trembling but with a faint smile. This was the opportunity of a lifetime.

Kasuma was already on top the green dragon's back, looking regal and terrifying. "Remember," she called, "walk forward with respect. Hands open to her. Head down. And whatever you do... do not move quickly or reach out, unless you want to lose an arm."

I swallowed, nodded. Taking my time, I approached. My chin on my chest. Slowly, I laid my hand gently on Big Red's warm scales. She rumbled deep in her chest.

With a deep exhale, I worked my way along her side with my hand trailing behind on her scales. I pulled myself up and positioned myself on her back. Kinnat repeated my motions, climbing behind me.

Wings unfurled in a blaze of red and gray, each beat stirring the air into a cyclone.

"Hold strong!" Kasuma shouted. "We have a long way to travel!"

And then we were rising.

The world dropped away beneath us. The first rush of air punched against my chest, warm and wild. Big Red's wings opened wider, so wide I thought she'd blot out the moon. And then we weren't falling anymore. We were *soaring*.

The forests of Irkalla stretched endlessly below, a patchwork of black and blue light. Every beat of her wings sent a deep vibration through me, and the air whipped through my hair.

Kinnat's arms locked around my waist, tighter than ever. I could feel her heartbeat through the layer of wool and leather, quick and unsteady, syncing with mine as Big Red climbed higher.

I wasn't sure if she was terrified or thrilled—probably both. I was too.

When I risked a glance back, her hair was snapping wildly in the wind, her eyes wide and shining. She caught me looking, smiled. And the smile quickly faded as we dropped in the air a bit. But that smile, her smile, hit harder than the wind.

I turned forward again, pressing a little closer so she wouldn't have to hold so tightly. That's what I told myself, anyway.

The sky above us was wide, the world below a blur. For the first time since leaving the Black City, the noise in my head went quiet. No plans, no fear, no what-ifs. Just the heat of the dragon, the rhythm of her wings, and Kinnat's breath against the back of my neck—steady, real, grounding.

I didn't know what waited for us in Atlantis, but for a few perfect seconds, I didn't care. I just wanted to stay right there, in the rush of wind and her arms, pretending we could fly forever.

52

Learning to Fly

Finley

"Finley."

If I ever met one of these supposed gods, I'd try to kill them in a heartbeat. And... probably end up dead in the process. Like dead-dead.

"Finley?"

They built the labyrinth. They put in an escape tunnel. They designed it so once someone went through, it would be sealed shut. I had no doubt about any of it.

And they locked me away from Braylor. I will *never* forgive them.

"Finley!"

Jonathan's voice finally tore through the fog in my mind. He stood over me, bending down, eyes searching my tear-stained face.

"What?" My voice came out cracked, small.

"What are we going to do now?"

I turned away, wiping at the never-ending tears. The rocky beach around us was jagged and cold; my world thick with grief and regret. The thin slab of stone we'd rolled from the tunnel lay behind us, silent and uncaring. The morning sun hadn't yet reached us, and the walls of the labyrinth still cast their long shadow.

294

"I don't know," I whispered.

My chest felt hollow. Braylor's laughter still echoed in my head. The way he'd grin after pulling off something reckless, the way he'd squeeze my hand before a fight. He'd promise we'd make it out together. He always kept his promises.

But not this one.

The gods had created things which had taken everything from me before—my home, my peace, my sanity—and I'd clawed back pieces of myself each time. But Braylor was different.

He was the piece I was not ready to lose.

The one who made this cursed place survivable.

He was gone, and I had nothing left to give but anger.

My chest felt like it had been scooped out with a dull knife. Air refused to fill my lungs. The world pressed against me, trying to remind me I was still here when he wasn't.

Jonathan squatted down. His shadow stretched long and thin across the wet stones, a stranger's outline in the light of dawn.

He grabbed my hand. "Look, I have no idea what you're going through. I can't even imagine. But..." he looked around at the beach. "We're out. We survived. He would want us to keep going. To make his death mean something."

I shoved his hand away, harder than I meant to. "You're just saying that because you're scared."

Because if I let myself believe what he said, believing Braylor's death could have meaning, I'd break.

"Right now, I don't think the Atlanteans know we're free," he said. "They have every reason to think the Minotaur killed us and ate us up. We should take advantage of this! Now. While we still can."

"By doing what?"

"I don't know. Find a boat, sail back to the mainland. Something!"

I stood up, anger flaring to cover the grief clawing at my throat. "Find a boat?! Are you fucking kidding me?!" I pointed at the sea water lapping against the rocks. "These people breathe underwater, Jonathan. There's probably a whole other city down there. A boat sailing away would be the first goddamn thing they'd see. We'd be surrounded in seconds!"

Exasperated, he looked around for an answer hiding among the shattered rocks. "Then... what are we going to do?"

I shoved past him, my boots scraping against stone. The tears rushed back, stinging my eyes, hot and useless. "I don't know about you... but I'm getting me some sweet revenge."

"Finley."

I didn't slow down. My body was a storm, all motion and no thought. Around the curve of the labyrinth, the island of Atlantis came into view, gleaming and distant. Mocking me. The labyrinth was nestled inside the curve of its C-shaped harbor, almost close enough to touch. Almost.

"Finley! Finley, what are you going to do?" He trailed after me, all nervous and clumsy.

"I'm going over there to kill Thalassa."

"By yourself? With no weapons? Against her palace guards?"

"Yes."

"You're talking about a suicide mission," he said. His voice softened, trembling around the edges. "I get it. But you need to have a plan."

"I have to try," I said. My voice cracked. I bit down on it, but the tears still came. "I can't sit here."

He opened his mouth, probably to tell me I was being irrational, but something in my face must've stopped him. Maybe the part of me that had already accepted I was done being careful.

Then his eyes went wide. "What?" I asked.

He stammered, pointing behind me.

I spun around.

A purple dragon cut through the sky, each wingbeat shaking the air. Zeranthyl. And clinging to its back, barely upright, was Pherric. Pallid, terrified, hanging on tight. They soared around the city once and then the dragon dropped out of the sky, disappearing behind the cliff and the towers of Atlantis.

"Holy..." I started.

Jonathan finished. "Crap." That's not what I would have said.

"She brought him here... on her dragon," I mumbled.

He blinked hard. A child seeing magic for the first time. "Dear god, that was.... a dragon."

"Now," I said, voice steadying for the first time since Braylor's death, "we have a plan."

He tore his gaze from the sky, dazed. "What? Wh-what's the plan?"

I reached up and closed his gaping mouth. "Save him."

"Who is he?"

"He's my mage. Pherric. He's the same as Ramil, only... not a dickhead. Well, kinda. They all are." My throat caught halfway through the sentence, because even making fun of someone hurt now. "But Thalassa wants my immortality potion, and she's not getting it."

Jonathan slowly recovered, resigned to his fate. "So, we're going over there."

"We are." I turned toward the edge of the water.

"Wait," he said, nodding toward the sea. "You said the Atlanteans are down there. They'll see us swimming."

I followed his gaze. The distance wavered with sunlight, impossible and mocking. He was right.

Dammit. But at least it gave me something to *do*. Anything was better than sitting still and remembering the way Braylor's hand had felt when he reached for me one last time.

"We don't have a choice. We—" A thought struck. I looked at Jonathan. "You!"

He blinked. "Me what?"

"You told me you can move shit with your mind. Telekinesis."

"And?" His face scrunched up, then went white as the idea hit him. "No. No way."

"Yes way."

"Finley, I can move a small tin cup. A pile of powder. I can't pick up a person!"

"Why not? Same concept. The physics don't care."

He planted his hands on his hips. "You're insane."

I almost smiled. "I'm grieving and desperate. Big difference."

He stared at me like I'd lost my mind, which, to be fair, wasn't totally wrong.

"I can't pick up a person," he said.

"Why not? It's the same thing. You're still moving an object with your mind. Your muscles don't lift... *you* do."

He blinked, incredulous. "How do you know?"

"Because we're going to find out." I crossed my arms, chin lifted. "Right now."

"Huh?"

"Pick me up," I said, because it *was* the most reasonable request in the world.

"Um..."

He hesitated, glancing around to the rocks for moral support. Then he sat cross-legged on a flat patch of sand and closed his eyes. "This is not going to work."

"Whether you think you can, or you think you can't... you're right."

His eyes cracked open just to glare at me. "Did you just quote motivational bullshit at me right after your boyfriend died?"

The jab hit harder than he meant it to. For a second, I couldn't speak. Then I exhaled through my nose. "Grief comes in flavors, Jonathan. Mine's sarcasm."

"Look. If we go flying over the water, won't the Atlanteans, down there, see us?"

"No. Well, even if they see two shadows flying above the water, they'll think it's birds or something."

He blinked. Looked guilty. But he closed his eyes again.

Nothing happened.

I waited. Encouraged him. Waited more. Still nothing.

After the fifth try, he jumped up and stormed to the water's edge, kicking at a rock. "This is pointless."

I followed, placing a hand on his shoulder. His tunic was damp and coarse, gritty with sand. I wanted to shake him. Slap him into trying harder. Or, maybe, telling him he was useless and he couldn't do it. Which probably would've worked on me. But I tried a different approach.

"Hey," I said softly. "It's okay. I've been there. When I first got here, I thought I'd die within a week. I couldn't fight, couldn't speak their language, couldn't even stand without tripping over my own feet. But look at me."

He glanced at me. His eyes were red. He trembled, but he listened.

"I'm still here. Still fighting. You'll get there. We could try swimming if this doesn't work. Maybe no one will see us."

He sighed. "Okay."

I nodded and turned toward the beach. But his footsteps didn't follow. When I looked back, he was sitting again, eyes closed.

A flicker rippled through the air. The fine hairs on my arms rose. The world felt... warped.

And suddenly... I moved.

Not much, not gracefully. But the ground *fell away.* As if I were standing on a rising platform. My stomach dropped, and a startled laugh broke out of me before I could stop it.

Then I toppled forward, spun in a circle midair, and crashed into the rocks below.

Jonathan scrambled over, panic on his face. "I'm sorry! Are you okay?!"

I winced, rubbing my elbow, then laughed again, and that sound was a little wild. "You did it!"

He stared. "What?"

"You just lifted me off the ground!"

The realization hit him. He looked at his hands, mouth parted. "I... did."

"You did!"

He actually smiled. A full, disbelieving grin. For a brief second, I saw hope. And maybe it was enough to keep both of us going.

The next hour was a mess of failures that led to bruises and curses.

He'd lift me a few inches, then drop me like a rock. Sometimes I fell sideways. Once I rolled into a tide pool and nearly lost a boot. But each time he failed, he tried again.

The lighter gravity on Tir Na helped. But it was a big ask.

Still, we kept at it. Because pain was easier when it came from falling than from remembering.

The hard part was getting him to move himself. And it took time and a kind of focus I could almost respect. He closed his eyes, trembling, until finally, he began to float.

When he opened them, hovering a few feet above the sand, I caught myself grinning.

We didn't talk about Braylor. I think he knew better. But when he said, "Ready for the big test?" his voice was softer, careful, not wanting me to break if he raised it too high.

"Ready," I said.

I stood at the edge of the waves, my boots sinking into wet sand.

"Do you want me to jump? Give you a helping hand, so to speak?" I asked.

"I really, truly don't know," he muttered. "Can't hurt."

I took a few steps back, filling my lungs, steadying myself. "Okay. Here we go."

He nodded.

I ran. Jumped. And landed in the shallow water. I thought it hadn't worked... until the air tilted and every organ inside me fell. I was *up*.

The wind ripped through my hair, the world spinning beneath me. I gasped and nearly screamed all at once, flipping end over end. He pushed me across the water. I'd go up and then down, but I kept flying. He must've lost his concentration, at some point. I crashed hard into the shallows on the other side. Sand filled my mouth. Saltwater burned my eyes.

But I was astounded. I rolled onto my butt, grinning ear to ear. As though I weren't someone who had lost everything.

"We did it!" I shouted.

Across the water, I heard his voice echo, "Yes!" Then quieter, when he realized how loud he'd been: "Yes..."

I wiped my face and motioned. "Your turn!"

He was drained but grinning, shaking his hands out the way sprinters do before a race. Jonathan squatted on the sand, eyes closed, slowly exhaling.

He rose, shakily at first, then steady. Floating.

Pherric had taught me about mindforms, about how magic wasn't always seen but *felt.* I reached out with my thoughts, not to take control but to brace him. I was the net under the tightrope walker.

He crossed the water, wobbling like a newborn bird. A third of the way across, he started to tumble. Spinning in the air.

His eyes snapped open, panic flashing there. He began to drop.

"Come on," I whispered. "You got this."

I doubled my focus. He stopped in the air, right before hitting the water, and regrouped. He floated up again—faster this time, controlled. Wobbling a little, but steady. He skimmed above the surface, then shot forward way too fast, bouncing off the shallow water and overshooting the beach. He became a skipping stone until he tumbled into a pile of rocks.

Boots splashing through the shallows, I sprinted to him. Jonathan lay twisted in the rocks, groaning.

"Are you hurt?" I hissed, dropping to my knees beside him.

He blinked, dazed, sand streaked across his cheek. "I don't... think so."

"Good." I grabbed his arm and hauled him up. "Move."

We scrambled toward the cliffs, our soaked clothes clinging to our skin. Every sound felt too loud: the slap of waves, the rasp of my breath, the rattle of pebbles skittering under our boots.

Above us, the city of Atlantis woke in the rising light. White-gold towers, tall and silent, catching the sun. The day hummed with tension.

"Down," I whispered, shoving Jonathan against the wall of rock. We pressed ourselves flat, chests heaving.

I scanned the beach. Empty. But not safe.

The crash we'd both made—the flight, the splash—it *had* to have been seen. Any second now, soldiers would be sprinting down the carved paths from the city. Tridents raised. Swords swinging.

But no one came.

Just wind, surf, and the far-off cry of seabirds echoing off the cliffs.

Jonathan's trembled beside me. I met his eyes. Fear. Disbelief. Maybe a little pride.

"We did it," he whispered, voice hoarse.

I nodded. "Yeah." My gaze stayed on the mountain holding up the city, watching for any flicker of movement. "We did."

A few heartbeats of silence stretched too long. Then he let out a shaky laugh. Half relief, half hysteria. "I can't believe it worked."

"Don't celebrate yet." My voice came out lower than I meant, almost a growl. "They'll know we're here soon enough."

He swallowed, following my eyes upward. The cliffs above were streaked with gold light, the city looming beyond them—beautiful, bright, and full of people who'd gladly see us dead.

I shifted my weight, muscles still tight from the flight. "Now comes the hard part."

53

Asymmetrical Fashion Choices Indeed

Finley

"So, what do we do now?"

"Ugh, I knew you were going to ask me that."

Jonathan was a pain in my ass, but he was right. I needed a detailed plan. My brain was still buzzing from the flight, that unnatural blur of wind and light that somehow hadn't killed us.

We crouched on a ragged stretch of shoreline.

"Finley..."

"I know, I know. Let me think."

I stared up at the cliff that carved a dark outline against the glowing city above. Citizens moved along elevated walkways that dangled between elegant spires. Soldiers stood guard in shiny armor that reflected the light of the sea.

There was no way to come at this like Hominans. They'd spot us before we even reached the stairs. The Atlantean soldiers would surround us and we'd be prisoners again. The thought made me queasy.

But what would Atlanteans do? They'd swim in. Of course they would. Half of them probably came and went through the water. I scanned the shoreline for some hidden passage, a cave entrance, anything. But the beach was bare, all slick obsidian and dark sand that clung to my boots.

"We can't go up the steps leading to Thalassa's palace," I said finally. "Too open. We'd be grabbed in seconds."

Jonathan shivered. "So...?"

"So we keep going."

I started down the rocky stretch, each step crunching louder than I liked. The low hum of the city above made the back of my neck prickle. Every splash of water made me think an Atlantean would surface at any second. The alarm bells would go off shortly after, I was damned sure of it.

The cliff ahead sloped lower toward the sea, and I took that as a small mercy. "Maybe we can find another way in," I said, though I didn't believe it.

Jonathan stumbled behind me, muttering something about my definition of "plan." The rocks grew slick, and the spray hit my face in cold bursts. For a brief moment, I almost envied the Atlanteans—the ease with which they moved between worlds, walking on land but breathing underwater. I was stuck clinging to stone like a shipwreck survivor with no idea which way was up.

We rounded a bend and spotted a wide beach ahead, pale and open like a stage. Way too exposed. I stayed in place, scanning for activity. Nothing but the rhythmic crash of waves and the distant glow of the Atlantean towers.

"This way," I whispered, pointing to a steep slope. The cliff face looked climbable. Barely.

Jonathan groaned. "You're kidding."

"Do I look like I'm kidding?"

It was slower going than I wanted, our fingers scrambling for holds, the rock flaking away beneath us. My arms burned halfway up, and Jonathan wasn't exactly built for stealth. Or heights. But we made it. When I finally pulled myself over the ledge and lay flat against the cool stone, I dared a look back. The ocean below wavered silver–blue below us. I reached down and hauled him onto the landing.

We hadn't been spotted. Not yet.

"Okay," I said. "Let's see how far we can get."

By the time we reached the edge of the city, my arms were jelly and my boots were covered with sea grit. There wasn't much grass or soil here, just smooth stone inlaid with mother-of-pearl mosaics that shone underfoot, patterned like waves frozen mid-motion.

Pools of water were carved into the walkways, some deep enough to dive into. In the distance, I saw people strolling along, graceful figures in fluid garments, their skin faintly luminous, their dark hair drifting in the wind. The sound of water moving through hidden channels whispered beneath the city, like the island itself was alive and listening.

But there were no citizens near us. I had hoped we might capture a few of them, borrow their clothes. Or at least grab a weapon. No such luck.

"Are we seriously going to just... walk in?" Jonathan whispered.

"Would you prefer to swim up through the sewers?" I hissed back. "If we stay out of sight, we might have a chance."

We crept between two narrow buildings carved from stone and seashell. If it wasn't terrifying, it might have been beautiful.

We were almost to the main causeway that wound toward Thalassa's palace when I stopped in my tracks and crouched down. A soldier stood at the far end of the alley, his back to us, a trident resting against his shoulder and a sword at his hip.

"Wait," I whispered.

Jonathan followed my gaze. "We could... sneak past?"

"Or knock him out."

He blinked at me. "You're serious?"

"I'm improvising."

Staying low, we hustled to the end of the alley. Jonathan went low; I went high. It was sloppy, but it worked... until the soldier's helmet clanged against the wall as he fell. It rolled out into the street, and the metallic sound rang out like a bell.

"Shit."

I grabbed the fallen soldier's sword and gestured for Jonathan to follow. "Run."

We sprinted down the narrow lanes as shouts erupted behind us. Boots pounded stone. More soldiers emerged, shouting as they tried to figure out what was going on.

"Left!" I whispered, yanking Jonathan into a shadowed side street. Ahead, a door led into a small house. I didn't think. I shoved it open, pulled him inside, and closed the door. There was no lock.

We collapsed into darkness. The space smelled like fish and maybe some seaweed. Probably a breakfast had been eaten in there. My eyes adjusted to the dim light, revealing a room carved smooth from pale stone, its walls slick with a pearlescent sheen. It wasn't cluttered, but every surface gleamed with purpose: shells arranged like art, coral tools laid neatly beside colorful glass bowls. A shallow basin on the floor in the corner brimmed with seawater, sloshing gently; a quick escape route, maybe, for anyone who preferred the ocean to a door.

I heard soldiers running near us outside.

"Stay quiet," I mouthed.

We waited. My heartbeat was loud enough I was sure they'd hear it.

When the footsteps faded, I stood and scanned the small home. Despite its size, the space hummed with quiet wealth. The faint drip of water echoed through the room, and somewhere beneath the floor, I could hear the deep, rhythmic pull of the tide through the city's structure.

"If we're going to survive, we need to blend in."

Jonathan frowned. "How are we going to do that? We don't look Atlantean."

"Maybe we can fake it?" I said, kneeling beside a low chest carved from white wood. Inside were layers of fabric. Short wraps and draped halters spun from something between silk and linen. Most were cut to leave the belly bare where Atlantean gills pulsed.

I swallowed hard. Mine, of course, didn't.

"Turn around," I told Jonathan.

"What? Oh," he did what he was told.

I removed my soaking wet tunic and found a length of thin green fabric, pulling it diagonally across my torso, covering the spots where gills should have been. The effect was more "asymmetrical fashion choice" than "land dweller in disguise," but it would have to do. I picked a pale blue wrap, light enough to dry in seconds, and wound it high across my chest, tucking and knotting it until the folds looked intentional.

The trousers were little more than soft black strips tied at the hips, leaving the sides of my legs bare to the air. When I moved, the fabric shifted and whispered like water. Atlantean clothes weren't made for modesty—they were made for movement, for skin that belonged to the sea.

I exhaled, tightened the wrap one last time, and hoped no one would notice I wasn't built to live underwater.

Jonathan just stared. "Okay, that actually does kind of work. Except for your hair."

I reached up to grasp my red curls. "Oh, yeah."

Glancing toward a bowl on the table, there was a cluster of dark berries glistening like ink pearls. I smashed a few between my fingers. The juice ran deep purple-black. Perfect.

I caught my reflection in a pane of polished glass, then rubbed the juice through my hair. It clung fast, streaking my red into dark waves. Messy, but effective. "What do you think?"

"You look kind of... scary," he said.

"Perfect."

Then came the sound that made us both stop dead. The sounds of boots on the cobblestones outside.

Voices. Two soldiers.

"Check inside!" one barked.

Jonathan's eyes went wide. I yanked him behind a hanging curtain near the back wall, fabric brushing my cheek. I quietly slid baskets and a tall box to the side, and we ducked in behind them.

The soldiers' soles scraped across the floor as they entered. Items in the room were picked up, pushed aside. They stepped closer. I could see their shadows moving through the thin fabric, one of them only an arm's length away.

Jonathan loudly gulped. I pressed my hand against his chest, mouthing *don't move.*

I held up my sword, ready to take the guy on.

The second soldier turned toward our curtain. A hand reached for the fabric.

From outside, a distant shout: "Over here! They went in this direction!"

Both men cursed. The hand hesitated, brushing at the fabric. I held my ground. Waited. But they turned and rushed from the small apartment, the door slamming as they ran off.

I exhaled, my knees nearly giving out on me.

"That," Jonathan whispered, "was *way* too close."

"Welcome to Atlantis," I muttered.

I checked the mirror again, slicking my hair back. The berry dye had darkened into a deep blue-black sheen. I squeezed out more juice from a berry and ran it across my lips. I managed to add some to my red eyebrows and lashes, but that burned like hell. Bad idea.

Next, I added a silver band from a bed table around my arm, completing the look. The woman staring back at me in the mirror didn't look quite like Finley anymore.

My big problem? I didn't find any male clothing. Jonathan was still wearing his tunic, black pants, and green robe. Not very Atlantean of him.

"Okay," I said. "New plan. I'm your captor."

Jonathan blinked. "Huh?"

"I caught you sneaking around my home. I'm taking you to the palace myself."

He opened his mouth, closed it, and then sighed. "You're certifiable. You know that don't you?"

"Probably," I said, scanning the room until I found a coiled rope. "Hold out your hands."

He hesitated. "You're actually going to tie me up?"

"Fake tie," I said. "You'll live."

I wrapped the rope loosely around his wrists and tightened it just enough to look convincing. The sword gleamed faintly at my hip. I straightened my shoulders, adjusted the wrap, and smirked.

"Alright, *prisoner*," I said, pushing the door open to the empty street. "Let's go find Pherric."

54

How Do You Feel About Fish?

Finley

We slipped down the street in the *opposite* direction from the soldiers. See? Occasionally, I made intelligent choices.

Jonathan pulled his hood low, trying to look inconspicuous, which somehow made him look guiltier. The green robe didn't help; it caught the light and drew a few stares from every direction.

I kept my sword angled low, its hilt hidden beneath the wrap at my hip, and forced my stride into something casual. Around us, Atlanteans filled the avenue. Vendors hawking steamed shellfish and shell trinkets, children chasing each other with ribbons soaked in dye that left streaks of turquoise on the pavement. The air wavered with morning heat and humidity, thick enough to taste.

A pair of merwomen across a narrow waterway paused their conversation to whisper behind their hands. One pointed toward Jonathan's robe.

Great. Perfect.

I shoved him lightly between the shoulder blades. "Move," I shouted loud enough for anyone close by to hear.

We veered off the main road, cutting through a smaller street where the walls closed in and the sound of the crowd dulled to a watery hum. When I glanced between the buildings, a glint of something caught my eye. There was a canal running alongside the smaller street over. It was narrow but deep and the surface a mirror.

I followed its path. It wound past the markets, under a carved arch, and toward the tall towers that crowned the city's heart. The palace sat at the end of it—pale, distant, and impossible to miss.

A shallow boat came drifting up the canal towards us. It was almost as wide as the canal and filled with crates and barrels mostly overflowing with a variety of fish.

An idea started forming. Risky, messy, probably smelly. But doable.

I looked at Jonathan. "Even newer plan. How do you feel about fish?"

"I'm not a huge fan—"

"Look. There," I said, nudging Jonathan. "That boat is full of fresh fish. Those barrels are likely headed to the palace. They probably have a lot of mouths to feed."

He blinked, then squinted. "We hop on and—?"

"We hide," I said. "In two of the barrels."

Across from us the fisherman stepped confidently off his barge, a man who owned every tide he'd ever sailed. He lugged a crate onto the dock and marched across the avenue to a tent. He immediately began a foul-mouthed ballet with the vendor over prices. While the two men argued, I motioned for Jonathan to follow. Staying low, we snuck onto the boat. The side dipped into the water, creating a splash. I watched the fisherman, but he never turned our way.

The wood barrel was damp and heavy, the lids slick with old fish oil.

We wrenched the lids off. The smell hit full. And it was intense, honest, and perfect. Together we dumped two barrels of fish into the canal.

Jonathan hesitated. "You want me to—"

"Get in," I said. "Climb in, curl up tight. Don't make any more sound than you have to."

"That won't be a problem."

He slid into the first barrel with the grace of a man who's cursed at the world more than once, but his knees bent like he'd been born to fit into small places. I placed the top on his and jumped into mine, the wood creaking, my palms catching on damp, splintered grain. I pulled the lid back on. A small crack gave me a decent sight line, if I moved my head back and forth.

The fisherman returned with his crate and muttered at the vendor. He tossed the empty crate, scratched his jaw, and pushed off with a long pole. The barge rocked gently; the nets rubbed against our barrels, and I felt the boat's breathing—the tiny, hollow, reassuring rise and fall you only notice when you're pretending not to be boxed inside a smell.

We drifted, the canal guiding us ahead. The buildings pressing close enough that I could hear a cook's tinny curse, a woman's laugh, the distinct slap of a fish skin being worked over stone. Light refracted off the water in a scatter of green and amber.

A shadow loomed: two guards on the dock, armor clinking, the hard professional silence of men whose mornings are made of checking lists.

One hailed him. "Hold!"

My heart did something clumsy. The boat slowed. The fisherman spat into the water and cursed—the universal response of someone who hates being given orders by people who have never mended a net.

"Why must you harass me?!"

"Two foreigners have been reported in the city," said a guard. "A soldier was assaulted."

"What does that have to do with me?" the fisherman snarled.

"They might be hiding on your boat."

"I've been on this canal since sunrise. Do not tell me I lost my eyes," he said, loud enough I felt it vibrate in the barrel wood.

One of the guards came forward, suspicious. He prodded a net with the trident-tips and his shadow passed over the barrels. I kept still until my shoulders cramped.

He tapped the wood with his spear, wanting to make it speak. The fisherman leaned in, eyes hard, and clapped a hand on the edge of the canal. "Unsalted stock for the palace kitchens, mate," he said with a grin that was all teeth. "You want it checked, check the barrel. You want trouble, you make me late, and the Queen's cooks will skin you for a trifle."

The guard frowned, then reached down, thumbed the barrel's rim, and took a quick sniff. The wet, oily scent answered—the right answer. He snorted, half-amused, half-annoyed. "Go on then." The trident lifted.

The barge pushed under the arch.

Inside, my lungs whispered betrayals.

We rode under several smaller bridges and continued along the canal. The fisherman made two more stops.

He guided the barge into the palace. When we eased to a halt, he leapt onto the dock on the palace side of the channel, calling out, "For the Queen's table! Fresh and salted!" His voice bounced off stacked crates and down a torchlit hallway. He hefted a crate of fish and set it in the webbed hands of a kitchen assistant.

We waited. The fisherman lingered, chatting with a porter in their language. When he finally followed the man into the hallway, their footsteps faded off against the walls.

"Hey," I whispered.

"Yeah?"

"Rock your barrel back and forth."

"Jesus," he hissed.

I began shifting my weight—forward, back, forward again—until the wood creaked under me. Jonathan followed suit, his barrel groaning beside mine. One last push sent me tumbling off the end of the boat and into the canal. The lid burst open with a hollow slap as the cold water closed over my head.

I surfaced just enough to see Jonathan fall in near me, his hair plastered flat, his eyes wide and glistening in the low light. I motioned for him to follow, hugging the wall of the canal and keeping the barge between us and the dock.

Voices rose behind us—angry, overlapping in Atlantean—as the fisherman and porter raced back to the water. The boat rocked under their weight. Barrels and crates clattered. They argued over who's fault it was, each blaming the other.

In the chaos, I caught Jonathan's gaze and nodded. *Now.*

We sank beneath the surface and swam hard, the murky current muffling everything. When I surfaced again, only my eyes broke the waterline. I looked back along the canal. Neither one had noticed.

"All right," I whispered. "We swim a bit farther. Look for a door that leads inside."

He nodded, and we pressed on.

The canal curved inward, deeper into the palace. I spotted a stone ledge and hauled myself up, dripping. The first door was locked. We wrung out our clothes, my sandals squelching as we crept along the narrow walkway until another door came into view. I pulled on the handle. It was unlocked, its hinges rusted but quiet.

I eased it open. Inside: a storage room stacked with crates, kegs, barrels, and coils of rope. A second door gleamed faintly in the gloom.

We slipped inside and closed the way behind us.

Jonathan exhaled. "We made it in. Now what?"

"I wish I knew." I pushed my soaked hair back, and dark streaks ran over my fingers. My dye job bled out, betraying me. "But we've got to find a way to the throne room. I bet that's where she's got Pherric."

He cracked the next door open, peered out, then nodded. "Coast's clear. But it's not going to be easy."

I gave him a half-smile. "Hey, we've come this far..."

The hallway beyond the storage room was empty, but we rounded the corner and the larger passage was alive with quiet motion. Servants padded past, balancing trays, carrying bundles of linens, or whispering to one another in the fluid, clipped syllables of Atlantean. Jonathan and I pressed to the wall at first, ready to duck back inside—but no one looked twice.

One servant even brushed past me, grumbling about kitchen troubles, too harried to notice two dripping strangers standing near the wall. I stared after her.

"They didn't even blink," I whispered.

Jonathan's mouth twitched. "Guess chaos looks the same everywhere."

"Then we blend in," I said, straightening. Confidence—thin, borrowed, but growing—settled over me. I took the cord from around his robe and re-wrapped his wrists, then held out my sword. We started walking.

We turned down a marble corridor where the floor was a vibrant black ice. That's when a man stepped out of an archway ahead. Not a guard— no uniform or a weapon—but something about him was too neat, too deliberate. The silver pin on his collar caught the light. Official.

He frowned. "You two. Where are you going—"

Before he could finish, I grabbed Jonathan's wrists and tugged the cord to make sure it was tight. Then I pressed my sword to his spine.

"Mind your business," I said flatly.

The man stilled in front of us, eyes darting from me to Jonathan and back again. Whatever authority he thought he had evaporated. He stepped aside, hands raised slightly, and disappeared down another hall without a word.

Jonathan exhaled as I let go. "Nice touch."

"Act like you belong," I murmured, sheathing the blade. My inner Genevieve glowed.

We moved faster now, turning corners guided by the faint hum of water through the palace's channels. Twice, we ducked behind columns as soldiers in scaled armor marched past, their tridents ready for blood. The sound of their boots faded into the distance.

Finally, the corridor widened. Through an archway ahead, a faint blue light spilled across the floor—rippling like waves. We crept closer and peered inside.

The throne room.

We slipped behind a column and ducked behind a heavy curtain, its fabric warm against my cheek. A long, wide table had been dragged onto the dais, crowded with vials, jars, powders—an entire traveling apothecary laid out. Pherric stood in front of it, his hands bound behind him, cheeks blotched with the mottled bruises from too many slaps. Blood traced a line from the corner of his mouth.

Before him stood two figures: a mage in green robes and Thalassa's gaunt Atlantean mage wrapped in bright silk. Between them, the Queen lounged on her throne of coral and gold like she was watching afternoon theater.

Jonathan went still beside me. His jaw clenched so tightly the muscle jumped.

"Ramil," he whispered.

"That the guy who was with you? The one who lied about me?"

He nodded once, fists tightening.

Ramil paced before Pherric, a storm contained by skin. Taller than Pherric and broader, tattooed heavily and confidently. He radiated menace.

Thalassa flicked her hand. "Now, create your immortality elixir, mage."

Pherric lifted his chin. "I need to see that Queen Finley is alive... and well."

A ripple of tension passed between Ramil and Thalassa. They did not have me. They assumed I'd died in the Minotaur maze.

"The insolent little one is alive," Thalassa said. "That is all you need to know."

"I will not do the work until I see her standing before me."

Ramil stepped closer, low and dangerous. "She is... formidable. Too formidable to be in the same room with her mage."

A thin smile cracked across Pherric's bruised mouth. "I see that you have dealt with her."

"I have," he said tightly. "And I will not do so again."

Thalassa slammed her hand against the arm of her throne. "Make him do it, Ramil!"

Ramil swept an arm over the table. "We have all the necessary ingredients. Begin."

Pherric's eyes flicked through the assortment. "You have... but I require assurance."

Ramil seized the front of Pherric's robe, nearly lifting him. "You know your queen well. Sense that she is alive. You can feel her heartbeat. You can feel her..."

His gaze drifted, his mindform powers rippling outward. He searched the room.

For a heartbeat, panic detonated inside my chest, a hot, bright spike of

I'm here, he sees me, he knows—

—and then I slammed it down. Hard.

I forced my lungs to slow. My pulse to quiet. Emotion was a beacon, and Ramil was far better at this than Pherric ever was. If I didn't smother every flare of fear, he would feel it—feel *me*—quivering behind the curtain.

His searching slowed. Tilted away. Not convinced, but no longer zeroing in.

"Her presence," he finished, though something in his eyes said he felt more than he wanted to. "Recreate the formula," he growled. "Now. Or I will order her death, and then yours."

A guard stepped in to untie Pherric's hands. The Queen relaxed back into her throne.

I started to draw my sword.

"I can't let him do this," I whispered, already shifting forward.

Jonathan clamped onto my wrist. "Finley. Don't."

"She can't have the immortality potion—"

"If you go in there now, you'll get us killed." He angled his head toward the Atlantean guards circling the room.

I paused. Every instinct screamed for violence. Jonathan's grip, steady and unyielding, was the only thing keeping me rooted.

"So what if she lives forever?" he added quietly. "No harm, no foul."

I glared. Hard. "Then what are we supposed to do?"

"Wait and see how it plays out? I don't know."

Pherric opened the *Arcanum Libellum*, fingers trembling only slightly as he flipped toward the final pages. His eyes jumped between Thalassa and the inked instructions, weighing every risk, every consequence. With a long, steadying exhale, he began. The memory hit me hard—him working beneath the arena, frantic and desperate, while I lay dying for the first time. He wasn't frantic now, but the precision remained: exact measurements, careful pours, slices shaved from the hide of the dead Ramidreju weasel-creature, mixtures stirred and checked and rechecked. He moved with the grim efficiency of someone who knew the cost of being off by an ounce.

Ramil loomed over him, arms crossed. Thalassa's mage watched intently, his hands moving slightly along with Pherric's, mimicking each gesture. Thalassa herself reclined deeper into boredom.

At last, Pherric stepped back from a bowl of steaming liquid. Ramil shoved him aside, inspecting the mixture. He sniffed, nodded.

Thalassa lit up. "It is ready?"

Pherric nodded once. "It is, your highness."

She turned. "Goran!"

I exchanged a glance with Jonathan. No explanation came.

The First Sea-Lord strode out from behind a curtain, all attitude and ceremony. Thalassa accepted the bowl from Ramil, and Goran thumped his chest with a fist, signaling he was ready to die for her.

"Drink," she commanded.

He swallowed the potion in one motion. His eyes bulged—yes, it burned. I remembered that—but he kept his expression grimly composed.

A long beat.

His hand went to his sword. "If you have poisoned me, sorcerer, it will be your last act," Goran growled at Pherric.

Pherric simply folded his hands and bowed his head.

Jonathan whispered, "What's happening?"

"Testing it on him first? Maybe?" I murmured back.

After a minute, Thalassa snapped her fingers. "Your sword."

Goran handed it to her instantly.

"If he does not recover," she warned Pherric, "your death will not be quick."

Without any ceremony, she turned and plunged Goran's sword up under his chest, just below a gill. The tip pierced the heart, if he had one.

He staggered, gasping. A look of shock and pain on his face. I knew that pain all too well.

But he looked down and then stood straight. He pushed the sword out and it clattered to the floor. A smile washed across his face. We watched in amazement as the blood stopped flowing. The gash in his ribs sealed up slowly. He shoved fingers against his new skin.

"I am," he muttered, "alive."

Thalassa all but squealed. "Repeat the process now. For tenfold the original amount!"

"Tenfold?" Pherric gasped.

She gestured dramatically. The guards stiffened. Anticipation rolled through the room.

Thalassa flicked two fingers toward a waiting servant. Guards brought up their heads. Something anticipatory tightened in the air, like the ocean pulling back before a wave hits.

They arrived with military precision.

Nine mermen and one mermaid emerged from different entrances—two from behind veiled archways, three descending the stairs from the terrace above, one rising from a recessed pool without a single splash. They converged without speaking, falling into formation.

Their armor was matte black scaled plating with gold edging, fitted close to the body to allow movement in both water and air. Each carried a trident taller than I was, the prongs flaring. They stood three rows deep, motionless, eyes forward.

Not guards. An execution squad with pageantry.

"The Deep Guard," Thalassa announced.

Pherric's expression curdled. "You wish to make them immortal? Nine more soldiers?"

She answered with a smile that felt like a door closing.

"Oh shit," I whispered to Jonathan. "She's not preparing for a war. She's preparing to win one forever."

"I will not do it," Pherric said flatly.

Goran lifted his sword, but Thalassa held up a hand.

"Ramil?"

He smirked. "I can do it, Thalassa."

Shoving Pherric aside, he began assembling ingredients.

"We can't let him do this," I muttered.

"Finley," Jonathan hissed, gripping my arm. "If you thought the odds were bad before... they've got the Deep Guard."

I shook with rage. "I don't have a choice. If I can take out Ramil before he—"

"Thalassa's mage was also watching him. You'd have to take out both of them. And probably Pherric, too, to stop this."

I clenched my jaw hard.

"We'll escape," Jonathan urged. "Warn the others. Fight them when it's not just you alone in a throne room full of warriors. Now, come on. Let's get out of here."

"No," I snapped. "We have to rescue Pherric."

Jonathan exhaled hard but didn't argue further. Smart of him.

We watched—thirty excruciating minutes—as Ramil and the Atlantean sorcerer reproduced the potion. The Deep Guard drank. Each survived fatal wounds.

Thalassa drank the final potion. No one dared to stab her. She'd seen enough and knew it would work on her as well.

A new army of gods. And an immortal queen.

Thalassa clapped, delighted. "Well done!"

Goran dragged Pherric forward, sword hovering at his gut. "What do we do with this one?"

"Rid me of him," she said lightly, waving him off as if he were an insect.

Ramil stepped in. "Thalassa, we may need him. As a bargaining chip."

She turned, intrigued. "What do you mean?"

Ramil scanned the room. He knew about me. Or sensed. Or suspected.

"I believe Finley is still—"

And then the world split open.

55

The Walls Came Tumbling Down

Finley

A sound—heavy, thunderous—rolled through the palace. The floor shook under our feet. Dust sifted down from the carved ceiling in thin drifts, like ash shaken loose from a dying fire.

"What was that?" Jonathan whispered.

Thalassa spun on a heel. Ramil broke the mindform he was using to try to find me. Even the rail-thin Atlantean mage stiffened as another crack reverberated through the palace—closer this time, deep enough to rattle the columns.

Shouts erupted in the hallways. Goran and the Deep Guard snapped to alert in unison, tridents angling toward the entrance.

The Queen didn't hesitate. With a whirl of silk and authority, she stormed toward the exit, barking commands. "With me!"

The Deep Guard surged after her, ten shadows of war moving as one. The throne-room guards followed, their boots pounding across the marble, weapons drawn. Even Ramil and the pallid sorcerer exchanged a glance and hurried after her, robes snapping in their wake.

In seconds, the dais was empty.

Except for Pherric. And one guard left behind—young, nervous, probably too green to be trusted with anything important. He stared after the departing elites, torn between duty and the instinct to run after his queen. His hand hovered over his weapon, indecisive.

Jonathan took a step toward the throne room, toward Pherric, but I yanked his sleeve. "No. Come with me."

Something surged inside me—hope I didn't want, didn't trust.

We slipped out through a side door, racing down a narrower hall and into a chamber that opened onto a wide balcony. Wind slammed into us, hot and gritty, carrying dust and the unmistakable sound of something enormous breaking.

Across the small bay, the island that held the labyrinth was coming apart.

Shivers ran through the ground beneath the palace. Then the sound hit us: thick, hollow, ancient.

The entire labyrinth was falling.

One wall at first. Then another. Then the entire maze began to collapse in sequence, stone slamming down against stone in rolling detonations that echoed across the water. Each crash sent up a plume of dust that twisted into the sky.

The ground vibrated with every impact. The balcony rail thrummed under my hands. I could feel the power of it.

Jonathan stood beside me, wide-eyed. "What the hell..."

There was no explanation. No spell. No storm. Just destruction, complete and unstoppable. The walls—those impossible, towering walls that had seemed eternal—buckled and folded as if made of sand.

A shockwave rolled across the bay, warm and wet, carrying heavy waves that crashed on the beach of Atlantis.

The labyrinth's perfect symmetry folded in on itself.

When the last wall went down, it was almost quiet. Just a low rumble as things settled. More waves crashed against the island.

Where the labyrinth had stood, there was nothing but ruin: a jagged plain of broken stone and soot. The air was heavy with it, churning in great clouds that drifted over the water and rolled toward us, dimming the sunlight. The wind carried the dust to my face, fine and pointed, and I blinked through it, refusing to turn away.

It took minutes for the haze to thin. The grit swirled, lifted, and began to fall away.

And then, through it all, I saw a figure sitting. Motionless.

He was just a shape at first, dark against the debris. But as the debris cleared, I saw him. Broad shoulders, hair wild and matted with blood, one massive hand gripping something curved and white.

Braylor.

He sat in the wreckage, surrounded by the death of the labyrinth, holding one of the Minotaur's horns. At his feet lay the monster's body, sprawled in defeat—massive and terrifying even in death. Its hide was split open in deep, brutal gashes; its twisted limbs bent at impossible angles, half-buried in dust and rubble. The creature that had hunted us through the dark, that had seemed unstoppable, was still at last.

Braylor looked carved from the same ruin that surrounded him. His shoulders sagged, his skin streaked with dirt and blood, his clothes torn nearly to ribbons. He was breathing, but each rise and fall of his chest cost him something. The horn in his hand trembled because he didn't have the strength to hold it anymore.

The morning light caught on the wreckage behind him. Shattered stone, shattered myth and, for a moment, I couldn't tell where the ruins ended and he began. He'd fought all night. All morning long. He'd given everything. And yet... somehow, impossibly, he was still alive.

My fingers slipped from the railing. My throat caught. "He's alive."

I said it once. Then again, softer.

He was *alive*.

And for the first time in a long time, I felt something bloom in my chest. Something bright and defiant and entirely mine.

"Come on, Braylor," I whispered. "Get up."

I crouched low, voice shaking as I stared down at him. The love of my life, sitting half-dead in the ruins of what used to be the labyrinth. All of the blood covering him hurt my heart.

He had to be beyond exhausted. Bruised and battered didn't even begin to cover it. He looked like the universe had taken a personal grudge against him—which, honestly, it might have.

But motion in the water caught my eye. Atlanteans. They were surfacing all around the island, their heads breaking through the waves in eerie unison. Dozens of them. Maybe hundreds. Word was spreading. The walls had fallen, the labyrinth was gone, and now they were coming up to see who had dared to bring it all down.

And when they found out it was *him*? The soldiers would come next, fast and merciless.

"Get up..." I thought out loud, the words spilling through my teeth—a plea and a command all at once. "Move."

Jonathan's voice broke through my panic. "Where can he go? There's nothing left."

I tore my gaze from Braylor long enough to scan what was left of the island. Shattered stone. Ash dust rising from fissures where the walls had collapsed. The once-magnificent labyrinth had been chewed up and spat out by an earthquake. No, not a quake. This had more to do with the gods. Maybe the maze was designed to fall once the Minotaur was gone?

"Well," I said, squinting through the haze, "if he can walk, and if he thinks about it... he might go through the tunnel we used to get to the island."

Braylor shifted. Barely. But it was enough to make my heart seize. With a great effort, he rose to his feet. He wobbled, caught himself, and for one terrifying moment I thought he'd collapse again. But he stayed upright.

"Good boy," I said, relief flooding through me. "Look around. Try to find the entrance to the tunnel..."

Atlantean soldiers were already climbing up the rocks. They were bugs crawling out of the sea, dozens of them, their tridents or swords catching the glow of the early afternoon sun.

Braylor staggered forward. He turned his head, looking up at Atlantis. At *us*.

I waved my arms, though I doubted he could see me from that distance. I motioned toward the far end of the island. *Come on, Braylor. Please.* Closing my eyes, I focused every ounce of my willpower, projecting the thought:

Walk toward the tunnel. Go to the tunnel.

His body jerked slightly. Something unseen nudged him. But he started walking. Each step was agony. His muscles trembled with effort. But he was on the move.

"He's doing it!" Jonathan exclaimed.

I exhaled a shaky laugh. "Of course he is. He's too stubborn to die."

But my relief was short-lived. More Atlanteans were hitting the beaches now. A tide of bodies, moving fast as they closed in around him. He dropped to his knees, half-buried in rubble, his broad shoulders rising and falling. For one horrible second, I thought they would finish him off.

My gut tumbled. "No," I whispered. "I need to go get him."

Jonathan squinted through the fog. "Finley, he's surrounded. There's no way—"

"He's alive," I cut him off. "He is alive."

"Barely. We need to go before they spot us. We can come back with help."

I shook my head so hard it hurt. "No. I thought he was dead. I'm not leaving him again."

"Finley," Jonathan said quietly, stepping closer. "If we stay, we die here. Pherric's still being held in the throne room. We can save him, get him out, find a ship, regroup—"

"And hope they don't kill Braylor first?" I snapped. My voice came out harsher than I meant. "She got her immortal warriors. She doesn't need any of us."

"We have to do something," Jonathan pleaded.

I turned to him, shaking my head. "No. I'll rescue him. We'll get Pherric and you'll get him out of here."

Jonathan hesitated. I grabbed his sleeve, pulling him along as we left the balcony behind and tore down the corridor.

The throne room was empty. Pherric was still there with his guard.

I snuck around the circular room, using the columns and curtains. Drawing on my stealth training from Kasuma, I snuck up quietly behind the merman. I pulled back on his forehead and let my blade slide across his neck. He crumpled to the floor.

I used my sword to slice through the ropes binding Pherric's hands.

"Where should we go?" Jonathan asked, still gasping.

I shrugged because I had no idea.

Grabbing Pherric's face, I met his eyes. "Are you okay?"

"I am," he said. His voice was steady, but I saw the shake in his fingers.

"Do you remember how to get back to where you landed on the dragon?" He nodded. "Did you see all those ships? That big dock?"

"I did indeed," he said, rubbing his wrists. Pherric grabbed hold of his *Arcanum Libellum* book.

I turned to Jonathan. "He'll show you the way. Can you sail?"

Jonathan gave me a shy grin. "Never sailed sober, but I've done a few booze cruises. I'll figure it out. Put up the sail and turn her into the wind."

"Good enough. Go."

He nodded, then paused. "Please don't go after him. You will be captured and—"

"Don't worry about me," I said, already listening for footsteps. "Head to the opposite side of the island. The east side! We'll meet you there. And... if we don't make it, keep going."

Before they could argue, I was gone.

I ran for the stairwell that led to the dungeon. My footsteps slapped against the stone as I retraced my path: past the cells, through the narrow passage, into the temple room where we found the tunnel entrance.

The tunnel door groaned as I forced it open.

As I leaned into the tunnel, I heard footsteps.

"Braylor!" I shouted.

Dozens of Atlantean soldiers were charging straight toward me through the tunnel, their armor catching the torchlight.

"Not today, Satan," I muttered.

I slammed the door shut. A moment later, the impact of their bodies rattled the frame. I staggered back. My brain was already calculating a dozen doomed options. The door started to slide open.

"Okay. Plan B," I whispered. "Run."

I spun and bolted up the stairs, back into Thalassa's throne room, heart hammering. They hadn't returned yet.

Think, Finley. Think.

Every idea slammed into the same walls. Every shadow felt like teeth. Jonathan's voice jumped into my mind: *We can come back to get Braylor later.*

Later would be too late. And I doubted I'd survive long enough to make "later" happen anyway.

I pushed onto the dais, trying to plan, to think clearly, to—

And then I saw it.

The orb.

Sitting on that pedestal where it always had, just behind the throne. Quiet. Terrifying. Important.

Instant leverage. It *had* to be. I could sense that it meant something to Thalassa.

Without hesitating, I sprinted to the pedestal. The sphere was heavier than it looked—dense, cold, offensive. My fingers tingled the second I touched it and my nerves didn't know how to interpret it. No time to think about that.

I whirled toward the alchemy table. Pherric's bag still sat open, collapsed on its side where he'd been working earlier. I shoved the orb inside, the leather sagging under the weight, and yanked the strap over my shoulder.

There. Something Thalassa cared about. Something she could not afford to lose.

Something that made Braylor's survival non-optional. Maybe. Hopefully.

I'll come back for you, Braylor. I swear it.

I tore across the dais and peeked out of the entrance—and stopped in my tracks.

Thalassa's voice echoed through the hall ahead of me. "...and Finley is dead as well. He was the only survivor."

Another voice—Ramil's—answered, tight and certain. "No. I sensed her earlier. Before the walls fell. She is here, in the palace."

Fuck.

I started into the corridor but held up as a guard sprinted past. I waited until the sound faded.

I needed to work my way to somewhere on the east end of the island. Jonathan and Pherric would come by in a boat. Not that I truly believed they'd pull that off, but...

Sticking to shadows, I made my way through the palace, ducking through empty hallways and sprinting as fast as possible. Twice, I paused as guards passed inches away. Once, I jumped into a storage alcove and waited until some servants passed.

When I reached the outer hall, a soldier rounded the corner and almost collided with me. His eyes widened.

I stepped forward. "Do you know where the bathroom is?"

The soldier hesitated, confusion firing across his face.

That didn't work. "There's a big, giant Fomorian after me! Please help!" I pointed down the hallway.

The fool stepped next to me, staring into the dark corridor. I threw my elbow into the man's jaw. The soldier crumpled, a lifeless puppet.

I pushed open the palace doors and chaos slammed into me.

The city was going crazy. Citizens ran in every direction. A bell rang from the watchtowers. Guards shouted orders no one followed. The collapse of the labyrinth had sent ripples of panic through all of Atlantis.

"Blending in is the order of the day," I mumbled.

The words barely left my mouth before I was running again, my sandals slapping against marble on the palace stairs.

The Atlantean city glowed under a haze of drifting dust, its once-pristine towers muted to shades of ash and pearl. A fine grit hung in the air, layered with the scent of pulverized stone and seawater... the smell of a thousand shattered walls carried on the wind. Bridges arched over canals streaked with silt, their mirrored surfaces clouded and gray.

I tore through the marketplace, past abandoned carts. The area buzzed with shouts and the murmur of fear.

A bell tolled again from one of the high towers, a shuddering sound that made my skin crawl.

I slipped into a side street slick with runoff from the canals. Orders being barked in Atlantean, the clang of weapons, the rhythmic pound of boots. They were coming after me.

To my left, there was a narrow bridge arcing over a canal.

I sprinted onto it. A group of citizens were pressed against the railings, trying to peer toward the bay where the labyrinth island had once stood proud. One of them turned, saw my fiery red hair, and screamed.

Instantly, heads snapped toward me.

The crowd parted in panic as I raced through, knocking over a cart piled with fish. One slimy little sucker slapped against my sandal and I nearly lost my footing.

I ducked beneath a series of archways carved with strange runes that pulsed faintly in the gloom. The air was warmer here, the scent of steam and metal stronger. I'd stumbled into their forge district. Sparks drifted from open windows where smiths had left their work.

There were voices. "There! Stop her!"

A squad of soldiers rounded the corner ahead of me, tridents ready.

I jumped behind a column as a volley of spears and a few tridents flew by.

"Any ideas, Finley?" I asked myself. I peered around the column. "Yeah. Don't die."

I lunged out, swung my sword, and cut into one of the soldiers. I threw my blade up at another and caught him in the chin. I pushed a mermaid soldier hard, flinging her into the canal water.

More were coming. Too many.

My eyes picked up a narrow stairwell spiraling up the side of a building.

I ran. My thighs screamed with every step, but adrenaline kept me going. Halfway up, I slipped. I managed to grab the railing and pull out of my fall.

At the top, I burst onto a terrace overlooking the city. The skyline was breathtaking, even in chaos. Below, canals crisscrossed. I still marveled at the beauty, even though it was trying to kill me.

I crossed the terrace, jumped down onto another rooftop, and kept running, leaping the narrow gaps between buildings.

Soldiers shouted below, tracking me like hellhounds. One of them raised a spear and hurled it upward. It seared past my shoulder and exploded against the wall ahead, showering me in debris.

I reached the edge of the roof and found nothing but open air. The street below was three stories down. I swallowed hard.

At the last second, I spotted a metal staircase. I raced to it and started climbing down.

The noise of pursuit grew louder. Behind me, soldiers spilled from alleyways, weapons at hand.

I ran again, pounding through the narrow lower streets as Atlantean soldiers shouted orders ahead. Iron gates screeched as they dropped into place, sealing off routes one by one. Chains rattled, the clang of metal echoing through the stone corridors. They were closing the city around me, tightening the noose.

I knew I needed to go somewhere they didn't expect. Translation: somewhere stupid.

The sound of pursuit echoed behind me. The city's lower streets funneled into a broad plaza where a great aqueduct loomed: an enormous spine of carved limestone stretching from the palace quarter all the way to the far end of Atlantis.

Water shimmered along its shallow channel, rippling as it carried the tides inland. Beneath it, a web of arches rose high above the ground, forty feet up at least. It was built for moving seawater, but right now, it was my only path out.

A ladder clung to the nearest support column. I scrambled up first, the metal cold and wet under my hands. Below, soldiers poured into the plaza.

I moved along the aqueduct's top, water splashing against my legs. The view from up here was dizzying—Atlantis stretched out in all directions: a vast maze of white roofs and winding streets, cloaked now in drifting dust from the ruined island.

Behind me, more shouts. Everyone was super-shouty.

I risked a glance back. A dozen soldiers were already scaling the ladder, shields strapped across their backs.

A bolt of crossbow fire whizzed past my ear and blew up the stone ahead. I flinched.

The next one grazed my arm, burning hot across the skin. I bit back a scream.

I crossed a narrow junction where the aqueduct split—one branch veering north toward the palace, the other east toward the cliffs. The path ahead was open, a single ribbon of stone bordered by low walls. Wind howled across it, carrying the distant crash of waves.

Ahead of me: the east end of the island. Where Jonathan and Pherric were supposed to meet me. Assuming they had, you know, even made it to a boat and managed to sail it away.

I ran harder. Below, the city moved—crowds surging, soldiers bellowing, banners snapping in the wind. Somewhere a bell tolled again, slower this time, like... the heartbeat of a wounded giant. My mind went to Braylor, but I shook the thought away.

A tremor shivered through the aqueduct beneath my feet. I stopped before taking another step. "What was that?"

I looked down at the aqueduct. The structure was old. The collapse on the smaller island may have weakened it.

Another tremor hit, stronger. Cracks spiderwebbed along the stone, water leaking through.

I tore forward as the aqueduct groaned, a beast waking from sleep. Ahead of me, part of the walkway crumbled into dust, dragging two soldiers down with it. The sound of their screams was lost in the roar of falling stone.

I leapt over open space—and my sandals hit the far side, hard.

I stumbled, rolled to a stop, chest heaving.

The aqueduct narrowed, its guard walls breaking away to open air on both sides. Below, the eastern quarter of Atlantis spread out—rows of whitewashed roofs, narrow streets crowded with people trying to flee the bay. The sea glittered in the distance, deceptively calm.

I was halfway across when a horn blared.

From the plaza behind, a full contingent of soldiers had reached the aqueduct. Scores of them.

Arrows hissed past, a few striking the channel beside me and sending up splashes of water. One hit the low wall inches from my hip.

I reached the next support arch where the aqueduct merged with another channel. Soldiers were racing along the new path. I spotted a pulley system built into the side—thick chains and wooden winches used to lift repair materials. A plan sparked.

I grabbed what had to be a release lever. I shoved my shoulder into the mechanism, and with a grinding roar, the chain tore free. The pulley arm swung out wide and smashed into the side of the aqueduct, breaking the edge stone away.

The first dozen soldiers on the walkway had no chance. The entire section collapsed beneath them, dropping them fifty feet into the square below.

The aqueduct curved gently upward as it neared the island's edge. The wind picked up, whipping through my hair. Ahead, the water channel poured straight into a cistern carved into the cliff face. It was a small reservoir that spilled runoff back into the sea. The stone path narrowed to a thin ledge beside it, barely wide enough for two people.

I could already hear them again. More soldiers were coming. The sound crawled up my spine.

I reached the end of the aqueduct and stopped. There was a small field of tall grass below. Beyond the cliff ahead, the waves crashed far below, flinging white spray high into the air. The sound of it swallowed everything.

I heard the thud of their boots. The Atlanteans rushed around the curve. The aqueduct shuddered beneath them.

I gasped. *It was too many people.*

Then came a deep, cracking sound as the island exhaled. The supports beneath me shifted. I felt it in my teeth.

We were all too heavy on the aged structure.

The next instant, the entire span lurched forward. The stone legs folded, the aqueduct tipping toward the cliffs. The soldiers screamed as gravity seized them. We all dropped with the collapsing structure, clinging to its slick surface as it tilted and dropped.

The world blurred—sky, sea, stone—a violent tumble that seemed to last forever. When the aqueduct finally slammed into the earth below, the impact tore through me. For a moment, all I could hear was the crash of waves and the hiss of dust.

The remains of the aqueduct launched the soldiers high, sending them over the edge of the cliff.

I collapsed, shaking and soaked. Below, the sea churned a murky blue, the water thick with silt and foam—but no Atlanteans surfaced. It wasn't a fatal fall, maybe twenty feet at most, which meant they'd probably survived. And if I jumped, they'd be waiting.

But before I could think, the pounding of new footsteps rose from the other side of the small plain: another wave of soldiers racing toward me through the tall grass.

I drew my sword. "Finley, your good luck has finally run out."

56

Option C

Finley

I held my sword up, sandals slipping in the mud. My lungs burned from the run, my heart from the hopeless math—one of me, maybe fifty of them. And a cliff at my back.

Great tactical positioning, Finley. Ten out of ten.

They could surround me, take their sweet time poking holes in me with those shiny tridents. I'd rather go down swinging than take my chances swimming with the same gilled psychos waiting underwater. So, yeah... ocean escape? Hard pass.

My gaze shot toward the southern horizon, to the edge where the cliff curved. I didn't even know what I was looking for, just that stupid and desperate hope of seeing a sail. Any sail.

The soldiers slowed their charge, spreading into a half circle. Goran—Mr. Seaweed (or Sea Lord) himself—strode out front, smugness practically steaming off him. He raised a hand and his men halted.

"Ah," he said with mock reverence, "what an honor to end the reign of the immortal witch queen."

I leveled my sword at his fishy face. "You talk too much."

He smirked, stepping closer. "This time, I will remove your head and feed it to Zeranthyl."

"And you're *still* talking," I shot back, then mentally kicked myself. Maybe shut up for once, Finley. Maybe stall. "Wait. Wait! You can't kill me. You *need* me."

Goran's eyes glinted. He danced just out of reach as I jabbed forward. "We no longer need you, dragonwitch. Your mage gave us the magic elixir. I myself cannot be killed."

My stomach tightened. Pherric and Jonathan. Did they have them?

"Well, you can't make more," I said coolly, "He's already escaped with the formula. You lost him."

He waved me off as if I were background noise. "He is no longer important. We can take our time. Where can he go?" They didn't have Jonathan or Pherric yet.

The soldiers closed in, the ring tightening one deliberate step at a time. My pulse thudded louder than their boots.

Goran tilted his head, smirking. "Do you wish to surrender—or die here in the dirt?"

I reached into the bag, pulling out the orb. I held it up.

Goran took a step back, his eyes wide. Fear enveloped him. *I knew it*! The orb was important to them.

"Stay back!" I yelled. "Or I swear to your gods, I will... smash this thing to pieces!"

He dropped his sword, holding his hands out.

"Do not... do that."

I stole a glance at the edge of the cliff.

"Listen, do me a favor. Let Thalassa know that if anything, and I mean anything, happens to Braylor, then this orb will be destroyed. You got that?"

"What?"

I talked very slowly for the idiot. "Do you understand what I just said?"

"Uh, y-yes..."

"So, what were my choices again?" I teased. "Surrender or die here in the dirt? Hmm."

"Finley..."

I sighed, pretending to consider. "I think I'll go with... option C."

I stuffed the orb back in the bag.

"Option C? I do not know—"

"*Jump!*"

I sprinted to the cliff's edge. The soldiers shouted, tridents flashing as they gave chase. The ground vanished beneath my feet. For a heartbeat, I was flying—arms flailing, hair whipping around my face—before a white sail filled my vision.

I hit the deck hard, sandals slapping wood. The impact knocked the air from my lungs as I rolled into the railing, white light bursting behind my eyes.

Pherric and Jonathan swarmed me, pulling me up from the deck. Jonathan thrust a waterskin at me; I drank half of it and spilled the rest down my barely-there clothing. Smooth.

The ship was small—maybe twenty feet long, maybe ten across—a baby boat with one stubborn sail that looked about as confident as I felt. And I quickly realized absolutely no one was paying attention to the fact that the boat was drifting sideways... straight toward the rocks.

"Fantastic," I muttered, pushing myself upright. "I survive the fall just to die in the world's slowest crash."

I stumbled to the stern, grabbed the rudder, and wrestled it hard to the side. The hull groaned in protest, the sail snapped, and the boat swung wide of the cliff face, skimming the foam below. My heart didn't start again until the rocks slid safely past.

When I looked up, Goran was still on the cliff above, sword lowered, face twisted in fury. He shoved one of his soldiers and shouted something I couldn't hear over the wind. I smiled sweetly and gave him a cheerful one-finger salute.

He went rigid, jaw tight, then spun and stormed away.

"Yeah, that's what I thought," I said, hands still shaking on the rudder.

Pherric dug into his worn leather satchel and pulled free a cluster of vials, the glass clinking together like nervous teeth. He handed one to me.

"Drink this," he said, giving me that unmistakable fatherly *don't argue with me* look.

I downed it. The liquid burned sliding down my throat, leaving warmth in its wake.

Pherric passed me a torn chunk of bread. "This was all I could steal on the way out."

I tried to thank him, but my mouth was full, and it came out as something between a grunt and a sigh.

"Uh... Finley?" Jonathan's voice cracked.

I turned and locked up. Webbed fingers were curling over the ship's railing.

I leapt back from the rudder. "Aim us away from Atlantis!"

Jonathan took my place, jerking the tiller as the Atlantean hauled himself over the edge. I swung my sword in one motion; he ducked, quick as a serpent, and lunged—snagging the green fabric at my waist. I rammed my elbow into his jaw. Bone cracked. He staggered, and I followed with a slash across his throat. His eyes went glassy as he gurgled and fell back into the sea.

I scanned the dark water—activity everywhere. I saw heads bobbing in the water, eyes glowering, and bodies that arched through the waves. We weren't free. Not even close.

A shriek split the air. Another Atlantean had Jonathan by the shoulders, dragging him toward the stern. I lunged, drove my blade down hard. She slipped away before I hit bone, smiling as she slid under the surface.

"You've got to help, Pherric!" I shouted.

"You know I cannot kill someone, Finley."

"That's not true!" I sprinted past him, slicing at a soldier climbing over the bow. "You stabbed that guy outside the wall at Shangri-La!"

"I did not," he said evenly.

"You did too!" I drove my sword through the Atlantean's side. "You said 'sometimes violence is necessary' or something!"

"I stabbed him in the thigh. I did not kill the man."

Two more attackers vaulted the railing, one on each side. I slashed at one, kicked the other straight in the gills. She collapsed against the deck with a hiss. I jumped at her and shoved her back into the water. I turned to face the remaining merman, and steel clashed against steel.

The wind filled the sail, and the boat surged forward, waves roaring around us.

A wall of seawater crashed over me, drenching me—and suddenly, energy flooded every vein. The world sharpened. My muscles hummed. I slammed the pommel of my sword into his chin, kneed his gill, and booted him clean overboard.

"What the hell was in that potion? Jesus-fucking-Christ, I feel *great!*"

Pherric chuckled without looking up. "A new elixir I have been testing. Something Cira would have appreciated. Thought it might be a potion to carry for... emergencies."

"My heart's trying to escape my chest! I think you might've invented cocaine!"

"That is a flaw I have not eliminated."

"Finley!" Jonathan shouted. Another Atlantean had him by the collar. I swear I *flew* across the deck. My sword punched through the creature's neck, spraying blood into the wind.

Atlantis shrank behind us, swallowed by mist and distance. We were flying across the waves.

"Try to breathe deeply. Slow and even," said Pherric, still calm as ever.

"That's easy for you to say!" I snapped, darting to the railing where more webbed hands reached up. I hacked one away, then another, stabbing down until blood splattered across my face and deck alike.

I laughed—loud, wild, maybe even a little unhinged. The sea itself seemed to pulse with me.

Eventually, the attacks slowed. One more dead. Another few nursing their wounds. Then everything stopped. I stood there panting, scanning the water for another shadow.

"Well, you are quite the sight," said Pherric, arms crossed and staring me up and down.

I looked at myself. I was drenched in seawater, sweat, and streaks of blood. My hands shook, but whether from the drug or exhaustion, I couldn't tell.

"Are they done?" Jonathan asked from the rudder, eyes locked on the sea behind him.

Pherric stepped beside me and pointed toward the horizon. "They have another plan of attack."

Two massive ships were breaking away from Atlantis, their black sails swelling as they turned toward us.

I swallowed hard. "You got any more of that stuff?"

57

What Waits Beyond the Mist

Jonathan

I sat at the till, steering in utter disbelief. *Flabbergasted... that was the word my father would've used. But it barely scratched the surface. These people were something else.

Death was still on our heels. Two black-sailed ships were cutting through the water behind us. But somehow, Finley and Pherric had pulled off the impossible. They got me out of Atlantis. My heart was still pounding. It hadn't gotten the message we were safe, and my hands shook on the rudder, even though I hadn't done a single thing to earn the adrenaline.

I felt small. Insignificant. Useless, even. Sure, I'd helped launch Finley and myself across the bay, but let's be honest, she probably could've swum across and made it work. While she was fighting off soldiers like some kind of myth come to life, I sat there frozen and terrified. And she did it all while *laughing* with Pherric the whole time. Laughing. How does someone do that?

She caught me watching and gave a small nod, that half-smirk of hers that somehow said *you're fine, rookie.* And Pherric? He couldn't have been more than a few years older than me, yet carried himself as a man who'd lived a lifetime already.

Then the guilt crept in. I'd come so close to poisoning Finley, and she'd risked everything to protect me anyway. She's terrifying and magnetic all at once—funny, feral, fierce, and more loyal than anyone I've ever known. And me? I'm just the stranger she saved. The one still trying to figure out if I deserved to be on the boat at all.

Spray hit my face again, the taste of salt sticking to my tongue. The waves were growing larger the farther we sailed from the island. The tiller quivered under my hands. Every muscle in my arms burned, but I couldn't let go.

Behind us the Atlantean ships clawed through the chop. They were larger, faster, and relentless. Their sails were storm clouds given shape, swelling with every gust. Our single canvas flapped and fought the wind, the little boat straining to keep going.

"They're closing," I said, though no one needed the reminder.

Finley crouched near the bow, braced wide as the deck pitched. Her red hair stuck to her neck, soaked through, but her eyes were fierce and calculating. "Is there anything we can do?" she asked. "Any way to go faster?"

I looked around at our boat. Except for us, it was bare. Nothing to cast over the side to lighten us up.

"I don't think so," I offered weakly. If she wanted to throw me overboard, I would not have been surprised.

Pherric, standing mid-deck with one hand gripping the mast, peered east. The light there was dying. A wall of gray swallowed the horizon, dragging mist and shadow with it.

"A storm is forming fast," he said. Calm. Always calm. "Too fast."

Finley turned. "Good. Let it come faster."

"You would rather us drown?" asked Pherric.

"I'd rather us not get boarded."

That seemed to be Finley: the kind of person who'd rather fight the forces of nature than men.

"What happens when we can't see?" I asked. "Now that Atlantis is gone, I've got nothing to go on. But when we go into a storm... I don't know. Anyone know how to navigate a boat in the open sea?"

Pherric's mouth twitched. He exchanged a hopeless look with Finley. "We do not."

We continued on, and I tried to keep the boat pointed in the same direction. From the maps I'd seen, I knew Atlantis was due south of Cíbola. While I still had sunlight overhead, I attempted to keep us on a northerly line.

The stormfront was close enough now that the air carried its scent—wet iron, ozone, and something that made my skin prickle, like the moment before a struck match flares. The sea ahead turned darker, flecked with ghost-gray mist that rolled low across the waves.

Finley, instantly next to me, clapped my shoulder. "Head for it."

I jumped at how quickly she moved. Then her words hit me.

"Head *into* it?"

"Unless you've got a better plan than 'die slower,'" she said, moving toward the sail.

Pherric joined her, pulling ropes with sure hands, dragging down the canvas. "Half-sail," he said. "Or the first squall will topple us over or tear us to pieces."

The boom groaned as they tied it down. The smaller sail eased the strain, though the boat still rocked violently with every gust.

I adjusted the tiller, angling us east toward the black wall. The Atlanteans didn't hesitate. I watched as both ships slowly veered after us, their sails billowing as they turned into the wind.

"Keep her steady!" Pherric shouted over the wind.

"I'm trying!"

The tiller jerked against me, slippery in my hands. Finley crouched near my shoulder, watching the horizon, reading something I couldn't.

"A friend told me to feel the wind," she said. "Not with your eyes. With your skin. That'll tell you what the sail wants."

"What *I* want is to not die."

She grinned. "That's a start."

We eventually drove headlong into the darkness. First, we hit the mist and our world shrank. The sea and sky became one gray blur. Sound changed—muffled, dampened. The rhythmic slap of waves turned into a hollow thud, but the breeze continued to waft into my ear. I could no longer see the Atlanteans behind us.

It was almost peaceful. Then the first gust hit.

The boom swung hard and low. I backed away instinctively as it whooshed past my head. Finley caught it with a curse, retying the line before it could break loose again. The sea sprayed across the deck, lashing us.

The rain came next. Sudden, heavy, cold. It flattened the mist into sheets and made the wood at our feet slippery as glass. Our lone sail strained against its knots. Pherric pulled another line taut, water streaming off his robe.

"Watch your angle!" he barked. "You will lose the wind!"

I wrestled the tiller along with the wave's push. My hands hurt and my arms shook. I felt the current fighting me, the boat trying to spin, to show its side to the storm.

"Hold her nose to it!" Finley called. "Feel for the swell! Ride it!"

"I *am*!"

The wind screamed. Lightning flashed inside the fog, a tight blue line through the gray. Thunder rolled, slow and massive. For a moment the sea glowed under the flash, every wave tipped in silver light, the next crest towering like a moving wall.

The boat rose. And dropped. Water slammed across the deck, filling my boots. My teeth chattered together.

The sea had a rhythm. Angry, uneven, but still a rhythm. I tried to find it, to steer not against the storm but *with* it.

Gradually, the tiller's fighting became something else. Resistance, but not rebellion. We reached an understanding.

Finley crouched near me, one hand on the side, hair plastered to her cheek. "That's it," she said, barely audible over the wind. "You're getting it."

"We still lost?"

"Oh, absolutely," she said, smiling through the rain. "But at least we're stylish about it."

We sailed on silently for another twenty minutes or so, but it felt like hours.

Pherric pointed ahead. "Mist's thickening. Stay on this line."

Lightning struck again. Farther away this time. The glow briefly revealed something far in the distance, high and uneven.

"Is that—?"

"Land?" Finley squinted. "Could be a bluff. Could be more clouds."

"Or we're circling back toward the Atlanteans," I muttered.

"No," Pherric said. "Wind has shifted north. We are holding course."

He said it with such quiet certainty I almost believed him.

Several minutes later, the storm intensified again. The waves reared. The sail snapped and flapped, begging for mercy. The boat pitched so fiercely that Finley had to grab the side to stay upright.

"Ease that line!" she yelled.

Pherric grimaced at her. "We will lose the wind!"

"Better that than our sail!"

He let the rope slip a few centimeters, and the boat righted enough to breathe again. Another flash showed the sea behind us. Empty. No black sails. No Atlanteans. Just the writhing gray of the storm.

"They can't follow in this," Finley said, half laughing, half panting. "We did it."

"Or they sank," I said hopefully.

"That would work, too. But... I doubt it. They've got a lot more experience than we do."

We sailed blind for hours. No sun, no shadows, no sense of time. Only wind, waves, and the occasional shout between the three of us to adjust course or a line. The world was nothing but gray and motion.

At some point, the thunder softened. The rain became drizzle and the mist lightened. My arms trembled from fatigue.

Pherric was a statue, scanning the horizon that was slowly, mercifully returning. "Do you see anything?" he asked quietly.

Finley frowned. "Nothing."

"We should return to a northern course," he said. "And hope our good fortune holds."

Finley grinned. "For once, I didn't bring any bad luck to a ship! Or, well, a boat."

I exhaled a shaky laugh. The guilt that had been sitting in my chest—the near poisoning, the cowardice, the uselessness—didn't vanish, but it shifted, lighter somehow. The sea had taken a share of it.

Ahead, the fog thinned further. A darker line broke the horizon, uneven and solid.

"Jonathan," Finley whispered. "I think you did it. Got us through. Keep us headed that way." She pointed toward the front of our vessel.

I nodded and steered us north. The little boat groaned but kept sailing along. Behind us, the storm growled in retreat. The black sails were gone. Ahead, the faint promise of shore waited —

—until the shapes emerged.

At first, I thought it was a coastline breaking apart in the haze. Then the lines sharpened. Rigid. Vertical. Moving.

"Pherric," I said quietly. "Tell me that's land."

He didn't answer right away. He leaned forward, squinting through the haze. His knuckles whitened around the mast. "Not land," he said at last. "Ships."

My stomach turned to lead.

"Atlantis?" Finley asked.

"I cannot tell."

Several massive silhouettes loomed out of the fog, side by side. Their sails hung half-caught, dark against the lightening sky. I felt the air change—thinner, expectant, deadly.

"They found us," I whispered.

"Not possible," Finley muttered, though her hand drifted to the sword at her waist.

One angled slightly toward us. Sails caught a white shaft of light, and for a moment my chest clenched.

We must have circled around. And there was no where to run.

58

Damn, Girl...

Finley

The mist had a mind of its own, sliding across the water in ribbons that licked the hull and then re-formed, thicker. I drew my sword and held it low.

The gray stretched endless ahead. Nothing moved but the water slapping the boards and the faint roll of thunder behind us. Jonathan's breath came quick and shallow; the tiller creaked under his grip. Pherric stood by the mast with that infuriating calm he wears whenever I'm about to make a terrible choice.

If they wanted a fight, I'd give them one.

A shadow flickered through the fog—a shape, then a flutter. Cloth catching wind.

A flag.

For a heartbeat it looked black, the kind of color that means no mercy. The storm's dying light made it worse, painting everything in dark shadows.

Then the mist shifted, and the flag border gleamed royal blue. Not ocean blue. Irkallan blue.

My hand loosened on the sword as recognition rooted me. The fear slid away, replaced by something heavier. Familiar and inevitable.

Heartbeat settling. Purpose returning. Irkalla's colors. My colors.

Pherric's voice came quiet and certain. "Irkallan."

I nodded once, eyes fixed ahead. "Yep."

Jonathan's voice wavered behind me. "Irkallan? Who—"

"Mine," I said.

I slid the sword back into my makeshift belt. A useless strand of wet hair had welded itself to my cheek; I tucked it behind my ear and straightened. The wind tested my balance, wild and insistent and salty-wet, tugging at my clothes to see if I'd lean. I didn't.

"That would be my navy," I said.

He blinked, still clutching the tiller. "You have a navy?"

"Small one," Pherric answered for me, dry as ever. "Only three ships."

The shapes emerged. Sleek hulls with their flared prows, sails trimmed tight against the wind, ropes neat as a drum. Lanterns sparked alight one by one across the decks, cascades of gold that softened the edges of everything. The glow traveled across the water and climbed our boat. The storm's color had been drained out of the world, and my ships had brought it back.

They turned slightly and floated alongside.

"Bring her in slow," Pherric called, and Jonathan obeyed. The tiller groaned. Our boat angled obediently toward the nearest hull. Voices began to carry across the gap: clipped commands, a laugh too loud, a curse, the comforting chaos of competent people doing what they've trained to do.

I stayed at the bow and let the wind pull at my hair again. The storm behind us lost interest at last and wandered away in grumbles. And my people had found me.

"Dat you, dragon demon?" came a shout from the deck above, rough and delighted. "Uh, yer highfulness, I meants to say."

Melcente. The grin hit me before the name did.

"Yes, captain!" I yelled, leaning into the sound. "It's me!"

"Damn," she said, not exactly happy with what the universe had brought her.

Pherric laughed, an actual honest sound from a man who mostly communicates in disapproval, and clapped my back so hard I rocked forward.

A crewman unrolled a rope ladder. It slapped the hull twice, then stuck, and I climbed without grace. The distance up was nothing, but I felt every rung was a small victory.

When I pulled myself onto the *Aegiros*, the deck felt as solid as a promise. The swell moved under us and the rigging sang and for the first time since the Atlanteans' door slammed behind me, my body stopped bracing for a blow.

That lasted three seconds.

It didn't hit me until I stood fully upright and everyone looked at me that I looked... awful. Soaked. Blood-streaked. Wearing the Atlantean outfit I'd thrown on in that cursed little house that left little to the imagination. I must've turned fifteen shades of red. Queen of Irkalla: half-drowned, half-dressed, wholly stubborn.

The deck went quiet in that respectful way I hate. Then knees bent up and down the line in a wave as almost everyone bowed. Everyone except Melcente, who gave me a slight nod with an expression that landed somewhere between smug pride and *you're a cursed woman who's going to get me killed.*

"How are ya?" Melcente asked, looking off at the water. We were just two sailors watching a simurgh flying around.

"Well, I'm exhausted. My head's pounding, my ribs ache, and I can't tell if my hands are still shaking from fear, cold, or the weird drug Pherric gave me. But I'm—"

"Imma stop you there. I was tryin' ta be nice. Didn't know it'd become a whole... thing."

I hugged her, because the world was tolerable again and she was in it. She made a strangled sound and tried to squirm out of my arms.

"Agh! Disgustin'!" she cried, pushing me back and wiping at the mess on her jacket with two fingers.

Footsteps behind us. Sandulf. He had the look of a man trying not to smile too soon. But when he got closer, a new reality sunk in and the smile died. He bowed in a fluid, perfect line, and before I could reach him, he dropped to a knee.

"Forgive me, your highness."

"For what?"

He stayed down, eyes locked on the deck. "I failed in my duties. I allowed for your capture by the Atlanteans. I can no longer act as your knight commander."

Something in me flared, protective and irritated. But fond. I hooked a hand under his big shoulder and hauled him up. I stared up at his handsome face.

"Stop trying to quit on me, Sandy. There was nothing you could have done."

"But I—"

"Ah! Nothing. You hear me? I brought this on myself, dragging you all down here. This was my fault entirely. You got that?!"

He blinked hard. Tears collected at the lower lashes and made his eyes bright as polished amber. "Yes, your highness."

For a heartbeat I let myself breathe. Deck under my sandals. Salt on my lips. Pherric counting heads, Jonathan being checked out by a crewman. Alive. We were alive.

And then the shape of what's missing slammed into me so hard I swayed. Braylor.

I saw it all at once, bright and unbearable—the last glimpse of him on the island, Atlantean weapons flashing as they surrounded him. I had run. No. I had survived. I chose the only path that didn't end in my capture. But the difference felt academic and ugly when there's an empty space where he should've been.

My insides went cold. The fear that kept me moving was gone. Guilt tried to braid itself around my guts; I cut it off with a hiss. Don't spiral. Not now. He is not a lesson. He is a person. He is my person.

I lurched to the rail before the thought finished forming. The sea below clawed at the hull. Atlantis lurked behind the gray clouds. Somewhere in that glittering city, they had him. They thought they could keep him.

No.

All the excuses line up: we're outnumbered, we need to regroup. Be reasonable, your highness. Reason has never once dragged someone back from a cell.

I gripped the rail until my knuckles ached. This ship answered to me.

"Pherric!" My voice cracked across the deck. He turned, already anticipating orders that point toward danger.

I jabbed a finger toward the specter of Atlantis.

"We have to go get him," I said, and there was no room in me for debate, only air and fire and a single, fixed star. "Now."

"Finley..."

"What? She has Braylor." It wasn't a shout. It was clean and cutting.

The nearest sailors went still as statues pretending to fiddle with lines. Several soldiers stopped pretending altogether and openly watched us. Great. An audience. I hate audiences when I haven't rehearsed.

Pherric spread both hands in that practiced way that makes men feel like they're being soothing but women feel like they're being manipulated. "I understand, your highness."

"But? There's a but coming, right?"

He met my gaze without flinching. "What is your plan? Three ships and a few hundred soldiers against the entire island of Atlantis... and their entire fleet? An island which may or may not even be found, if we go looking?"

I snarled, absolutely did the foot stomp, and folded my arms. I was every petulant princess in every song I've ever made fun of. "Why do you have to ruin everything?"

"I completely understand and I do agree with you. Something must be done, but—"

The sentence ended in a new sound. A deep, rhythmic thumping that made the canvas tremble and the rigging hum. It wasn't the storm or the sea. It was the beat of something enormous carving the air into order.

The whoosh came down in a wave that rattled the ropes against the mast.

The unmistakable arrival of a dragon.

"Shit! Zeranthyl!" I screamed.

Pherric threw his hands up, backing away. "What?!"

"Thalassa's purple dragon! The one that brought you to Atlantis!"

The word slammed through the crew faster than a bell. *Dragon.* People behaved exactly as people do when they hear "fire" in a theater: an immediate, chaotic scattering. Men and women sprinted for whatever cover a ship can provide: coils of rope, barrels, the brief mercy of a mast. A dozen directions at once. Someone tripped. Someone else hauled them up by the collar without looking.

I ran to the rail. Pherric shouted my name. "Finley!"

"No!" I turned, pointing at the fog that now moved. "It's okay!"

Big Red burst through the gray. She was all muscle and leather and fire-gold eyes, the ridges along her spine glossy with rainwater. Two riders clung low to her back. She checked herself with a thunder-loud beat of wings and hovered for a heartbeat over the narrow world of deck and rigging. There was nowhere to land. No stretch of deck would hold her weight. The taut lines a delicate prison cage.

She inverted cleanly, a lazy show-off of a flip that sent her riders sliding free. They dropped straight down and vanished into the sea with two heavy slaps that just about threw spray up to the railing. Big Red snapped up, red membrane flashing, beat downward once more, roared loudly, and pulled altitude until the low clouds swallowed her.

A green dragon flew in after her—smaller, fast as a thrown knife. One rider. She leaned into a curve over the mast and at the apex she was suddenly not on the saddle anymore. It was Kasuma! She leapt off the dragon's wing and reached a rope. Her hands found it without looking. Momentum swung her in toward the sail, where she snagged a second line, braced her thin black boots, and slid the last distance to the deck like she was stealing home.

Kasuma landed light and set her feet as if she had always belonged there.

"Wow," I said, stepping up as she bowed her head with the kind of precise respect that included amusement. "You know how to make an entrance."

"And you..." she said, looking me up and down with a slow assessment that took in the wounds, the too-bold Atlantean fabric. "...know how to stay alive."

"I try. So, who are the two deep sea divers you brought with you?"

She held out her hand, and we moved toward the rail together.

The first woman who climbed onboard was all straight lines and purpose—gorgeous with that spare, unornamented beauty some warriors carry without trying. Dark leather clung to her in soaked sheets; dark hair and eyes; a face that would look serene if she weren't clearly deciding three ways to kill anyone who threatened her. She was light-skinned, slightly taller than me, trim, taut, fierce even as water dripped from her lashes. She reminded me of Gunnr.

I silently hoped we were on the same side because I did not have the energy for that problem today.

The next head that emerged was dark curls and stubbornness. She was dark skinned and slightly shorter than me, which was its own small surprise—most Hominans tower over me on principle. She struggled over the rail, coughing water, blinking hard to clear her eyes—and Jonathan quickly jumped in. He was there, hands on her shoulders, hugging her like he'd been drowning and she was air.

Kasuma gestured to the warrior woman. "This is Kinnat."

I nodded and smiled. Her face went white so fast I thought she might topple.

"Is this... the queen?"

"This is Finley Maguire, Queen of Irkalla."

The poor girl tried in vain to wipe water off her face with her wet fingers. She smoothed her soaked hair back in a gesture so humble it tugged at me. She bowed deeply. "Your highness."

Kasuma motioned for the other woman to join us. "And this is someone you already know."

"I do?"

She lifted her thick, dripping curls off her face and the world did that thing where it narrows and widens at the same time. My body knew before my brain did. The breath I took was not ladylike. Or gentle.

"*Genevieve?* Genevieve!"

I rushed at her. She backed away, panic bright in her eyes, and then recognition flared and burned clean through it.

"Finley?"

"Yes!" I got my arms around her and crushed her to me. I did not care that I was staining her with blood or that she was soaking through me or that half my crew was now looking pointedly anywhere else. The relief was physical, and something heavy levered off my chest.

"Finley," she said again, and then it hit her all at once. "Finley!" She stepped back and we stared at each other, both grinning, both trying not to cry, both failing. I took her in, the defined line of her cheekbones, the defiant set of her mouth, the thousand tiny changes that make time a thief and a gift.

I was so utterly, completely shocked to see my best friend standing not only on the *Aegiros* but on the planet. She wasn't supposed to be here. Not in *my* nightmare-turned-home.

Genevieve straightened, and it hit me how different she looked. She'd always been gorgeous—annoyingly so—but now she was something else. Beyond fierce. A survivor. The kind of strong that doesn't come from gym memberships and green smoothies, but from bleeding and not dying. Her eyes told me everything I didn't want to know. She'd fought. She'd seen things. She'd *lost.*

There were new lines around her mouth, her eyes, faint but sharp enough to cut me open. And somehow, she looked ten years older—the world had aged her faster just to keep up with the pain. It made me grab her again, harder this time, as I tried to squeeze the old her back into existence.

"How are you *here*?!" I screamed.

"I got no idea. But here I am," she said into my shoulder, her voice soft and frayed at the edges. Then she pulled back to look me over. "Let me see you."

Her gaze swept over my mess of scars, blood, and attitude. The disappointment stung, but there was pity there too. Recognition. "Damn, girl," she said, a slow grin tugging at her lips. "You are one badass mother now!

"And you! You look like you eat monsters for breakfast now. With protein powder."

"Only on leg day," she said. "You look... alive. Which was not on my bingo card."

"Same," I said. "Pretty sure I died at least once getting here!" I let out a laugh.

She poked a finger into my shoulder. "Since when do *you* stand like that? You've got a whole 'don't try me' thing going on, girl!"

I turned to glare at Jonathan. "I grew into my villain arc," I said. "You missed it."

Jonathan stared at deck, kicking rocks and feeling guilty.

She snorted. "Figures. You get get kidnapped, missing for several damn years, and become terrifying."

Her friend, Kinnat, was giving me the serious side eye. For some reason.

We were talking over each other now, words tumbling out.

"Oh, my god, everyone must've been so worried—"

"—no, wait, what the hell are you wearing—?"

"—well, do you remember that time—"

"—you owe me a coffee, by the way—"

"—WITH OAT MILK," we shouted in unison.

We froze in place.

Then lost it.

"Holy shit," she laughed. "You're still impossible."

"And you're still late," I said. "You literally missed my reign of terror." I shot Jonathan another look. I was never going to let him live down trying to kill me. Ever.

"I can't believe you're a queen!"

"I can't believe *you* survived this place. Well, I can."

"What the hell happened to us?!"

I laughed; awkward, broken, but real.

I wanted to sit down, right there on the spot, and trade every horror story and every victory, cry, scream, *laugh.* But—

"Finley?" Pherric's voice cut through the moment. Because.... yeah.

I rolled my eyes. "What now?"
"We have work to do."
Dammit.

59

Love and Other Resurrections

Genevieve

I could not get over it. Finley was there. Alive. Standing in front of me, dripping seawater and blood, looking like she'd fought her way through hell and laughed at the gatekeeper on the way out. I wanted to throw every word I'd ever held back at her feet—every story, every sleepless night, every stupid, beautiful memory we'd left unfinished. I wanted to hear her voice tell me what madness she'd survived, what impossible things she'd done this time.

Finley squeezed my hand and started to move across the deck, still holding on like she always did when she didn't want to say goodbye.

"Don't worry," she said with a new grin that could command armies. "We'll catch up. I promise."

I believed her. Of course I did. We'd rushed here to save her—to save _Pherric_, even—and somehow she'd managed to save herself and everyone else in the process. She seemed unstoppable. But to me, she wasn't a queen. She was Finley Maguire. My best friend.

She was always a bit shy, introverted, but funny as fuck. She was beautiful but had no idea. And now she was a queen?

I watched her argue with Pherric. Finley, who used to hide in hoodies and carry softness she apologized for, was lean and strong now, all clean lines and quiet strength. The stolen Atlantean fabric didn't leave much to guess at; scars crossed her like a map of places she'd fought, and she didn't flinch at being seen. Her voice stayed low as she pushed back on Pherric, but the people on the ship shifted toward her anyway, drawn by the certainty in her eyes. This was new, a steadiness she never owned in Manhattan, and it fit her better than any crown.

A blur tugged at the edge of my vision. Kinnat stood off to the side, arms crossed so tightly she seemed to hold herself together. She turned her gaze from me to follow Finley—harsh, wounded, almost accusing. Finley had stolen something sacred. I watched the fire in her eyes falter; her shoulders sagged, and she looked away, blinking fast.

And right then I knew. She wasn't angry. She was *hurt.* Jealous. Which could only mean one thing...

When she looked back up toward Finley, there were tears trembling on her lashes.

Oh.

Oh no.

"Kinnat," I said, before I could talk myself out of it.

She flinched at the sound of her name. "Genevieve," she replied quietly, eyes fixed beyond me.

"Can you—" My mouth kept moving. "Can you come here? Please."

She hesitated, then crossed the deck toward me, every step careful, braced. As if she expected this to hurt.

I didn't give myself time to think. "I need to say something, and I'm probably going to say it badly, so please... don't stop me."

Her brow furrowed. "Gen—"

"I know this isn't the moment. I know everything's chaos and Finley's back and this world is nuts. Sure, you drive me crazy and I know I'm on your last nerve. But I keep thinking you're going to leave at some point, and I'm pretending I'm fine with that. But I'm not. I like you. Kinnat, I really do. And I don't mean grateful-like-you, or you're my best friend, I mean—"

I was still talking when her hands came up, firm and decisive, cupping my face.

Then she kissed me.

Not tentative. Not asking. She kissed me as if she'd reached a conclusion and was done waiting for permission.

My thoughts vanished. The deck, the sea, all the people around us, everything. Just gone. There was only her mouth, warm and sure, and the way she exhaled like she'd been holding that breath for years.

When she pulled back, her forehead rested against mine.

"You talk too much," she murmured, voice unsteady.

I laughed, breathless and shocked. "You kissed me."

"Yes." Her thumbs brushed my jaw. "Because if I let you finish, I would have lost my will."

I swallowed. "You... feel something too?"

Her eyes softened, something old and lonely moving beneath the surface. "I have always known I was not like the other women around me," she said quietly. "I did not wish for a mate. Well, not a male one. And because of that, I know there is something wrong with me." Tears rained down her cheeks. "So, I assumed I was meant to live in this world alone. And I accepted that. I would serve, protect, endure... and that would be enough. This is why I push you away. I could not let myself believe an amazing one such as you would truly care for me. In that way."

"Oh, there is nothing wrong with you! At all." I stopped trying to fight off the tears.

She inspected my face. "I am not sure of that. But when you arrived, loud and fragile. Impossible." A small, wry smile. "And I found myself wanting a thing I had never allowed myself to want."

My chest ached. "Kinnat..."

She kissed me once more, gentler this time. "I am female. And I did not know you could... or would choose me."

"I am choosing you," I said without hesitation.

Behind us, someone cleared their throat—badly.

"Oh my god," Finley said. "Did I just interrupt something amazing?"

I turned, still holding Kinnat's hand. My heart felt too big for my ribs.

"Finley," I said, smiling so hard it hurt. "This is Kinnat."

Finley tilted her head. "I'm aware," she said, half-smiling. "We just met when you came onboard."

"No," I said, shaking my head. My hand tightened on Kinnat's. My voice broke somewhere between terror and joy. "I mean... I want you to meet *my love*. And I-I don't know for sure, if she feels as much as... the same way about me, but I-I'm crazy about her."

I reached up, cupped the back of her neck, and pulled her down for another kiss.

Finley clapped her hands and practically bounced. "I'm so happy for you!" She turned to Kinnat with delighted emphasis. "And for *you* too! God, I *love* that!"

I laughed through tears I couldn't stop. Kinnat's forehead pressed against mine again.

Finally, I broke away and turned to Finley, cheeks burning, heart still beating out of rhythm. "Sorry to interrupt," I said, half-laughing, half-weeping.

Finley waved a hand, her grin wide and wild. "Oh, for *that?!* Any goddamn time!"

She caught my hand again, squeezed once—firm, reassuring—and then, with a grin toward Kinnat that managed to be both queenly and conspiratorial, she patted her shoulder and turned back to Pherric. Nothing in the world could surprise her anymore.

But she looked back once, over her shoulder. And the pride in her eyes... that was the kind that could light an empire.

I held Kinnat's hand, my heart still fluttering from everything that had just happened, and wanted to steal her away to some quiet corner of the ship—to fall even harder for her where no one could see.

"Wait," Finley called.

We turned as she strode toward us, sea wind whipping her hair. She caught both our hands, her grin bright and breathless. "I know you two probably have so much to talk about, but... I don't want to exclude you. I'd love it if you'd join us. We've got to rescue *my* love, and I could use your help. But I know you've been through a lot, and I'd understand if you didn't want to—"

Kinnat squeezed my hand. "We are at your service, your highness."

I looked up at her—so steady, so sure—and I could not possibly love her more than in that moment. "Yes, Fin. We're here for you. Anything we can do."

"Come with me," Finley said, tugging us back toward her circle.

Kasuma, Pherric, and Jonathan greeted us with brief smiles and curt nods. The air around them thrummed with tension.

"So," Pherric said, squaring his shoulders, eyes locked on Finley. "You were saying?"

Finley tried not to grin at the two of us, then forced herself to refocus. "Oh! Right. Sandulf, you mentioned you searched for me and couldn't find the island? Well, I know why you couldn't find Atlantis."

Kasuma inclined her head. "Continue, your highness."

"Stop calling me that. It's just us, okay?" Finley's discomfort showed in the small twitch of her smile.

"Yes," Kasuma replied smoothly, "your highness."

Finley rolled her eyes. "All right, fine. Atlantis, from far away, looks like a tiny fishing village stuck on a rock in the middle of the ocean."

Sandulf frowned. "What do you mean?"

"She's right," Jonathan said quickly. "I saw it with my own eyes. They can... fold space. As you approach, the island sort of unfolds itself and the real city appears. It's amazing. And deeply unsettling."

"I saw it, too," Finley added. "When they kidnapped me. At first, it's this sad little outpost with a couple of huts, and the next—bam—everything shifts. The edges blur, buildings double, then click into place like someone put reality on shuffle. Bridges appear where there weren't bridges, court-yards pop into existence. The whole island rearranges itself depending on where you're standing."

She shuddered. "It didn't grow. It didn't change size. It just... opened. Like a book you didn't realize had hidden chapters. Pherric, you saw it when you flew in on the dragon, right?"

Pherric rubbed his chin, brow drawing tight. "No. I am afraid to admit my eyes were closed the entire time."

Finley laughed at him, shaking her head.

He continued, "But this sounds like more magic. From the gods."

"Yes!" Finley grabbed his sleeve, practically vibrating. "I don't know how they do it, or why it works, but it explains why the place is impossible to find unless it *lets* you."

Pherric's eyes sharpened. "What else can you tell us?"

She reached into the leather satchel at her waist and pulled out... a sphere. A very ominous, very *weird* sphere.

Pherric recoiled a half-step, his eyes widening to perfect circles. "What is that?"

"No clue." Finley held it up with both hands. "But it's very, very important to them. I threatened to smash it right before I jumped on your boat. That Goran guy was about to melt from sheer terror. It was on the pedestal, behind her throne."

"That... I did see." He reached for the orb—slowly, reverently. He turned it over in his fingers, testing its weight, tracing its unnatural smoothness. The matte surface warped the reflection of his fingers as if the orb couldn't quite decide what reality to show him.

Jonathan leaned in beside her. "A little large for a bowling ball."

Finley grinned but Pherric ignored him entirely. His expression shifted through awe, confusion, calculation. He held it close to his temple.

Finley exhaled deeply. "So here's what I'm thinking. We sail right back to Atlantis and offer a trade. This, for Braylor."

Pherric finally tore his gaze from the orb. "No."

Finley groaned. "How did I know you were going to say that?"

"What I mean," Pherric clarified, lifting a finger, "is that we *cannot* get too close. If we approach with three ships, they will overwhelm us with ease and reclaim the orb. But..." He tapped the sphere lightly with his thumb. "We may be able to arrange a trade. At a neutral location."

Finley threw her hands down, pacing away. "That takes *time*, Pherric! Negotiations mean letters, messengers, waiting around while they decide terms! And travel and delays and—no." Her voice cracked. "The longer she has him, the less chance she keeps him alive."

Pherric hesitated. His throat bobbed. "How do you know she has not already…" He struggled. "…executed him?"

"I told Goran to tell Thalassa she'd better keep Braylor alive, or I'd smash that thing." She jabbed a finger at the orb. "Right in front of them."

Pherric gave her the kind of look a wise mentor gives an impulsive apprentice—equal parts pride and exhausted concern. "Then we *do* have time."

Finley shot me a look that said plainly: *See what I'm dealing with?!*

Pherric gently placed the orb into her hands, as though returning a living thing. "You have done well, Finley. I can sense… something within this. Something beyond craftsmanship or artistry. This was not created by any species on this world."

Finley blinked. "It's from the gods?"

"Most certainly." His voice dropped to a hush. "And it may hold the key to everything. You have done exceptionally well."

Finley stared at the orb—heavy, cold, humming with weirdness—and for a moment, her anger quieted.

Leverage.

Hope.

A chance.

60

Miss Fire

Finley

Pherric all but dragged me into the ship's quarters to rest. He didn't have to say it. I knew I was useless, worn out, hungry, and shaking. I fought him anyway, because fighting was easier than feeling. But in the end, he was right. I'd be no good to Braylor if I couldn't even think straight enough to form a plan.

Sleep came in shards—fitful and cruel. Every time I closed my eyes, the dark turned on me. Nightmares bled into flashes of memory, and then panic—tight in my chest, hot behind my eyes. When I couldn't take it anymore, I slipped onto the deck, barefoot and breathless.

The night was quiet except for the restless sea. The moon hung low, its light washing the ship in ghostly blue. Everything looked unreal. My ships bobbed on the dark water, waiting. For what, I wasn't sure. Orders, maybe. Based on some far-fetched miracle idea from me. Right.

I wanted to move, to act, to *fix* something. But every idea ended in blood. I had to get Braylor back... that much was certain. Even if it meant storming onto Atlantis alone. I knew these sailors, these soldiers, would die for me if I asked. But that kind of loyalty was a weight pressing into my spine. The kind of weight a crown leaves behind.

Still, the truth was plain. Atlantis—and their queen, Thalassa—had started this. She'd kidnapped me, tortured me, and stolen the man I loved. All to create a crew of immortal soldiers. And to make herself live forever. Whatever happened next, I had every right to make them pay.

But that didn't make my decisions any easier.

The sea had a sound that night, a restless and uneven heartbeat that matched my own. I leaned against the railing, the chill of the wet wood biting into my hands, trying to steady the shake.

For a moment, I thought I could almost find calm there. Almost.

And that's when a sound interrupted everything.

A soft *slosh*. Then another. Slow. Purposeful.

Every muscle went rigid. I scanned the dark water. Someone was down there. Climbing up the hull, maybe. Atlanteans... come to finish the job.

Oh, shit. Immortal soldiers.

My pulse spiked, and I fumbled for my dagger. I bent over the railing, waiting for a hand to break the surface.

What surfaced wasn't a hand. It was a shadow under the water. Long. Sinuous. Sliding beneath the moonlight with a grace no merman had.

I blinked, trying to make sense of it. The shape rippled through the black water, scales sparkling like bits of shattered starlight before vanishing again. I followed it along the rail as it drifted past the bow.

It wasn't attacking. Just... moving. Watching.

A strange pull rooted me there. I should've been terrified, and I was, but something about it was familiar. Déjà vu in my bones.

And then I knew.

My dream. The eyes. The fire. The creature that had made dragons look small.

The Leviathan.

The memory hit me: those blood-red eyes cutting through the fog, the heat of her fire against my skin, the way she had *looked* at me.

I gripped the rail until my fingers ached. It couldn't be real. That dream had been nothing but fear and fever. But there it was, moving beneath the ship, a god from the deep.

For a heartbeat, I thought maybe it was here for me.

And suddenly I heard—

"Sea serpent!"

The voice ripped through the night from the mast above.

Everything exploded into motion.

Men and women poured onto the deck, shouting, shoving, boots slamming against the planks. Bows were drawn, swords unsheathed. The air turned to chaos.

"No!" I screamed, shoving past a sailor. "Hold your fire! Don't shoot!"

But panic spreads faster than sound.

The first arrow flew, cutting through the dark with a deadly hiss. Then another, and another.

The sea erupted.

The Leviathan rose in a tower of water, its scales flashing blue and silver beneath the moon. When it opened its jaws, fire poured out—white-hot, blinding, alive. The heat shot straight into the night sky, not at our ships.

Screams tore through the air.

"Stop!" I shouted, voice raw. "Hold your fire!"

A few heard me. The rest didn't. More arrows flew. Someone threw a spear—it bounced off the creature's scales. The Leviathan reared back, its roar splitting the night.

And then it looked at me.

Finley.

Did I hear that? Time slowed. The world seemed to tilt. Those eyes— those impossible, furious eyes—locked onto mine.

It saw me. Knew me.

For one moment, I thought it might understand. That maybe it had come here to help. To warn.

Arrows continued to bound off the thick scales.

Then it exhaled—a long, guttural sound, sighing in disappointment— and sank beneath the waves. The fire went out with it.

The water boiled for a few moments more before settling back into the rhythm of the tide. Smoke clung to the air, thick and sour.

I couldn't move. Or breathe. Whatever the Leviathan had been, whatever it had *wanted*, it was gone now.

The silence that followed was worse than the confrontation.

All around me, the crew and soldiers stood still. They were wide-eyed, trembling, the kind of fear that doesn't leave easily. Someone was sobbing quietly near the foremast. Another still clutched a bow, arrow half-drawn, shaking.

Sandulf appeared beside me, panting, sword in hand. "Your highness, are you hurt?"

I shook my head, but the motion felt distant, disconnected. My eyes stayed fixed on the black water.

"You shouldn't have fired," I whispered.

He followed my gaze, then glanced at the charred planks. "We thought the serpent was attacking—"

"It wasn't." My voice cracked. "It wasn't."

For a heartbeat, no one spoke.

A crewwoman near the mast whispered a silent prayer to the gods, muttered something about curses.

I wanted to tell them we were safe. That we had misunderstood. That the creature hadn't come to destroy us. That I'd *seen* it before, that it had known me. But what good would that do now?

The weight of everything pushed invisible and heavy on my shoulders again. I was supposed to protect them. And instead, I'd led them into the wrath of something ancient.

I took one last look at the dark sea, the ripples smoothing over as though it had never been disturbed, and whispered, barely loud enough for the wind to carry it away—

"I think we just made a terrible mistake."

61

Ship Happens

Finley

At some point in the dark, chaos stopped knocking and just moved in.

"No! You gotta go!" shouted Melcente, storming across the deck and shrugging into her leather coat. "I done made da mistake a lettin' your cursed ass on ma ship!"

Pherric intercepted her, hands on her shoulders. "Now is not the time."

He turned to me. "You are well?"

I nodded, a lie if there ever was one.

I marched into my quarters with both of them following me. I threw on a fitted linen shirt, a leather jerkin, and the closest pair of boots. I tucked my trousers in and buckled on my belt—dagger and sword where they belonged. I tied my hair back with a strip of red cloth. I sighed and grabbed my chainmail shirt.

"What happened?" he asked, lifting my chin gently, inspecting me.

"Once again," Melcente cut in, "she nearly got us killed!"

"Captain," Pherric warned, his tone harsh.

"Well, she did," Melcente muttered, stalking off to check the crew.

I exhaled, trying to slow the spin in my head. He walked back with me as I returned to the deck. "I forgot to tell you about it, but I had a dream on the trip down here. The Leviathan visited me. She said my name. And…"

Pherric frowned. "Are you sure this was a dream and not a mindform? You have been in communication with a number of… entities in your time here."

"I have no clue! But… maybe it was. And now I wonder if the Leviathan was trying to help or something. Maybe trying to warn us. Warn me. I don't know. But we blew it! We fired on it! Her… I think it's a her, don't ask me why."

He gave a quiet laugh, the kind meant to calm the crazy person. "There was nothing you could do. None of this was your fault."

"But I'm in charge, Pherric. Me! I'm responsible for everything. And now a giant ass sea serpent is pissed at me. Not good."

"No, it is not good. But we will make the most of our situation."

I took a step back. "Make the most of what? We've only got three ships, a baby-sized army, and we're up against an ocean full of people who live underwater. Throw in a vengeful sea serpent and a small army of immortal soldiers and we're basically eating a dog-shit sandwich, Pherric. There's nothing to make the most of."

He gave a small, almost playful smirk. "This does seem dire. Worse, perhaps, than our battle with Kane."

I arched a brow. "Wow. You are still *terrible* at pep talks. Have I mentioned that lately?"

"You have not."

Before I could reply, a shout tore through the dark.

"Sails!"

Every conversation, every creak of the ship fell silent at once.

Up in the rigging, the lookout leaned so far over the crow's nest I thought he might drop into the sea. "Two ships!" he cried. "Off the bow!"

Melcente's head snapped up. "Where away?"

"Southeast! Two, maybe three axims out!" came the reply. "Black sails!"

Those last words struck me hard.

The crew didn't need an explanation. They knew who sailed under black.

Melcente stormed toward the helm. "Sound yer watch! Warn dem other ships!"

Pherric and I raced up to the top deck for a better look. Out beyond the rolling waves, two dark shapes cut through the reflection, long, low, and sleek. The light caught on the edges of their sails.

The Atlantean ships.

"Dammit," I murmured. "They found us."

"Perhaps that was your... warning," Pherric mumbled beside me.

Melcente snatched a spyglass from the sailor at the wheel and nearly tore it in half extending it. She squinted through it, cursed, and spat into the wind.

"Atlanteans, no doubt." Her voice dropped, low and dangerous. "To ya stations!"

The deck exploded into motion—boots pounding, ropes snapping, metal clanking against wood. Crew members shouted orders that vanished into the sea wind. Lanterns flared to life across the deck, painting everyone in trembling gold light.

Pherric turned to me. "We should not act rashly. They have not yet—"

"They don't have to!" I cut him off. "Look at them. They're headed right for us."

The wind ripped across our deck, snapping the sails and raising goose-bumps along my arms.

Pherric's gaze never left the horizon. His voice was quiet, but it carried. "They must know you stole the orb. They are coming to reclaim it."

"What do we do? Run? Stand our ground? Or, I guess... our water? Stand our *groundwater?*"

He blinked at me. "That is not how that phrase works."

For a few precious seconds, everything stilled. Only the whip of canvas and the slap of waves beneath us.

"Unless." Pherric turned toward the aft rail and the two ships anchored behind us. "We take advantage of our numbers."

He marched to Melcente. "Captain, have your other vessels extinguish their lights."

"Why would I—?" she began, but the question died halfway out of her mouth. Understanding lit her face, wicked and eager.

"Have 'em pull back," she growled, "then swing 'round and return on our flank!"

I stared between them. "Is someone going to tell me the plan before I accidentally help the wrong side?"

Melcente barked orders to a sailor, who sprinted down the steps. Within seconds the deck buzzed with motion again, sails lowered and ropes hauled tight. Behind us, the *Thalyra* and *Skathis* vanished into darkness as every lantern blinked out, leaving only silhouettes against the moonlit sea.

Pherric pointed as the wind carried them away. "The Atlanteans saw this ship... but perhaps not the other two."

Realization clicked hard and fast. "They think we're just one ship."

"Aye," Melcente said, teeth flashing. "Let 'em come close, nice an' confident. Den we ram da bastards."

I swallowed, gripping the spyglass tight.

Off our port side, the Atlantean vessels crept nearer, their hulls faintly aglow—two predatory stars against the endless dark.

But mere minutes later, the Atlantean ships were no longer distant shadows.

"They're getting kinda close," I muttered.

Melcente didn't answer. Her eyes were locked on the water, jaw tight, hands on the wheel.

The Atlanteans angled inward, side-by-side but offset, moving with the smug precision of predators that had already decided how we would die.

"Melcente?" I tried again.

"Wait now..." she murmured, almost tenderly, as if coaxing the sea itself.

Pherric swallowed audibly. "Captain, they will intercept us within—"

"Shh. Not yet." Her gaze flicked upward to the sails, then to the oncoming ships. "Let 'em commit first..."

The Atlantean bows surged on, slicing through the sea.

"They're really close," I hissed.

"Aye," Melcente said. "Just a *tish* more..."

The wind gathered like it understood her intent.

The Atlantean ships raced into their final approach, perfectly aligned, ready to strike.

Melcente grinned, bright and triumphant.

"Now! Full sail!"

Canvas exploded overhead as sailors hauled ropes with frantic precision. The *Aegiros* jumped forward, catching the wind cleanly, pushing ahead enough that the Atlanteans overshot their approach angle. Melcente grinned with all her teeth and spun the wheel.

"Hold tight!"

The ship swung in a wide arc, and we leaned over hard. The stern yawed until both Atlantean ships lined up behind us.

They took the bait.

Pherric braced himself beside me, cloak whipping in the wind. "They committed both ships. They believe we are alone," he murmured.

"Good," I growled. "Let them."

Behind us, the sea swallowed all light... until two blacker shapes ghosted out of the dark.

The *Thalyra* and *Skathis*, lanterns dead, sails low.

They moved quietly through the shadows.

Melcente lifted a finger, waiting for the moment the Atlanteans drew too close—when turning would be impossible.

"Now."

From opposite sides, the *Thalyra* and *Skathis* slammed into the Atlantean hulls with the sound of mountains colliding underwater. Wood screamed. Metal rang. One Atlantean ship buckled inward; the other was forced tight against it, the two vessels smashed together in a violent embrace.

Shouts erupted across the water.

Melcente ran to the rail. "Pull back!" she ordered, and her captains obeyed. Both my ships wrenched free, leaving the Atlantean ships crippled and locked against each other, their formation broken.

Melcente didn't hesitate. "Bring us alongside!"

The *Aegiros* surged forward and swung parallel to the closest Atlantean ship.

Sandulf vaulted the stairs to the high castle. "What is your plan?!"

I had no idea. "I don't know! You're the expert! Kill them?"

He flashed a rugged grin and rushed off, blasting orders to the Irkallan troops waiting on deck.

"Attack!" I screamed, pulling out my sword.

Our archers lined the side. Arrows firing in a blur of black.

But the Atlanteans were ready and returned fire. They had crossbows. And they did a lot of damage. Their bolts went clean through a body, most of the time, and hit anyone standing behind.

I leaned against the high castle rail. "Fire quickly! Aim for those bow shooters!"

Our archers were able to reload much faster. Sandulf had them shooting three or four arrows for every crossbow bolt that fired.

"Ropes! Ropes left!" Sandulf ordered. "Boarders with me!"

Lines went taut. Knots bit into palms. My soldiers swung over to the other ship, landing in their midst.

I didn't wait. I raced down to the main deck and grabbed the nearest line. I felt it cut into my hand as I launched across the gap. The Atlantean deck rose to meet me and I rolled as I landed. A merman in breastplate moved to intercept, but Sandulf met him mid-swing. The Atlantean stumbled, and Sandy took him down with a short, efficient strike.

What truly impressed me was when I saw Kinnat and Genevieve fighting at the far end of the ship. Kinnat was a different kind of thunder. She was fierce and each step measured. Her sword skills were raw, but she had the eye. An Atlantean soldier charged, and she ducked under his swing and sliced along his gills with ease. His mouth went wide; his legs buckled as if the deck itself had melted him into syrup. He fell, and those behind him hesitated, a dangerous gap in their discipline.

That's when Genevieve moved. She threw herself into the gap, blade flashing across a soldier's face and down his chest. The man staggered back, and for a heartbeat, everything around her went still. Her breath stopped, eyes round; the horror crept in right behind the adrenaline.

First kills always do that.

I noticed the fear and disbelief fight for space behind her eyes. I had seen it before—in others, and once, long ago, in a reflection of my own.

"Hold the line!" I screamed, driving forward. I felt the scrape of metal along my wrist as a sword nicked me. I drove my shoulder into the Atlantean's hip and knocked him into his comrade; the two of them went down in a tangle of limbs and swallowed curses.

On our deck, bow archers aimed low to stop boarding parties from taking hold; our stern archers fired at their crossbows who had stepped clear of the fight.

The tinny ring of steel on steel was a percussion line under the shouts.

"Boarders!" an Irkallan bellowed behind me. Back on the *Aegiros*, a group of Atlanteans clambered over the rail at the bow, up from the water. Their swords flashed in the moonlight. They were trying to pinch us off from behind. But they hadn't counted on what waited below.

A set of double doors burst open on the back deck, and a dozen Irkallan soldiers surged up from the hold—blades singing as they cut off the boarding party before they could fan out.

That was Sandulf's idea. Clever bastard. I made a mental note to give him a raise—if we lived through this.

The fight pitched and rolled with the sea. Men slipped on wet planks and blood and kept fighting. I knocked a merman's trident aside with the pommel of my sword and slit his throat before he knew where he was. It was clean and ugly and necessary.

Through the clash of metal, my gaze found Genevieve again. The fight had drained from her—she stood leaning to the side, blade limp at her side, staring at the man she'd cut down as if expecting him to rise again. An Atlantean surged toward her, but Kinnat was quick. She stepped in front, catching the blow with a violent twist of her sword, her snarl cutting through the din. "Eyes up, Genevieve!" she barked. The words seemed to drag Genevieve back into her body. She fought on, but her eyes were glassy. Luckily, she had Kinnat at her side.

A dozen minutes later, our other two ships slid alongside and out front of the damaged Atlantean ships. Their arrival changed everything. The Atlanteans flinched at the sight of reinforcements. Arrows from those ships began to pepper their decks, and our soldiers heard the roar of more of our people joining the battle.

The fight didn't end so much as it unraveled. One by one, the remaining Atlanteans broke ranks, eyes staring toward the sea like animals spotting an open gate. Some leapt without hesitation, armor and all, vanishing beneath the waves in white bursts of foam. Others scrambled after them, abandoning weapons and dragging away the wounded. Within moments, the decks that had been thick with movement emptied out.

There was the scent of blood, and the decks and sea below churned with the dead.

I made my way back to the high castle just as Pherric emerged from hiding, his expression unreadable as he took in the aftermath. Bodies were being hauled and stacked on the deck below, our win measured in weight and silence.

"A costly victory," he said at last.

With the two ships destroyed, a reckless thought crossed my mind—to head straight for Atlantis and be done with it.

"And I fear the cost will only rise," Pherric continued, "now that I've made the error of rendering Thalassa and several soldiers immortal."

Shit.

I had almost forgotten about Goran and the death squad.

"Fantastic," I muttered. "Now we have two problems."

"Braylor," Pherric said simply. "And the Deep Guard."

I tried picturing possible scenarios. "What is she going to do with ten undying soldiers?"

He finally looked at me, his expression grave. "Braylor will live... as long as we possess what she wants. My greater concern is this: she will send the Deep Guard after you next."

"Because of the orb."

"Because of the orb," he confirmed. Then his voice dipped, barely above the wind. "And because nothing terrifies a queen more... than losing something she loves."

The world went still.

The waves kept crashing. The rigging kept creaking. But inside me, a hollow and aching quiet.

Was he talking about Thalassa?

Or... me?

My throat tightened, the words I might've said dissolved before they reached my tongue. For a long, suspended moment, all I could do was stare at the dark water where the Atlanteans had vanished, feeling something settle beneath my chest.

Pherric did not clarify.

And I did not ask.

62

Accidental Leader, Do Not Perceive Me

Finley

I spent most of the morning pacing the upper deck of the *Aegiros*, pretending to look busy while avoiding everyone like the plague. Every few minutes someone would approach—crew, sub-commander, random bystander—asking what we were going to do next. I had no idea, but that didn't stop them. I waved them all toward Pherric. He was better at sounding authoritative while saying absolutely nothing.

Our forces returned to the ships. We really now have five in total, if you counted the damaged ones we had taken by force. Five ships against Atlantis. Five ships against a queen who commanded an impressive fleet, an army that survived underwater, and a squad of soldiers who could not die. Yeah, those odds sounded fantastic.

The Atlantean sailors who'd swum off hours ago were probably halfway home by now. The second she heard, she might get angry and kill Braylor. She was seriously unstable.

And I wasn't about to let that happen.

Even if she didn't, I would do everything in my power to get him back. I'd search for Atlantis for months. For years. I was not going to give up. Ever.

"What is your plan?" asked Pherric. Kasuma joined him at my side.

My arms folded automatically in a makeshift shield. I'd been dreading that question. The crew and soldiers kept sneaking glances at me, waiting for a command, a miracle, anything. They knew that whatever decision I made meant life or death.

So many lives already lost because of my choices.

I swallowed hard. I couldn't let the emotion show. Not the fear, not the guilt, nor the crushing pressure of being everyone's answer when I barely knew my own.

"We're returning to Canela," I said finally.

Pherric blinked. Kasuma's eyes narrowed. I'd just shocked two people who literally live for strategy and command decisions.

"That is... a wise decision," Pherric said slowly.

I laughed, too loud and too fast. "I finally got one right?"

"In this case," he said, weighing his words, "yes."

"Wait, really?!"

His lips twitched. "I am proud of you, your highness. You are showing remarkable restraint. I am genuinely surprised you are personally not steering these ships toward Atlantis right now."

I sighed. "Okay, yeah, that sounds more like me. But since we've got her magical orb, I just have to hope she doesn't kill him, right? Canela is our only option, I think."

The words felt like surrender.

But they were the only way to win.

While Pherric relayed our sailing instructions to Melcente, all I heard was the wind rattling through the ship and the distant churn of the sea. My own problems looped in my head—Braylor, Thalassa, the orb, the immortal squad—each one a hungry hellhound snapping at me.

Then my gaze drifted across the deck... and snagged on someone far worse off than me.

Genevieve.

She stood near the mainmast, still and small against the chaos, staring in the opposite direction—as if waiting for something to come *from* the shadows instead of out of the light. There was blood on her clothes, none hers, and her hands hung limp at her sides, fingers still curled because they hadn't decided to stop fighting.

Here I was drowning in what-ifs while she was drowning in something real.

Something I'd dragged her into.

I exhaled hard and pushed away from the rail. Whatever storm I was trapped in could wait; she needed someone who wasn't falling apart.

Kinnat was off having a healer tend to her wounds.

I made my way to Genevieve carefully. When I slipped my arm around her shoulders, she jolted, snapping out of her thousand-yard stare with a too-bright smile.

"Hey," she said, voice brittle. "How are you doing?"

I clasped her hands in mine. "It's okay, Genevieve. I've been there too."

Her brows drew together. "Been where? What are you talking about?"

"I'm talking about killing that guy," I said softly. "I know it wasn't easy."

She gave a laugh that didn't sound like her. "Naw, I'm fine. Really. No big deal."

"Genevieve," I said again, quieter this time. "It's me."

Her head lifted, defiant as always, but the tears were already forming. "I'm all right, girl. You know that."

"I *know* you're tough. One of the toughest people I've ever met. On Earth." I paused, glancing at the bruised sky. "But this isn't Earth. Tir Na changes you. It demands it."

She tried to deflect. "Yeah, I know. Look at you, *Queen Badass*. You've changed so much. I love it."

I sighed and sank to the deck, tugging her down beside me. "Years ago, Kasuma and I ambushed a camp of soldiers. She told me to take one while she handled the rest. And, of course, I completely screwed it up. But I managed to... do the deed."

Genevieve's gaze dropped to the floorboards between her knees. For a long time, neither of us spoke. Then, barely above a whisper: "How did you deal with it?"

"I didn't. Not at first." I rubbed my thumbs over the backs of her hands. "I was practically comatose for a day. Couldn't eat. Couldn't think."

Tears spilled freely down her cheeks. She tried to swipe them away, but they kept coming. "I'm not a killer, Fin. I don't know what I was thinking. They attacked, I jumped across to that ship, and I just... reacted. I didn't think. I just *did*. And now—" Her voice broke. "That's not who I am."

"I know," I said. "It sucks. You hate yourself for it, and then you hate that you don't hate yourself enough. I actually apologized to the next guy I killed."

That pulled a choked laugh from her. "Does it get easier?"

I tilted my head. "It has to. On this world, violence isn't just an answer... it's the question. I hate it. I hate every damn bit of it. But if I've learned anything here, it's that life doesn't care what's fair." I gave her hands a squeeze. "But I'm here. You're not alone in this."

"I know," she said finally, her voice small but steady. "I just... I want to go home."

"Yeah," I whispered. "I get that."

We sat there a moment, the roar of the ocean filling the spaces between our words.

Then I said, "When the time comes, I want you back in Irkalla. You and Kinnat. You don't need to be part of this war."

She turned toward me, calm but firm. "No. You need me. You need *us*."

"Genevieve, we're headed to Canela. To regroup. Yes, I need to find Braylor. And stop Thalassa. But I've got trained warriors. Your part in this is over."

"You still have fighting to do. You are my friend. I will always be by your side. So, I guess I need to suck it up."

She stood, squaring her shoulders, brushing away the last of her tears. The transformation was instant—raw emotion reforged into steel.

I rose with her. "You don't have to do this. Not anymore. I've got help now." I gestured toward the ships around us.

She shook her head, a grin tugging at her lips. "Finley, you were the quietest, most introverted girl I ever met. I used to drag you out of your dorm just to make you talk to people. To go out. Try and have a little fun. And now look at you: warrior queen, savior of this world, and still somehow managing sarcasm at the end of it all."

I smirked. "So if *I* can do it...?"

"...then I can too," she finished, gripping my forearms tight. Her eyes burned with determination. "I can do this. For you. And for me."

"Are you sure?"

"Yes."

"Good," I said, slinging my arm around her shoulders and steering her toward the railing. "In that case, you're holding your sword way too tight. Relax your wrist or you'll sprain something. And by the way—"

Laughing, she shoved me off with an eye roll. "Girl..."

The word lingered between us, warm and familiar—the first true piece of home I'd felt in quite a while.

Genevieve's grin lasted for half a second.

Then it shuttered out, as though someone had blown a candle from across the room.

Her entire body jerked tight. Her head snapped upward, eyes widening, irises dilating. Her breath caught, tense and unnatural, and her fingers spasmed around her sword hilt.

A cold spike of dread shot through me.

"Gen?" I whispered.

She didn't look at me. Not really. Her gaze slid *past* me, *through* me. She was staring at something I couldn't see. Her jaw clenched hard enough I heard the tiny grind of her teeth.

Then her face twisted into something feral.

A guttural sound ripped from her chest. She was raw, stripped of everything human.

Steel flashed.

I barely reacted in time.

Her sword whistled past my cheek, slicing a curl of hair clean off as I stumbled backward.

"Genevieve!" I shouted, scrambling away from the next strike. "Stop!"

She didn't.

She lunged again, faster, stronger, her whole body shaking with lethal intent.

Crew members shouted. Someone screamed. Boots thundered on the deck as soldiers surged toward us.

"Stay back!" I roared, flipping over a coil of rope as her blade carved into the deck where my leg had been. Splinters exploded upward.

Genevieve didn't even flinch.

She pivoted, bringing her sword up in a vicious arc that would've cut my head clean off if I hadn't dropped flat to the floorboards. I rolled, came up in a crouch, and darted behind a capstan.

She smashed into it full-force, steel shrieking against iron.

"Genevieve, listen to me!" I pleaded. "It's Finley!"

She answered with a scream that rattled the air.

"Mindform!" Pherric shouted from across the deck. "She is under *mindform compulsion!*"

"Huh?!" My heart plummeted. "How? No one here is—"

I avoided another swipe of the blade and scanned the deck. My eyes fell on Jonathan.

Jonathan's face drained of color. He held up his hands. There was fear in his eyes—this was not his doing.

"What's going on?!" I yelled at him, backing up across the deck as Gen lunged again.

"Ramil," Jonathan mumbled.

"Jonathan?"

"Ramil! He, uh, he said she was his backup plan. He must've planted a dormant spell. Back at the Scholomance Academy. A buried mindform." His voice broke. "Finley, he turned her into a *weapon.*"

Cold terror flooded my veins.

Three soldiers tried to rush her at once. She grunted and sliced into two of them and shoved the other to the deck. I had no idea she was such a capable fighter.

"I can't hurt her!" I yelled back, as she turned back to me.

"Genevieve! No!" Kinnat's scream cut through the noise.

She came barreling onto the deck, half-bandaged, blood still soaking through the wrappings on her arm. She tried to reach Gen, sobbing, hands outstretched, begging her by name like it might anchor her back to herself.

"Gen, please!" Kinnat yelled. "Look at me. It is me. You do not have to do this!"

She surged forward, and two soldiers caught Kinnat in time, arms locking around her shoulders as she thrashed and screamed. She fought them hard enough that a third had to rush in, pinning her back as she broke down, crying Gen's name over and over, watching helplessly as the woman she loved turned her blade on me.

I ducked as Genevieve swung overhead, burying her blade in a mast support beam. She ripped it out with a grunt that wasn't her at all.

"Your highness, she will not stop!" Sandulf shouted, reaching for her from behind.

"Don't touch her!" I screamed.

He hesitated, and in that slit-second, Genevieve back-kicked him in the knee so hard he tumbled to the deck, collapsing with a howl.

She didn't even look at him.

Her focus was solely, completely, on me.

Kinnat reached out her hand. "Please! No!"

The world narrowed to the sound of her ragged breathing and the scrape of a sword on wood.

I bolted toward the stairs leading to the quarterdeck. She gave chase, sprinting after me with inhuman ferocity. I vaulted the railing back down to the lower deck; she *jumped from the stairs* and landed behind me in a crouch, sword ready for a killing thrust.

Every instinct screamed to fight.

But I refused.

I dodged sideways, slamming into a barrel. Her sword cut clean through it, water exploding outward. She swung again, forcing me up the rigging ladder.

I scrambled halfway up before she grabbed the back of my boot and yanked hard. I fell, twisting midair and slamming onto the deck, rolling to avoid her blade stabbing down where my heart was right before.

Crew members flooded in, trying to form a barrier.

"No!" I shouted. "Let me try to stop her!"

A sword was shoved toward me. "Your highness, take it!"

"I will not kill her," I stated, trying to inhale as much air as I could.

"She will kill *you!*" Pherric shouted from the deck above, voice breaking.

Genevieve charged again, swinging wide. I ducked under the mast beam, skidding on my knees. She swung at my face, missed by inches, and cut a lantern rope instead. The lantern dropped, smashing at my feet and spilling fire across the deck. Soldiers rushed off to grab water.

The flames reflected in her blank, murderous eyes.

"Genevieve!" I begged as I leapt over the fire line, lungs burning. "It's me! It's Finley! You don't want to do this! Snap out of it!"

No recognition.

No hesitation.

No mercy.

She climbed through the fire.

I stumbled backward into the mainmast, trapped.

Her voice tore out, a guttural, wordless sound of rage and agony intertwined. She raised the sword high.

"Pherric!" I cried. "Break it! Do something!"

His voice reached me, frantic and helpless. "I cannot! Ramil was a master. He certainly instructed her to kill or be killed!"

The order.

To kill me.

Jonathan's voice yelled out through the haze. "Finley, Ramil meant for this. He meant for her to assassinate you! You're... going to have to stop her."

Genevieve didn't want this. She wasn't choosing this.

She was trapped inside her own mind, screaming for help while her body obeyed someone else's command.

Her sword shook in her grip. She was fighting it, but unable to win.

Kasuma had started to move in close, a dagger in her hand and deadly design in her eyes.

Crew members swarmed closer again, desperate to intervene.

"Stop!" I ordered, voice shaking. "All of you! Fucking stop! Now!"

"We'll lose ya, girlie!" Melcente shouted, sword half-drawn. "Not that it'd be a bad ting..."

"I am not fighting her!" I screamed back.

And then I understood what I had to do.

It wasn't bravery. Or nobility. It was the only way to save her.

My eyes met hers. They were blank, tortured, beyond wild.

"I'm sorry, Gen," I whispered.

I lowered my arms.

Her body pitched, completing the motion the compulsion had demanded all along.

The sword drove straight through my chest.

The world went blinding white.

I heard someone scream my name. Jonathan, or maybe Pherric. The ship twisted under me. Or maybe I twisted under it. Probably that.

Genevieve's face flickered—anger, then confusion, followed by horror and pain in micro-seconds. She collapsed to the deck, released from the spell the instant I was mortally wounded.

The cold rushed in. It always does.

My body crumpled.

My pulse fluttered once, twice.

And as everything dimmed, a single thought beat through the fog:

Please let me come back from this death.

Because I cannot bear for Genevieve to live with what she's done.

I died.

63

Back From the Dead and Already Behind

Finley

I won't rehash how bad it blows to come back from the dead after many months. I've explained it to death (haha! See what I did there?! Sorry.)

What I will say is: waking up felt like dragging myself through wet sand while someone rang temple bells inside my skull. Again.

I groaned and lifted a hand to shield my eyes. Sunlight poured over me—actual sunlight, warm and golden, but I was not on the ship in the captain's quarters. A soft breeze drifted across my face, carrying the sea air and distant shouting.

I blinked hard, forcing the world into focus.

Okay, I was... inside.

The ceiling above me was tan stucco with wooden beams darkened by age. The air smelled faintly of citrus. I turned my head. The pillow crackled under me, stuffed with something that was definitely not feathers and definitely not comfortable.

To my right: an open window.

No glass, just a wide arch framed with creamy curtains that fluttered lazily in the warm wind. Beyond it, terracotta rooftops sloped toward a glittering blue horizon. The Tir Na version of seagulls wheeled overhead, screaming like they were gossiping about me.

To my left: a bare wall, the color of sun-baked clay, decorated only with a single iron lantern and a cracked ceramic bowl on a wooden table. Everything was simple—functional—nothing like the grandeur of Irkalla.

The bedroom was small. This was a cheap room.

Southern kingdom. Warm-weather architecture. Open-air windows.

Canela, maybe? Likely. I was nowhere near—

Genevieve.

I sat up too fast.

Pain lanced through my chest—a feeling I was now very familiar with. Had someone had forgotten to remove the sword? I hissed and pressed a hand against the spot where I'd died, but there was smooth skin now, tender and ghostly.

The bed creaked under me. Sheets scratchy enough to exfoliate the dead skin right off you. Outside, sounds drifted up: merchants begging, hooves clacking against stone, waves slapping the harbor wall.

It was peaceful.

It made my heart race. Because peaceful meant time had passed.

And time meant everything might have ended badly.

"Okay," I muttered, pushing hair out of my face with a shaky hand. "Where the hell am I? And how many disasters happened while I was busy being... medically inconvenient?"

No answer.

Just the warm Canelan wind, and the quiet terror of waking up alive when too many people needed me.

I swung my legs over the side of the bed... and nearly collapsed.

So, yeah. Resurrection hangovers? Zero stars. Do not recommend.

"Pherric?!" I yelled, immediately regretting it as my skull throbbed.

Footsteps shuffled on wooden floorboards. Someone murmured outside the room, then hurried off, no doubt to fetch my mage.

Tall, dark, and eternally disheveled Pherric finally appeared and perched on the edge of the bed. "You are alive."

"In theory," I groaned.

"I feared the worst. You—"

I reached out—or tried to—to grab a fistful of his green sleeve. "Genevieve?!"

"You need to rest after—"

"Genevieve," I repeated, louder this time. "Tell me. Is she okay?"

He exhaled. "She is doing well, considering what occurred. And no, I will not bring her to you."

I was absolutely going to ask for that next. "Where is she?"

"She has been confined to a room in this inn. We could not risk another... attempt on your life or anyone else's."

"Confined? For almost four months? That's ridiculous!" I tried to sit up again and instantly regretted it as my head performed a coup.

"That is a subject we need to discuss," he said, choosing his words with surgical care. "Did you ingest any poison while you were imprisoned in Thalassa's dungeon?"

"No," I said—and then hesitated. Maybe some had gotten on my lip. Maybe. "Why?"

"You have been gone for over five months. We feared you would not return at all."

"Five?" My voice pitched. "What the *fuck*?"

"There appears to have been a change in the pattern," he said. "I worried you had been poisoned, as your return took far longer than normal." He pressed his hand to my forehead, then checked the pulse at my neck.

"Well, I need to see her," I said. "She's probably—Oh, shit. Five months. What the hell has been happening? Any word on Braylor?!"

"No news," he said softly. "As far as we know, he remains alive. Thalassa has not... delivered his head to anyone."

I tried to laugh at that. It hurt too much. "Fair."

"We will explain everything," he said, patting my arm, "but first, you must rest."

I tried to argue, but an inn attendant appeared with a pitcher of water and a bowl of broth, and the smell alone made me realize I could fall asleep face-down in it. I managed a few hours sleep, maybe more. When I could finally stand without feeling as if I was made of wet laundry, I got dressed.

Someone had kindly laid out an outfit: light riding trousers, a breezy linen shirt, and a short, padded vest that looked both comfortable *and* stab-resistant. The boots were soft enough to sprint in. Still, I put the whole thing on. Priorities.

I wobbled toward the room where Pherric had set up a temporary command post.

The entire second floor of the inn had been secured in anticipation of my resurrection. Cute.

I wanted to see Genevieve first—needed to—but Pherric insisted on bringing me up to speed before I went anywhere near her.

A table and chairs had been dragged into the center of the room. Sandy, Kasuma, and Pherric were already seated, the air heavy with expectation.

I gulped down the water in front of me. "All right. What did I miss? Give me all the bad news at once."

Pherric unrolled a massive world map across the table. There really can't be a meeting on Tir Na without a map involved.

"Commander?" he prompted.

Sandulf stood, smoothing his jacket. "Your highness, I am glad to see you alive again." He offered a curt nod as I stole his water mug and drained it. "Queen Thalassa of Atlantis has been... active in the time you have been away."

I leaned toward Kasuma and whispered, "I assume he knows about the whole coming-back-from-the-dead thing?"

She nodded. "He watched you die on the Aegiros."

"Right. Go on."

"First," Sandulf said, pointing to the coastline, "our ships are moored west of Canela. Your army is encamped in the hills outside Magoria."

"Get to Thalassa," I said, rubbing my aching temples. "My head is going to melt."

He nodded. "She has seized every major port along the southern coast— from Svarga in the east to Elysium in the north."

"Seized? As in, she's in control? How is that possible?"

"Atlantean forces invaded Svarga and took Amarashila," he said, sliding his finger along the map. "Then Tamalindra. Then the coastal cities of Cíbola. Several weeks ago they captured Caerwyn Harbour and Llyr's Gate in Elysium."

"What about Canela?" I asked Kasuma. "We're in Canela, right?"

"We are," she said, her tone ice-cold.

I blinked. "The Atlanteans are in *this* city?"

Pherric leaned in on his fists. "Canela is under siege, your highness. We remained only because we did not wish your body moved. We hoped you would awaken before the city fell."

"We're in danger. Got it. We need to leave soon." I rubbed my face. "Okay, how did they pull all this off?"

Sandulf traced the ports again. "By blockading every harbor with multiple ships. Then a small force invades, led by members of Thalassa's Deep Guard. They kill or capture the leadership and take control."

"I'm sure it's messier than that."

"For brevity," he said. "They are efficient, merciless, and frightening. Rumor spreads quickly that her soldiers do not die."

I shared a look with Pherric.

"What afflicts me," I said slowly, "also afflicts a handful of her Guard. But unlike me, they don't stay dead for a day or a month—they don't die *at all*. Ever. Thankfully, she only has about ten."

"I see," Sandulf murmured. I don't think he saw.

"You have the book, right?" I asked. "She can't make more immortal soldiers?"

Pherric patted the leather satchel at his side. "The *Arcanum Libellum* is safe."

"Okay. If she's taken these ports, what's everyone else doing? Is anyone fighting back? I can't imagine Queen Urraca letting that slide."

"Most kingdoms have resisted," he said. "But the Atlanteans hold the ports. Queen Urraca nearly reclaimed Ifrīya's Landing, until the Deep Guard arrived and drove her out."

I frowned. "They showed up that fast?"

"They are spread thin," Kasuma added. "One... immortal Guard commands each city, but they reinforce each other as needed."

"Which could make them vulnerable. Okay, the ports are screwed. Trade's screwed, too, I bet?"

"Utterly," Sandy confirmed. "Grains, spices, fruits, timber—everything. Thalassa controls distribution and demands heavy tribute. Ships avoid the coast altogether for fear of being given only a few coins or having their cargo confiscated entirely."

I leaned forward. "And Braylor? Any message? Any demand for the orb?"

"Nothing," he said. "I am sorry."

I swallowed hard. The words hit hard, echoing into a place inside me I didn't want to look at.

If she wanted him dead, she would have sent a message. Or his head.

At least... that's what I told myself.

But the truth surged up, cold and choking:

I'd been *gone* for five-plus months. Anything could've happened. Five months where he could've been tortured, moved, hidden, executed. And I wouldn't have known. Wouldn't have been able to stop it. Couldn't have been there to hold him or fight for him or even say goodbye.

Five months where the world kept turning without me, and he might have died thinking I abandoned him. That I wasn't coming.

I felt suddenly weightless, hollow, a ghost haunting a life that had moved on without me.

I didn't cry. Not yet. But something inside me twisted hard enough to bruise.

I stood abruptly. "Take me to Genevieve."

Everyone leaned forward, their bodies in one collective flinch.

"Your highness—" Sandulf began.

I shot Pherric a warning glare. "Do not even try—"

"She poses a risk," he said.

"I don't care." I marched toward the door. "She kills me again, it's on me."

They trailed me down the hall. Sandulf strode ahead and stopped at a door, blocking my way.

"I must bind her hands," he insisted.

I shoved his hand off the latch. "Nope. Not happening."

He didn't stop me, but he didn't move aside either.

I pushed past him and opened the door. Stepping through, I slammed it shut.

Genevieve shot up from the cot in the corner, eyes wide, and let out a short gasp. For a split-second, relief flooded her face—raw, desperate relief—before it crashed into something like terror.

"Finley?" she whispered. She wasn't sure I was real.

She took one instinctive step toward me... then flinched back as if I were a hot stove.

"I... I shouldn't—" Her hands flew behind her back, to hide the shaking. "You shouldn't be here."

"Genevieve," I said softly.

She shook her head so hard her hair whipped across her face. "No. No, Finley, you don't get it." Her voice broke in the middle. "I killed you."

The words shredded her. Her knees nearly buckled.

I crossed the room in three steps and caught her before she hit the floor. She gripped my arms.

"I remember talking to you," she whispered. "At the mast. I remember what you said. I remember almost crying. And then—"

She choked on the next sound.

"And then nothing," she said. "Just... black. And when I woke up, I was—"

Her whole body shook violently.

"I was holding the sword, Finley. It was covered in your blood. You were on the deck. Your body—" She squeezed her eyes shut, sobbing. "You were dead because of me. I... I killed my best friend."

I pulled her tight into my chest as she broke. Hot tears soaked into my shirt; mine stung behind my eyelids but didn't fall. Someone had to stay upright.

"It wasn't you," I murmured into her hair. "You hear me? It wasn't you."

She jerked away suddenly, anger slicing through the grief. "It *was* me! My hands! My sword!"

"But whose mind?" I countered.

Genevieve blinked. Confusion, guilt, and terror tangled together.

And then she seemed to recall something. A memory.

Her eyes widened. "Him."

"Who?" I asked.

"Ramil..."

Her inhale was fast. "Finley... Finley, I think he... He did something to me."

I guided her to sit before she fell. She clutched her belly with one hand, her head with the other, forcing the memories into place.

"He grabbed me," she whispered. "Back at the academy. He... he dragged me to my room. He put his hand on my wrist and he started chanting." Her fingers twitched at the memory. "My skull was splitting. He-he was... digging around inside."

He'd used a mindform on her for certain.

"He said he wanted me to forget something I saw," Genevieve said. "And I fought it. I thought I won. I thought I held on to everything just to spite him." Her voice cracked. "But I didn't win anything, Fin. I think he left something in me. Maybe it was a command. I was brainwashed or... I don't know."

"Yes. He did. It was a mindform. The kind Jonathan knows how to use. To move things." I said, my voice soft. "I think he planted a... mission into your brain. To kill me if you were ever alone with me."

She swallowed hard. "He turned me into something that, that—"

"He turned you into a weapon." I cupped her face in my hands. "*You* didn't kill me."

Her voice was barely a whisper. "I did."

"No," I insisted. "Ramil did. He used you. When he decided to pull that string, you had no choice."

She pressed her forehead to mine, crying openly now. "I'm sorry. God, Finley, I'm so sorry. I would never—"

"I know." I gripped her shoulders. "I know you wouldn't. And I won't let anyone punish you for something that wasn't yours."

She tried to breathe but it came out as a tremor.

"I was very scared," she confessed. "Every day. Locked in here. Wondering if I'd snap again. If I'd pick up something sharp. If I'd hurt someone else. I can't sleep. I don't eat. I just—I just kept seeing your body on that deck."

Her voice dissolved again.

I pulled her into me. "Look at me. I'm alive. I'm back."

She nodded against my shoulder, still crying.

"We don't need to fix anything," I murmured. "Whatever spell he left in you, whatever control he thought he had...... it's gone now."

She clung to me harder, voice muffled. "Don't leave me again."

"I won't," I promised. "Not for anything."

Outside the door, I could hear Sandulf pretending very hard not to hover. Pherric's soft footsteps a little farther back. Kasuma's exhale.

None of them mattered right now.

This was the girl who dragged me out of my dorm in Manhattan, who taught me how to live a little, who believed in me long before I ever believed in myself.

I pressed a steadying hand to her back.

"Genevieve," I said quietly, "let's get you out of here."

She flinched. "But... what if I—"

"You did what *he* wanted," I cut in gently. "Not what you wanted. And you haven't attacked me in all the time I've been with you. Now tell me, when was the last time you saw Kinnat?"

A small, broken laugh escaped her. "She sits outside the door every day."

"That's it? Just sits there?" I shook my head. "Yeah, that stops now."

I slipped my arm around her shoulders, and together we stepped out of that suffocating little room.

Pherric and the others in the hallway stiffened, eyes jumping between us—fear, concern, silent pleas to reconsider radiating off all of them.

I ignored every single one.

Genevieve walked beside me.

Exactly where she belonged.

64

No Room at the Inn

Finley

We barely managed three steps down the corridor before Pherric swept in ahead of us, a worried mother who also happened to dabble in necromancy.

"Your highness, may I beg you to reconsider?"

"No, you may not," I said, sidestepping the pleading expression.

"Finley—"

I spun on him, heat flaring across my face. "Pherric. I *cannot believe* you locked her up for five goddamn months!"

"She tried to kill you."

"Right! And I was *already dead.* She couldn't do anything worse! And keeping her away from Kinnat too? Did you think she was going to kill her girlfriend next? I—I don't even know what to think about you right now. You're usually the smart one in the bunch."

He exhaled. There was more he hadn't confessed.

"What else did you do?" I demanded.

"We kept Jonathan... away. Since I could not determine his state of mind."

I stared. "Aw, Pherric. You're kidding me, right?"

"I am not."

"Jesus-fucking-Christ. Where is he?"

Pherric started to point down the hall—when a Cíbolan woman sprinted up the stairs, rounded the corner, and collided with us. Her rough linen skirt was dusty from the street, a faded shawl slipping off one shoulder as she gasped for air. She spotted me, hesitated and seemed unsure if she should bow, then hurried straight to Pherric.

"You must leave at once," she panted. "They have been alerted to your presence in the city."

"Do they know we are at this inn?" Pherric asked.

"I do not believe so, but they may have heard whispers."

"They will start with the inns," he muttered. "We must get you out. Immediately."

"Only if she comes with me," I said, tightening my hold around Genevieve. "And Jonathan."

Pherric's mouth twitched. He expected that answer. "We will certainly get them out. That will not be difficult. *You* will be difficult."

"Oh, yeah," I said.

Genevieve scrunched her face. "What's so difficult about her?"

I twisted a curl of my red hair. "This. They call me *firehair* here. It's really rare, apparently."

Sandulf stepped in behind me, a wall of discipline. "Pherric, you take Jonathan and Genevieve. I will ensure the queen exits the city."

"How will you do that?" Pherric asked.

"Yeah, Sandulf... what's the plan?"

"We have no time to waste," he said briskly. "If the Atlanteans know you are in Canela, they will increase security before their search begins. This is what I would do. We must leave now, your highness."

I was still too exhausted from being *alive again* to argue.

He pressed a silk headscarf into my hands and ushered me down the hallway. I tried to give Genevieve one last reassuring look, but Sandulf had us around the corner and down the stairwell before I could do anything.

"How did you happen to have a scarf on you?"

He shoved open the inn's doors, scanning the narrow street. When he saw no soldiers, he guided me onto the sun-baked road. Dust coated everything in a film of despair. The bright paint on the buildings was still there, but the color seemed... tired. Everything had given up trying.

When we landed here five months ago, Canela was loud and vibrant and full of life. Now shutters hung half-closed, shop signs creaked in the wind, and the only voices were whispers. Even the air felt muted, as if the city itself was dying a slow death.

"I have feared this day would come," Sandulf murmured. "I keep that scarf and a pouch of coin on me at all times."

He handed me a small leather purse. I slipped it inside my vest, the coins rattling softly—one of the few sounds in a city that used to hum with life.

"I did not wish to remain here once the other ports fell," he continued. "But Pherric insisted, especially after you failed to... return to us."

I tied the scarf tightly around my head.

"Keep your head down," he ordered. "We will go out the largest gate."

"The largest?" I blinked at him. "Shouldn't we try a smaller one?"

"That is where they will concentrate their search. More guards, stricter inspections. The main gate because..." He gave a grim half-smile. "chaos works in our favor."

We hurried through Canela's winding streets. The banners that flew overhead were gone. The vibrant pottery I remembered had vanished from balconies, replaced with empty hooks or broken clay. A few vendors sat beside bare tables, staring hollow-eyed at nothing in particular. No sizzling smells drifting from street grills, no sweet burst of orange blossoms on the breeze, no spices perfuming the market stalls. It was hot, dry, empty.

The other missing ingredient. Children laughing, playing, running around. There were none to be seen.

Except one.

A small boy ran out from an alleyway and tugged at my sleeve, hand open, eyes too old for his tiny face. Instinctively, I reached for my hidden coins, but Sandulf's fingers clamped around my wrist.

"No," he whispered. "If you give him coin, ten more will swarm you.

And someone desperate enough might try to take the rest... by force."

He pulled me along the street and the boy drifted away without a word, swallowed by a thinning crowd.

We pressed on, passing shuttered bakeries and boarded-up taverns. A karkadann-drawn wagon clattered by, piled not with goods but with people fleeing... whatever this place was becoming.

Finally, we stepped onto the broad thoroughfare leading to the main gate. Once bustling, it was now a wound—wide, raw, bleeding citizens who streamed toward escape with whatever they could carry. A few vendor tents still stood, but most were empty, canvas flapping weakly in the breeze like abandoned sails.

We hugged the walls as Sandulf led me through the gathering throng. He moved with the precision of a man who'd mapped every possible escape route months ago.

At last, we reached the outer gates. Very few were coming in; most were leaving.

He nudged me into the line of foot travelers leaving the city. Wagons and carts were being stopped and inspected at the large gate, but pedestrians passed through a smaller iron side-gate—quicker, less scrutinized.

A Canelan guard, broad-shouldered and bronze-skinned, wearing a scuffed plumed helmet, looked each person up and down before mindlessly waving them through. His eyes were sunken, exhausted. For once, luck seemed willing to give me a scrap.

Only a handful of people stood ahead of us.

Naturally, that's when two Atlantean soldiers marched up to the gate.

They whispered to the guard. His posture snapped straight. His eyes swept the crowd with new intensity.

And I bet he'd been warned to look out for a shorter, red-haired woman.

Shit.

"This is not good," I murmured.

Sandulf's grunt said he agreed.

The guard began inspecting people more thoroughly: lifting hats, checking satchels, demanding their thin coats be removed.

If he asked me to take off my scarf... I was done.

Sandulf leaned in. "Follow me."

We slipped out of the line and into a side street. Sandulf scanned the area and we ducked into an alley. He turned to me. "Wait here."

"Okay, but—"

He was gone before I finished.

Seconds later, he returned with an empty bottle of liquor. An elderly man snored in the dirt at the end of the alley.

Sandulf splashed the bottle's remaining drops into his palm and smeared it across his mouth. "When the time is right, slip out the small gate. Do you understand?"

"Yeah, but when will I know—"

"You will know. Come."

He placed me back in line and took a spot several people behind me. I kept my head low as the line crept forward. I had a vague idea what he planned—but zero clue how it would actually work.

The guard was only two people away from me.

"Bygods, hurry it along!" came a slurred voice.

Sandulf.

He staggered out of line, pretending to chug the bottle.

"I got to... get home!" he bellowed and then burped.

The guard's head snapped up. "Get back in line!"

Sandulf swayed. "I am in a *rush*! I have no time for this!" He flung his arm dramatically, bottle in hand, pushing those around him away. I stepped back too.

The Atlanteans leaned in, away from the wall, hands drifting toward sword hilts.

The guard stormed at him. "Oy! Back in line or I will throw you in a cell, ya drunkard!"

Sandulf tipped the bottle upside down. Not a drop came out. He tossed it. Glass shattered. Karkadanns shuffled. People gasped. Heads turned.

Perfect distraction.

"Drunkard? *I* am not drunk! *You* are drunk!" he shouted.

I drifted backward, pressing against the city wall.

As the guard shoved Sandulf and sent him sprawling, the Atlanteans stepped forward—and I slipped through the small gate.

I hurried along the outer wall, not daring to break into a run until I turned the corner. Footsteps echoed. A hand clamped around my arm.

Expecting Sandulf, I turned—

—and found myself face-to-face with an Atlantean soldier.

"I saw you!" he barked.

He reached for my scarf.

Instinct took over.

I stepped forward and wrapped my arms around him in a desperate hug. "Oh, gods be with you! I was frightened!"

"What... hey!" His arms were awkwardly splayed.

I hugged him tighter.

"Let me see under that scarf!" he demanded, pushing me back.

His hand reached out.

I held up the dagger I stole from the belt at his waist.

And plunged it into his side—once, twice, three times—pressing my body to his so the movement blended into the embrace. He sagged in my arms as life left him. I eased him to the wall.

A woman passing nearby gasped. I pointed to the fallen soldier.

"He's tired," I lied weakly.

I feared she would sound the alarm, but when she saw the blood, and the dagger in my hand, she ran. And then, I ran too.

I sprinted across the dusty clearing, boots slipping in loose gravel, the city wall shrinking behind me. A low hill rose ahead, dotted with stubborn patches of dry grass, and I threw myself over it. Only when I plunged into a scraggly patch of woodland—more a collection of half-dead trees than a real forest—did I let myself slow.

If you ever die and come back, don't try to run. Trust me.

I braced a hand against a rough trunk, listening. Nothing but the rasp of insects and my own ragged breathing.

Still... I looked over my shoulder.

Again.

And again.

Every shifting shadow seemed to be an Atlantean soldier materializing out of the heat. Every crack of a twig sent my pulse spiking in my neck.

Sandulf had planned how to get me out.

He had *not* planned what I'd do once I was out.

I stuck close to the thin tree line, ducking beneath branches that snagged at my scarf, moving parallel to the edge of the forest. The soil here was sandy and bright, scattered with jagged stones and thorny brush that tugged at my boots. Between the gnarled oaks and stunted pines, slivers of sky glared down. It was too bright, too exposed.

After a long while, the trees thinned, and a wide stretch of packed dirt came into view beyond the last row of trunks. Wagons rattled past, pulled by karkadanns. Merchants shouted. Wheels groaned. A column of dust drifted lazily into the sunlit air.

The main road.

I hadn't even realized I'd been angling toward it the whole time.

I crouched low behind a cluster of brambles as a carriage rolled by, its passengers oblivious. I waited until it passed, then crept down to the roadside, keeping low. Every time a wagon approached, I ducked behind a fallen log or slipped into a shallow ditch, heart thumping until the sound faded.

They would be searching for me now, especially if they found the dead Atlantean.

Eventually I collapsed onto a flat rock beneath a twisted old tree, breath leaking out of me in shaky bursts. My legs trembled. My head pounded.

Hopefully Pherric and the others would make it out clean.

And hopefully they'd take this road.

Otherwise... I was fucked.

65

Tied Up and Pissed Off

Finley

I was being followed.

Kasuma had drilled the instinct into me so well it was a reflex, an itch under my skin, a tingle at the back of my neck. That night, under the thin, unnatural slice of Tir Na's fake moon, I crept through the light forest, staying alongside the main road out of Canela and pretending I didn't notice the shadows tailing me.

There were three of them.

Breathing too heavy. Steps too wide apart. The weight distribution of adult men. Women tended to fall lighter on their heels, but men compressed the earth. These guys were making the dirt *sink*. They were big and strong. Three distinct cadences. Three bodies adjusting their stride when I adjusted mine.

They formed a loose triangle around me, one behind and two on the flanks, trailing me without actually closing in. Waiting for something.

I debated scrambling up one of the scraggly, half-dead trees lining the road, but the branches were too thin to hide me. One glance up and they'd see me perched there like a very confused, very doomed owl.

They might have been Atlantean, but honestly? Didn't matter. Anyone following me this long, this far, wasn't planning to invite me to a party.

Why didn't they just get it over with? A rush. A few blade strokes. A quick "welcome back to life, now die again" moment in the woods.

But instead, we danced this stupid dance for over an hour—me pretending not to notice, them pretending they were hunters and not three dudes who kept stepping on branches.

Fine. But I was tired and hungry.

I doubled back silently, slipping off my path and into a patch of trees. Picked the widest trunk I could find and flattened myself against it. I steadied myself until even the night insects seemed louder.

When I stopped moving, they figured it out and stopped too. Confused. Good.

Then they started again, very slowly closing in, but they had guessed my location wrong. They thought I was farther along. I let my eyelids fall shut, focusing on sound alone.

There.

The nearest one.

He moved carefully, but not carefully enough. Dried leaves cracked under his sole. His boot scraped the dust. He exhaled heavily. Nervous or annoyed, not sure which.

I could take him from behind. Quick. Quiet. Knife to the neck, then drop him down. But he was just out of perfect range. Close enough I'd reach him, far enough that any sound from my own boot might give me away.

Still... I had to try.

I opened my eyes. He was tall, wrapped in black leathers that blended into the night—clearly someone who'd done this before. But he wasn't looking behind him.

I slipped from the shadows, weight placed feather-light, step by silent step. My hand reached for his forehead, knife poised to open his throat—

He stopped.

Straightened.

Fuck.

Had he heard me?

"Do not," he whispered, voice barely audible.

I remained motionless but kept the knife lifted.

"I am not here to hurt you," he added.

My fingers crept closer to his neck anyway.

"I am Eryd."

"I couldn't give a damn," I muttered.

I pressed the tip of my blade at his back. He lifted his hands slowly, compliant.

That's when the other two emerged in their dark leathers, flanking me. But they stayed back.

Eryd took a deliberate step forward and turned to face me, hands still up.

"I am not from Atlantis," he said. "I am from Elysium. We come in good faith."

"Why?"

"You have been summoned."

I slid my eyes toward the others—they stayed away, hands near their weapons but not attacking. And I wondered who had summoned me, but that was a distraction. He was stalling me, trying to get my drop my guard.

"Okay," I said. "Then why all the cloak-and-dagger shit? You know, the lurking, the stalking, the '*I'm a shadow! Fear me*' routine? If you wanted to talk, you could've just yelled 'hey.' Simple."

Eryd blinked, clearly not expecting the feedback.

"You are a formidable warrior," he said carefully. "We were unsure if you would come willingly."

"What makes you think I'll go now?"

Before he could answer, a hood slammed down over my head.

A fourth man.

Silent as a ghost.

He was good. I never once heard a fourth man.

Shit, shit, shit!

I'd been played. The other three were the loud decoys. He was the predator.

I was shoved to the dirt, hands yanked behind my back and bound. I thrashed, but the weight of two bodies pinned me down. My knife torn from my grip.

"This is a shitty way to summon someone, dickheads!" I spat.

"Forgive me," Eryd said, maddeningly gentle. "I was not given a choice."

I never saw the fourth man's face.

Yep. Me being kidnapped yet again. Starting to see a pattern?

Well, they marched me for several axims, keeping close but not within kicking range, as we followed the quiet main road. Every so often I tried something new: asking questions, insulting their mothers, you know, just being my charming self. But these guys had taken vows of silence or were physically incapable of banter.

Nothing worked.

Not even when I questioned whether they were compensating for something with all the leather.

Eventually, they shoved me into a carriage and tied my hands to a wooden door pillar. The carriage lurched forward. Karks pulled us along. We rode for an hour, judging only by how many times my head smacked against the damn carriage wall. Then the wheels turned and screeched and we changed direction. Another long stretch of rattling and bumping followed until we finally slowed.

New sounds drifted through the hood: karkadanns snorting, footsteps crunching over packed dirt, doors creaking open and slamming shut. Voices. Muted, tired, too few to be a proper town. A small village, maybe. But it was late at night.

We stopped. Hands clamped around my arms and dragged me out of the carriage, across a dirt lane, between two buildings by the sound of our feet echoing off the walls, and through a door heavy enough to groan in protest. They halted me somewhere warm.

I stood still and listened. A fire hissed nearby, popping now and then. Torches crackled along walls. The air smelled of ale, old wood, and... god, stew. Meat stew. My stomach let out a traitorous growl loud enough that anyone in the room would have heard it.

The hood ripped away.

Light stabbed into my eyes. After a few blinks, the room sharpened into view: wood-plank walls, crates stacked high, kegs of ale lined in rows, bottles of wine gleaming in the firelight. Hooks on rafters, burlap sacks, more barrels. It was a back room. A storage room for a tavern, but a large one.

"Well, that was fun," I said dryly, spotting Eryd standing beside me. "Next time, maybe just send an invitation instead of the whole kidnapping spa package?"

The rickety wooden door I had been brought through creaked open.

Torchlight spilled across the floor... followed by enough political power to start (or end) a continental war.

King Ferghas of Elysium staggered through the doorway first, because, well... yeah. He barreled into the room like he expected applause. His curly red hair stuck out wildly, his beard a masterpiece of chaos, and he was holding—*I swear to god*—another tankard of ale. During my kidnapping.

"Your majesty!" he boomed, grinning wide enough to show every tooth. "Good to see ya!"

"I can't believe you're still alive," I muttered before I could stop myself.

"What was that?" he called, cupping a hand to his ear.

He drank a lot, so I plastered on a smile and said louder, "I said, I can't believe you're here."

Behind him swept Queen Urraca of Ogun, all crimson and gold and lethal grace. Two of her spear men followed, formation tight even in a tavern storage room. I noted she had a few new scars. Likely from her battle against the Atlanteans.

She gave me a single cool nod. Regal. Measured. Judging me and the décor simultaneously.

"You look well," she said.

"Well? I was *kidnapped*," I snapped. "Did that part not make it into your briefing?"

Urraca blinked once, the royal equivalent of a spit-take.

Then the room shook.

Jarl Trym Baldrson had to turn sideways to fit through the door. He still scraped both shoulders. The thin furs, the braids, the sheer glacier-sized mass of him—he brought two axe-bearing warriors behind him, because apparently this needed to feel more like a raid.

He slammed one fist to his chest in greeting. "Dragonwitch."

More shadows filled the doorway.

The Prominan king was next. I did not know him yet, but he was tall, and his fur gleamed in silver. His sea-green robe caught the torchlight. He moved with slow, deliberate calm, the exact opposite of everyone else, accompanied by a pair of ape-men whose expressions suggested they regretted being alive that day.

Then another figure appeared. Alone.

King Dagda of Mag Mell ducked inside, towering even among giants. His bluish-black beard hung past his chest. He was broader than Trym, with a heavy brow ridge casting deep shadows over eyes the color of stormwater.

Next came King Longzhe of Oceantis, wings folded and buried beneath a dark cloak. His Tenguans lined up behind him, silent and disciplined.

And then, just when I thought the room couldn't get any more crowded, the final figure entered, flanked by three armed guards in polished Cíbolan plate.

The reason I have trust issues, rage issues, and will have at least three future therapists on standby.

The man I've wanted dead more than anyone who's ever lived.

My peak-level, *final-boss* mortal enemy.

Lord Diago of Cíbola.

My mouth dropped open. Tall, elegant, and infuriatingly composed, with long silver hair tied back in a sleek ponytail. His tailored coat—deep obsidian trimmed with hammered gold—fitted him perfectly, each silver ring on his fingers catching the firelight with smug precision. Even his boots looked expensive enough to feed a small town.

His smile spread easily, charmingly. He was simply greeting an old friend instead of the woman whose death warrant he'd basically signed.

"Queen Finley," he purred, bowing with infuriating grace. "It is... an honor."

I didn't think. I lunged.

Bound wrists, aching limbs, sleep-deprivation, still-technically-recent resurrection—none of it mattered. Rage did the moving for me.

His guards reacted instantly, swords drawn, crossing glowing-steel blades inches from my face. The closest one stepped forward, blade pressed so near my cheek I could feel the heat of the forge it came from.

"Stand down!" Eryd growled, grabbing me around the waist and hauling me back before I could launch myself teeth-first at Diago's throat.

"Coward!" I snarled at him. "Traitor! You sold me out to Malek, had my friends killed, and now you *dare* to walk in here?!"

Diago's smile didn't falter. If anything, it intensified.

Eryd grabbed my arm.

"Don't you—" I jerked, twisting out of his grip.

"Your majesty," Eryd hissed, pulling again.

He turned me around to face a long, rectangular wood table, already set up behind me. This was the world's worst surprise party. Eryd tried steering me toward a chair.

He managed, through sheer stubbornness, to sit me down. I immediately fought against the ropes binding my wrists, leaning forward ready to launch myself at Diago.

The rulers began positioning themselves around the table as if this were all perfectly normal.

Ferghas thumped into his seat, sloshing ale onto the floorboards.

Urraca took hers with precision, already radiating the kind of patience one learns by ruling a nation of warriors.

Trym dropped onto his chair hard enough he seemed to want to break it first.

King Dagda's bench bowed ominously under his weight.

Longzhe folded into his seat with calm, the picture of unshakable diplomacy.

Diago—gilded Basilisk that he was—sat last, his three guards positioning themselves behind him.

Their attendants poured drinks. Not any tavern servers. This was a private meeting. The rulers settled in and everyone pretended I wasn't tied to a chair vibrating with barely-contained murder.

I fixed my stare on Diago.

"The hell is he doing here?!"

Longzhe lifted a hand. "Finley—"

"No." My chair screeched as pushed forward. "No, we're not doing *anything* until someone explains why Lord Backstab-and-Smile is sucking in the same air as me!"

Diago's smile widened just enough to make me want to throw myself over the table and throat-punch him.

Eryd's hand hovered near my shoulder, ready to restrain me. Again.

Longzhe exhaled. "We will address that, I promise you. But allow me first to—"

I interrupted. "Because unless we're hosting a war crimes trial, there is no fucking way he should be in my face right now!"

Dagda took a loud sip of something alcoholic. "She does have a point."

Diago's guards tightened their grips on their swords.

I yanked at my ropes. "Let me out of this seat and I'll provide exhibit A."

"Queen Finley," Longzhe said more firmly, leaning forward, wings folding tighter. "We will *get* to Diago's presence. But first—on behalf of all rulers gathered—I must apologize for the manner of your... retrieval."

"Retrieval?" I barked. "You mean kidnapping. The thing kidnappers do."

Ferghas raised his mug. "We did send Eryd. You should count it as a courtesy."

"Try that shit again and I promise one of you will be eating through a straw."

Ferghas laughed and cheered me before taking another drink.

Urraca tapped her fingers on the table. "We feared you might not come willingly."

I glared at Diago. "Oh, trust me, there's nothing *willing* happening with that man in the room."

"Speaking of trusting you..." said Urraca out of the side of her mouth.

"What's that supposed to mean?!"

"Finley," Longzhe said, calm as ever, "please. Listen. We are united for one purpose, and you are central to it."

"I'll listen," I growled. "But the second you're done explaining, I want him gone."

Diago looked at me the way someone appreciated fine art.

Longzhe inclined his head, unfazed. "The situation is as dire as the one we faced with Malek and Kane. Perhaps more so. Information reached us that you had been taken by Queen Thalassa to Atlantis, and subsequently hidden away in Canela for several months. We did not know if you were alive, compromised, coerced, or... altered."

"Altered," I repeated, staring at him. "You mean brainwashed? Enchanted? Or turned into Thalassa's personal hype woman?"

Ferghas snorted ale through his nose.

Longzhe continued carefully. "We needed to ensure our safety... and yours. When word reached us that you had slipped out of Canela, King Ferghas sent Eryd to retrieve you with... discretion."

I glared at Eryd. "Discretion? You hog-tied me like a satyr!"

"Respectfully, your grace," Eryd murmured, "you are very difficult to tie."

"Not helping!"

Longzhe lifted a calming hand. "We are here in secrecy because the Atlanteans control every major Southern port. If you had been compromised, even unintentionally, the risk to all gathered here would be catastrophic."

"Wonderful," I said. "Truly stellar justification for assault and abduction."

"I ask," he said, voice low but commanding, "not as a ruler, but as someone who has stood beside you in battle—be patient. Hear me out. Hear *all* of us out. What we face now is larger than any grudge, even one as justified as yours."

My jaw flexed. My pulse raced.

But every ruler in the room was watching me as if my answer might decide the fate of the world.

I exhaled once more.

"One minute," I warned. "And if Diago so much as twitches, I'm strangling him with my bare hands and several lifetimes of suppressed rage."

Ferghas lifted his mug. Again. "Gods, I have *missed* her!"

66

How to Start a Fight with Every Monarch Alive

Finley

My rage faded.

Slightly.

The realization of what they wanted slid into place, a blade settling between bone.

Across the table, the Prominan king kept his massive arms folded, fur bristling, eyes narrowed with open suspicion. His heavy brow cast a shadow that felt more accusatory than any words.

I shook my head, trying—failing—to shove thoughts of murdering Diago into a locked emotional cupboard. "I see what this is…"

Longzhe's brows pinched. "I apologize. I do not understand—"

"You want to organize our armies again. Get everyone back together." I waved a bound wrist at the assortment of monarchs—and shot Diago the most potent stink eye I could muster. "Yeah. Fight off the Atlanteans the same as we did against Kane. Sure. That makes sense."

Their faces shifted, some hopeful, some tense, some trying not to look directly at my wrists as if they weren't the reason I was tied to a chair in a tavern storage room.

"I get why Ogun, Elysium, and Cíbola—fuck you, Diago—are here. But why Mag Mell, Kunlun, and Valhalla? They haven't invaded your ports. Hell, I don't think there *are* ports in Mag Mell."

Trym cleared his throat. "We simply wish to come to the aid of—"

"No, no," I cut in. "That's not it. Not out of the *goodness of your heart.*"

Dagda leaned forward on the bench straining under his weight. "We, um, simply want to open the lanes of trade once again."

I grinned at him. "Oh, why don't you just admit that you depend on other kingdoms for food and other resources?"

His eyes flitted guiltily around the table. "We are a proud land. We rely on no one and want for nothing."

"But...?" I coaxed.

He wilted. "We do enjoy fruits and vegetables that come from the south, this is true."

Trym took a long drink, slamming his mug down. "And it is only a matter of time before they move north."

The king of Kunlun lifted his furred chin. "We believe our ports are next."

"I'm sorry, your highness," I said. "We haven't met."

"No, we have not."

I looked down at my tied hands, then back at him. What a fantastic first impression. "My sincere apologies, your highness. Not exactly the most dignified way to meet a fellow ruler."

That seemed to appease him. Proud Prominan. All about formality. He gave me a curt nod.

"I am called Fu. Let me simply say that you have lived up to your reputation."

Pretty sure that was an insult. Then... oh no. Fu. *King Fu.* His name was King FU!

I almost wheezed. It took everything I had not to laugh. These Prominans, always bringing it the joke names.

"Thank you. I think. I look forward to proving my value to you... some day."

Another brief nod.

"So, we're forming an alliance then? That the plan?"

"Yes, that is our intent," admitted Longzhe.

He motioned for Eryd to cut my restraints.

Ferghas grinned. He was ready to take out popcorn for the upcoming show. He was hoping I'd go after Diago again. Eryd cut the rope.

Trym exhaled. "Are you sure that is wise?"

"Queen Finley understands what is at stake now. Do you not?" Longzhe asked.

I rubbed my wrists, debating whether to vault the table and stab the Lord with a fork. "I do."

But I pointed straight at Diago. His guards immediately tensed, hands on hilts. "So, you didn't come to our aid to stop Kane and his army. And now you expect *us* to help you? Is that it?"

"Young lady, I simply wish to do what is best for the entire continent."

I exploded up out of my chair, sending it clattering backward. Eryd grabbed my arms before I got anywhere.

"What was best would've been helping us back then!"

Diago lifted his palms. "I made a grievous error in judgment and—"

"No. You tried to back what you thought was the winning side!"

"My people were starving. The same as the other kingdoms. But ours was not a rogue nation. Many others did not come to your aid."

"Yes," I snarled. "But you also turned me in! You got my friends killed! For that... you will die."

"Queen Finley, please..." Longzhe implored, rising to his feet.

"She is right," Diago said quietly, infuriatingly calm. "I erred in the most unforgivable way. I understand your anger. Truly."

"By my own hand. You understand that? That is how you die."

"I do. But let us focus on the task at hand. You will need my warriors."

"Why?! We didn't need them at the Battle of Shangri-La!"

He looked away for a beat, then forced a smooth smile. "Because of that battle, the strength of all our lands has been greatly diminished. Yours included."

I dropped into my chair with crossed arms—pure defiance.

Silence strangled the room until Ferghas snapped his fingers at his attendant. Drinks were poured. Someone placed a steaming bowl of stew in front of me, and the scent nearly made me faint in the chair. God, I was starving.

"All right," I muttered, breaking the silence mostly so I could eat. "What's the plan?"

Longzhe relaxed for the first time, sitting up straight. "We have begun to amass our troops, every kingdom and Cíbola as well. Our goal is to regain the ports and drive the Atlanteans back to their island."

I shoveled in a bite. "You mean by attacking Atlantis, right?"

He blinked. "We mean to confront them where they are, of course. Starting with—"

"Starting with Ogun," Urraca snapped. "As we have agreed."

"We have agreed on nothing," Diago said. Selfish dick.

Ferghas leaned in. "Elysium should be the first prong of engagement! The Prominans, Valhallans, and Fomorians will be sailing directly by my land!"

Arguments erupted. Urraca rolled her eyes. Trym banged a fist. Diago muttered something smug. Ferghas reached for more bread.

I shoveled stew with the single-minded fury of a *skritcher* loose in a grain cellar.

Fu said nothing. He simply watched me with that heavy, unsettling stillness.

Longzhe tried to restore order. It failed spectacularly.

With a sigh, I pushed my bowl away and drank deep from my wine. "Stop!"

The command cracked. Fu slammed a massive hand onto the table, rattling mugs and spilling ale. I saved my wine mug out of sheer reflex.

Silence fell. All eyes swung to him.

"I wish to hear what the queen of Irkalla believes to be our best course of action."

My throat dried. "Me?"

"You." He stood and planted both fists onto the table. "I was fighting in the valley at the Battle of Shangri-La. Wounded and dying. Had you not brought the dragons, had you not rallied my people, had you not driven the enemy back from the city walls... I would not be here."

"Well, I kinda got lucky and then—"

"What would be your plan?"

Deep inhale.

"Okay," I began slowly. "I get why you think fighting them at the ports makes sense. Overwhelm them, push them back into the sea. But that's a tiny bandage on a gaping wound."

Urraca groaned. "Here she goes again."

"Listen to me," I snapped. "Thalassa has a handful of immortal soldiers. Even if you wipe out her regular forces, they'll regroup and retake every port the second we leave."

"They would not dare!" Dagda barked.

"They would. You don't know her the way I do."

"And there is our exact problem!" Urraca jabbed a finger at me. "She is in league with the Atlanteans! I said this would be true!"

Longzhe exhaled through his nose. "We know nothing to be true, Urraca."

"I'm not in league with her!" I shouted. "She tried to kill me! She has my boyfriend!"

Trym folded his arms. "Then he is why you wish to attack Atlantis directly? Instead of the ports? To retrieve your mate?"

"No! I—I..." Every ounce of confidence shattered. "No. That's not it."

"Then why attack Atlantis?!"

"First of all—" I stalled, absolutely winging it. "First of... Look. She took over too many ports. She only has ten soldiers in the Deep Guard. They can't be killed, but they're spread too far out."

Glances crossed the table. Some skeptical. Some curious.

"Go on," Longzhe urged.

"We attack each port and we probably take them back. At least some of them. She knows that. And she'd just send her immortal squad back in once we left. But if we go *straight at her*, her soldiers will have to rush home. To defend the homeland."

Trym grunted. "But that is a problem. Atlantis is their home. They would have the advantage."

"Oh, I'll admit it. They've got a huge navy. Great weapons. But we have numbers." I glared at Diago. "Well, assuming Cíbola actually shows up this time."

Diago's jaw clenched.

"We've got ships, warriors, and the element of surprise. Thalassa will expect us to hit the ports. And there are no walls around Atlantis. If we take the island, we win the war."

"And you can find the island?" asked Longzhe.

"I can. It's hidden, but I know where and... *how* to look."

As soon as I said that a dozen arguments erupted instantly: troop distribution, ship counts, Atlantean weaponry, who's in charge... all that shit.

I leaned back, sipping my wine like I wasn't internally screaming.

Fu reclined as well, giving me the smallest, most satisfied nod...

I had *no idea* if any of this would work. Not even a little.

Because if we didn't get this right... If this alliance fell apart, or if I hesitated, wavered, or failed—

I would never see Braylor again.

"Atlantis," I murmured to myself, fingers curling into a fist. "I'm coming. Just... hold on."

I wasn't sure if I was praying or promising. Maybe both. I sat in my chair, wine forgotten, stew cooling, heart hammering with a single truth:

This wasn't about politics. This was about Braylor.

And I would burn the ocean itself if that's what it took to bring him home.

67

In the Event of War, Please Board Quickly

Genevieve

It was night, which was usually when bad ideas started feeling reasonable.

The shoreline outside Magoria was quiet in a way that felt staged. The world had paused just to see who would screw up first. The waves didn't crash. They barely moved, slipping up the sand in soft, useless motions. I didn't trust it. I never trusted calm.

Out on the water, three ships waited.

No lanterns, no reassuring glow to prove there were people on board. Just massive shapes floating in the dark, motionless enough to look abandoned. Dead in the water. If I hadn't known better, I would've sworn they were traps—set there to see who was desperate enough to come close.

The *Thalyra*. The *Skathis*. The *Aegiros*.

Saying their names in my head didn't make them feel more real. Just heavier.

I told myself I was fine. That this was just another bad decision layered on top of worse ones, and I'd survived those, and clearly I'd survive this too. Confidence was easier when no one could see your hands shaking.

We stayed low near the shore, a few miles beyond the outer edge of camp. My Irkallan helmet was tipped forward just enough to shadow my face.

Cold sand pressed into my hands—gritty, damp, the kind that worked its way into your skin no matter how hard you scrubbed later.

Torchlight rippled along the beach as soldiers moved past in short lines. There was no chatter or bravado, only boots and purpose. Everyone here knew exactly where they were going.

Between them and the ships were the ferries.

Flat-bottomed boats rocked gently as they touched shore. Crews shouted counts while soldiers boarded in tight groups. Once full, the ferries shoved off, oars hitting the water, and vanished into the dark.

We were not on the list.

The realization sent an intense, electric thrill through my chest. Fear and excitement tangled together until I couldn't tell where one ended and the other began.

Kinnat crouched beside me, so still she might've been carved out of the night itself. Her shoulder brushed mine when she breathed—slow, steady. Familiar.

"Last few waves will be going out," she murmured. "After that, I doubt they will be counting as closely. At least I hope that is the case."

I nodded. If we missed it, we missed everything.

Waiting always did this to me. Standing still gave my memory room to stretch, and memory never waited to be invited.

I thought of Finley. The guilt was still there. It hadn't vanished just because she'd returned from the dead. Guilt didn't evaporate, it adapted. Learned how to sit quieter and when to surface.

A few weeks ago, she'd looked me straight in the eye and told me it wasn't my fault. No hesitation. No softness. Just truth. Ramil had taken my mind. Used my body like a borrowed knife. And I believed her.

That didn't mean I'd forgiven myself.

Five months ago, I'd been sure the weight of what I'd done would crush me completely. That I'd keep waking up screaming or sobbing or hollowed out beyond repair.

Instead, something else happened.

I hardened. Not in a brittle way but in a way that sank deeper. Before all this, I thought I was tough. I strutted through New York as though I owned the sidewalks, talked big, laughed loud, never let anyone see when I was scared. I thought confidence was armor.

It wasn't. It was noise.

Real toughness was getting out of bed every day knowing exactly what your hands had done and choosing not to let that be the end of you. It was surviving mind control and deciding the person who did it didn't get to keep you.

Ramil had taken my body once. He would never get that chance again. I didn't know if he'd be on the island—but if he was, I was damn sure getting my revenge.

I stared out at the water as ferries raced back toward shore.

"Sometimes I wish none of this had happened," I said, only realizing I'd spoken aloud when the words were already gone. "That it was all a dream."

Kinnat's brow lifted. "You wish I were a... dream?"

I turned to her and kissed her, quick and certain. I needed the reminder.

"No," I whispered. "You're a dream come true."

My hand found hers. She squeezed back, steady and warm, and for a moment the fear loosened its grip.

If all of this insanity was real, at least I wasn't facing it alone.

My gaze drifted back to the water, and more memory followed.

Finley had vanished escaping Canela. When Sandulf was finally released, he took Jonathan, Kinnat, and me to Magoria. He'd led her to the gates of the city—and then lost her. Days passed with no word. No sign. No certainty that she was alive.

Then, suddenly, she was back. A carriage had rolled up and deposited her at the camp.

When I went looking, she'd already been swallowed by command tents and council circles—maps, messengers, decisions stacked on decisions.

I caught a glimpse of her once across the camp. Thinner. Tense. Furious in that quiet way that meant something big was coming.

Word spread fast after that. Faster than a fire ever had. A bunch of the kingdoms had come together. She had met with them after she left the Canela. There was to be a grand alliance. They were going to war. With Atlantis.

When I heard, I didn't hesitate. I went straight to Pherric. He was rushing across the camp and I caught up.

"I'm going," I told him. "With you guys. To fight them."

He didn't slow down. "No."

I matched his stride, heat flaring in my chest. "You don't get to decide that."

He stopped so abruptly I nearly ran into him. His eyes were hollow in a way that scared me. "I do," he said quietly. "Because I won't put her in danger again."

"I'm not a danger. You checked me out! You said you could sense nothing else in mind. And she trusts me!"

"I do not trust you, Genevieve." And he walked away.

I tried Sandulf next. Different man. Same wall.

At least with him, the rejection didn't feel like a door slammed in my face. He was gentle but firm, bracing the door shut with his *whole* body.

When he finished drilling an elite squad of Irkallan soldiers, I pulled him aside. Sweat darkened the collars of their tunics, bodies taut with discipline and exhaustion, eyes bright and unflinching. These weren't trainees. These were people who had already accepted the possibility that they wouldn't come back.

Without waiting or looking me in the eye, Sandulf exhaled and said, "I know what you want but I cannot allow it."

The words hit anyway.

"Did Finley tell you to keep me away?"

That finally made him look at me. Genuine surprise crossed his face. "No. But you have not completed any training. You have not held up in battle. You are, simply, not ready. I could not have your death on my conscience."

I swallowed. Hard. "Dude, are we leaving *tomorrow*? No! I will be ready. Kinnat and I will train. We've gone through months of training at the Scholomance," I begged, hating the way my voice leaned toward desperate.

He turned and pointed at his troops—men and women tightening straps, checking blades, quietly laughing. Even though it was the last calm moment before hell. "These soldiers have been training their whole lives. And many will not walk away from the island of Atlantis. You cannot be my responsibility."

That did it. Not anger. Not pride. Reality.

I wanted to argue. I wanted to say I'd survived worse than drills and blood and fear. But nothing reasonable came to mind. He was right. And that might have been the worst part.

So, instead, I walked away. The camp felt louder somehow. Metal clanking. Fires crackling. Orders barked across the clearing. Everyone moving with purpose, and I'd just been told to sit still and wait.

When I found Kinnat, she knew before I opened my mouth. She always did. "They said no."

"Yeah," I said, the words flat in my chest. "They said no."

"Then we will go." That was it. No bravado. No dramatics. Just a decision.

So we stole uniforms.

Late that night, when the camp had quieted into a restless half-sleep, we slipped into one of the supply tents. The smell of canvas and oil clung to everything. We moved fast, careful, hearts thudding—not from fear of punishment, but from the thrill of crossing a line we couldn't uncross.

We made off with two sets of armor that would fit well enough. Kinnat stitched mine tighter with practiced hands, adjusting straps and seams because she'd been doing it her whole life. I'd still probably stand out. I was shorter. Lighter. Less carved by years of war. But I looked the part.

And we trained our asses off. Weeks blurred together in sweat and bruises and aching muscles. Blades rang. Feet burned. My hands toughened. My reflexes improved. And through it all, Kinnat was there—correcting my stance, knocking me flat when I got sloppy, hauling me back up again without comment.

I got to spend precious days with her. Stolen hours. Fragile hours. Loving

Kinnat hadn't softened during the months we were kept apart. It had distilled down to the essentials. Her voice through a closed door. Her presence on the other side of silence. The knowledge that she stayed.

Now that I could touch her again, train beside her, and share the same space, every moment felt borrowed. I didn't know if we'd make it back either.

During our training, I recalled the first time I got to see her when Finley let me out of that room. Kinnat stood there, eyes rimmed red, unable to move. Her hands clenched because she was afraid I'd disappear again if she took a step.

I tried to speak. To apologize. To explain. None of it made it past my throat.

She crossed the room and held my face, memorizing me. This was something she'd practiced in her head to survive the days without me.

"What happened did not change how I chose you," she said quietly. Then, softer, "And know that I would've waited longer."

That was the moment I understood something fundamental. Not everyone loves like a fire. Some people love like a vow.

"Now," she whispered.

The present snapped back into place.

The final ferry nosed toward shore. Soldiers surged forward. Someone shouted a count.

Kinnat grabbed my sleeve and pulled me with the flow.

Heads down. No hesitation.

We stepped into line at the very back.

Boots thundered behind us as late stragglers sprinted in, helmets half-fastened, shields banging. The line compressed until I could feel breath on my neck. Too close.

I squared my shoulders and stood tall as we walked forward.

The officer raised a hand. "Stop."

Everything inside me went cold.

Then his eyes moved past us. Counting. Not suspecting.

"All of you... break off," he snapped, pointing toward another ferry scraping onto the sand. "You are heading to the *Thalyra*."

Damn it. I had hoped to be on Finley's ship, but those were the breaks.

We boarded as the ferry shoved off, Magoria shrinking behind us. The night was warm enough that sweat trickled down my spine, but I still felt cold, the hair on my arms lifting. My body knew something I hadn't said out loud yet.

I curled my fingers into a fist.

Finley trusted me. More than I probably deserved.

I wasn't staying behind. And I wanted a shot at Ramil.

Kinnat glanced at me. "You are thinking loudly."

"I do that."

She gave a devilish grin.

"I'm scared," I admitted. "But I'd rather be moving."

Her mouth curved. "Good."

The ships loomed larger.

Atlantis waited.

This time, I would choose where my sword landed.

68

Simply Unfinished

Jonathan

The sea was angry.

It had shaken off its stillness. Long swells moved beneath us now, lifting the ship in slow, deliberate rises that made the deck groan. It felt transitional; the moment before a reaction tips and there's no returning to equilibrium.

I stood at the rail of the *Aegiros*, boots planted wide as the deck shifted beneath me, and watched the sea with a focus that felt almost clinical. It didn't change. It didn't break. It simply existed, uninterrupted.

Behind us, the *Thalyra* and the *Skathis* cut through the water at full sail, their lanterns held in careful formation. More ships followed beyond those, with lines and angles spreading outward until the fleet felt less like an armada and more like an equation that refused to resolve.

So many banners. All these kingdoms moving in the same direction, not because they agreed, but because they had arrived at the same conclusion from different fears. That kind of unity could work—temporarily—but it was narrow by design. When pressure shifted, so might the alignment.

Atlantis waited somewhere ahead. I tried not to dwell on it. I didn't need to. The knowledge sat in my chest anyway, solid and persistent, alongside everything else I'd been avoiding since Finley came back to the camp in

Magoria and nothing felt simple anymore.

I rested my hands on damp wood, watching the dark water slip past us. Night pressed in from all sides, the sea stretched flat and endless, broken only by the low silhouettes of other ships cutting through the water alongside us.

Finley had come back to camp changed. More intense, but quieter. Whatever had happened in her meeting, it had adjusted something in her. She hadn't said much, just enough to make it clear that war was no longer theoretical.

I hadn't been invited into any of that planning. No councils. No strategy circles. No whispered decisions over maps.

But at least I'd been invited onto the ship. I wasn't sure what that said about me.

Mostly, I'd done nothing at all.

Sure, I had changed my mind about poisoning Finley. And figured out how to lift us and throw ourselves over to Atlantis to escape. But other than steering our boat away, I'd done nothing.

My brain decided to pick a fight with the memory of how close I'd come to killing her. That thought lodged itself in my head, uninvited and unwelcome.

She'd forgiven me. Or at least, she'd said she had. I wasn't sure I deserved it.

The deck creaked softly beneath me as the ship cut through the water. Wind pulled at me, cool against my skin.

A presence settled beside me.

Pherric stood there, his green cloak stirring in the breeze, eyes fixed on the ships beside us. He looked unbothered by the vastness of it all.

"You have been quiet," he said.

"Not much to say, really."

"You are truly a wonder. What you are capable of? Most fully trained mages spend decades failing to achieve that. You are remarkable."

"I'm not really sure about that," I said, trying to smile.

He folded his arms. "Jonathan, what you can do should not be possible for someone newly awakened to mindforms. Finley told me you were able to throw her and yourself across the water. She has been able to affect a touch, one time, in a tavern against a foe. But not again. I have never been able to do such a thing."

I shrugged, uncomfortable of praise. "It felt less like strength and more like... desperation. And I don't know how it happens, it just does."

Pherric smiled faintly. "And yet that is precisely what makes you remarkable."

That word again. I wasn't sure it fit. But I knew enough about Pherric to realize he wasn't one to flatter. He was studying me, trying to piece together something he hadn't yet understood.

"I have seen many variations of mindforms," he continued. "But what you do is older. Wilder. To move matter with pure will..." He shook his head slightly. "I have only heard of it mentioned in long forgotten books. Legends from before the dragons."

"Ramil said something similar," I admitted. "He told me it was rare... maybe impossible now here on this world. He also said—" I hesitated, remembering that strange conversation. "He said most people who can use mindforms here are... what did he call them? *Strorgrir*. Cold. Detached. They don't feel much of anything. They have no empathy."

Pherric's expression darkened. "Yes. The word means something similar to 'unmoved.' Those who master the mindforms learn to quiet the heart. To still compassion until nothing stirs the water within. It is the only way most survive the training."

I gave a tired laugh. "Then I'm a terrible fit. I feel *everything*. It's all noise in my head half the time."

"Yet you are the one who succeeded." Pherric leaned closer. "Do you not see? Ramil sought power without conscience, but he required someone with conscience to wield it. He needed your empathy to bridge what he himself could never reach. In the end, that was his downfall."

His words settled. "You think that's why he chose me?"

"I know it." Pherric's gaze didn't waver. "He believed he could bend you, that your compassion could be redirected—turned to anger, then loyalty, then obedience. But he misjudged what empathy truly is. To feel deeply is not to be weak. It is to be rooted. You could not be twisted because you care too much. You were too... Hominan."

The ship rocked, and for a long moment neither of us spoke. The sails above caught the breeze, and I thought of Ramil's face when he'd first told me I was "unique." I'd taken it as a compliment, maybe even a sign of destiny. Now it sounded more like a trap.

"I should have seen through him," I murmured. "I wanted to believe I was special. That I finally mattered."

"You *do* matter. But not because of what you can lift with your thoughts. You matter because you did not become what he wanted you to be."

I looked down at my hands. They were calloused, trembling slightly, the veins standing out beneath skin that looked too sickly. "He said empathy was rare. Dangerous, even. That it clouds reason."

"Of course he did," Pherric said. "Those who crave control always call compassion a weakness. It frightens them, because they do not have it and it cannot be commanded."

I met his gaze. "You think that's what makes me different?"

"I think," Pherric said slowly, "that your heart gives your mind its strength. You have touched something beyond mindforms. What you're doing, moving matter with intent born of care and not dominance, hasn't been seen in centuries. You reach *through* things instead of *against* them. That is why it works for you."

The deck shifted, and moonlight cut across his face, gilding the acute line of his jaw. For all his stoicism, there was warmth there too... the kind born of respect.

"Ramil thought he had found a weapon," Pherric went on. "Instead, he found a mirror. He looked at you and saw what he had never had: caring, connection, the ability to love without fear."

I exhaled. The pounding in my temples eased slightly. "So what you're saying is... being decent is my superpower."

Pherric chuckled, deep and genuine. "If you wish to call it that, yes. But do not diminish it. We have built a world rich in power and strength, but poor in kindness."

The sea glittered in fractured blue light, and for a moment I felt a quiet kinship.

Pherric shifted his stance, the movement subtle but deliberate, and his gaze slid away from me toward the upper deck.

The breeze chilled me. I tightened my cloak. The ship rolled beneath us, steady and indifferent.

"You are not useless, Jonathan," he said at last. His voice was calm, certain. "You are simply unfinished."

The words caught me off guard.

I frowned and turned to see what he was looking at.

Kasuma stood alone near the forward rail, her wings folded awkwardly against her sides. One hung a few degrees down—subtly, but unmistakably—throwing off her balance, her posture strained in a way that made my chest tighten. She wasn't watching the fleet or the sky. She was staring down at the water, head tilted slightly, waiting for it to answer a question it hadn't heard yet.

She looked... stranded.

Pherric watched her in silence, his expression no longer distant. Something had shifted there. Not concern, exactly, but focus. Calculation. Possibility.

69

Desperate Times, Improvised Measures

Finley

The captain's quarters were too quiet for a ship carrying part of an army.

Maps lay spread across my table, weighted down at the corners. I stood over them without really seeing anything, listening instead to the low creak of wood and the steady push of water against the hull. Every decision had already been made. All that was left was following them through.

A knock sounded at the door.

Before I could answer, it opened. Pherric stepped inside, his shoulders brushing the frame, Jonathan trailing a half-step behind him, entirely unsure why he'd been summoned.

Pherric inclined his head. "Your majesty."

"Pherric," I said, then glanced over. "Jonathan."

He nodded awkwardly. "Hi."

Pherric wasted no time. "Did Genevieve and her companion succeed in boarding?"

A smile tugged at my mouth. "Yes. She made it. She's on the Thalyra."

Jonathan blinked. "Wait? She did? She's here?" He frowned. "She thought you were ignoring her or mad at her or something. She said you

430

hadn't spoken at all in weeks."

"I know," I said calmly.

"Then why?" He looked genuinely confused now. "Um. Your highness."

"Because I needed to be sure," I said. "Sure she wouldn't try to come along because she felt obligated. Or guilty. Or afraid of disappointing me." I met his eyes. "I needed to know she was choosing this. Choosing the fight. Choosing the risk."

Jonathan swallowed. "And... you were okay letting her think you were angry?"

"I was okay letting her decide," I said. "If she's going to stand and fight with us, she needs to want to be here. Not because of me."

Pherric nodded once, approval flashing briefly across his face.

"Good," he said. Then, almost casually, "There is something else."

Jonathan stiffened.

Pherric turned slightly, angling his body back toward the door. "Kasuma's injury."

"What about it?" I said.

"I believe," Pherric said, "that Jonathan may be able to help her. To... heal her."

My attention snapped into place.

"Wait a minute. You!" I jabbed a finger toward Jonathan before the thought could cool.

"What?" He pointed to himself, startled. "Me?"

"Yes, you. You have telekinesis!"

I'd seen him hesitate every time the subject came up.

"Yes," he said warily, already backing away. "But no. No!"

"Why not?" I pressed.

"Because I'm not a doctor!" Jonathan blurted. "I—I would never try anything like that!"

Pherric folded his arms, rubbing his chin. "It might work."

"No way!" Jonathan waved frantically, tangling himself in his own sleeves.

I crossed the space and caught the front of his robe before he could retreat any farther. "Will you please try?"

Before he answered, I pulled him from the quarters. I looked all around until I saw Kasuma standing on the high castle. Jonathan complained as I dragged him up the stairs.

She turned to us, confused. "Yes?"

"He's going to help you!"

Kasuma eyed him up and down, eyebrows furrowed. "How do you mean?"

"They want to operate on you," I said before I thought about that. The words came out too fast. "Pherric wants Jonathan to use his mind powers to fix your broken wing."

She stared at me, face blank.

"Yes," Pherric said. "That is what I would want him to try."

Kasuma's gaze took in Jonathan's panic, Pherric's stillness, my barely contained hope.

She nodded once. "I am willing."

Jonathan looked as though he might fold in on himself, chest rising fast, breath tightened with every second. "I'm—I am not—I don't know how to—"

I steadied him, both hands firm on his arms. "Hey. It's okay. All I'm asking is that you try. Just like you did on the beach."

"Your highness," he rasped, "you've seen how inept I am. I moved you across the water, but I practically dropped you. I crashed myself into the beach. And I-I don't know enough about human anatomy to even—"

"Tenguan," I cut in.

He blinked. "What?"

"She's Tenguan," I said. "Not Hominan."

"That doesn't help," he said desperately. "I can't do it."

"Jonathan," I said. "I'm not asking you to throw Kasuma. Just use your mindform to... poke around in there a little." I gestured to her damaged wing. "You picked up grains of poison in my cell and dropped them into my food. This isn't much different."

"But moving a bone won't heal her," he said.

"How do you know?"

He hesitated. "I'm assuming your bones are hollow. Because you can fly?"

Kasuma nodded.

"Then they might get crushed! I can't fix that!"

I softened my grip on his robe, lowering my voice. "Will you please try? For me?"

Jonathan groaned, squeezing his eyes shut, unable to meet my gaze.

"I'll do it."

70

A Wing and a Prayer

Jonathan

To say I was scared was a massive understatement.

Terror parked itself on my chest, making every breath harder than the last.

Pherric signaled to several crew members to fetch a wood table.

The deck rolled beneath me, the ship groaning as waves struck the hull in uneven rhythms. Night swallowed what little light there was.

Kasuma climbed onto the table without hesitation, as though this were routine instead of insanity. She lay flat on her belly, wings spread just enough for access—one strong and steady, the other slack. Even injured, they were astonishing: silver-gray, tan, and white feathers layered with impossible precision, built for a physics I barely understood.

I didn't belong there.

Finley hovered, tense but quiet. Pherric stood a few paces back, arms folded, eyes assessing. But not interfering. They were trusting me with something I wasn't qualified to do.

"I need... room," I said, my voice barely cooperating.

They stepped back without argument.

The night air felt too warm, sweat already crawling down my neck despite the chill rising off the water. I threw off my cloak and wiped my hands on my trousers, inhaled, exhaled, then closed my eyes.

Darkness rushed in.

Then the familiar hum, the pain behind my eyes. Fear tried to claw its way back in, breaking my concentration. I opened my eyes again, grounding myself. I looked to Finley, her smile set, blue eyes fierce and steady.

She believed.

I closed my eyes again and let go.

The deck vanished. The sea disappeared. My awareness slipped inward, past the rough weave of the cloth on Kasuma's back, past cool skin, into something deeper. Muscle gave way beneath my focus, then bones—light, hollow, elegant. Built for flight.

Kasuma's heart fluttered beneath my awareness, fast but steady. She didn't move. She trusted me.

I shifted my attention to her uninjured wing first, mapping it carefully with my brain. The thick joint. Heavy tendons. The alignment. The way tension distributed itself naturally through bone and muscle. I memorized it the way you would a blueprint.

Then I moved back to the injured one.

The difference was immediate. That heavy joint sat too high—not shattered, not crushed, but displaced. Wrenched from its proper position, like a door forced off its hinge.

"I–I think... it's dislocated," I said quietly. "Not broken."

Finley exhaled softly. "Okay. Stay with her."

I focused harder. In my mind, I tried to wrap invisible fingers around the joint and the bones, feeling resistance. When I pushed my mental pressure on her, she groaned.

I eased off. "Kasuma," I said, voice tight. "This will hurt."

"I am ready," she quickly replied.

I braced myself and pulled. Mentally.

I tugged on the joint. There was no sound. I expected a popping noise or a crack. But everything was silent. However, Kasuma's scream ripped through the night, intense enough to make my vision blur. I recoiled instinctively, staggering back as my focus shattered.

For one second, I was sure I had failed.

Kasuma slid off the table, clutching her shoulder, chest hitching with harsh gasps. Her skin darkened with pain, sweat glistening along her temples.

Then she straightened.

Slowly, cautiously, she lifted the injured wing.

It trembled. Shuddered. But it moved.

A stunned silence settled over the upper deck. Even the waves seemed to hesitate.

Kasuma flexed again, testing the joint. Pain flashed across her face... but beneath it, something else flickered. A grin.

She looked at me, eyes wide. "It is... aligned."

My legs almost gave out.

Finley made a sound that hovered on the edge of a laugh. "You did it."

"I reset it," I said weakly. "That's all. It's not healed."

Kasuma barely seemed to hear me.

She stepped back, rolling her shoulders, wings lifting higher this time. Higher than before.

"Kasuma," I said. "Don't."

She crouched anyway.

Fear punched through me as she leapt.

For a heartbeat, the wind caught her wings, enough to lie convincingly. Then the injured joint failed. Her body twisted, and she hit the deck hard, the sound rough and unmistakable.

I was at her side instantly.

"Don't move," I said, gripping her shoulder before she could rise. "You might tear it or dislocated it again."

Her breath came fast, teeth clenched against pain. "I will fly."

"Not yet," I said, forcing calm into my voice. "You need time. Ligaments don't reset instantly. You can't force recovery."

She sagged slightly, frustration burning hotter than the pain.

Finley knelt beside us, guilt shadowing her face. Pherric joined her, silent for a long moment, studying Kasuma's wing with a careful, assessing gaze.

"She will heal," he said at last. "Not tonight. But she will."

Kasuma closed her eyes, wings trembling faintly, no longer twisted in agony.

The sea rolled on beside us, dark and relentless. The ship pressed forward toward Atlantis, indifferent to our small victory.

I sat back on my heels, hands shaking, heart doing a tap dance. I hadn't performed a miracle. I hadn't rewritten nature or undone damage with a thought.

But I'd done something real. Finally.

Pherric's voice reached me again, quieter now. "You did not merely lift or pull," he said. "You understood what you touched. That is rarer than power."

I looked up at him, surprised.

He met my gaze and inclined his head slightly. "You will matter in this war, Jonathan. Perhaps not in the ways you expected."

Something in my chest loosened.

For now, that was enough.

71

Found Atlantis, Immediately Regretted It

Finley

Two days later, the sea decided to behave.

That alone made me uneasy.

Late afternoon light spilled across the bow of the ship, turning the water into sheets of shiny gold as I stood at the prow. Pherric, stoic as ever, stood at my side. Sandulf was there too, broad and unyielding, his gaze fixed ahead as if everything might blink under enough pressure.

We had been searching for hours.

Atlantis did not want to be found. That much was clear. If that place had a sense of humor—and I suspected it did—it enjoyed watching sailors doubt their own eyes.

I lifted a hand and gestured back toward the helm.

Melcente saw me and orders were passed without raised voices. The sails eased to half mast, canvas whispering as the ship slowed, not stopping so much as *waiting*.

Ahead of us lay a small island.

A sad blob sitting still in the sea. Low surf. One solitary tower rising from its center, almost an afterthought. A small fishing village.

Was that it? We'd gotten two other small islands wrong the day before.

I stared harder, refusing to let doubt creep in. *Come on*, I thought. *Don't make me look stupid in front of so many people.*

The Elysium ship, the *Carnwennan*, drifted alongside us, her bronze-plated hull catching the sun and setting the water aflame. Shields rimmed her rails—blue and gold, scarred but defiant. King Ferghas leaned casually at her bow, one boot propped high, a tankard of ale dangling from his hand.

He squinted at the island, took a long drink, then barked a laugh.

"I do not see a damned thing!" he shouted across the gap. "You slowing us down for another speck of sand?"

I didn't rise to it. Just lifted my arm and pointed.

"There," I called back. "That island."

Ferghas followed my gesture, snorted, and shook his head. "That is no fortress. No city. That is barely a place to drown properly."

"Wait," I said. "Wait for it..."

He scoffed, but he paused. We slowly sailed forward, the sea lifting us up and down.

The air changed first. Not wind. But a weight. The edges of the small island shimmered. And it didn't seem like magic either. It was uncertainty. Large rocks on the beach vibrated. Lines softened. A straight edge bent into something curved.

"...Ah," Ferghas whispered.

The island did not grow.

It *resolved*.

The lone tower began to multiply before our eyes. Empty space filled itself in. Bridges stretched. Structures layered atop one another in impossible geometry, scale snapping violently into place.

Atlantis unfolded in front of our fleet, vast and undeniable.

I finally let myself feel the proverbial sigh of relief.

"Found you."

And then something on both sides of the Atlantis bothered me.

Not action, but *shapes*. Lines where there hadn't been lines before. Angles that didn't belong. Dark slashes at the periphery of the island, too precise to be natural, too still to be harmless.

Ships.

They slid into view from both flanks of the shore—vessels that had been aligned perfectly with the island's false contours, waiting to see if we would commit. Black sails unfurled in unison, drinking in the wind.

One. Then several more. Then enough that counting became beside the point.

They weren't charging blindly.

They were closing a trap.

At least thirty Atlantean vessels surged forward in tight formation, hulls dark as ink. They did not hesitate. They were already coming for us.

Sandulf's hand tightened on the rail beside mine.

Pherric exhaled once. "They were waiting."

Ferghas drained his tankard and flung it into the sea. "Well," he said hoarsely, squaring his shoulders. "That answers that."

My heartbeat kicked into something piercing and focused. Fear, yes— but also clarity. This was it. No more wondering if we were ready.

I broke into a run as the first black sails cut closer across the water, boots slamming against the deck as the ship swayed beneath me. By the time I reached the high castle, Melcente was there, hands locked on the wheel, jaw set.

"I got dis," she snarled, hauling the helm hard to port. "But ya wreck ma ship, and I'm goin' ta want me another. Only bigger. And better."

I braced myself against the rail as the *Aegiros* swung wide, the sea foaming angrily along our flank. "You'll get it," I said, eyes never leaving the oncoming Atlantean line. "Just stick to the plan."

"Aye," she said, satisfied.

The *Aegiros* slipped sideways just as another one of our vessels surged into the gap we'd created, shields flashing along her rails. The fleet was moving now—not as a single mass, but as interlocking parts, each group sliding into position.

An Atlantean ship lunged for us, its prow reinforced with dark metal shaped into a spearhead. But it was too slow. Melcente spun the wheel, and the ram missed us by a hair. Sandulf's archers were already in place along our starboard side. He gave one quick gesture.

Fire.

Arrows streaked across the distance between us, shafts vanishing onto the enemy deck. A few Atlanteans fell. Others held up shields, disciplined under fire. They answered in kind, a storm of crossbow bolts rattling against our hull, some punching through canvas, one lodging itself inches from my shoulder.

We were past them before they could correct.

"Keep moving!" I shouted. "Do not get pulled into a standstill!"

Melcente glared her glare at me.

Behind us, the sea fractured into violence.

Ships from Mag Mell surged forward with terrifying grace, their bows adorned with antlered crests, their thin frames slicing clean paths through the water. They didn't ram blindly—they struck at angles, ramming the fronts or rears to avoid getting caught up, crippling maneuverability before slipping away.

From Elysium came sleek vessels with light sails, moving in quiet control. Their crews worked with unsettling calm, boarding hooks flying, grappling lines snapping taut as they drew Atlantean ships close and turned decks into brutal, close-quarters chaos.

The Prominans came on as battering rams. Their ships were thick-hulled and brutally practical, reinforced with layered timber and iron bands, built less for speed than for surviving impact. Broad decks swarmed with them—tall, powerfully built figures with heavy brows, long arms, and thick-corded muscle, their faces set into fierce, simian scowls that made them look carved from anger itself. They shot arrows first relying on great, heavy shafts that flew in dense volleys, striking with punishing force and brutal accuracy. At range, they were devastating. Up close, less so. When boarding became unavoidable, they relied on momentum over finesse, grappling and overwhelming rather than fencing, trusting raw strength to finish what their bows had begun.

Above it all, the Tenguans took to the air. Launching from their rigging and rails, their wings beat hard against the wind. Their silhouettes streaked overhead, staying high and out of range, their arrows raining down in tight, lethal arcs. Atlantean crews scrambled for cover, some firing upward, others breaking formation as panic rippled through their ranks.

The Valhallans thundered forward, their longships cutting straight through the heart of the fray. War cries rolled across the water, oars rising and falling in brutal rhythm. They didn't slow. They rammed, boarded, and began to overwhelm, axes flashing as they surged onto enemy decks with savage joy.

And, holy shit, the Cíbolans were actually helping too! Their banners snapped in the wind, their ships heavier, broader, built to endure pun-ishment rather than avoid it. They took hits that would have splintered lighter vessels and kept coming.

The Ogun—Ogunians? No, not that. Just the Ogun. They moved differently. Their ships held back from the front lines, crews working heavy, iron-bound wooden mechanisms bolted into the decks, massive springs wound tight beneath their frames. With a deep, grinding roar, long and weighted spears launched in low arcs, smashing into Atlantean hulls with concussive force. Ships staggered, veering off course or slamming into their neighbors. It wasn't meant to destroy. It was meant to *break momentum.*

But the Atlanteans adapted fast.

Black sails shifted and their formations widened. The smaller vessels peeled off, attempting to flank, to isolate. Larger ships advanced in pairs, overlapping fields of fire, forcing our allies to break speed or take losses.

They were good. Too good to underestimate.

"Hard to port!" Melcente barked.

The *Aegiros* swung again as another Atlantean ship tried to cut us off. The rudder adjusted to maintain wind. We skimmed past close enough that I could see their faces: focused, determined, utterly unafraid.

Sandulf fired arrows again, striking the soldiers on their deck before slipping by. The Atlanteans answered in precise volleys, firing more crossbow bolts that hissed across the gap, tearing into shields and dropping archers and soldiers alike before some could duck for cover.

Pherric and Jonathan sprinted for the injured. He knelt beside the first wounded soldier and showed Jonathan how to pack a wound, how to tie cloth slick with blood, how to ignore the screaming and work anyway. Jonathan swallowed, nodded, and dropped to his knees beside another, hands moving clumsily at first, then surer, staying there longer after Pherric had moved on.

We were getting closer to the island now. Close enough that Atlantis loomed—vast, terrible, beautiful in its wrongness. Towers watched us. Shiny bridges glared down.

Braylor was in there.

I clenched my fists, locking everything down. *Get through the ships first. Then the city. Then him.*

Another wave of Atlantean vessels surged forward, but our fleet met them head-on this time. Ships locked together. The sea churned into froth and wreckage.

For the first time since the black sails had appeared, I allowed myself a thin, fierce smile.

We weren't breaking.

We were advancing.

I scanned the battle unfolding behind us and watched banners flying, ships sailing, wings cutting the sky.

"We're holding," I said, more to myself than anyone else.

Wings. Wait... The thought snagged.

I turned and my heart kicked once, hard. Kasuma stood right there. Once again, she got me. My own personal accusation.

I caught her shoulders on instinct, holding her gently. "Kasuma, can you—"

"Yes."

I blinked. "You don't even know what I was going to ask."

She looked past me, eyes fixed on the distant curve of the island, the hint of a smile tugging at her mouth. "You want me to find Braylor. Free him from whatever hole they have buried him in. If he is moving instead of imprisoned, he cannot be used to lure you into surrender."

I stared at her. "I—" I stopped, shook my head. My flabbers were gasted. "Yeah. That. How did you—"

"You are predictable," she said calmly. "Wild and dangerous, but predictable."

"Wow," I stammered. "I feel so seen."

Then I hesitated, the real question pressing against my ribs. "Can you... fly?"

Her expression didn't change. "We shall see."

Before I could argue, she stepped away. Kasuma walked toward the stairs leading up to the high castle, the highest point of the ship. Sailors and archers glanced up.

She spread her wings, crouched, and jumped.

For half a heartbeat, she lifted.

Then gravity reclaimed its due. She came down hard, feet and knees striking the deck with a crack. She rolled, caught herself on one hand, and stayed there, shaking with the impact. The deck fell silent.

"Kasuma," I called, already moving. "You don't have to—"

She pushed herself upright.

Her jaw was set now, eyes dark with something stubborn and old. She didn't look at me. She broke into a run.

Straight across the deck.

Soldiers scattered instinctively, archers flattening themselves against rails as she barreled through. Her wings flared for balance, clipped a mast line, and she stumbled—slamming shoulder-first into the steps leading upward. The impact knocked the air from her. She slid back a step, feathers shuddering.

For one awful second, I thought that was it.

Then she growled. Actually growled.

Grabbing the railing, she hauled herself up, ignoring the hands reaching for her, ignoring my voice. She stood balanced on the rail, the sea yawning beneath her.

The ship pitched. The wind surged. She didn't wait for perfect conditions.

She dove.

My heart fell with her.

She dropped fast, wings out as wide as they would go—and the entire deck rushed to the side. Someone swore and another shouted a prayer.

Then her wings caught. Not smoothly. Not cleanly. But enough.

She dipped once more, too close to the waves, then rose. She was awkward, uneven, but rising. The motion wasn't graceful. It was effort. Muscle and will and pain welded together into flight.

Kasuma climbed, each beat stronger than the last, until she cleared the ships and angled toward Atlantis.

A cheer broke loose below me, ragged and disbelieving.

I didn't join it. I could only watch her go, hope and dread tangling together.

"Go," I whispered. "And don't you dare get caught."

The battle raged around us.

But for one breathless moment, a wounded Tenguan flew again. Straight into the heart of the impossible.

72

A Reasonable Amount of Murder, All Things Considered

Kasuma

I am Kasuma, Tenguan daughter of Longzhe the Seventh, King of Oceantis.

Finley has insisted that I record my account. I did not see the necessity. I survived. That should suffice.

But she was persistent, and I was tired.

This is what happened.

I was flying hurt.

That is the truth. Not pain meant to be noticed, but pain meant to be endured. My wing did not fail me, which I appreciated. It did not forgive me either.

The sea lay dark beneath me, broken by the distant glow of battle behind. I did not look back. Looking back invites hesitation, and hesitation gets you killed. I flew low at first, then climbed gradually, letting the wind do what my body could barely manage on its own.

Atlantis revealed itself the way it always does. Reluctantly.

From above, it seemed modest. A light crescent of stone and sand, white marble catching the fading light, towers rising with calculated elegance.

446

I approached from the west side of the island, keeping the falling sun behind me. The city stirred below, but unevenly—too few guards where there should have been more, activity rushed and poorly spaced. War had pulled their attention outward.

They believed the palace itself was protected.

I landed atop a high spire, my shoes making no sound on stone worn smooth by centuries of wind. I folded my wings and tested the injured one once. It answered. Reluctantly. Good enough.

The palace was not difficult to enter. It never is. Power prefers beauty over caution.

I moved downward through open arches and polished corridors, blending with shadow and reflection, following the logic of the place. Throne rooms sit at the heart of palaces. Dungeons sit beneath them. Atlantis was no different.

The dungeon was empty.

Not abandoned but maintained. Clean enough. Cells prepared and waiting. There was no Braylor. No signs of recent imprisonment. No guards lingering from boredom... or cruelty.

I searched carefully. I am very good at careful.

He was not there.

I moved upward again, this time to the throne room itself. I was hoping to relieve the queen of Atlantis of... her duties, but the room was vacant. It was also vast and offensively symmetrical. Pools of water flanked the central path, their surfaces perfectly still. The throne rose ahead, carved from gray stone and entitlement.

Braylor was not there either. I almost left then.

Something felt wrong.

Behind the throne hung a curtain, thick and heavy and embroidered with scenes of conquest rendered in pearl and gold thread. It did not belong. Curtains are for hiding flaws. Atlantis pretended it had none.

I slipped behind it.

The room beyond was not a room. It was a vault.

Artifacts lined the walls: weapons that hummed faintly, jewelry that bent the light around it, relics scattered about. There were glass cases throughout the room. Cages. Some were empty. Some were not. In one particular smaller cage I saw large shapes resting beneath the surface of deep water—scaled, still, unmistakable.

Dragon eggs.

I did not linger. Awe is a distraction.

I exited the vault silently and found a guard alone at the far end of a hall. He never heard me approach. My blade rested against his throat before he understood he had little time to live.

"Where is the Fomorian?" I asked.

He trembled. I adjusted the pressure slightly. Courtesy is optional.

"The guest wing," he whispered.

"Where?"

He pointed toward the south end of Atlantis.

I unburdened him of his life. He fell quietly.

For a moment, I stayed there, watching the blood spread in a thin red pool across the white marble.

It was beautiful in a way I will not write about.

The guest wing was less guarded. That should have concerned me more than it did.

I heard Braylor before I saw him. His voice carried—loud, thick, menacing. I slipped into the room through an open balcony door just as he turned.

Recognition flashed across his face.

Then vanished.

He attacked without hesitation.

Steel came for my head. I ducked, rolled, barely clearing the edge of his blade as it bit into wall. He was faster than I expected. Stronger too. His actions were precise but empty, like a man following commands he did not understand.

"Braylor," I said once. "It is Kasuma. Your friend."

He did not respond.

We circled. He struck. I avoided. The room was chaos. Furniture shattered, stone cracked, the sound of steel ringing far too loud. He nearly took my wing. That would have ended poorly.

He did not speak. He growled. Did not hesitate. And when our eyes met again, there was nothing there that knew me.

That hurt more than the blade would have hurt.

I disengaged. Distance is sometimes the only victory available.

I leapt for the balcony, caught the railing, and threw myself into open air.

The drop was long. My wing protested. I ignored it.

I fell.

Then I rose.

The wind took me hard and uneven, but did give me what I wished for. I climbed fast, forcing my body to obey while the palace receded beneath me. A few shouts followed. Arrows did not.

Atlantis folded back into itself as I gained altitude, shrinking into something harmless and false.

I did not retrieve Braylor.

I did not free him.

I did not kill him.

These are facts.

I left before the island could reconsider its mistakes.

The wind argued briefly. I ignored it as well.

That is all.

Finley insisted I add something... positive.

Here it is:

I did not die.

73

So This Is What Competence Feels Like

Genevieve

The hold of the *Thalyra* smelled of sweat, old wood, and fear pretending to be bravery.

We were packed shoulder to shoulder with soldiers who knew what they were doing. Men and women checked belts, tightened grips, and whispered to themselves or no one at all. The ship groaned around us, timbers flexing as waves struck hard and close. Every so often, something heavy slammed against the hull above and the whole world jolted.

I braced my boots wide, fingers curling around the leather wrap of my stolen blade.

I had fought before against them. That was the lie my brain kept offering me, trying to make it easier if I repeated it enough times.

I had *survived* before. I had panicked. I had killed someone and spent the rest of the night trying not to think about how his face appeared when it happened. That wasn't the same thing as this. This was organized and very intentional. Everyone here knew exactly what kind of shit waited for them.

Including me.

The *Thalyra* shuddered violently.

Someone swore. Someone else laughed, harsh and wild.

Above us, archers shot their arrows. I could hear it in the sound of the strings, tight and rhythmic, and then the *whoosh* of the feathers flying. The answering thud of their arrows striking wood followed almost immediately, some of them punching clean through planks overhead. A splinter rained down and caught on my helmet. I hated wearing a helmet.

Kinnat's hand found mine.

She didn't squeeze. She didn't look at me. She just *linked* us, and it was the most natural thing in the world.

A voice cut through the noise. It was deep, carrying, edged with command.

"Listen to me!"

Our captain stood on a crate near the ladder, helmet tucked under one arm, sword held loosely in his fist. He looked calm in the way people look right before doing something stupid on purpose.

"We board on the next pass," he said. "Atlantean vessel is damaged but not dead. They will fight like cornered animals because that is what they are!"

A ripple of grim agreement moved through the hold.

"Stick with your line. Do not chase. Do not freeze. If you fall, get up. If you cannot get up, make it hurt for the bottom-feeding fish who put you there."

A pause. His gaze swept us.

"And if you are scared," he added, not unkindly, "good. Means you are paying attention."

The ship slammed again, harder this time. The impact knocked the air out of me and sent a few soldiers staggering into one another. Ropes creaked. Somewhere above, wood snapped.

"It is time!" the commander barked. "Go, go, go!"

The stairs surged with bodies.

Kinnat pulled me with her.

The moment we hit open air, the noise exploded.

Clanging steel. Shouting in several languages. The Atlantean ship bobbed beside us, close enough to kiss if either of us wanted to die dramatically.

Grappling hooks screamed past my head.

Iron claws struck wood, rope, and sail—some skidding uselessly, others catching with a sound that shook my bones.

Lines yanked tight.

"Now!" someone yelled.

Kinnat ran and I went with her.

We grabbed the line together, and for one weightless, insane second we were swinging over open water.

Then we hit the other deck. Hard.

I stumbled, boots skidding on slick planks, heart trying to escape my chest. An Atlantean surged toward us immediately—tall, armored, face painted in dark streaks that made him look carved rather than born.

Kinnat leapt first.

Her blade flashed, precise and economical. The man went down, surprise collapsing into a wet, choking sound. She didn't pause to watch him fall.

Another came at me from the side. I raised my sword too slowly, barely deflecting the strike meant for my shoulder. The impact rang up my arm and into my teeth.

Too loud. Too fast.

For half a second, my thoughts scattered. So many inputs and screams, coming from every direction.

This is where I die, said a small, annoying voice in my head.

No. Not today.

I forced my breathing down. In through my nose. Out through my teeth.

I followed Kinnat's lead. Not with my eyes. With my body. She shifted left and I shifted left. She ducked; I ducked. She struck; I covered.

Someone lunged at her from behind. I didn't think. I stepped in and blocked, our blades screaming as weapons collided inches from her spine. The Atlantean snarled at me, eyes wide with delight.

"Wrong target," I told him.

Then I shoved him back and slashed low, striking his thick thigh.

He fell.

I didn't watch. I couldn't. I just pushed the thought from my mind. And remembered that Finley said she apologized to the second guy she killed.

"Sorry," I whispered to myself. "Not sorry." I drove my blade down into his neck. And looked away.

Chaos closed in again.

Arrows hissed overhead. A man screamed as he went over the side. Someone tripped and didn't get back up. Blood sprayed hot across my forearm and for one horrifying second my brain tried to catalog it instead of reacting.

I shut it up.

The world narrowed. Enemy. Friend. Space. Timing. That was it.

A trident came out of nowhere.

I felt it before I saw it and a white-hot line of pain crossed my ribs as the prongs scraped instead of pierced. I saw black spots dancing in my vision. I staggered back a step.

The Atlantean holding the weapon grinned.

Something in me snapped yet again. It was becoming a fucking habit. But I did not break... I focused. Fear burned down into energy, clean and usable.

I went forward, knocking the trident aside and closing the distance before he could recover. I threw my shoulder into his chest. We went down together. He tried to roll, but I stayed on him, sword finding the gap under his arm.

The sound he made was ugly.

So was the sound I made, apparently, because Kinnat glanced over at me mid-fight, eyes assessing.

I nodded fast. I was fine. I was more than fine.

Another came. Then another. I didn't hesitate this time; I fought.

Blocked. Struck. Kicked a knee. Twisted away from a wild swing that would have taken my head off if I'd still been thinking about anything else. My arms burned. My sides throbbed. My lungs were lined with fire.

But I kept going.

Somewhere in the madness, I realized I wasn't panicking anymore.

The noise faded into nothing. The deck became minor obstacles instead of threats. Even the blood—slippery and everywhere—registered as something to account for, not hide from.

This wasn't grace. It was choice.

An Atlantean charged me, bigger than the rest, armor dented and blackened, eyes locked on mine because he'd decided I was next.

Good.

We circled once. He struck. I parried and felt the jolt up my arms, felt the weakness where I was tired, where I was human and bleeding and very much not trained for this. I didn't back up. I stepped *in*. My blade slid into his gills, turned, and bit deep.

He went down and I stood over him for half a second, chest heaving, sword dripping.

Then Kinnat was there again, shoulder to shoulder, and the moment passed.

The Atlanteans were pulling back now, heading over their rail, toward their officers, to anything that looked like order. Our people surged after them, momentum snapping fast, a rope drawn to full strain.

And then it was finished.

Not clean. Just... done. The deck was littered with bodies, blood everywhere. I turned, sword up, searching. No one came.

"Fall back!" someone shouted.

I took a step forward anyway.

Kinnat's hand closed around my wrist. "Genevieve. Enough."

I stopped.

The world rushed back in. The screams returned, the ring of swords back into sheaths could be heard. My grip loosened and the blade dipped. Finley was right; I was holding it too tight.

"We leave now," Kinnat said, already turning us toward the lines.

I raced after her, my hands starting to shake only once my boots hit our own deck.

I leaned over, fists on my knees, gasping hard. Blood dripped off my sleeve. Some of it was mine.

Kinnat nudged me with her shoulder.

"You did not hesitate," she said.

I laughed once, a little hysterical. "I absolutely hesitated."

"Not when it mattered."

I straightened slowly, pain flaring along my side, and looked back at the Atlantean ship as it drifted away, bloodied and abandoned.

My heart was still racing. A healer inspected me. She placed cloth against the wound and quickly wrapped my midsection tight.

But I was standing. And this time, when I looked at the deck, I didn't need to puke.

I wiped my blade clean.

"Okay," I said hoarsely. "I think I'm done warming up."

Kinnat's mouth tilted, just barely.

Then someone screamed, high and breaking.

"Dragon!"

That word ripped across the deck.

Soldiers locked up. Someone dropped their shield. I felt it before I saw it—the way the air shifted, the way every instinct I had... suddenly agreed on one thing. Whatever came next was not meant to be fought like this.

I looked up.

74

This Is the Part Where I Do Nothing

Finley

I stood on the high castle of the *Aegiros* with my hands locked around the wood, knuckles bright white against dark wood slick with seawater.

The ship surged forward beneath my feet, every inch of her committed to the long arc that would take us around the crescent and toward the palace side of Atlantis. Toward Braylor, the whole fucking reason I had dragged half the known world into a war.

Kasuma should have been back by now.

That thought didn't sit in my brain politely. Kasuma didn't dawdle or get distracted. If she wasn't back, it meant one of two things: she was dead, or she was still searching.

Or he was gone. Nope, that was not an option.

I chose that she was still searching because it let me stand upright without collapsing. That was the bar. Anything more ambitious felt reckless.

Then the screaming started in the distance.

Not the usual you hear during battle. The loud, warlike kind that runs on adrenaline and bad bravado. This was different. The kind that emptied a person out in one blow and made trained soldiers forget what they were

456

holding and why.

"*Dragon!*"

I heard it from across the water.

The sky was no longer empty. Thalassa's dragon, Zeranthyl, tore through it like a bruise made solid.

His scales caught what little light there was and threw it back in flashes of indigo and violet. His wings were enormous—very broad, too deliberate— and each downbeat punched the air hard enough that I saw the sails push in. It seemed to rattle my teeth, but that was most likely fear. My body wanted to crawl inside itself for safety.

He didn't roar because he didn't need to.

The dragon circled once, slow and almost thoughtful, as he decided what—or who—to ruin first.

And everything screamed at me to turn the ship. I glanced at Melcente, but her eyes were wide and fixed on the distant shape of flying death.

It was instant. Animal. Clean. Every instinct I had gathered from surviving this world shouted the same thing: you don't leave your allies in a battle.

But the palace lay ahead. Braylor.

And behind me, Zeranthyl acted.

Fire erupted from his throat in a torrent so bright it hurt to look at. A fierce orange-white heat that washed over one of the Elysium ships. The sails caught instantly, canvas blackening and curling in on itself. The rigging went next, ropes flaring and burning through, lines dropping across the deck.

Burning cloth rained down onto the deck.

I could see sailors scatter, bodies jerking into motion before their minds could catch up. Fire spilled across planks, licking at boots, catching tunics, crawling angrily along ropes. Someone stumbled with their sleeve aflame and slapped at it with frantic hands that only spread the fire higher. A man hit the deck and stayed down, and I couldn't tell from this distance whether he was dead or simply swallowed by smoke and panic.

The dragon climbed again, wings beating hard, drawing more fire.

Flames climbed the mast, consuming everything that had ever made that vessel a vessel.

The mast groaned, an awful and living sound, before splitting with a crack that echoed across the sea.

Then the fire found something it liked. Pitch, stores, dry wood. I had no idea. The flames surged and spread with terrible purpose, racing the length of the deck, climbing the smaller masts as the ship fed them. The vessel didn't explode. It simply began to die, fast and loudly.

The Elysium ship began to list.

Soldiers and sailors leapt overboard, some of the poor bastards burning. Armor dragged at them as though the sea itself had hands. I watched them hit the water and thrash, trying to swim, to stay afloat, and understand how they'd gone from "sailing" to "dying" in the span of a minute.

What gutted me was the Atlantean ship closest to the Elysium floating funeral pyre. I watched its crew shed armor in practiced motions, metal hitting the deck as they ran. Daggers and short swords went into their mouths. They slipped beneath the surface without hesitation, diving straight down in a clean, smooth motion.

Then there was a pause. Too long and quiet.

I knew what was happening before the people in the water did.

The Atlanteans weren't fighting where the soldiers or sailors could see them. They were swimming under the wreckage, beneath the people, into the blind spots.

From the deck, it seemed harmless—just survivors clinging to floating timbers, gasping, calling out to one another. Then someone's eyes went wide. And another choked, a wet, startled sound bubbling up as blood spilled from their mouth. Another body was simply... gone. Pulled under cleanly enough it left nothing behind but a ripple.

Panic spread far too late. People turned to each other, scrambling, grabbing at shoulders, shouting questions no one could answer. They didn't know why the person next to them had stopped moving. And they had no idea what was below.

I did.

There was nothing I could do but watch as the water took them one by one, as it was just another task waiting to be finished.

Zeranthyl wheeled again, shadow sweeping the water, and something cold tightened behind my ribs. We had planned for Thalassa's dragon. We had counted on it, even. Our idea was to push our ships closer to theirs, forcing the Atlanteans into tighter formations where dragonfire would cost them as much as us.

But Zeranthyl was better than that.

He never clipped an Atlantean sail. Never scorched one of their decks. He found the gaps we couldn't close and burned only what he was meant to burn. And so there was no longer any version of this where everyone survives.

When he descended again, he chose a Prominan ship.

Fire slammed into its deck and washed over it in a roaring cascade that turned wood to cinders and the ape-men to screaming shapes. Prominans were strong on land—broad, heavy, strong, built for crushing enemies—but in water they were slow, clumsy. When the flames drove them overboard, they hit the sea hard, thrashing, sinking faster than they could swim.

I watched many disappear.

And I hated myself for how my mind immediately tried to calculate it. That's what I had become. A queen. A strategist. Someone who could watch people die and still keep moving.

But I wanted to turn the ship.

The thought came again, sharper now, almost physical. One word to Melcente and the *Aegiros* would swing wide. I could throw myself back into the chaos, scream orders, fire arrows, call allies, do something instead of this slow, deliberate agony.

The palace lay ahead.

And if I failed there, if I let Queen Thalassa keep him, then all of this death would have been meaningless. Wasted.

I dropped to my knees on the deck.

The wood was damp. The ship rolled gently, indifferent to my crisis.

Somewhere way behind us another mast cracked and fell. Fire roared. People screamed, a chorus that rose and fell.

I steadied what needed steadying. Not because I felt calm. Because I needed to be functional.

I can't stop him, I admitted to myself. Not from here.

But I could call for help.

My mind reached inward, past fear and noise and grief, to the place where the *mindform* lived. It wasn't a tool to me, but a presence—something I could reach with thought as surely as I could reach for a sword with my hand. I simply called a single name and put everything I had behind it.

Big Red.

Her name wasn't dignified. It was something silly I came up with at the time. But it carried warmth, memory, familiarity—an anchor in a world that kept trying to tear itself apart.

Come to me.

I pushed the thought outward hard enough that it made my skull ache, trusting that somewhere, beyond the smoke and fire, she would sense it.

Over and over. *Come. Please... help.*

Then I stood again, eyes lifting in time to see Zeranthyl bank and dive.

His target was an Ogun ship.

The bright orange fire struck low, smashing into the iron-bound mechanisms along the deck, heat warping metal with a shriek that carried even over wind. Flames crawled outward. The Ogun crews scattered with manic speed, but few could outrun dragonfire. The ship's path faltered as smoke billowed upward, black and ugly against the sky.

Hold, I urged silently. Just hold.

Zeranthyl climbed, wings beating powerfully, smoke trailing behind him. He was making another pass, choosing another ship, and turning this battle into a slaughter by himself.

And I could do nothing but stand there and watch.

I made my choice.

Now I had to endure it.

"Please," I whispered to the wind, to the sea, to whatever gods may still be watching over this deadly planet. "Hurry."

Zeranthyl folded his wings and dropped. I could only wait for help to arrive—and prayed it would arrive before there was nothing left worth saving.

75

Braylor: Alive, Murdery, Enemy-Adjacent

Finley

"Melcente—"

The word stuck in my throat, thick and desperate, because my hands were gripping the side hard enough to hurt and every instinct I owned was clawing in the same direction. Turn the ship. Go back. Do something that actually helped instead of this long, sickening forward glide leaving burning allies and screaming in the water.

Zeranthyl was flying in the distance, purple scales flashing as he wheeled for another pass. Smoke smeared the sky. Fire crawled across the surface of the sea where ships had been, and people had not lasted long enough to matter.

"Melcente," I said again, louder this time, my voice already tipping toward command. "Bring us about. Hard to—"

A shadow cut across the deck.

Not a dragon. Smaller. Faster. Out of order.

Someone shouted. I heard another curse.

I turned in time to see Kasuma fall out of the sky.

She didn't land cleanly. She was on borrowed strength, spent down to nothing. Her thin boots hit first, then one knee, wings flaring wide before snapping in tight as she absorbed the impact. The deck ignored her because she was so lightweight. She stayed down for a heartbeat too long.

I was moving before my brain caught up, crossing the deck in a blur of boots and sails and shouting names. I dropped in front of her, hands already finding her shoulders, solid and real and very much alive.

"You're back," I said.

"Yes." Her voice held steady even as the rest of her didn't.

"Are you hurt?"

"No."

I opened my mouth again—Braylor, the palace, anything—but she looked up at me, really looked at me, and the words died where they stood.

"You should not attempt to rescue him," she said.

It wasn't a plea. It wasn't even advice. It was information.

I glanced past her, reflexive, toward Melcente at the wheel. Melcente's eyes were wide, flicking between the dragon-stained sky and the two of us.

Kasuma followed my gaze and shook her head once. "Not yet."

My pulse slammed hard. "Kasuma. What are you saying—"

"He is... alive."

She pushed herself up without help, favoring one side just enough that I noticed. Her healed wing trembled faintly before she folded it tight against her back.

"Tell me," I said, because I needed the truth before I shattered something with a bad decision.

"Braylor is compromised."

The word landed heavy.

I felt the deck tilt, though the *Aegiros* held her course. Smoke drifted past the bow. Somewhere behind us, wood cracked and collapsed. I barely heard it.

"Compromised how?" I already knew I wasn't going to like the answer.

Kasuma's eyes didn't leave mine. "Ramil."

Cold slid straight down my spine.

"No," I said. "No. Not—"

"The same mindform," she continued. "The same fracture he used on your friend. Genevieve. He knew me. And did not. He attacked without hesitation. And then harder again without recognition. Without restraint."

The world narrowed to a tight, brutal point.

Genevieve's face flashed in my mind—blank, furious, not hers. The blade in her hands. The way my friend had looked through me? She had been instructed to destroy.

My hands curled into fists.

"You didn't kill him," I said, because I needed to hear it.

"No."

"Could you have—"

"No."

"We still have to go get him."

Pherric and Jonathan rushed to me, once they saw Kasuma return. She gave them the bad news about Braylor.

Turning away, I dragged a hand through my hair and paced two steps before stopping myself. Zeranthyl roared again in the distance, the sound vibrating through bone and memory. Another ship burned. I didn't look to see which one.

Pherric turned to me. "We have to ignore Braylor. He is no longer part of your plan."

I looked at Jonathan. "He's right," he admitted.

"How do you know?"

Jonathan, covered in the blood of the wounded, stood up straight. "Ramil will have learned his lesson with Genevieve. He commanded her to assassinate you, but he didn't have her cut off your head. If that's how you truly stay... dead, then he will have made sure of that with Braylor. I know it. He's smart."

"In other words," I said. "Braylor won't stop until he's dead or I am."

Kasuma inclined her head. "That is accurate."

I laughed once, harsh and humorless. "Fantastic."

Melcente cleared her throat. "Orders?"

I looked at the wheel. At the sea. At the smoke-streaked horizon behind us where people were still dying while I stood there thinking.

Then I looked at Kasuma again.

"Did he hesitate... at all?" I asked.

"No."

Being the queen still sucked.

"All right," I said. "Let's rejoin the battle. Maybe we can help."

I glanced back at the dragon carving circles through the darkening sky. "But I wouldn't put money on it."

I nodded to my captain. Melcente's hands tightened on the wheel.

There was a subtle change in the *Aegiros'* angle, the way the deck leaned just a hair too far under my feet. The crescent of Atlantis began to slide out of alignment with our bow.

The island started to recede with infuriating slowness. I stared at it as if willpower alone could drag it closer, as if Braylor might feel me turning away and understand.

I am not abandoning you, I told the distance. I am not done.

Kasuma's words echoed in my skull. *He was altered... he did not know me... he attacked.* The idea of Braylor standing somewhere in that palace, alive and unreachable, shattered something sharp and ugly in my chest. Worse still was the thought I couldn't quite outrun: what would happen when he finally came for me? The man I crossed the ocean and kingdoms to save was waiting on the other side with a blade and Ramil's voice in his head.

I swallowed it down. I could grieve later. Right now, there were ships burning behind us.

Help them first, I told myself. Survive this. Then go back.

Sandulf was already barking orders, his voice carrying over the chaos. "Shields up! Prepare for boarding! Eyes ahead!"

Pherric and Jonathan returned to the wounded amid coils of rope and scattered arrows.

I opened my mouth to call out—

And the sea answered.

A scream rose from the starboard side.

Someone shouted, "Enemy at the rail!"

Atlanteans came over the side of our ship, determined nightmares crawling out of a shared dream. Hands gripped the wood, hauling bodies up with terrifying ease. Without armor, blades clenched between teeth. Water poured off them as they vaulted onto the deck, eyes bright, maneuvers smooth and confident.

They were already among us.

"Attack!" Sandulf roared.

Steel rang. Someone went down hard. Another scream cut off mid-word. I didn't think. I moved.

"Pherric! Jonathan! *With me*," I snapped, grabbing Jonathan's sleeve and hauling him upright. "You do not fight."

"I can—" Jonathan started.

"You absolutely cannot," I said, shoving him toward the captain's quarters. "And you won't."

Pherric didn't argue. He stepped in behind Jonathan instinctively and pushed him along. I carved a path ahead of them, sword flashing as an Atlantean lunged for us.

He was fast. I was faster.

My sword caught him in the groin. I kicked him back and turned, slashing again as another came at my flank.

"Inside," I ordered, ramming the door to the captain's quarters open with my shoulder. "Stay there. Lock it. Do not open it for anyone unless it's me."

Jonathan's face was ashen. "Finley—"

"Now."

Pherric hauled him inside. I slammed the door shut and turned back to the deck.

The *Aegiros* was a war zone.

Atlanteans swarmed from both sides now, dragging themselves up from the water in relentless waves. Our soldiers fought back hard. They dropped bows and drew swords, their shields locking with the enemy.

One of them vaulted over a fallen body and came straight for me, trident flashing. I parried and twisted inside his reach, slicing low. He went down choking on blood.

Another took his place. One after another. My arms burned. Somewhere nearby, Sandulf bellowed a command and a shield wall slammed together just in time to catch a surge of Atlanteans trying to split the ship in half.

An Atlantean jumped from behind a mast. I caught the motion at the last second and barely turned the blade aside. Pain flared along my shoulder as his dagger sliced skin. I answered with a hard, brutal cut that sent him sprawling.

I fought my way toward the center of the deck, shouting orders, cutting down anyone who got too close to the captain's quarters door.

Blades clashed again. Someone slammed into me from the side and we went down. I rolled, came up on one knee, and drove my sword upward into soft flesh. Warm blood sprayed my face.

I wiped it away and kept going.

We were taking heavy losses. The ship groaned, as more Atlanteans tried to climb aboard.

Hold, I thought grimly. *Just hold.*

I backed toward the captain's quarters, blade up, gasping for air, my heart hammering.

I wasn't done.

"Come on then," I muttered, bloodied and shaking and very much still standing. "If you want this ship, you're going through me first."

I realized that they wanted the orb.

My hand reached down to the leather bag at my side. I still had it. It was still close, but they would not stop until the orb had been recovered.

The doors behind me flew open.

Jonathan emerged from the captain's quarters, crossing some invisible threshold and leaving hesitation behind.

Pherric was right there, one hand steady on Jonathan's shoulder—not holding him back, not pushing him forward, just grounding him. Both of their eyes were closed, and that, more than anything else, sent a cold ribbon of shock through me.

Jonathan lifted his hand, fingers shaking slightly, not with fear but with strain, and the air around us seemed to tighten.

The Atlantean charging from my left never reached me.

He was yanked backward mid-stride, webbed feet slapping uselessly against the deck before gravity lost its argument altogether. His body lifted, weightless and without control, and then he was gone—flung cleanly over the rail in a wide, ungraceful arc that ended in a distant splash. The sound was almost anticlimactic.

I stared, my sword half-raised, pulse roaring in my ears.

Another Atlantean surged forward, trident leveled at my chest. I shifted my footing, already moving to meet him—

—and Jonathan flicked his wrist.

The man slammed flat onto his back, the impact rattling the deck. He lay there stunned, blinking up at the sky, his weapon skidding out of reach.

Sandulf didn't hesitate.

"Press!" he bellowed, voice cutting through the chaos. "Now!"

His soldiers surged forward with renewed ferocity, seizing the opening Jonathan had torn into the fight. The stunned Atlantean didn't rise again.

Something inside my chest loosened, just enough to let air back in.

Jonathan stood rigid, with his jaw clenched. Sweat darkened his hair and ran down his temples, his hands shaking now with the sheer effort of holding the world at bay. Blood dripped from his nose. Each action he took was small, precise, and he seemed terrified of using too much force and breaking something he couldn't fix.

An Atlantean vaulted the rail behind him, blade raised.

Pherric stepped forward instantly, his voice low and calm. "Left."

Jonathan reacted without opening his eyes.

The Atlantean was wrenched sideways and smashed into the mast with bone-cracking force. He slid down in a crumpled heap, and Sandulf's troops finished what Jonathan started.

I felt awe bloom, honest and welcome, right alongside fear.

This wasn't a warrior's fury. No rage or swagger or desperation made loud. This was control—fragile, hard-won, and terrifying in its restraint.

Another wave of Atlanteans pressed in against us, moving fast, coordinated. This time Jonathan didn't throw them into the sea.

He dropped them.

All five hit the deck at once, weapons flying from their hands. One groaned. One lay still. The third tried to crawl away, dragging himself through blood and seawater before a blade ended the attempt.

The rhythm of the battle shifted.

Not all at once, but enough that I felt it—the hesitation creeping into the Atlanteans' movements, the way their eyes shot toward Jonathan instead of locking onto targets. They hadn't planned for this. They'd prepared for swords and arrows.

They hadn't planned for an unseen hand.

Jonathan staggered as he flung another attacker overboard, this one spinning wildly before vanishing into the waves. Pherric tightened his grip, murmuring something I couldn't hear—guidance, reassurance, a reminder to relax.

An Atlantean officer shouted orders in their own tongue, loud and urgent.

That was when they broke.

Some dove back over the rail, abandoning the ship entirely. Others scrambled toward the edges of the deck. Jonathan caught two mid-leap and hurled them hard into the side of the ship with the sound of bones cracking against wood.

When it ended, it wasn't glorious. No final stand. There was no dramatic flourish.

Just bodies, the tang of blood in the air, and the sea quietly reclaiming what it always did.

More than half of them were dead. The rest fled.

Jonathan lowered his hands slowly, afraid the world might still be attached to them. His knees buckled, and Pherric caught him before he could fall.

Silence crept back onto the deck, broken only by distant screams and the crackle of fire somewhere far behind us.

Sandulf wiped his blade on his sleeve and exhaled what might have been a laugh.

"Um," he said, eyeing Jonathan with reverence, "Well done."

I crossed the deck toward Jonathan, sword finally lowering, my hands shaking now that there was space for it. He opened his eyes.

They were terrified. And alive.

I stopped in front of him, chest heaving. "Hi," I said hoarsely.

He swallowed. "Hi."

A laugh tore out of me. "That was... *neat.*"

He shook his head at me, wiping away the blood at his nose.

"Remind me to never to underestimate you again," I added.

Pherric grinned.

The dragon still ruled the sky. Atlantis still waited beside us. But for the first time since this battle began, we had pushed back.

And I intended to keep doing it.

76

How Not to Park a Ship

Finley

"**S**hip!"

We all heard the shout from the lookout, high on the mast.

The word cracked across the deck from high above, loud with urgency and a little too late to be comforting.

"Jesus Christ… what now?" I was already running, boots skidding on wood as I cut toward starboard. Smoke smeared the horizon to our side. For one dangerous heartbeat, I hoped it was one of ours—late, limping, alive.

It wasn't.

The Atlantean ship came out of the haze, low and fast. She wasn't angling to board. She was aiming to hit us broadside and break our spine.

"Hard port!" I shouted, though Melcente had already seen it. Her hands flew over the wheel, muscles stood out along her arms as she hauled the *Aegiros* into a desperate turn.

But it was far too late.

We'd been distracted. By boarders, the wounded, and the illusion that we'd bought ourselves breathing room. The Atlanteans hadn't rushed. They'd waited. And now they were close enough that I could see the man standing there.

Goran.

He waited there, an unpleasant inevitability, grinning as though this were all going exactly to plan (which, depressingly, it probably was.)

The First Sea-Lord of Atlantis didn't hold a weapon or issue a command. He watched us with the relaxed interest of someone who knew the outcome, and was mildly entertained by how long it was taking us to realize it.

"Brace!" someone screamed.

The impact punched our world sideways. Wood shrieked. Metal screamed. The deck leapt violently under my feet as their prow sliced into our hull. I pitched forward, barely catching the side as seawater fire up through the breach, cold and furious and very much inside the ship now.

The *Aegiros* was wounded and furious.

Melcente fought her, spinning the wheel with a feral snarl. The ships ground together, hulls scraping. She managed to turn us just enough that we weren't dead in the water... but not enough to break free.

And the Atlantean captain knew exactly what he was doing.

Their ship didn't slow.

"Why aren't they stopping?!" I shouted over the noise. "Trying to board us?!"

Pherric was beside me instantly, eyes already tracking the shoreline rushing closer. "They do not try to sink us," he said grimly. "They are running us aground."

That understanding was cold water down my spine.

"They want us alive?"

"They want the orb," Pherric corrected quietly.

Of course they did.

Arrows began to fly, crossbow bolts whizzed past us and shot into my soldiers. Sandulf threw everyone at the rail where our ships connected and steel rang out, blades flashed as a few Atlanteans leapt the gap. They were testing our defenses, keeping us pinned while the coastline loomed larger in a way I absolutely did not like.

The *Aegiros* groaned as she was pushed forward, her wounded side screaming with every yard, her bow turning not by our will but by theirs.

Atlantis grew faster than it should have.

But the water beneath us began to change—not the color yet, or the depth, but the *behavior*. The sea didn't just roll; it drew back in places, swelling unnaturally in others, as something massive shifted beneath the surface and the ocean itself tried to make room.

My skin prickled.

A sound rolled up through the hull. Not a crack or a groan, but something that pushed into the ship and stayed there.

"What is that?" Pherric whispered.

The water *blew the fuck up.*

Well, not upward, but out. A wall of spray surged beside the *Aegiros* and the Atlantean ship, drenching both decks and blotting out the sky in white foam.

Out of the water rose two eyes. Twin points of bloody red light cut through the mist, unblinking and impossibly large.

No. No, no, no—

The Leviathan surfaced.

My mind struggled to contain it. Her body rose from the sea, a living battlement with scales the size of shields. Her neck uncoiled higher and higher, water cascading from it in sheets, until she hovered above both ships at once.

The Atlantean ship fired crossbow bolts and arrows. Tridents bounced off the skin and bolts vanished into the water against its hide.

The Leviathan answered with fire.

Not a focused stream like Zeranthyl's, but a wide, brutal blast that washed over *both* ships indiscriminately. Flame slammed into the Atlantean deck—and then rolled across our own, heat pressing the air from my lungs as crew and troops screamed and scattered.

"She's certainly not here to help us!" I shouted, more to myself than anyone else.

Pherric's voice was tight. "But... she is not choosing sides."

The Leviathan reared back and *rammed.*

Her massive body slammed into the space between the ships, the impact splitting us apart with violent force. Hulls screamed. The *Aegiros* was flung sideways, men and weapons skidding across the deck. The Atlantean vessel took the hit even harder, its bow crumpling inward as the serpent's scaled flank smashed into it again, teeth flashing as she snapped blindly at anything within reach.

Fire rained down in wild arcs, igniting wood, sails, bodies. Smoke swallowed the air. The Leviathan thrashed between us, battering hulls and sending burning debris raining into the sea.

She wasn't hunting but she was *angry*.

At *all of us*.

And then, as suddenly as she had come, she dipped low again, her massive body sliding beneath the surface, leaving the sea heaving and boiling in its wake.

The ships drifted apart—both burning now, both mortally wounded, still moving inexorably toward the island.

I staggered to the rail, coughing smoke, staring at the burning Atlantean vessel as it struggled to regain control.

Atlantis was still coming.

"Shallow water!" someone screamed.

The warning barely registered.

I looked back once, scanning the water where the Leviathan had vanished. There was no sign of her, just waves and floating wreckage.

She wasn't gone. She'd simply decided we weren't worth finishing.

"Everyone off the ship!" I shouted hoarsely. "Now!"

The flames climbed higher and the island loomed. Fire raced along, eating through everything with hungry snaps. Smoke rolled across, stinging eyes and turning every breath into a gamble. Somewhere below, the hull groaned as water poured through the breach faster than their buckets could manage, the ship shuddered.

The color of the sea had changed again, from a deep blue giving way to murky green, as the sandy shelf rose to meet the hull. Burning debris fell over the side in hissing arcs, steam rising where flame kissed water. The

Atlantean ship drifted into us, its own deck ablaze now, pushing us harder until—

Impact.

We shook violently as the keel bit into sand. The Atlantean ship turned away somehow and began drifting back with the current.

We were beached.

"Everyone off!" I shouted. "Now! Do not stay on this ship!"

Sandulf relayed the command with brutal efficiency, his soldiers already running as flames licked the mast. "Over the sides! Swim if you can! If you cannot, find something that floats and pray to the gods!"

"No!" I screamed, the words bitter on my tongue. "They'll be waiting beneath the surface! Swim underwater!"

But no one heard me.

Jonathan appeared at my side, pallid and soaked in sweat, Pherric half-supporting him as smoke curled around us in choking waves. "Finley—"

"Can you swim?" I snapped. He was exhausted but he nodded. "Go!"

Pherric didn't wait. He grabbed Jonathan and hauled him toward the rail, already scanning for a break in the chaos as another section of rigging collapsed in sparks behind us.

Above us, wings beat hard.

Kasuma swooped in low. She snatched a fallen bow from the deck, yanked arrows free from a dead soldier's quiver, and took to the sky again in one smooth motion, smoke sliding past her wings.

She didn't look at me. "Go now!" she shouted, already firing an arrow that dropped an Atlantean mid-leap as flames burst out.

Pherric shoved Jonathan over the side. I watched until they hit the water and vanished beneath the surface.

Then I followed. The cold slammed into me. Everything went green and dark, sound reduced to muffled thuds. I kicked hard, forcing myself along instead of up, every instinct screaming for air.

Shapes moved beneath the surface.

An Atlantean came at me from below, eyes bright and unblinking, webbed fingers clawing for the leather bag at my hip. The orb tugged against its straps as he seized it, jerking me sideways.

I tried to swing my sword. But it was useless. Too slow, way too much drag.

I let it go and yanked the knife from my boot instead, driving it down in a blind, furious stab. The blade bit. Bubbles burst from his mouth as he recoiled, but his grip tightened. Not on the bag. On my leg.

He dragged me downward with terrifying strength, fingers locking around my boot, pulling as the water darkened and pressure closed in. My lungs burned. Panic edged harsh and immediate.

I kicked, flailed, twisted. Finally, I broke free, managing to surface with a choking gasp. Kasuma's shadow streaked overhead. She fired, but the water distorted everything and her arrow vanished into green nothing.

Hands yanked me under again.

I fumbled, fingers slick, heart screaming. I slashed at him with my knife to no effect. I reached down, grabbed the heel of my boot, and kicked it free—leaving it in his grip.

The sudden release snapped me upward. I struggled with everything I had, hit the surface, and swam like hell.

Hovering above, Kasuma fired another arrow into the water. The Atlantean jerked, convulsed, an arrow buried deep between his shoulders. He sank, before he could grab me.

Looking back, the water bloomed red.

I went as fast as I could, half-expecting hands to seize me again and drag me under. But the water shallowed abruptly and I crawled forward, coughing, palms scraping sand as waves slapped against my back. Around me, soldiers staggered and collapsed, some hauling themselves clear, others lying where they fell.

Jonathan lay a few yards up the beach, Pherric already dragging him upright, both of them soaked and shaking but alive.

Melcente was further up the sand, bent over and gasping for air. Another death stare from her.

Behind us, the *Aegiros* burned.

Flames crawled along her deck unchecked now, smoke pouring from her.

She became a funeral pyre. The mast leaned at a dangerous angle, rigging glowing orange before snapping loose and crashing down in sparks.

Kasuma landed hard nearby, wings flaring, bow already raised again as she tracked motion in the surf. A few Atlantean heads popped up and she fired until her arrows were gone. She took out at least four of them.

By the time the last of us staggered clear of the water, the cost was undeniable.

Far too few had made it to the beach.

I stood on the sand, soaked and bleeding and shaking, the orb still miraculously heavy at my hip, and stared back at the burning ship stranded behind us.

We survived.

But Atlantis and the Leviathan had taken what they thought was theirs.

I rolled my shoulders, tightened my grip on the bag, and turned toward the city.

"Somebody give me a goddamn sword," I said loudly. "And a spare boot. Left. Size nine. Nine and a half would work, too."

Apparently, we were doing this the hard way.

77

Dragon Problems, Now in 3D

Genevieve

The sky had gone off.

Not just smoke and fire—that I understood—but it was warped, stained, like something had busted it. Even the light looked like it wanted out, bending away from the worst of it and leaving shadows where shadows didn't damn belong.

Kinnat stood beside me at the railing, close enough her shoulder brushed mine when the ship rolled.

The fleet was coming apart.

Ships didn't burn cleanly. They failed in pieces. One moment they were ships; the next, they were shapes—dark red silhouettes swallowed by fire. I watched an Elysium vessel take a glancing hit. The fire moved fast. Sailors ran until they didn't. Then they jumped. One after another.

On the edges of the chaos, Atlantean ships had drifted outward. They were not fleeing, but repositioning. Their crews watched from the sides, unhurried, eyes tracking the destruction with the patience of predators who knew they didn't need to rush.

That was when I understood this wasn't just a battle. For them it was a process.

The _Thalyra_ surged forward, our captain barking orders, the crew scrambling to keep pace with the shifting lines of battle. We angled closer to an Atlantean vessel, sliding alongside it just enough to deny the dragon a clear strike.

For a while, it had worked.

Then the light changed.

A shadow slid over the deck. I looked up just in time to see the purple dragon descending, wings spread wide enough to make the sky feel suddenly smaller.

His scales caught the failing light in hard, jagged flashes, and his wings erased what little sun we had left. Someone screamed. The captain yelled something I didn't catch.

Fire followed.

The blast slammed into us, heat biting anywhere skin was exposed. Kinnat and I dropped behind our shields as the deck screamed around us. Pain flared bright across my cheek, the air itself burning. Kinnat slapped at my hair without looking, smothering the flame before it could spread.

Fire spilled across the deck.

People ran. Or tried to. Smoke swallowed them. I smelled it before I could think about it—the sulfur, and then the *other* smell. The one that doesn't need explanation. A sailor staggered past me with his shirt burning, eyes empty, hands uselessly patting at flames that climbed higher. Another went down screaming.

The ship staggered as people jumped over the sides.

"We have to get off the ship!" I shouted.

I took a step toward them before Kinnat's hand snapped around my wrist.

"Look," she said again, forcing my gaze back to the water.

Below, the sea churned with activity. The Atlantean swimmers were already there. Waiting for us.

I was caught between fire and being sliced up from below, so no real choice at all.

The dragon climbed again, circling back for another run.

And then—

Something tore through the sky.

At first, I thought it was more fire. A trick of the light, maybe, or a nasty hallucination. But then the shape resolved, massive and unmistakable, scales gleaming in the dying sun.

Big Red.

She hit the purple dragon mid-air.

The impact was violent enough to feel in my chest. A loud *thump.* The two dragons spiraled together, claws locked, wings beating furiously as they fought for balance.

Fire met fire.

Big Red unleashed a blast straight into the other dragon's chest, flames colliding in an explosion of heat and light that turned the sky white for a heartbeat. The purple one roared this time, the sound echoing through my heart, and retaliated with a savage swipe that sent Big Red spinning.

They dropped.

Fast.

The dragons plummeted toward the water, bodies twisting, tails lashing, teeth gnashing against scales too hard to shatter. They hit the surface in a towering spray, vanishing beneath the waves.

The entire deck gasped as one.

Soldiers and sailors raced for the edge, hands gripping scorched wood. We leaned forward together, staring down at the churning water.

The captain shouted, "Put out the fires!" The sailors raced away.

The dragons had vanished beneath the surface.

For a brief moment—nothing. Just rippling waves and the fading echo of impact, the sea closing over them.

Another heartbeat passed. Then another.

Bubbles broke the surface. Not small ones. Great violent blooms of heat surged upward, rolling and popping in frantic clusters.

The water began to boil.

A roar detonated from beneath the surface—muffled, distorted, but unmistakable—and then fire exploded upward through the waves, punching out of the sea.

Two massive shapes burst free, water cascading from them as they thrashed violently, locked together in a snarl of claws and wings. Big Red surged up first, jaws clamped hard onto the purple dragon's neck ridge, her teeth scraping his scales as he writhed and snapped back at her face.

The impact sent waves crashing outward, rocking ships already half-dead. Sailors stumbled as the dragons slammed against the surface again, tails lashing. Purple reared, wings half-spread, trying to gain air, while Big Red drove him down, forcing him back into the water with brute, furious strength.

They fought like titans drowning.

Purple tore free with a scream, snapping his jaws shut inches from Big Red's eye. She answered with fire at point-blank range, the blast ripping across his chest and turning the water around them into roiling steam.

Then Purple did something desperate.

He kicked hard against the sea, wings beating in frantic, uneven strokes, and surged upward. Water streamed from him as he clawed his way into the air, climbing fast, furious, and wounded.

Big Red did not hesitate.

She launched after him, wings snapping wide as she burst free of the water in a crimson spray, her roar splitting the sky as she chased. The two dragons climbed in spiraling arcs, fire streaking between them, as they twisted higher and higher.

The deck erupted into sound all at once—shouts, laughter, sobs, curses—but I stayed still, eyes locked on where the battle had returned to its proper place.

I had never seen anything like it.

This wasn't the clean brutality of soldiers clashing or ships colliding. This was ancient violence, raw and elemental, forces of nature given teeth and will. The purple dragon lunged, jaws snapping inches from Big Red's neck. She twisted away, spiked tail slamming into his flank with heavy force. He retaliated with claws that raked her hard.

They lost altitude again, spiraling so low I thought they would crash straight into the fleet.

At the last second, a third shape streaked in from the side.

Green.

The other dragon that Kasuma had ridden! He was sleek and fast, and he hit the purple dragon hard, driving him off balance. Purple shrieked, wings faltering as the two dragons pressed the attack together.

For the first time since this began, the purple one retreated.

He pulled away hard, wings pumping as he climbed, pursued by Big Red and the green dragon as they chased him toward the open sky, fire and fury snapping at his heels until they vanished into the distance.

Cheers broke loose again, ragged and disbelieving. Sailors laughed, cried, clutched one another. Someone dropped to their knees. Someone else shouted thanks to their gods.

And there was no damn way any of their gods were listening.

The captain barked orders and the crew snapped into motion, stamping out fires, cutting away burning lines, hauling the injured clear. The *Thalyra* lived. Barely. But we were still floating.

I didn't cheer.

I couldn't have, even if I'd wanted to. My body knew better. Cheering was for moments where we won, and this didn't have that feeling.

I looked out over the water and finally let myself see the cost.

The sea was no longer a battlefield. It was a graveyard. Ships still burned in uneven patches, flames chewing through hulls and rigging with stubborn persistence. Some vessels leaned at sick angles, their decks half-submerged, sails hanging in blackened ribbons. Others drifted aimlessly, abandoned and silent, smoke coiling upward in slow spirals.

Debris covered the water in every direction—broken masts bobbing, entire sides of ships floating by, shields without owners. I saw a helmet floating upside down, filling slowly with water, and my brain tried to decide whether that was better or worse than seeing the person who'd worn it.

A few survivors clung to wreckage, too still to tell whether they were resting or simply waiting for a merman to kill them. The tide nudged them together and apart with quiet patience, the sea sorting them by weight and worth.

Half the fleet was gone. Not damaged. Not limping. But fucking gone.

The empty spaces between ships felt louder than the battle ever had.

Somewhere behind me, someone laughed, high and shaky, and then cried. Orders were being shouted again. Fires were being beaten down. The living were already moving forward because stopping meant thinking.

I stayed there a moment longer.

Because if I didn't look now, if I didn't let it register while it was still raw and real, I knew exactly what would happen. It would be forgotten.

A ship slid into view beside me, the bronze-plated hull cutting the water with stubborn refusal to sink. She was battered, smoking, but very much alive.

The Elysium king, a burly red-haired guy, with a mug in his hands, stood at the bow.

Smoke curled around him. He took in the scene with the same expression he might have worn while surveying a ruined banquet hall: disappointed but not surprised. When his eyes found me across the narrow stretch of water between our ships, he lifted his cup in a brief, wordless salute.

I returned it by not falling over.

He nodded. An acknowledgment. You're still here. So am I. We'll sort out the rest later.

He leaned over and spat into the sea, watching it vanish among the debris.

"Well," he called, voice carrying easily over the water, "that went poorly."

I huffed out something that might have been a laugh if I'd had the energy to pretend.

Behind him, his crew was already moving—cutting lines, hauling wounded, stamping out flames. They worked around the bodies without ceremony. No one said anything but there were some prayers being muttered.

He took one quick look at the same aftermath I had seen. His mouth tightened into not quite a frown but also not a smile.

"Best not linger," he shouted over, more to the water than to me. "The sea remembers, even when we don't."

Then he lifted his mug again, draining it.

He turned to the people on his ship. "On with the attack!"

He gave me a final wink as his slightly singed sail lowered and the ship lurched in the heavy breeze.

Kinnat placed a hand on my shoulder, smirking at me.

And what was left of the fleet surged forward again.

<h1 style="text-align:center">78</h1>

Do the Hardest Thing First (Or Die Trying)

Finley

I knew I had to find Braylor.

I also knew that if I did, he wouldn't hear a single word I said. If he was compromised—really compromised, not just shaken or manipulated around the edges—then the man I loved was going to try to kill me. And if he was fully himself, full-strength Braylor, rested and furious and no longer holding back? He'd succeed. He was too damn good at violence when he put his mind to it.

But I didn't have a choice.

It wasn't as though I could just leave him on Atlantis and hope things worked themselves out. That wasn't how this world operated. That wasn't how *I* operated.

My grandfather used to say you should do the hardest thing in your day first. Get it over with, and everything after that feels manageable by comparison.

The problem was, I wasn't convinced I'd *have* a rest of my day once I faced Braylor.

We moved fast through the city outskirts, boots crunching over stone and ash, the air ruined by smoke and heat. Resistance was... light. Too light. The streets weren't empty, exactly, but the guards we encountered were young—barely more than boys, eyes wide and hands shaking around weapons they weren't sure yet how to use properly.

Sandulf's soldiers cut them down quickly, without cruelty. The good ones were out there, at sea.

We took a hard turn east, toward the cliff side overlooking the water. Away from the palace I'd once fled and then jumped into the stolen boat to get away. And there I was, back again.

I'd underestimated how stubborn I was.

We ran and climbed until my legs burned, and the city fell away and the sea opened up below.

That's when my heart broke.

The battlefield stretched farther than I realized. There were ships scattered across the water in the aftermath of devastation. Smoke rose in thick, oily columns. Some vessels still burned, flames still crawling along masts and rigging with terrible intent. Others tilted hard, some with ships so far down the sails were half-submerged, and crews scrambling or gone entirely.

We'd lost so much.

Not all of them. I could still make out allied colors on the water—banners from Valhalla, Elysium, Kunlun, Mag Mell, and, unfortunately, Cíbola, still waving from the ships that hadn't been lost yet.

"The fleet is in shambles," I muttered.

Sandulf brought me back around. "We still have more than half our ships," he said, calmly. Then his gaze focused. "What is our plan?"

"I'm going to find Braylor."

Sandulf frowned. "He is compromised. You said so yourself. I will go with you."

I stepped closer and pressed a hand to his chest, feeling the steady thrum of his heart beneath armor scorched and dented from battle. "If this turns into chaos... and it will, they'll need you. You're their anchor."

"Your highness—" Sandulf started.

"And Goran was on the ship that rammed us," I cut in. "He's immortal. If he's here, the Deep Guard might not be far behind."

His jaw tightened.

"If you run into one of them," I continued, "don't take them on alone. Ever. You throw everything you have at them at once, and you *cut off the head.* That's the only way they stay dead. If you can burn them, do it. If you can't... run. There's no shame in that game."

He nodded curtly. "Understood."

I started to take off for the palace.

"Finley," said Kasuma. She would have only used my first name if it was important.

I followed her long finger out to the sea.

"She has changed her target," she said quietly.

I squinted as the shape resolved itself. It was long, massive, unmistakable. A shadow beneath the waves, moving straight toward the heart of the remaining fleets.

The Leviathan was back at it.

The Atlanteans fleet had pulled out to the edges of the battle while their dragon did the dirty work. And they were between our fleet and the sea serpent. Which meant we still had time.

My brain scrambled. I needed to come up with something. Fast. We had not accounted for the Leviathan in our plans. She had torched our ship and Goran's in a heartbeat. With her fire, size, and speed, it would be over—for all us—in no time at all.

Think. Think. What can we do?

I tore my gaze away and turned south, toward the enormous port that stretched away from the Atlantis coastline. Stone and wood docks in deep water. A chance. It was slim and ugly, but it was real.

"Can you fly again?" I asked.

"Yes." There was no hesitation in her eyes. Just readiness.

"Fly to every ruler, every ship, still out there," I said, forcing myself to sound like I wasn't watching a living catastrophe pick its next victims. "Tell them to dock. All of them. As fast as they can. They need to get off the water *now!* You've seen what she can do!"

Kasuma didn't reply. She unfolded her wings and launched herself skyward, already angling toward the nearest ship.

More screams carried over the water.

I turned in time to see the Leviathan rise.

She didn't break the surface so much as replace it. The sea around her rolled, ships pitching hard as if even the ocean wanted some distance.

Then she opened her mouth.

Fire came out in a wide, lazy sweep, catching two Atlantean ships at once. Not precise. Not tactical. Just enough to ruin everything.

Their decks dissolved into chaos.

Merfolk scattered, their clean efficiency I'd seen earlier gone completely. Some jumped overboard without hesitation. Some made it a few steps before fire caught them.

The Leviathan lingered long enough to make her point. Smoke curled from her nostrils as she dipped back beneath the waves, leaving behind burning ships, screaming survivors, and water swallowing the evidence.

Kasuma streaked down toward an Elysium ship, arrows from the enemy already flying as their own vessels burned.

The Leviathan surfaced moments later, slamming into another Atlantean hull with devastating force. The ship tilted violently, water pouring in as they screamed and scrambled.

Kasuma lifted off again from the Elysium ship, already redirecting toward a Fomorian vessel.

And that Elysium ship began to run, turning away from the Atlanteans and sailing toward the docks. Hopefully the others would follow.

Braylor would have to wait. I needed to be down on those docks when our ships arrived.

I watched the chaos for one more heartbeat and lead the others away from the cliff.

<h1 style="text-align:center">79</h1>

Exhaustion, Efficiency and Extinction

Jonathan

I followed Finley and Sandulf because there were only two viable options: stay behind and likely die or hide and attempt to recover while everything important happened without me. Neither would be useful.

Finley walked at Sandulf's side, her pace steady, her jaw tight. There was blood on her sleeve. Hers, I suspected, but she didn't seem to notice. She carried herself with the brittle focus of someone who had already made too many decisions that day and was bracing for the next one. Occasionally, her hand flexed near her side, as though resisting the urge to touch the orb in the bag.

My legs felt disconnected from my intent, a fractional delay between decision and execution that had not existed before I pushed my mindforms beyond any reasonable margin. Nothing came easily anymore. I cataloged the symptoms automatically: muscular fatigue disproportionate to exertion, tremor in the hands, mild narrowing of peripheral vision. Overuse. Shock. Not immediately dangerous, but trending in a direction I did not like.

Pherric stayed close. He did not touch me, which I appreciated, but he adjusted his stride so I never had to hurry or lag. His presence acted as a stabilizer, a constant in an increasingly chaotic equation.

The docks emerged through the smoke in fractured glimpses.

Atlantis had built its harbor with aesthetics in mind. Arched bridges. Broad stone quays. Water channels designed to reflect light and grandeur. Now those same features funneled us into narrow killing lanes. Atlantean soldiers waited for us at the edges of the buildings in tight ranks, tridents braced, shields overlapping, crossbows aligned.

I counted without thinking about it. Forty. Possibly more, depending on what lay beyond the visible lines.

Sandulf raised his fist.

Our group halted.

The stillness before the clash was unnerving—not because it was quiet, but because everything in it was contained. Motion compressed into potential energy. I felt it in my chest, the way the soldiers adjusted without moving, hands tightening on hilts, every body keyed to the same moment. Finley stood motionless beside Sandulf, eyes forward, expression unreadable.

If I had been stronger—if my reserves had not been hollowed out earlier—I could have assisted before the first blades crossed. A lateral displacement, applied unevenly, would have collapsed their front line inward.

The thought lingered long enough to become dangerous.

Pherric's hand closed around my wrist.

"Jonathan," he said quietly.

I turned, already knowing the answer to the question I had not asked.

"No," he continued, calm and immovable. "You are not ready."

He was right. The evidence was there. Attempting another mindform at that level risked loss of consciousness at best and brain hemorrhage at worst. Acknowledging this did not make the restraint easier.

The Atlanteans charged.

Initial crossbow fire cut down several of Sandulf's soldiers immediately. But the rest rushed forward, shields up, before they had time to reload. And the collision that followed was immediate and violent. Swords rang out and Sandulf's troops absorbed the impact, driving forward in controlled surges. They rotated fighters out of the front line before fatigue could become failure.

It was methodical. Efficient. Brutal in the way only experience allows.

I focused on patterns instead of blood.

Every movement had intent. Every death followed a sequence of advantages or errors. And a lot of luck. When an Atlantean fell, it was not because they were weaker, but because their formation broke half a second too early—or because Sandulf anticipated a feint and countered before it fully manifested.

Finley was a blur. She stayed low, moved in close, and took advantage of every bad move an enemy made. Twirling and ducking down, spinning away, and hitting at a weak point before delivering a death blow.

In all, I think ten of ours went down while more than thirty of theirs did not rise again.

The survivors ran away, injured or frightened. Sandulf did not pursue. He had an objective and was determined to reach it.

I exhaled slowly. My hands began to shake now that the immediate demand for control had passed.

"That was," I said, recalibrating, "remarkably efficient."

"Efficiency keeps men alive," Sandulf replied, already turning. "We move."

Finley said nothing. She stood there gasping, wiping blood from her blade. When she looked at me, her face was streaked and spattered.

The look in her eyes scared me, even knowing who she was, and I realized with a chill that this was simply what surviving here required.

The ground vibrated beneath our feet.

At first, I assumed structural damage—resonance from distant impacts—but the frequency was off. Too low and broad. The sensation climbed my spine and settled behind my eyes.

Something enormous was moving through the city.

Finley felt it too. I saw her stiffen, shoulders lifting, her attention snapping upward before any sound reached us.

There was something happening beyond two towers to our right.

The dragons crashed into view without warning.

Big Red and Zeranthyl were locked together, wings tangled, claws embedded in scales, tumbling down another street leading to the docks with enough force to crack stone and send debris flying.

We scattered instinctively, diving for cover as masonry exploded into dust.

Behind them, the green dragon followed. His wingbeats were lower, slower, and uneven.

Zeranthyl's tail lashed out before he landed.

The blow caught the green dragon and hurled him sideways into a collapsed market structure. Wood shattered. Stone gave way. He vanished into a cloud of debris, his momentum carrying him into stillness that lasted too long.

I went still. "Is it—"

"He's alive," Finley said without hesitation. "Injured. Not dead." She sensed it somehow.

Zeranthyl turned back toward Big Red.

Finley went very still. Her eyes were fixed on the dragons, hands clenched at her sides. I noticed that she closed her eyes as Zeranthyl reared back and launched himself onto the red one.

For a moment, I thought she was bracing herself.

Then I felt it... a faint, unstable energy at the edges of perception. A mindform. She was trying to reach the dragon. Not Big Red. Zeranthyl.

I recognized the signs: the inward focus, the minute tension around her temples. A gentle, pleading, restrained by sheer force of will. It had to be an effort to communicate, to de-escalate, to stop what was happening.

But it had no effect.

Zeranthyl bit into Big Red and then launched himself upward, landing on one of the harbor bridges. That elevation granted him a clear advantage.

From there, he reared back, jaws opening wide. Nothing emerged. No flame. Only smoke and a sound that was closer to rage than triumph.

Big Red surged forward regardless, claws scraping against stone as she attempted to close the distance. But height matters and Zeranthyl struck downward with brutal precision, driving her away from the arch of the bridge, forcing her into retreat.

Zeranthyl threw down a wing and caught Red on the head, all but scratching away her eye. But Big Red vanished beneath him. The bridge shuddered. Stone cracked. She came up behind him with heavy force, slamming into his flank and driving him off balance. Zeranthyl tumbled from the bridge in a cascade of shattered stone, striking the ground hard enough to leave a slight crater.

Finley gasped.

Big Red did not hesitate. She took to the air in a single powerful beat and landed squarely on his back, talons sinking deep. Zeranthyl thrashed, snapping blindly, trying to twist free, but she held on, jaws closing around the base of his neck. There was no fire left for either of them. Only strength.

She bit down. Twisted. The sound was not loud, but it was final.

Zeranthyl went still.

Finley's knees buckled.

Sandulf caught her arm before she could fall, steadying her without a word. Her face had gone pale, eyes glassy with something that was not shock but grief.

Big Red stepped back, chest heaving, wings half-spread. She roared once, a sound that rolled across the harbor and displaced smoke.

But what she did next was surprising. She lowered her head. The green dragon stirred and dragged himself closer, limping but alive. He nudged Zeranthyl's body gently. Big Red did the same.

They backed away and sat there together, massive and silent. Heads bowed. Eyes closed.

No victory display. No assertion of dominance.

Only recognition.

Sandulf stared at the two great beasts, his voice hushed with disbelief.

"Two dragons... slaying one of their own. Not for territory. Not for dominance. For *her*." He swallowed, still watching them. "I never thought I would live to see such a thing."

No one dared to move. And not from fear, but from the cognitive strain of witnessing something ancient and irrevocable.

Finley had not opened her eyes.

When she finally did, they were wet. And she looked... smaller. Not weaker. Just unguarded.

Whatever bond she had with these creatures, whatever frequency she moved on that I could not touch, had just gone silent.

I felt the weight of it settle somewhere deep in my chest. Finley had bent this world in ways no one ever had. Dragons likely didn't change their nature—but somehow, for her, they did.

Sandulf's hand tightened briefly on her shoulder. "Your highness," he said quietly. "We have pressing matters."

She swallowed hard.

"Yes," she said. Her voice was steady, but it cost her something. "We do."

And we moved on, leaving three dragons reduced to two—and the world, somehow, quieter for it.

80

So Much for a Soft Landing

Genevieve

Kasuma hit our deck with the kind of precision that made you forget she was built to fly. One heartbeat she was a blur dropping out of smoke, the next she was there. Her tiny thin boots skidded, wings snapped in tight, and her voice cut through panic the way scissors glide through wrapping paper.

"To the docks," she told our captain, the word a commandment. "All ships. Now. The Leviathan is attacking indiscriminately."

Indiscriminately. That was a polite way to say we were *all* fucked.

Our captain didn't waste time arguing. He didn't even ask if this was part of the plan, because plans were a cute thing you had in the morning, before dragons and sea monsters began editing your life with fire. He barked new orders and the *Thalyra* turned hard, her bow cutting through chop and wreckage as we aimed for the Atlantis harbor.

I made my way to the rail with Kinnat at my side, the two of us braced against the ship's pitch. We were near the back of the fleet and had the longest distance to go.

Columns of smoke rose in uneven bursts.

We watched as the Leviathan moved beneath the surface in long, terrible shadows, as it took down another ship. And every so often, those twin points of red would flare under the smoke, and someone would scream "There—there—!" and then either the sea would ignite or it wouldn't, and the not knowing was its own kind of cruelty. She had knocked out a ton of Atlantean ships and was starting on ours.

There was no method to her madness.

Our ship sailed on anyway. As fast as we could. Sailors fought fires, ran lines, and turned sails, their voices tight with that focus people get when they're trying not to picture themselves burning.

Kinnat hadn't said much since the attacks began. She didn't waste time on what couldn't be fixed.

I watched the water and found myself grinding my teeth.

My hand held hers. When she shifted, I noticed the bag at her hip—the same worn leather satchel she had carried since Pandæmonia, since that farmer had shoved supplies into our hands and told us to live. It always sat against her. It belonged there. She touched it once, absentmindedly, checking its weight.

I wondered briefly what she still had in there, but I didn't ask. Kinnat had her secrets and she didn't hand them over just because the world was ending on schedule.

Our other ships rushed into the harbor, slamming into the docks and soldiers pouring out to face waiting Atlanteans.

The shout from behind, raw and panicked. I turned in time to see the water behind the *Thalyra* moving—not in waves, but a deliberate surge as the sea humped upward.

Foam boiled outward in a widening V, and for a horrifying heartbeat I realized we were about to be overtaken before we ever reached land. Ahead of us, the docks waited—wide, solid, and lined with Atlanteans already braced to fight. Behind us, the ocean itself was charging.

"Faster!" someone screamed.

The Leviathan surfaced with violence instead of grace. Her neck a living tower, the sheer size of her blotting out the background.

The ship shuddered as flame erupted from her jaws in a harsh blast. Fire hit into the stern, racing along lines and into the tight sails.

We ducked to avoid the fire as sailors behind us screamed. The captain burst into flames, hands still on the wheel. The ship lurched hard as the blast threw us forward, not gently or mercifully. We were *tossed* toward the dock like debris.

The impact came seconds later. Wood exploded. The *Thalyra* smashed into a wooden dock. The front bit deep as burning ropes started to collapse around us.

There was no pause, no clean moment to regroup. Only fire and smoke.

"Over the rails!" someone bellowed as Atlanteans tried to surge forward through splintered timber.

Kinnat grabbed my arm and we jumped together, boots hitting boards as fire expanded and roared behind us.

The Leviathan's shadow loomed at our backs, the enemy charged our front, and there was no choice left except to race forward and fight.

An Atlantean leapt at me immediately, trident thrusting for my gut.

I moved without thinking, knocking the shaft aside and stepping in close, too close for the length of his weapon. My blade shot up and across his throat. He made a startled sound and went down.

Kinnat was already fighting on my left, every swing clean and tight, her shield high, her sword doing what it was supposed to do. She wasted no energy and she didn't posture. She simply removed threats from the world.

The Atlanteans didn't fight the same as the ones we'd boarded earlier. These were dock guards, yes, but they were in their own territory, and there was a different kind of ferocity. A tight, offended rage. They were defending their city.

Crossbow bolts snapped past my ear and punched into a soldier's chest behind me. He hit the dock hard, eyes wide.

I adjusted my helmet and pushed forward.

A mermaid slashed at my thigh with a short blade. Pain flared hot. I kicked her hard in the gills and felt her fold. She grabbed for my boot. I yanked free and drove my sword into her back.

Kinnat's shield slammed into an enemy's jaw with a nasty crunch. She stepped past him as he crumpled, her face impassive. Someone's trident scraped across her shoulder guard, throwing sparks.

"Right," she stated, calm as sunrise.

I turned in time to block a strike aimed for my neck. The impact rang up my arm. My grip tightened but my lungs were hating on me.

"Dry land," I panted. "Much better."

"Focus," Kinnat said, which was rude, because I was focusing. On *not dying*, which I felt was a reasonable goal.

Another merman drove into us, shield-first, trying to split us up. The force knocked me back. My heel caught on a broken plank and my balance stuttered.

The Atlantean saw it.

He dove.

Kinnat's blade cut across his forearm. Blood sprayed. He hissed and retreated half a step, enough for me to recover and toss my shoulder into his chest. He stumbled, and I pushed my sword into his side.

His eyes widened in shock—he couldn't believe a land creature had managed to puncture him.

"You're welcome," I told him, shoving him down.

The dock was chaos now. Our soldiers were jumping from the ship in waves. But the Atlanteans were pushing back. They surged along the narrow channels between dock structures. There was no way to get around and pin them in. They used their shields and they had the long tridents that stabbed low, aiming for heads and legs. Nets flew—actual nets, weighted and clever—trying to tangle boots and drag warriors down.

One caught a soldier near me and he went down hard, shouting as an Atlantean moved in to finish him. I jumped in and parried, my sword catching the trident's shaft mid-thrust. I kicked the net away and hauled the soldier up by his collar.

"Get up," I hissed. "If you die here, you'll just haunt me... and I'm in no mood to deal with that!"

He grinned and stumbled forward, eyes wild.

Kinnat stayed controlled, though the edge had intensified. A thin line of blood ran down her temple where something had grazed her.

"You're bleeding!"

"I am aware," she replied.

"Okay. Cool. Just checking that you weren't... I don't know... decapitated."

She shot me a look that somehow managed to be both irritated and affectionate, which was an impressive multitask.

An Atlantean slammed into us from the right with enough force that my shoulder screamed.

I went to one knee, teeth clenched. The Atlantean raised his trident to drive it through my chest.

Kinnat stepped between us.

She caught the trident on her shield, braced, and then shoved forward with a grunt of effort, knocking him back enough for me to rise. I came up behind her, swinging, and caught him across the face. He reeled back, falling into the water.

We pressed together, shoulder to shoulder, fighting as one unit because separating was how you got killed.

And still the Atlanteans held.

They just kept coming. Their eyes too bright and their attack too sure. They fought as though the sea was beneath their feet, because they could always retreat into it. Maybe that was the confidence. And the reason they didn't panic.

We stopped making progress and started getting pushed back toward the burning ship.

My thigh throbbed. My wrists burned. The world narrowed to the next strike and the brief opening it offered. Four Irkallans pulled us back and took our place.

And then something huge hit the dock beside us.

The entire structure jolted. The dock screamed and most of us stumbled to our knees. One soldier behind me fell into the sea.

A shadow fell over us.

I turned, heart thumping, and saw the bow of a ship that had rammed into the teetering dock. It was broad, heavy, carved with brutal designs that didn't bother pretending to be elegant.

A Fomorian ship?

But of course it was. And those massive giants came tumbling over the sides.

A hundred of them, easy, pushed past us in a wave of muscle and fury. They were huge, at least seven and eight feet tall. Just pure, thick, brutal strength. Their faces were heavy-boned and harsh, brows thick, mouths wide, teeth bared. In another world, I might've thought "Neanderthal" and felt guilty for how unfair that sounded.

We held back as they bounded forward and hit the Atlanteans. There was no finesse or precise rotation. Or any delicate timing. Just the crushing wave of long, fat swords slamming into shields, snapping tridents like toothpicks, and splitting skulls.

Atlanteans who'd been pressing us suddenly found themselves facing a wall of screaming monsters.

One Fomorian grabbed an Atlantean by the collar and *threw him* hard into the deck and then tossed him dead into the sea. Another drove a blade down through a trident wielder's shoulder and pinned him to the dock.

The Atlanteans faltered.

It was the first real hesitation I'd seen from them.

Kinnat exhaled once. "Now," she said.

"Yeah," I mumbled, and we moved in behind them, finishing off the wounded.

With the Fomorians breaking their line, we rushed off the dock and onto a wide stone landing. Kinnat and I finally had room to fight the way we needed to—offense instead of pure survival. We ran forward, slicing into openings, moving around fallen bodies, striking at exposed throats, hands, and unguarded joints.

An Atlantean tried to slip past us toward the water. But Kinnat hooked her shield into his gills and slammed him back. I finished him.

Another went for Kinnat's hip. But she reacted faster than I could, pivoting and stabbing low. The warrior folded with a raspy exhale. Her hand went to the satchel for a heartbeat, making sure she still had it, and was right back in the fight.

We fought in a blur.

The Fomorians roared and laughed as they killed, which should've been horrifying, but honestly? After dragons and sea serpents and underwater massacres, my emotional meter was broken. I was grateful for anything that made the enemy look surprised.

The last few broke and ran, stumbling back toward the city or jumping in the ocean.

There wasn't silence. Just... a lot less screaming and hacking.

I stood there panting, sword dripping, my legs burning, my arms shaking. The harbor beneath my boots was slick, the air thick with smoke, the smell of death in my nose.

Kinnat leaned in, her shoulder bumping mine hard. "You are still standing," she said.

"Barely," I replied hoarsely.

She laughed hard.

Finley pushed through the aftermath with a cluster of soldiers. Their faces set with the grim focus of people who hadn't had time to process what they'd just survived. Sandulf and Pherric brought up the rear, moving fast despite the chaos, already scanning the shoreline and docks. Jonathan, anemic and unsteady but upright, rounded out their group.

My heart did that weird wobble.

Finley threw her arms around me. "You're safe!"

I pulled back. "You're not mad at me? For being here?"

"Hell no!" she laughed, hugging me again.

Several Tenguans dropped from the sky around us, wings snapping open at the last second as they landed. The Elysium king arrived with his soldiers in tight formation, armor scorched but intact, while the Fomorian leader strode up moments later, his massive frame cutting through the crowd with unsettling ease.

Finley, her arm around me, turned to the red-haired guy. "King Ferghas, did you manage to save any ale? I could use a drink."

"Ah, a wee bit premature, I believe."

He nodded toward the sea. We followed his gaze.

Hundreds of Atlanteans rose from the water in a rolling surge, all gleaming eyes and wet weapons catching the light as they hauled themselves on the docks and embankments. The sea vomited them up, row after row.

"Shit..." exclaimed Finley.

All the soldiers who had hunted beneath the waves returned to defend their island.

"Aye," said Ferghas. "Shit indeed. Still want that drink?"

"Yeah, but... you know."

"All too well," he sighed.

More allied ships were still unloading across every dock—Valhallans, Prominans, Cíbolans—pouring exhausted soldiers into the harbor. There was no ceremony, no pause. Wounded men were dragged aside. Fresh ones took their place. Shields locked.

A bigger battle was forming, right here, right now.

Finley backed up, shouting to everyone. "Remember the plan! Go, go, go!"

The leap into action was immediate. Troops broke from the docks and surged inland, away from the advancing Atlanteans, forming up on a wide, flat stretch of land bordering the harbor.

We didn't know "the plan", so Kinnat and I raced alongside Sandulf's Irkallans, their shields already forming a solid wall.

Prominan archers claimed the rise in back, kneeling in staggered rows, arrows loaded. Ogun warriors took the front line, long shields overlapping, spears angling forward. Valhallans stood behind them, axes resting on shoulders, faces carved in grim anticipation.

Tenguan archers adjusted quivers and tested bowstrings before lifting off, wings beating fast. Fomorian giants gathered beside the Valhallans, massive silhouettes rolling their shoulders and cracking necks and warming up for sport.

Sandulf threw his blade up and shouted orders, his voice cutting through the chaos with effortless authority. Ferghas led his soldiers back to reinforce the ape-like archers, their long arms steady as they took aim.

It was as if they had done this before.

And then I remembered the story I'd heard about the Battle of Shangri-La... and realized they had.

I lifted my sword again, felt the weight settle into my hand, and let my fear and anger dissolve into something cold.

"Okay," I muttered to Kinnat, staring at the wave of Atlanteans marching toward us. "Let's get this done."

81

Everyone Chose Violence

Finley

Atlanteans hauled themselves onto stone and timber, eyes locked on us. Tridents rose in tight formations. They did not hesitate or shout.

They ran.

"Hold!" I screamed, my voice barely cutting through the chaos. "Stick to the plan! Now!"

The Prominan archers answered me.

The first volley darkened the purple and pink sky.

Arrows fell, burying themselves deep into the front ranks of Atlanteans before they could gain real momentum. Bodies pitched backward off the deck into the water. Others collapsed forward, weapons slipping from slack hands. There was no cheer, no wasted sound from the Prominans. Just smooth, relentless motion—draw, fire, reload—each archer already selecting the next target before the last one hit.

It slowed them. But it sure as hell didn't stop them.

More surged up over the fallen, without breaking stride.

"Ogun line!" I shouted, my voice raw from smoke. "Brace!"

They bounced their shields on the ground and grunted in unison. Hundreds of spears reached forward with purpose. Atlanteans crashed

504

into the shield wall hard enough to stagger even the strongest, but the Ogun did not bend. Spears punched through gaps, withdrew wet and dark, and struck again. Broken tridents snapped under the force of the impacts, their wielders shoved back into the press behind them.

For a moment, just a moment... it held.

Then Sandulf raised his blade.

"Now!"

On either side, we moved as one.

Irkallans and Cíbolans swept inward. I ran with them, sword ready, my focus narrowing to timing, distance, and the next opening.

I struck an Atlantean from the side, my blade sliding into his ribs. Another turned on me instantly, a sword thrusting toward my throat. I knocked it aside, stepped inside his reach, and drove my sword into his chin.

There was no pause to confirm the kill. You never had time for that nonsense, because another attacker replaced them immediately.

The world fractured into a blur of swords and sound. Shouts cut off mid-cry. Blood sprayed across me, and I barely noticed.

To my right, Sandulf carved through the enemy, his blade rising and falling to where he wanted it to go next. To my left, Cíbolans fought in pairs, one drawing attention while the other struck low and final.

And Genevieve—

I saw her through a break in the press, and pride flared.

She moved with confidence now, no hesitation left. She and Kinnat fought together, shields overlapping for a heartbeat before splitting apart, blades swinging in clean, hard arcs. Gen ducked beneath a sword, drove her blade across an Atlantean's throat, and spun away before the body fell.

"Yes!" I screamed out for her, but only I heard it.

The Atlanteans hit us hard, desperation increasing with every strike. This was no longer about reclaiming territory. This was about their survival. Every step back meant more of us holding their island.

I felt the shift. It always happens. The moment when formation gave way to instinct, when the battle stopped being lines and became bodies.

That's where you got killed, sometimes by your own troops.

The Ogun wall buckled under the pressure. Shields pushed aside. Spears broke. Those awful screams of death.

"Watch your sides!" I shouted.

And then it was everywhere at once.

Swords clanging and warriors grunting. The press closed in until there was no room to swing, only thrust and shove and strike. I parried a trident, slammed my elbow into its wielder, and felt skin tear as I brought my blade down. A sword, from somewhere, had stabbed my shoulder. Pain flared, distant and irrelevant.

Another Atlantean came at me. Then more.

I gave ground without realizing it, blade moving on muscle memory alone, lungs burning as I forced space where there was none. My good arm shook. My thighs screamed. Sweat and blood blurred my vision.

I swung heroically. And by heroically, I mean I missed the mermaid entirely and nailed the back of a Cíbolan helmet.

"Sorry!"

He turned, gave me a glare that promised my immediate and creative death, then went back to killing things that were not me.

We were holding.

Barely.

More Atlanteans raced in from the water, faster now, less orderly, shouting harsh commands to one another as they closed the distance. The Prominan arrows slowed, then stopped entirely as the field became too crowded to shoot without hitting our own.

A Valhallan axe missed my shoulder by an insultingly small margin. My muscles seized.

This is when I officially confirmed that battles of this size are ninety percent luck and ten percent *please don't let me die like this.*

And this was taking too long.

Someone screamed behind us. Not in pain. But surprise.

I turned to see Atlanteans spilling out of the city streets behind our lines. Not soldiers alone. Citizens. Mermen and merwomen armed with mismatched gear: blades, staffs, kitchen knives, anything that could be turned into a weapon. They were running hard and furious straight into our backs. No elders. No children. Only those who could fight.

"Behind us!" someone shouted.

Too late.

They slammed into us from the rear, shattering what little cohesion we had left. The pressure was immediate and crushing. We were surrounded now.

This was how armies died.

I fought my way toward the center, shouting orders that dissolved into noise. My arm burned. Someone crashed into me and sent me sprawling across stone.

I rolled in time to avoid a blade meant for my neck.

This was it.

And then the air changed. Not wind. But there was a weight. Something invasive... deep. A vibration that settled behind my eyes and made my teeth buzz.

Jonathan.

I felt it before I could spot him, a surge that set every nerve on edge. I turned as he raised his hands, his eyes unfocused, blood already trickling from his nose.

"No!" I shouted. "Jonathan! No! Don't—"

He did it anyway.

The wave tore through the battlefield with devastating force.

Atlanteans—soldiers and citizens alike—were lifted from their feet and hurled backward into walls, into one another, into the ground. Shields flew. Weapons scattered. The space around us cleared in an instant, bodies slamming down in heaps. Bones breaking. Only a few of our soldiers were affected, but there were hundreds of Atlanteans dead, dazed, and lying hurt on the ground. I mean hundreds. It was crazy.

For one stunned heartbeat, everything and everyone froze.

Then Jonathan collapsed.

Pherric tried to catch him before his head hit the stone, but he was too late. He dropped to his knees as blood poured freely from the back of Jonathan's head. And from his nose, eyes, and ears.

"Oh gods," Pherric whispered. "Jonathan…"

He did not respond.

Rage fired through me, acute and incandescent.

"Push!" I screamed. "Now! Do *not* let that be for nothing!"

We surged forward with everything we had left.

Irkallans and Cíbolans hit the stunned Atlanteans hard. Ogun warriors reformed around the gap, shields coming back together, spears punching through weakened ranks. The Valhallans swung their heavy axes with devastating force. The massive Fomorians charged with a roar that would have unsettled even a seasoned serial killer. And their sheer mass and fury broke the resistance wherever it tried to reassemble.

Genevieve was there again, bloodied and relentless, dragging a wounded ally clear before turning back to the fight without missing a step.

I cut down an Atlantean who tried to reach Jonathan. Then another. Then another.

They attempted to rally. But it was not graceful. We drove them back toward the water, step by brutal step. Some fled into the sea. Others dropped their weapons and ran for the city.

Eventually they stopped coming.

Exhaustion settled over a battlefield that had finally decided it was done killing.

I staggered to Jonathan's side.

He was breathing. Shallow. Uneven. Blood crusted his face and soaked Pherric's hands.

"He lives," Pherric said, voice shaking. "But he went too far."

"I know," I said.

I let out a shaky breath. "Well. That's one way to clear a room."

His eyes were glassy, but he managed to focus on me.

My gaze held his. "You idiot," I whispered. "You're not allowed to save us by dying."

"Not my… best… idea," he managed.

I looked around.

At the beginning of the fight, we were outnumbered five to one, at least. But against every expectation, we were still alive.

I'd seen bodies before, spread across battlefields, that used to belong to people—but it never got easier. It never stopped making me nauseous. If anything, knowing what it took to get here only made it worse. The entire harbor was choked with it: Atlantean soldiers sprawled where they'd fallen, allied fighters slumped against stone, weapons dropped where hands had failed. Smoke drifted, blurring the edges of everything, making it hard to tell where blood ended and shadow began.

The sun had fully set now, leaving the world lit by fire and torchlight alone. Flames flickered along the docks, and torches mounted along the harbor walls cast long, warped shapes that stretched and twisted over the stone. The light made the devastation feel unreal, almost staged—faces half-illuminated, armor gleaming dully, eyes staring at nothing.

I wiped my blade on a fallen soldier's tunic, my hands shaking.

Sandulf approached, his shoulders sagging, the fight visibly drained from him. Blood streaked his face, and there was a deep weariness in his eyes that no victory could erase.

I looked up, still pulling air into my lungs. "Were there any Deep Guard among them?"

He exhaled and gestured toward the bodies. An Irkallan knelt, reached down, and lifted the severed head of an Atlantean by the hair. A moment later, a Fomorian stepped forward and produced another, this one still dripping.

"Two," I said quietly. "Only two?"

Sandulf shrugged, a small, unhappy motion.

I pushed myself upright and scanned the battlefield. "And Goran was here," I said, my voice tightening. "Unless the Leviathan burned him into ash. But... where are the rest?"

"Perhaps they did not return in time," Sandulf said.

I rubbed at my aching elbow, wincing. "Great. That's *only* seven more nightmares we haven't dealt with yet. That should be easy."

He focused hard, trying to remember something. "*Quand les poules auront des dents?*"

I let a proud smirk fall out. "Yeah, Sandy. When the chicken have teeth."

"However," Sandulf said, a grin crossing his bloodied face. "Her army is defeated."

My gaze drifted back to the bodies, to the torches flickering along the harbor, to the sea pretending it had nothing to do with this.

"We should start to—"

"Shit," I exclaimed.

Sandulf's head snapped up. "What?"

"Braylor..."

If Thalassa knew her soldiers had been beaten back, she might not wait. She'd use him. Or end him.

I rammed my sword back into its scabbard and broke into a run, boots slipping on stone as I tore into the streets of Atlantis.

"Finley!" Sandulf shouted.

Pherric and Genevieve called after me too, their voices blurring together behind the rush of blood in my ears.

I didn't slow down.

I wasn't going to be too late.

82

I Really Hate This City

Finley

I sprinted inland toward the palace and Braylor. To the hardest thing I would ever have to do, knowing full well it might be the last thing I ever did.

But I ran.

The city rose up to meet me, white stone and shattered calm, the same streets I'd fled not that long ago now rushing past in reverse. I cut through alleys and arches. I passed the fountain where I'd hesitated. The steps where I'd looked back. The turn I hadn't taken fast enough the first time.

The farther I went, the quieter it became. Not a comforting kind of quiet. It made my skin shrink and the hairs on my neck rise. There were no guards or even crowds running. No one seemed to be peering out windows or from behind doors. There was only smoke dragging low across the stones and the distant fallout of war behind me.

I burst through an archway and skidded to a stop in a wide plaza, swallowed by night. Only a few torches burned at the edges, throwing thin and nervous light across dim square. Shadows stretched and snapped back as the fire danced, turning columns into looming ghosts and open space into something that felt haunted. The center of the area stayed dark, untouched by the torchlight. As if the flames refused to touch it.

Then something moved. Because it always did…

He stepped out from behind a column, trident dragging against the stone with a sound that made my teeth rattle.

Goran.

Half his armor was gone. One side of his face was burned raw, skin blistered and split, one eye swollen almost shut. He looked furious. And delighted. The First Sea-lord of Atlantis stood alone in the wreckage, shoulders squared, exactly where he wanted to be.

"Well," he said pleasantly. "You live."

"You too, I guess," I said, lifting my sword. "Unbelievable. The Leviathan had *one job*."

He laughed and came at me without another word.

Goran was fast. Faster than he had any right to be. The trident whistled through the air, its prongs tearing through the air where my head had just been. I ducked, came up slashing. He deflected with ease and kicked me hard in the stomach. He quickly punched my wounded shoulder. Just for fun. Pain flared white-hot. I staggered back and barely avoided the follow-up strike that would've pinned me to the plaza floor.

"You are too small," he mocked, circling. "Too soft."

"Yeah," I said, gasping. "That's kinda my brand."

I lunged. But he did not turn away. And my blade sank deep into his side, sliding deep into his gut with a sickening give. I twisted, ripped it free, already bracing for blood.

He looked down at the wound and up at me.

And laughed.

The sound scraped my nerves as his flesh knitted itself back together. The blood remained, but the skin crawled closed like it had never been broken.

"Oh," he said. "Did you think that would be effective?"

"I was optimistic," I said. "It's a flaw."

He hit me again with the back of his fist, sending me sprawling across the stone. My sword skittered away. I spun away in time to avoid being skewered, came up empty-handed and panting, my vision narrowing.

This was it, whispered the sensible part of my brain.

He stabbed at me again and I leapt for my sword. I scooped it up before the prongs of the trident stabbed me and staggered to my feet.

The other part of my brain—the stubborn, furious, absolutely-done-with-this one—noticed something.

His trident.

Long. Heavy. Awkward.

Goran reared back for the killing thrust.

I didn't dodge.

I stepped in.

The prongs bit into my bad shoulder. Pain coursed through me again and I almost passed out. But before he pulled back, I grabbed the shaft with one hand and *held on*, even as he snarled and tried to wrench it free.

"Got you," I said, smiling.

I yanked him forward with everything I had and drove the tip of the blade up into his chin. Steel bit hard, closing his smirking mouth.

I leaned back. With all the strength I had left, I swung in a full arc and cut into his neck, at the base of my sword.

For one impossible heartbeat, Goran's body stood there, trident still buried in me, his face frozen in shock as his head fell to the side, hanging on by skin alone, and finally separated. It hit the tile with a dull, final thud.

Then the body fell.

I dropped to a knee, ripping the trident from my shoulder, and staggered away, with even more blood soaking my sleeve. I didn't look at the body again.

Immortal, my ass.

I turned and ran.

The palace loomed over of me, dark and waiting, and I forced my legs to keep moving.

Braylor was in there.

83

Shit. So Much Shit.

Finley

I slipped into the palace through main doors. It was quiet and dark. No force was waiting to greet me.

Two guards died without ceremony. One never saw me; the other did and barely had time to regret it. I caught this body before it hit the floor, eased it down, and kept going. The palace didn't echo. It absorbed sound the way deep water swallowed your scream.

An attendant stepped into my path at the worst moment. Her eyes went wide and her hands shook so badly the tray she carried rattled against her chest.

I lifted my sword. She opened her mouth. But I knocked her unconscious with the pommel before she could finish whatever warning she was about to scream. I told myself it was mercy. I didn't stay to argue with me, because... I'm rarely right.

The doors to the throne room stood open.

I was going to sneak inside, but stopped pretending to hide and marched in.

The space swallowed me whole—that circular, vast area that made my spine tingle. Columns rose into a domed ceiling painted with living myths that shifted slowly overhead. The room watched me and waited.

Thalassa sat on her throne, legs crossed and mouth grinning.

She looked exactly as she always did: composed, regal, untouched by the war outside her walls. Because cities would burn for her convenience.

Braylor stood at her side.

I inhaled deeply. He looked whole again. Strong. Grounded. The damage I'd last seen—bruises, blood, the results of his fight with the Minotaur—was gone, replaced by barely contained power and restrained anger. His eyes snapped to me the moment I stepped into the open, and the sound he made was barely Fomorian. It came from deep in his chest, a low, warning growl that vibrated through the stone beneath my boots.

Then I saw the collar.

Metal, fitted cleanly at his throat. Polished. Intentional. A silk ribbon trailed from it, bright and elegant.

Thalassa held the end of it loosely in one hand.

Ownership made decorative.

My grip tightened on my sword.

A flicker of a shadow beyond the throne caught my eye, behind a curtain heavy with woven fabric.

Ramil. He seemed nervous. Sweat on his upper lip. He hid back there, watching me and looking past for any friends I might have brought along. He knew he was in trouble because he'd bent Braylor's mind and probably proclaimed it to be loyalty. Now, he looked very aware there was nowhere left to run on an island.

I stepped fully into the light, lifted my chin, and met Thalassa's gaze.

"It's over, Thalassa."

The words sounded steadier than I felt. That seemed like a win.

"Is it over? Truly? While you still exist?" she replied. "I think not."

"Your army's gone. Your Deep Guard will be hunted down. And Goran?" I lifted my sword a fraction. "He's not coming back."

Her lips curved, slow and deliberate.

"Is that true?" she purred. "What a shame. But are you not forgetting someone?"

Her fingers tightened on the silk ribbon. Braylor jerked forward with a snarl, the sound enough to make my heart ache. Not anger. Not hatred. It was worse.

"The eleventh and latest addition to my Deep Guard," Thalassa continued smoothly.

I swallowed.

Reason number #97 on the continually expanding list of why she needed to die. Tonight. Preferably in a lot of pain.

"Don't do this," I muttered, though I wasn't sure who I was talking to.

She rose from the throne with unhurried grace and stepped to the edge of the dais.

"I get to watch you be slaughtered by your lover," she said, almost fondly. "And then I will simply slip away." She gestured lazily toward the pools of seawater flanking the chamber. "Only to return once your kind has tired and sailed away. I will rule again. You have not won anything, child."

My jaw clenched.

"And if Braylor doesn't defeat me?"

Her hands settled on her hips, her posture both proud and defiant, as she dared the universe to contradict her.

"You are wounded, Finley. Exhausted. And you will be facing one of the most capable warriors there is." Her gaze shot to Braylor with open satisfaction. "He defeated the Minotaur alone. When he was isolated and weak. I have little doubt about the outcome."

Unfortunately, she wasn't wrong.

What she hadn't mentioned—what she didn't need to—was that I wasn't sure I could bring myself to fight him at all.

Not really.

"So," she said lightly, "let us end this once and for all..."

She lifted the ribbon. And let it fall from her fingers.

Braylor's snarl tore through the chamber. He stepped forward, thick boots striking the smooth black tile as he mounted the first step.

Shit.

I retreated instinctively, pain flaring hot as my shoulder protested the movement. Blood slid warm down my arm. My other elbow barely cooperated when I tried to flex it. Every breath felt earned, dragged from lungs that had already given too much.

Braylor reached for the broadsword at his side.

The sound of steel leaving its sheath was slow. Deliberate.

He descended the stairs one at a time, heavy footfalls echoing through the throne room. He wasn't rushing. He was savoring this. Or whatever part of him was still capable of savoring anything was.

I shifted into a fighting stance out of instinct more than confidence, feet braced, sword lifted.

I still didn't know what I was going to do.

Braylor raised the blade over his shoulder and brought it down in a killing arc.

I didn't block. I rolled. There was no universe where I wanted my blade anywhere near his.

"Braylor, don't do this!" I hissed, scrambling to my feet. "Please!"

He answered by baring his teeth and lunging.

I jumped sideways, just clearing the reach of his broadsword, my boots skidding as I backed away across the slick floor. The throne room felt small now—too close and too exposed, every echo amplifying how alone I was.

"It's me!" I shouted. "Finley!"

His eyes snapped to mine.

They were wild. Unfocused. Spit flew from his lips as he swung at my waist. I arched back in time, the blade whispering past my tunic close enough that I felt the wind of it against my skin.

When the sword came back down, I reacted on instinct. I brought my blade up to parry.

The impact rang through my arms.

The force of it almost tore the sword from my hands. I barely kept my balance.

He was impossibly strong.

Before I could reset, his free hand came around in a brutal arc. The back of his fist caught my cheek.

The world went bright white and I nearly lost consciousness.

I flew backward and skidded across the floor, stopping short of one of the glowing pools. Pain exploded behind my eyes, stars scattering across my vision as my head cracked against stone.

I lay there for half a heartbeat too long.

His sword slammed down as I shifted away from his next strike. Tiles burst apart in small fragments.

I twisted, gasping, barely managing to get my knees under me.

"Braylor!" I cried. "Look at me! It's Finley! You don't want to do this!"

He answered with a snarl and another backhand that sent me reeling, fury radiating off him in waves.

"I love you!" I screamed, the words ripping out of me before I could stop them.

Tears blurred my vision. My grip faltered. For the first time since I'd stepped into this room, my resolve cracked.

"Dammit..."

Thalassa's footsteps echoed as she descended the stairs, unhurried, pleased. She looked entirely too comfortable watching this unfold.

"Do not consider surrendering to his strikes, child," she said calmly. "You will die... and he will not stop." Her smile grew intense. "He has been instructed to kill you. And remove your head."

Which was... unfortunate.

I'd briefly entertained the idea that letting him kill me might break whatever hold she had on him.

Apparently not.

"Come back to me, Braylor!"

I bolted, racing around the perimeter of the chamber, ducking, jumping, sliding away from every swing. Each near miss chipped away at my stamina, and each failure fed his rage. He roared and charged harder, faster, his attacks growing less controlled and more violent.

"You have to remember me!" I shouted over my shoulder. "Small, annoying, love of your life? Please—Braylor—please!"

I wiped at my eyes without slowing.

That was my mistake.

His broadsword caught the top of my thigh in a shallow but vicious slice. Pain erupted, hot and immediate. My leg gave out, and I stumbled, barely staying upright as blood soaked me.

I could still walk.

Barely.

I backed away, limping now, chest heaving.

This was not going well.

Not even a little.

84

Insufficient, But Enough

Jonathan

I was upright only in the loosest, most technical sense of the word. Pherric had one arm hooked under my shoulder, his grip firm enough to keep me vertical without crushing anything vital. Kinnat had the other side, smaller but somehow more immovable, her presence an anchor point my body kept circling whether I asked it to or not. Genevieve walked directly in front of me, backward, eyes locked on my face like she expected me to dissolve into vapor if she blinked.

"You need to stop," Genevieve said for at least the fourth time. Her voice was thin, the strain unmistakable. "Seriously, you've done enough."

We made our way slowly through the deserted city.

"Jonathan," she added, not shouting. "You're bleeding from places people aren't supposed to bleed from."

"I'm aware," I said. My tongue felt thick. The words took a moment to assemble. "That is not the primary concern."

"That's not comforting," she replied.

When we arrived at the palace, they rushed me through the open doors. No guards were there. Only a few bodies. Finley's handiwork, no doubt.

Inside, the main corridor seemed to shift. Not dramatically, but enough to remind me that my body had lodged a formal complaint and was no longer cooperating.

I thought of it as a reaction gone uncontrolled. Too much force introduced too quickly, no time for equilibrium. Heat without a release valve. Byproducts accumulating where they shouldn't exist. The copper taste in my mouth was the telltale sign that the system had started producing something toxic. In other words, my brain was bleeding.

Still not the primary concern.

Finley was probably in that throne room.

Braylor was with her. And he was trying to kill her.

I had not said it aloud, but the thought pressed in relentlessly: this was my fault.

Not all of it. Not the battle, not Thalassa, not the Deep Guard. But Ramil? Ramil had gained access because I believed him. Because I wanted his theories about me to be right. I wanted to believe that Finley was an anomaly instead of a variable.

I had helped him put his hands on Braylor's mind.

That weight did not lift just because I was injured.

We reached the main doors.

They stood open, the echoes of violence spilling through in loud, metallic bursts. I heard Finley before I saw her—her voice raw, desperate, cutting through the striking of steel. I forced my eyes to focus.

She was moving constantly. Not fighting, but surviving. Braylor towered over her, every swing heavy enough to slice her in half.

She wasn't trying to hurt him.

I scanned the room beyond them, vision swimming, searching for patterns instead of faces.

And there—

Behind the far curtain, barely visible in the torchlight, a familiar face.

Ramil. He was hiding. Watching.

I exhaled. "There," I said, lifting a trembling hand. "Behind the drapes. That's him."

Kinnat was already gone. One moment she was bracing my weight, the next there was only air. I didn't see her move. I simply registered her absence.

Genevieve followed my gaze. Her expression hardened instantly. "You guys go. I'm going in," she said. "I can help her."

"No," I said, harsher than I intended. The word scraped out of me. "I need your help. And…. Kinnat has disappeared."

Genevieve looked all around for her.

Pherric cursed.

Ramil must have seen us then, because he vanished. The curtain stilled.

"He's running," I said. "We have to—"

My legs wobbled.

I caught myself on the doorframe, fingers digging into carved stone, forcing my body to obey me through sheer will. The room swam violently, but I locked my knees and stayed up.

"I can stand," I said, because it was important that someone believed that.

Genevieve didn't argue. She threw herself under my arm.

We turned down the side corridor together, toward the direction Ramil had run.

The palace beyond the throne room was quieter, narrower. Torches burned low, their light uneven, shadows sliding along walls. My footsteps echoed too loudly. Every sound did.

We found him in a junction hall, racing around the corner. Ramil straightened when he saw us, drawing himself up with practiced authority. "You are obstructing matters of great importance," he said coolly. "I suggest you step aside."

"No," I said with determination.

Without asking, Genevieve shoved something into my hand. She knew what I wanted to do.

It was a dagger. It felt heavier than it should have, or maybe that was my grip failing.

"Do this. For me." She closed my fingers around the handle. "And make it fucking hurt."

His eyes went to the dagger.

Something in his expression shifted.

Not fear. Calculation.

"I know what you did," I said. Each word took effort. "To Braylor. To Genevieve. Hell, to me. You lying son of a bitch."

He smiled thinly. "Then you understand why you cannot stop this."

"I understand," I replied, "that you hollowed him out and turned him into a killing machine."

"He was already that," he snapped, losing composure for the first time. "I gave him a purpose."

I saw the sweat trailing down his temples. I had never seen him fear anything before.

Ramil turned to run and slammed straight into Kinnat. She smiled at him.

His fury flared, and in one quick, desperate motion, he tore a knife from her belt. Kinnat lunged for him, swearing, but I moved forward too.

My vision narrowed, my body screaming, as I forced one last surge out of failing muscles.

It wasn't a charge. It was a stumble disguised as one.

He turned to come at me with Kinnat's knife.

I slammed into him hard enough to throw him off balance. Pain exploded through me, white and harsh, but Ramil reeled, his grip faltering as he tried to recover.

I looked down. The entire blade was deep in his gut.

Ramil gasped, shock finally stripping the arrogance from his face.

We stared at each other for a heartbeat.

Then he collapsed.

I stood there, shaking, staring down at him, waiting for something to happen. Relief. Satisfaction. Justice.

Nothing came.

Genevieve shoved past me and dropped beside him, fury stripping her voice bare.

"You made me kill Finley," she whispered in his ear. No tremor. No mercy. "You wore my body like a costume."

Ramil gagged, blood bubbling at his lips.

"I will never forgive myself," she continued. "But you?"

She leaned in. "You don't get forgiveness. You don't get peace. You don't even get a clean death. I hope it hurts, motherfucker."

Pherric touched my arm. "We have to go."

Whatever victory this was for me—and it was something I had dreamed about for a long time—it was insufficient. But it was enough. For now.

We ran back toward the throne room, my vision still blurred, my grip on the dagger loosening as my body finally began to fail in earnest.

I did not know if I could help her.

But I knew I had to try.

85

The Choice That Broke Us

Finley

He drove the blade down again.

And again.

And again.

Each strike rang through my arms, through my shoulders, the bones in my spine, until I couldn't tell where the sword ended and I began. My blade was locked above my head, both hands around the hilt, elbows screaming as he hacked away in a brutal, downward rhythm that left me no room.

Braylor was a storm over me.

Every blow forced me lower, boots sliding across the polished stone, knees bending against my will. Sparks burst where swords met. My injured shoulder screamed in protest, blood slicking my arm.

I could hear Thalassa laughing.

Not loudly. Not dramatically. Simply a soft, pleased sound, as she watched the play reach its final act.

"Look at you," she whispered. "Still trying."

I didn't look at her. I couldn't afford to.

Braylor's face was inches from mine now, shadowed and wild. Sweat ran down his face, soaked into his hair, dripped from his jaw. The muscles in his arms stood out in defined relief as he raised the broadsword and brought it down again.

I cried out, a raw, involuntary sound, as my knees slammed into the floor. The blade hovered close to my face, my sword the only thing keeping it from splitting me open.

He leaned into the pressure, forcing my arms lower.

"You will die," he said.

The words were flat. Certain.

Not shouted. Not snarled.

And that chilled me deep.

Something inside my chest cracked.

That wasn't rage talking. Or Thalassa's voice echoing through him. That was Braylor, stripped down to function and command, delivering a conclusion he believed had already been reached.

I stared up at him through shaking arms and felt something terrible and final settle into place.

He was gone.

The thought hollowed me out.

"I love you," I whispered, the words tearing out of me.

His brow furrowed, just slightly, but the weight didn't ease.

"I love you," I said again, louder this time, my voice breaking. "I love you. I love you. I love you."

I didn't know what else to give him. I had no clever plan left. No strategy. No hidden strength waiting to be unlocked. Just the truth, offered up like prayer.

His arms shook.

The blows came slower. Still brutal. Punishing. But no longer as harsh and relentless.

He lifted the sword again and brought it down, teeth bared now.

"I love you," I said again, hoarse. "Please. Come back to me."

Another strike.

Slower.

His jaw clenched. His eyes shot—just for a heartbeat—to the side. Not toward Thalassa. Away from her.

I saw it.

Hope flared, fragile and dangerous.

"I know you're in there," I whispered. "I know you are. You don't want this. You never wanted this."

His sword came down again.

"No," he said.

The word ripped out of him, edged and strained.

But he struck again.

"No."

Again.

"No—"

Each denial came with a blow, his body obeying commands his mind was trying to refuse. His swings were losing precision now, the arc of the blade less controlled, his footing unsteady. He staggered half a step, then corrected, fury and effort warring across his face.

I twisted, barely managing to deflect a strike that would've split my skull. The force sent me skidding across the floor, my sword shrieking as it scraped stone. I gasped and rolled, barely getting my blade up in time to catch the next blow.

"You don't want this," I said, forcing the words through clenched teeth. "You don't want to kill me."

He struck again.

"No," he said, louder now, the word cracking.

I pushed up, shaking, and met his next swing head-on. The impact jolted through me, but I stayed upright. Barely.

His eyes were glassy now, darting, unfocused, as though he were trying to see past whatever had been laid over his thoughts. The sword trembled in his hands.

Thalassa's smile faltered.

"Finish it," she snapped, irritation heightening her voice. "Kill her."

He spasmed.

The command hit him hard enough that I felt it, a pulse in the air, a tightening that made my skull throb. He roared and lunged, all restraint tearing loose in a final, desperate surge.

I deflected the strike by instinct alone, twisting aside as the blade screamed past me. Stone shattered where it struck the floor.

He stumbled.

Just a step. But enough. I could have stabbed him.

"Braylor," I said, rushing toward him, ignoring the pain screaming through my body. "Come back to me. Please. I'm right here."

He stared at me.

Really stared.

And for the first time since I'd entered that room, I saw him.

Not the weapon. Not the warrior.

Him.

"I can't," he said. "...stop."

The words were quiet. Broken.

My heart dropped.

Before I could reach him, before I could say anything else, he flipped the broadsword around in his hands.

"I will not kill you..."

Holding the sharp steel in his hands, he drove himself down on his blade.

"No—!"

The scream tore out of me as the sword punched through his stomach, the force of it staggering him backward. Blood spilled instantly, dark and awful, staining the dark tile.

He collapsed to his knees with a choked sound, one hand braced against the floor, the other still gripping the metal as if afraid to let go.

I dropped beside him.

Braylor rolled onto the floor, the broadsword fell away.

"No, no, no, no," I sobbed, hands shaking as I tried to hold him, to stop the bleeding, to undo something that couldn't be undone. "You don't get to do this. You don't get to leave. Not like this."

Every inhale was a visible effort.

"I love you," I whispered desperately. "I love you. I'm here. I've got you."

His eyes found mine.

And for a moment—just one—

They were clear.

Then he sagged against me, the weight of him heavy and real and terrifying in my arms.

And I screamed his name into the echoing chamber, refusing to let go.

86

Of Revenge and Ruin

Genevieve

I hit the throne room at a run and almost slipped on the polished floor. My sword was out and ready to take on that huge beast of a boyfriend.

But they were no longer fighting.

Finley was on her knees. No longer screaming. Simply making this small, broken noise I had never heard from her before.

Braylor lay sprawled across the black tile, his massive frame impossibly still except for the short rise and fall of his chest. Blood spread beneath him in a red circle, soaking into the thin channels carved into the floor. His sword a few feet away.

Finley's hands pressed uselessly against his belly, her fingers red and quivering. Her hair had come loose and clung to her face with sweat and tears. She looked completely hollowed out.

Pherric stumbled in beside me, Jonathan sagging between him and Kinnat. Jonathan's face was gray, his eyes unfocused, but when he saw Finley, something darkened in his expression that made my throat ache.

For a long moment, no one moved.

The bitch I assumed was the queen of Atlantis was still there, alive and standing by a pool of water, but none of us paid her any attention. She didn't exist in that time. Nothing did except the girl on the floor and the giant dying beneath her hands.

"Pherric," Finley sobbed suddenly, turning wild and desperate eyes toward him. "Please. Please. You have to do something. One of your elixirs. Something from your book. Anything. I don't care what it takes. Please."

Her voice shattered completely on that last word.

Pherric stepped forward slowly, afraid anything might crush what little hope remained. He knelt across from her, careful not to jostle Braylor, and examined the wound with a grim precision that felt cruel in its calm.

I hated him for that calm.

He pressed two fingers lightly against Braylor's neck, then put his hand over his heart. His jaw tightened.

"I am sorry," he said quietly. "I have nothing that can undo this. My art does not mend what the body has already chosen to relinquish."

"No," Finley said, shaking her head hard. "No, that's not true... You brought *me* back! You made the Deep Guard immortal. You—"

"That was not healing," Pherric replied, his voice heavy with something that sounded dangerously close to regret. "I do not have the ingredients, and I do not have time."

Braylor's breathing was a wet, painful sound that ripped through Finley.

She collapsed forward, pressing her forehead to his chest, sobbing. "I'm sorry. I'm so sorry. I didn't want this. I didn't—"

I dropped to my knees beside her without thinking. I put a hand on her back, feeling the tremors running through her. I wanted to fix it. To do something useful. I wanted to scream at the world for being this relentlessly cruel.

Jonathan sank down heavily behind us, Pherric catching him before he tipped over. Jonathan didn't look at Braylor. He stared at Finley, eyes shining, jaw clenched, guilt carved into every line of his face.

Then I noticed Kinnat.

She hadn't moved closer.

She stood still just inside the threshold, eyes round, one hand hovering over the worn leather satchel at her hip—the same one she'd carried since that farm in Pandæmonia.

Her eyes met mine.

Something passed between us. Recognition. A silent question.

I had no clue what she wanted so I slowly nodded.

Kinnat fell to her knees and pulled the satchel open.

Finley didn't notice at first. She was too lost in her grief, whispering apologies into Braylor's blood-soaked body, brushing his hair back with shaking fingers.

Kinnat's hand emerged holding a single flattened leaf.

It was crimson and glossy, veins glowing faintly. The edges shimmered, seemingly serrated, and the surface pulsed with a slow, steady light that reminded me unpleasantly of a heartbeat.

Bloodfern.

I remembered back to that day on the farm.

How Kinnat had warned me before we crossed the fence that we shouldn't steal. How I'd rolled my eyes and told her I was hungry and morality could take a day off. We'd spent hours harvesting bloodfern in the heat, our hands stained red as we stripped the resin from the leaves. I remembered her explaining that the stuff could seal flesh in seconds, that crushed and prepared correctly it could knit wounds closed and stabilize broken bones.

Staring at the leaf glowing in her hand, I realized she hadn't left that farm empty-handed.

Pherric gasped. "Bygods," he whispered. "Where did you—"

Kinnat didn't look at him. She knelt beside Finley and held the leaf out gently. "I kept it," she said simply. "In the event Genevieve was hurt."

She looked up at me. She'd taken it for me. I let the tears loose.

Finley lifted her head, eyes red and swollen, confusion bouncing around her mind. "What... what is that?"

Pherric leaned in, awe and fear battling in his expression. "This is bloodfern. The resin can accelerate healing."

Finley grabbed onto that phrase like a lifeline. "Then do it. Please."

Pherric hesitated before nodding. He moved with practiced urgency, crushing the leaf with his fist on the hard floor.

"Get me some water."

I rushed to scoop up water from the glimmering pool with both hands. I returned and let it splash on the black tile next to him.

Pherric swirled it together with his finger. The liquid glowed a deep, living scarlet, steaming faintly as it resisted the air.

Braylor's eyes fluttered open as Pherric slid the mixture into his hand.

Looking into her eyes, Braylor focused on her with effort.

"I'm here," she sobbed. "I'm not going anywhere."

Pherric tipped his hand with deliberate care and pressed the red, milky substance to Braylor's lips.

"Slowly," he murmured. "Swallow it all."

Braylor choked, but he managed to down the makeshift potion. Pherric didn't hesitate. He rubbed the remaining mixture directly over the gaping wound in Braylor's stomach.

The effect was immediate.

The bleeding slowed... then stalled. Beneath the pool of blood, the torn flesh began to draw together, knitting itself closed in uneven, almost desperate motions. It was hard to see clearly through the mess, but there was no mistaking it.

The wound was healing.

"No!"

The scream tore through the throne room, shrill and feral.

I barely had time to register her leap before Thalassa was on Finley, fingers clawing at the bag at her waist. The queen's grip was frantic now, ugly, all pretense gone. She wasn't regal. She was desperate.

"Get off her!" I shouted, already moving.

Finley stumbled under the impact. She was exhausted. Anyone could see it. Her sword arm shook, her shoulders sagged, blood soaking through her outfit.

Thalassa nearly tore the rounded bag free.

Finley kicked backward, heel slamming into Thalassa's knee. The queen shrieked and lost her balance. The bag flew open and the orb rolled loose.

We didn't know what it did, but my instincts labeled it immediately as *Important Object We Were Not Supposed to Drop.*

Time slowed in the worst possible way.

The orb rolled across the throne room, dark and reflective, catching torchlight and warping it into something practically alive. I dove for it, boots slipping on the polished stone, fingers stretching—

I missed.

Thalassa scrambled past me, eyes wild.

I twisted mid-fall and slammed into her legs with my shoulder. We both went down hard. She screamed in fury and pain as I kicked out, catching her ribs.

But she was already leaping back up.

Finley was faster.

She stepped on Thalassa's hand with brutal precision.

I might've heard bones crack.

Thalassa howled, thrashing as Finley bent, picked up the orb, and straightened with it clutched in her shivering hand.

"This?" Finley panted. "This what you want?"

The look on Thalassa's face was pure hatred. She screamed something ancient and charged.

"Why is this thing important? Why does it matter to you?"

I had never seen Finley that calm when she was that angry.

"Because Braylor was important to me. And you tried to take him away," she said, her voice steady in a way that scared me more than shouting ever could. "So... I'm going to take this away from you..."

Finley didn't hesitate.

She threw the orb.

"No!" screamed Thalassa, her hand reaching out for it.

It struck the far wall—

And shattered.

The sound wasn't just loud. It had the unmistakable quality of something going catastrophically off-script. Light exploded outward in a blinding wave that knocked me back. I hit the floor hard, ears ringing, vision swimming.

Thalassa screamed again.

The palace answered.

The floor lurched violently. Columns groaned, stone grinding against stone as cracks raced up their length. Water surged violently in the pools, sloshing over the edges in shimmering sheets.

"The sea will not forgive this! Or you!" Thalassa shrieked, terror finally ripping through her fury.

"Good," replied Finley, her tone cold and harsh. "And I sure as hell won't forgive you."

Finley dropped down on her.

I scrambled up in time to see Finley straddle her, pinning her flat against the stone. Thalassa fought wildly, clawing, striking—but Finley didn't flinch.

"Something," Finley said, her voice shaking with rage and grief and something worse underneath it, "I've wanted to do for a very long time."

She leaned close.

"I ruined your fucking day."

Finley pulled her knife.

And cut Thalassa's throat.

Blood sprayed across the floor, hot and sudden. Thalassa gurgled, hands grasping uselessly at Finley's arms.

Finley didn't stop.

She hacked again. And again.

I did nothing. Not because I wanted to stop her, but because there was no way I would have tried.

Finley screamed with every strike, sound tearing out of her chest as stone cracked overhead. Pieces of the domed ceiling broke free and smashed into the floor, spraying dust and fragments across the room.

Finally—

Thalassa's head came free.

It rolled across the floor and splashed into one of the glowing pools.

Gone.

The palace screamed.

Cracks split the walls wide open. Columns crumbled. Chunks of marble crashed down around us. Water surged violently, slamming against the sides of the pools.

"Finley!" I ran to her, grabbing her shoulders, hauling her backward as another section of ceiling collapsed where she'd been kneeling seconds earlier. "Finley! Look at me!"

Fighting for air, she fought me for a heartbeat, wild and shaking.

Then she saw Braylor.

Pherric and Kinnat had him upright, arms hooked under his shoulders. He was alive. Shallow. Pained and weak. But alive.

"Help us! He is too heavy!" Pherric shouted. "The island is failing!"

The floor tilted beneath us.

We rushed over and, all of us together, lifted Braylor.

He was impossibly heavy, every step a strain, his boots dragging as the palace tore itself apart around us. Stone shattered. The seawater in the pools started to rise, spilling out on the floor.

We dragged Braylor out of the throne room.

Out of the palace.

Out as the world started to collapse behind us.

87

This Is a Terrible Time for Heroics

Finley

The palace steps cracked beneath our feet when we burst into the open air.

Atlantis was dying. And it was not poetic, it was messy.

The crescent bay stretched out below us, moonlight obscured by smoke. Farther out, silhouetted against the dark water, the *Skathis* sailed in tired and wounded—its hull scorched, rigging torn, one sail hanging like a ripped wing.

My last ship had survived. Melcente stood at the helm, alive and steady, hands firm on the wheel. Kasuma had made it too, circling the ship in a tight, vigilant arc, ready to dive in if anything went wrong. Her bow was still strung, the blood of others darkening her clothes.

Braylor sagged between me, Pherric, Gen, and Kinnat, his massive weight pulling at us with every step. Each ragged sound he made scraped raw, but he was still alive—and that mattered more than anything else.

I was still shaking. Not from exhaustion or grief, but from the echo of what I'd done.

Thalassa's blood was still on my hands. I could feel it even after wiping them on my ruined clothes, a phantom heat that clung beneath my skin. Rage had carried me through her end, dark and absolute. Now it drained

537

away in uneven pulses, leaving behind something hollow and buzzing.

Atlantis chose that moment to remind us there was no time for reflection.

A deep, grinding crack tore through the palace behind us. One of the outer towers sheared sideways, stone screaming as it collapsed into the lower tiers. Stone dust rolled across the steps in choking clouds.

"We need to go!" Pherric shouted. "Now!"

Down below, a small boat had detached from the *Skathis* and was rowing hard for the base of the steps. Help was coming. Barely.

Genevieve took my place and they began carrying Braylor down the stone stairs.

I stared back at the palace doors.

Something pulled at me. Not fear. But duty.

"Finley," Genevieve looked up at me, following my gaze. "What are you doing?"

I turned to her. "Get him to the ship."

Her eyes widened. "Finley—"

"Now," I snapped. "The island is going under. Get everyone to safety!"

"And you?" Pherric threw a shout over his shoulder.

I was already stepping backward.

"There's something I have to do."

Kinnat's grip tightened on Braylor's arm. "There is no time."

"I know." I backed toward the shattered doors, eyes never leaving them. "That's why I'm going."

Genevieve swore. "You are *not* going back in there!"

I smiled at her. Not a real one. "Watch me."

I threw open the doors and limped inside, the cut on my thigh intensely annoyed with me.

The palace groaned—enormous, furious. A section of the roof caved down the corridor, the sound rolling through the stone beneath our feet.

The heat hit first, hot air rushing outward as interior fires found fresh air. Then the noise. Stone splitting. Water pushing up through ruptured channels. The palace had gone from controlled elegance to panicked collapse in minutes.

I staggered through halls already half-destroyed, dodging falling debris and tumbling over cracks that opened without warning. The floor shifted at odd angles now, water sluicing across tiles in uncontrolled sheets.

Thalassa's domain was coming apart exactly the way it deserved to.

I skidded around a corner into the throne room. Thalassa's body still lying there, lifeless. I hobbled up the stairs and past her throne. Then tore through the hanging curtain, plunging into a chamber that reeked of wealth and old power.

Her treasure room.

My eyes locked immediately on the glass tanks in the middle of the floor.

"No time," I warned myself, already moving.

An old axe lay among the weapons—a brutal thing, all weight and purpose, its edge dull with age but still eager. I snatched it up and swung.

The glass exploded.

Water burst out in a violent surge, slamming into my legs hard enough to push me back a few steps.

Inside the shattered tank, cradled in woven coral supports, lay nine eggs.

The dragon eggs.

I lifted two of them carefully. Their shells were dark, veined with faint, ember-colored light that pulsed slowly, steadily once exposed to air.

"Oh," I gasped. "You are still alive... still in there."

Rage flickered again. Controlled this time. Focused.

I turned and shuffled away.

The corridor was worse on the way out. More collapse. Less patience. A beam crashed down behind me, showering dust and grit as it struck stone. I crawled over rubble and skidded through ankle-deep water, clutching the eggs tight to my chest.

The night air hit me as I burst back onto the palace steps.

They had dragged poor Braylor to the boat. Genevieve was already running back up the steps. Her mouth opened, a million questions ready to pour out.

"Dragon eggs," I said, already shoving them into her arms. "Real ones. Alive. Get them to the boat!"

Her face did something complicated. "You're kidding."

"Nope."

She stared at them. Then at me. Then back at the palace behind me. "You are going back in."

"Yup."

"Finley!"

I was gone.

The second run hurt more. My leg was screaming now, and exhaustion finally clawed its way through what little I had left. The palace had shifted again, stairs partially collapsed, forcing me to climb over fallen statuary and duck hanging slabs of ceiling.

Back into the treasure room. Two more eggs. And I didn't hesitate.

Then out to the palace steps.

Kinnat caught me this time, eyes wide as I thrust the eggs at her. "Guard these with your life."

She nodded once, fierce and silent.

"Finley! Stop!" Pherric shouted as he raced up the stairs, over the roar of collapsing stone.

"No can do!"

And I was back to it. I had to save as many as I could. The palace shuddered violently—hard enough to throw me off balance. I hit the floor on one knee, pain flashing bright and hot, but I forced myself up.

One more run. I could feel that this would be my last. And my heart broke. I wasn't going to be able to save them all.

The chamber was already half underwater when I reached it. Water poured through cracks in the walls, swirling around my knees.

I started to reach for two more eggs and considered trying to take a third. But the floor erupted at my feet. The water surged, knocking me back. I scrambled forward, chest burning, and reached blindly into the wreckage.

Two more eggs. That was it. If I wanted to live, too.

I wrapped them in my arms and stumbled away.

The ceiling came down behind me.

Not all of it, but enough.

I didn't look back.

The palace doors were barely standing when I burst through them one last time, lungs on fire, eyesight blurring. I hit the steps hard, boots slipping on water and dust, and staggered forward.

"Finley!" Genevieve screamed.

I stopped and slowly lifted my head.

The others were off to the sides of the stone steps, recoiling in fear.

What?!

That's when I saw her.

The Leviathan. She had hauled herself from the water and slithered up the stairs.

Her massive body was writhing along the lower steps, scales wet and gleaming in firelight, steam curling from between them. Her head rose higher than the palace entrance, eyes burning a deep, furious red as they fixed on me.

On the eggs.

On the ruin behind me.

The island groaned again, final and failing.

I tightened my grip on the eggs and squared my shoulders, heart slamming loud enough to drown out the world.

"Well," I said hoarsely.

The Leviathan hissed, a sound that scraped across my spine and sank deep into my chest.

"I was hoping you'd show up."

88

The Day I Got Promoted by a Sea God

Finley

The words were barely out of my mouth when I realized how stupid they sounded.

The Leviathan glared at me. Her gaze fell to the two final dragon eggs in my arms once again.

When her eyes locked on me again, reality stopped existing.

And I'm not kidding. Reality fucking ended...

The stone steps beneath my boots lost their meaning, the roar of the collapsing palace faded to an echo, and the weight of the dragon eggs in my arms suddenly felt irrelevant. All I could see were her red eyes—and everything else slipped away.

I didn't fall. But I was floating.

The air diminished, then thickened, became something else entirely. Cold pressed against my skin, but it didn't hurt. The light bent, stretching into long blue ribbons that sank past me, curling and folding as if the sea itself were deciding how to receive me.

Water closed over my head.

I should have panicked, accidentally inhaled and died and woken up screaming, because it was all a dream.

Instead, I inhaled. And didn't drown.

Not air. Not water either. Something in between. A suspension. A permission.

I stood—no, *existed*—on a plain of dark stone far below the surface, lit by slow-moving currents of moonlight filtered by bluish green water. Enormous shapes drifted in the distance: coral structures the size of cities, skeletal remains of creatures I couldn't name, ancient shipwrecks half-swallowed by the seabed and history.

And hovering before me was the Leviathan.

She rose from the dark with impossible grace, her body spinning in vast, patient arcs. Her scales were deeper blue here, shot through with veins of molten gold and green. Scars crossed her hide, old and healed and earned. Her eyes burned red—not with rage, but with awareness.

This was her domain.

I was a guest.

She lowered her head until one eye filled my entire field of vision. Her presence pressed against my chest, not crushing, but demanding.

Then she spoke. Well, not with sound but it was sort of all in my head.

Why did you save the eggs?

No accusation. No preamble. Just the question, laid bare.

I swallowed. My throat worked even though I wasn't sure it needed to.

"Because they were going to die," I said. My voice echoed strangely, carried through water and thought. "They didn't ask for any of this. And someone had to. There aren't enough dragons in the world anymore."

The Leviathan did not respond immediately.

Her gaze slid past me, *through* me, and I knew she was seeing them—the dragon eggs, fragile and warm and alive, cradled in my memory even now.

They are not yours.

"I know," I said quickly. "That's kind of the point."

A pause.

Then—not amusement, exactly—but something softened in the immense tension hovering around her.

You could have taken weapons. Power. Relics. You chose life instead.

"I'm not great with long-term planning," I admitted.

Her massive body shifted, currents rolling outward as she circled me. The seafloor trembled beneath her passage.

The surface believes destruction is decisive, she said. *That if something threatens them, it must be broken. Burned. Claimed.*

"That tracks," I muttered.

Her eye snapped back to me, piercing.

You destroyed an island.

"I destroyed a tyrant," I shot back. "The island did the rest to itself. That was the gods' planning, not mine."

The Leviathan's form wavered. The water rippled, light folding inward, compressing.

She stood before me as a woman.

Tall. Naked. Light-skinned. Dark hair floating around her shoulders, caught in a current only she could feel. Her skin held the faint sheen of scales at the temples, along her collarbone. Her eyes were still red. Still ancient and terrifying.

But now... understandable.

"I warned you," she said, this time with a voice that brushed against my ears. "In the fog. On the water."

"I remember," I said quietly. "I remember thinking it wasn't a dream."

"It was not."

She floated to the flat, stone plain and slowly drifted past me, fingers trailing through glowing strands of plankton that bent toward her touch.

"The sea has been patient," she continued. "Longer than your kind understands. We endured empires. Gods. Monsters. Atlantis was not unique."

"Then why attack everyone now?" I asked. "Why burn everything?"

She turned.

Because now, she did not have to explain gently.

"I have offspring," she said.

The words landed hard.

"One has been born to replace me," she went on. "The deep has been quiet for too long. And the surface would not allow it to remain so. Your kind create more and more danger. Objects and ideas that threaten the sea."

Images flooded my mind. A vision of fishing fleets casting vast nets, stripping the water bare. Ships tearing across the surface, newly-invented steam engines screaming, their wakes churning everything beneath them into chaos. I saw vessels burning and sinking, their wreckage tumbling down into the dark. Oil blooming across the waves in rainbow slicks. The thunder of weapons not yet created.

I was seeing prophecy—visions of a future this world hadn't but would soon reach, or echoes pulled straight from my own. From Earth. From everything we'd already done to our seas without ever looking back.

Beneath it all, I saw great bodies curling inward, massive spines arcing protectively around smaller, glowing forms—fragile things hiding in the deep while the surface tore itself apart.

"You weren't fighting a war up there," I whispered, "just for the hell of it."

Whether the vision was real or not, I saw the wreckage of one of our ships sinking behind her, tumbling down through the dark until it settled into the sand at the bottom of the Triton Sea.

"No," she said, her voice vast and unyielding as the ocean itself. "But you were poisoning a cradle."

She let the image of the dead ship crawl into my mind and take up permanent residence.

"Atlantis made the sea a weapon," she continued. "Your people made it a road. None of you will listen when the currents shift."

"So you decided to make us listen," I said.

She slid before me once again and her gaze did not waver.

"Yes."

I clenched my fists. "And now?"

She studied me again. Not my body but my *intent*.

"You shattered the anchor," she said. "The object that bound Atlantis to what it stole from the deep. The island will fall. The sea will reclaim it."

"And me?" I asked.

A long pause.

"You stand at an intersection," she said. "You carry destruction in one hand and preservation in the other. You are capable of becoming a storm that never ends."

I swallowed.

"Or?"

She stepped closer, close enough that I could see faint lines at the corners of her eyes. Weariness. Pain.

"Or you become something rarer," she said softly. "A boundary."

The water around us stilled.

I thought of the dragon eggs. Of Braylor bleeding out on palace stone. Jonathan collapsing under guilt. Genevieve pulling me back from rage. Kinnat saving something she wasn't supposed to, just in case.

"I don't want the sea to hate us," I said. "I don't want any of this to keep happening."

Her lips flexed slightly—not a smile, but recognition.

"Then understand this," the Leviathan said. "I am pleased you chose life. I did not come to stop you tonight."

"Good," I whined. "Because I'm very tired."

She almost smiled.

"I came to see whether you would stop yourself."

The ocean brightened.

Pressure lifted.

The world began to lean again.

We will watch you, Dragonwitch, her voice echoed as everything dissolved. *Protect the future you steal back from ruin or become another tide we must end.*

And then—

The stone steps were beneath me again.

The eggs were heavy in my arms.

The Leviathan loomed before me on the palace stairs, massive and real and waiting.

Time resumed.

And I knew, absolutely and terrifyingly, that she meant every word.

They were shouting my name before I fully came back.

Hands grabbed my arms—solid, real, too warm after the cold vastness I'd just been pulled from. Someone swore. Someone else sounded like they were trying not to panic. The world lurched, color and sound snapping back into place in jagged pieces.

"Finley." Genevieve's face swam into focus first, eyes wide. "Finley, what the hell just happened?"

I blinked. Once. Twice.

The Leviathan slithered down from the stairs, leaving only the echo of something enormous having been there.

Jonathan and Kinnat were on the boat, halfway to the *Skathis*. Genevieve and Pherric stared at me as though I'd just appeared out of thin air.

"How long was I gone?" I asked.

Pherric inspected me. "The Leviathan met you at the top the stairs, stared at you, and then slithered back to the sea. Mere moments."

Genevieve tightened her grip on my arm. "You went still," she said. "Like—like you weren't here. Your eyes—"

"I know." I swallowed hard. My mouth tasted of brine and something bitter underneath. "I was... somewhere else."

Pherric's gaze locked in tight. "A mindform?"

"Not mine." I shook my head slowly. "Hers."

Silence fell but not the comfortable kind. The kind that waits for bad news.

"She didn't come to finish the fight," I said quietly. The words felt strange in my mouth, too small for what they carried. "She came to ask me something."

Genevieve blinked. "Ask you what?"

I thought of the eggs cradled in my arms. And the way her stare had gone from those fragile, impossible shapes back to me—not with fury, but with something hard and assessing.

"Why I was saving them," I said.

Kinnat's head tilted, just slightly.

"I didn't even answer out loud," I went on. "I didn't have time. But I knew the answer. I knew it in that way you know something before your brain gets involved. Because they didn't choose any of this. That bitch had locked them in glass and called them a treasure. And if we keep destroying everything because it's in our way, there won't be anything left to win."

No one interrupted me. That alone told me how bad I looked.

"She showed me things," I said. "Not just here. Not just Atlantis. Patterns. Over and over again." My stomach tightened as fragments pushed back to the surface. "Ships over-fishing the waters. Fire sinking beneath the waves. The sea turning into a dumping ground for wars that were supposed to stay on land."

Pherric went very still.

"She wasn't defending Atlantis," I said. "She didn't care who ruled it. She couldn't give a damn about Thalassa. Or us." I paused, the words catching anyway. "She cared that we turned the sea into a battlefield. That we poisoned a cradle."

Pherric went very still. "A... nursery?"

"Yeah." My voice cracked, just a little. "For her. For others. Things older than dragons. She's seen this before. Different ages. Same ending. People fight. The water pays for it. And then nothing comes after. And it will only get worse as we develop more tools and more... weapons."

Genevieve stared at me. "Then why didn't she kill you?"

I looked down at the eggs. "Because I wasn't trying to win," I said. "I was trying to save something that couldn't fight back."

Behind us, something cracked—stone giving way as the palace continued to tear itself apart. The island groaned, because it already knew how this ended.

Genevieve exhaled hard. "So what now?"

I looked out at the bay. At the dark water stretching away from us, deceptively calm. At the ship waiting, scarred but still floating.

"Now?" I said. "Now we leave. This island is sinking. But in the future? I wouldn't recommend that we fight on the sea unless there's no other choice." I met each of their eyes in turn. "And if we forget that... she won't."

The wind shifted. Somewhere far out, the water rolled, heavy and patient.

Genevieve carefully took one of the eggs, easing my burden.

"She wasn't our enemy," I said softly. "She was just tired of cleaning up after us."

"I'm confused," admitted Genevieve.

"Well, congratulations are in order. I think I've just been promoted to Head of Tir Na's very angry version of Greenpeace."

Pherric cocked his head in the way he always did.

I added. "I guess I'm not just the Dragonwitch anymore. I'm also the ocean's customer service representative."

89

Elegy in Flame

Finley

I was one step away from jumping on the boat when the shadow fell over the stairs.

Heat washed over my back.

Big Red landed hard on the broken stone, talons biting deep as the island groaned beneath us. Her wings beat once, twice, sending ash and spray whipping across the steps. Somewhere behind me, someone shouted my name.

I didn't turn right away. I already knew. I looked into her eyes.

"She wants something," I said hoarsely. "From me."

Genevieve grabbed my arm. "Finley, no. Whatever that is—no."

I looked back at the *Skathis*, bobbing in the bay. Braylor was on board. Alive. That alone should have been enough to make me run.

But the dragon wasn't looking at the ship.

She was looking past the palace.

"I think I know what she wants. Go. Have them sail over to the docks and meet me there."

"Finley!" Pherric shouted. "The island—"

"I know," I snapped. "Trust me. I have a dragon…"

Big Red lowered herself, neck arching, one massive eye fixing on me as I climbed onto her wing and hauled myself up. Her warmth soaked through me instantly, steady and furious and alive. She did not wait for a command. The moment I settled between her shoulders, she launched.

Atlantis dropped beneath us, cracking open in long, violent seams. Towers slid into the sea. Water surged up through streets that had never known tides. Fire hissed and died where it met the waves.

Big Red beat her wings hard and fast, angling toward the far edge of the collapsing island.

Toward Zeranthyl.

The green dragon waited there.

She circled low, tight loops over the fallen body, a sound coming from her throat that was not a roar or a cry, but something ancient.

Big Red landed beside the body with a thunderous crack of stone.

I slid down her back and hit the ground, boots skidding on wet rock. The tremors were not quite as bad here. The land shuddered in uneven pulses. The island was taking its last gasps.

I walked toward Zeranthyl.

Up close, he was enormous. Bigger than I realized. His scales were scorched and split, his neck broken because his betrayal had caught up to him. One wing was half buried beneath rubble, the membrane torn to ribbons.

He looked... quiet.

The green dragon lowered his head. Big Red followed.

Then they lifted up and breathed fire together. Not in fury and or attack, but to dissolve.

Their flames poured over Zeranthyl's body in slow, deliberate waves—red and orange fire weaving together, heat roaring against the encroaching sea. The stone beneath my feet glowed. My face burned hot.

I had done this before. A dragon funeral. So, I sank to my knees, ignoring the way the ground bucked beneath me, and bowed my head.

For a long moment, there was nothing but fire and the sound of the island breaking apart.

When the flames died, Zeranthyl was no longer flesh. Only bone remained. Blackened. Gleaming in the smoke-covered moonlight.

A dragon reduced to what endured.

The green dragon stepped back first, giving me space.

Big Red watched me closely.

I swallowed and limped forward, hands quivering as I reached for the nearest fragment—a rib the size of a tree limb, still warm. I pulled and practically the entire skeleton crumbled. I dragged the bone across the stone, my injured leg screaming, and lifted it as high as I could.

Big Red dropped her head.

I placed the bone in her jaws.

She closed her mouth gently, reverently.

I turned to the green dragon and did the same. Smaller pieces. A shard of wing bone. A section of spine. Each one felt heavier than it should have, not with weight but with meaning.

The island faltered violently.

A crack split the ground between me and Zeranthyl's remains, water surging up through it in a roaring burst.

I staggered back, barely keeping my footing.

"Okay," I muttered. "Okay, message received."

I grabbed one last black bone and placed it into the green dragon's mouth. She rumbled softly, eyes never leaving me.

The ground heaved again. And stone gave way. Water rushed in fast now, swallowing what remained of Zeranthyl piece by piece.

I backed away, chest tight.

"We can't save any more," I said, voice breaking. "I'm sorry."

The green dragon hesitated, then lifted his wings.

I waved him off. "Go. Get out of here."

He launched, vanishing into the smoky sky.

Big Red didn't move.

She stood between me and the collapsing cliff, eyes locked on mine. She leaned down, nudging me with her snout—hard enough to bruise, gentle enough not to break me.

I grinned. "I know. I know."

I pointed back toward the Triton Sea.

The *Skathis* had sailed closer, fighting the currents, her crew shouting and waving frantically. The small boat was already rowing toward the rocks.

"They're there," I said. "I'm not staying."

Big Red hesitated.

Then she reached down, carefully, and hooked Zeranthyl's skull with one curved tooth.

The massive bone lifted free.

She reared back and launched.

I watched her go until she was nothing but a red streak against the black night.

The island chose that moment to give up entirely.

The ground collapsed beneath my feet.

I staggered to the beach. Water surged after me, fast and furious. Rocks cracked and slid. Everything shifted, violently.

Hands grabbed me at the edge of the sand.

I fell into them, coughing, soaked, shaking.

The boat pulled away hard as the beach vanished beneath the waves.

From the deck of the *Skathis*, I watched Atlantis slowly sink.

I had gotten some payback, but it didn't feel like any win. There was only pain and heartache and desolation.

A quiet understanding that some moments don't ask whether you succeeded. They only ask whether you survived.

And whether you remembered who mattered when the world fell apart.

90

Of Fire, Bone, and What Endures

Finley

We anchored off the coast of Kunlun at dawn days later, the wounded ship creaking softly as if relieved to finally rest. Melcente had turned the bow of the *Skathis* toward home the moment we were clear of Atlantis.

I instructed her to land us in view of the tallest mountain range in Kunlun once we had sailed far to the west and turned north.

Braylor was finally stable. I stayed with him night and day in the captain's quarters, nursing him back to health.

When we arrived at the coast of Kunlun, I knew he wouldn't be fit for the journey inland. He stayed aboard with Pherric, who tended him in my absence.

Although I had to tease my mage about remaining behind because dragons terrified him. Always had. It was kind of funny, in a way that hurt too much to laugh at. I'm still trying to imagine Pherric's journey from Irkalla to Atlantis on the back of Zeranthyl. I would've paid money to see his face.

The rest of us—Genevieve, Kasuma, Jonathan, Kinnat, and me—packed provisions and took to the mountains.

We carried the dragon eggs.

Six of them. Warm. Heavy. Alive.

The march and eventual climb was brutal. Pherric had done his best to heal up my leg, but it wasn't enough.

Kunlun rose hard and unforgiving from the sea, its slopes cut with old scars of fire and stone. The oxygen thinned as we climbed, the world narrowing to careful footing and shared quiet. No one complained. No one rushed. Each egg was cradled as if it might hear us, understanding the care we took with every step.

I carried one myself.

It was larger than the others, its shell a deep, dark red veined with faint gold. It pulsed faintly against my arms. A reminder that something waited inside, patient and stubborn and unfinished.

As we climbed, grief followed me.

I wasn't able to save the three eggs that remained in Thalassa's palace when Atlantis fell. Buried under stone and water and the weight of a city that had not decided if dragons were treasures instead of family. I tried not to picture them. Tried not to imagine silence where there should have been heat and and maybe a heartbeat.

But grief and hope are not opposites. They walk together whether you invite them or not.

By the time the path rose high and narrowed, and the land opened into the old lava slice running down from the bowl of the ancient volcano, I knew we had arrived.

The Valley of the Black Bones waited exactly as I remembered it.

Its floor carpeted in obsidian shards that glittered like broken stars. Dragon bones lay everywhere—massive ribs stacked with care, skulls turned toward the sky, entire skeletons curled in final rest. Some were black, others bleached white by sun and time. None were disturbed.

This was their cemetery.

We stopped at the edge of the valley. Even Genevieve, who rarely hesitated at thresholds, went still. Jonathan stared openly, awe stripping him of words. Kinnat inclined her head, a warrior's acknowledgment of sacred ground.

I walked forward first.

Every step felt measured. Intentional. The obsidian shifted under my boots, but I barely noticed. All my attention was on the egg in my arms and the presence waiting ahead.

Big Red lifted from the far end of the valley with a roar that rolled through me. She took off and flew toward us.

She was enormous in the open air, her wings spanning the width of the valley as she rose. Sunlight caught along her scales, igniting them into fiery brilliance. The green dragon followed her—sleek, powerful—and behind them, a younger black male and a blue female circled lower, watchful and alert.

Big Red descended slowly.

She landed among the bones with care. The others settled on the cliff, looking down over the preceding. The ground cracked softly beneath her weight. She folded her wings, lowered her massive head... and closed her eyes.

She bowed.

To me.

No dragon had ever done that. Certainly not to me. Probably not anyone.

The sound that tore out of me was ugly and raw and unstoppable. I didn't bother to contain it. Tears fell hard. I crossed the remaining distance and set the egg gently on the shards between us, my hands shaking too much to trust myself for long.

Then I stepped forward and pressed my forehead to the broad curve of her face.

Her scales were warm. Solid. Real.

I saw a fresh set of dragon bones stacked nearby. They were bigger than the rest. Big Red followed my gaze and dropped her head. Zeranthyl. Even though they fought, she and the others still mourned the loss of another one.

"I'm sorry," I said, the words breaking apart as they left me. "I'm sorry for your loss."

Images pressed into my mind—not words, not speech, but shared memory. Flight. Fight. Loss. Zeranthyl's death, our makeshift funeral of fire, and the echo that followed. Grief vast enough to hollow mountains.

But beneath it... there was that hope again. A careful, fragile, pesky little thing.

I wiped the tears from my cheeks and smiled, then laughed awkwardly.

Big Red exhaled slowly and nudged her forehead against mine, a gesture so gentle it undid me completely. We stood there together amid the black bones, and I cried again at what had been lost.

Behind me, the others approached.

Kinnat knelt to place her egg, her movements precise. Jonathan followed, eyes round and overwhelmed, his hands lingering as if unsure to let go. Kasuma was a little rougher than the others, but still respectful as she lowered her egg. Genevieve laid hers down last, her expression unreadable until she straightened—then I saw it. Relief. Wonder. A fierce, quiet belief that this mattered.

When all six eggs rested on the floor, Big Red stepped forward and carefully lifted one in her jaws, holding it with impossible delicacy. With two powerful beats of her wings, she rose and flew to the crest of the valley, where the young black dragon waited. She placed the egg before him, nudging it closer with the side of her snout.

Then she returned for another.

This one went to the green male dragon, who closed his eyes in acknowlededgment as the egg was set before him. Finally, each had three. The males settled in around their charges, bodies curving protectively, tails drawing shallow lines in the stone.

Caretakers.

I hadn't known that the males cared for the offspring. But somehow, it felt right.

I stepped back, the ache in my chest heavy and light all at once. This was not my place beyond this point. The valley did not belong to me. I had brought something back to it—but it was not mine to keep.

I turned and walked away.

The others followed without being asked. No one spoke. No one needed to.

At the edge of the valley, I stopped and looked back once.

Big Red stood among the bones, wings half-furled, her head lifted toward the sky. All the eggs rested with the males where they had been placed, whole and waiting. The future, fragile and stubborn, lay warming itself on ancient ground.

I guessed they were waiting for us to leave before lighting them with their flames. That was private to them.

Then I turned and led us out.

I left the Valley of the Black Bones behind—unchanged, and yet utterly transformed.

And for the first time since Atlantis fell, I believed we hadn't only survived the ending.

We had delivered a beginning.

91

I Wanted You to Know

Finley

The Cíbolan first family's tower was quiet in the way places built for powerful men always were. Thick stone walls muffled the world beyond them, as if nothing ugly could reach this high. Lord Diago's chambers sat above Quivira. A monument to gains he never paid for.

He stood at a washbasin, sleeves of his robe rolled, water dripping from his fingers. Candlelight flickered across gold-threaded tapestries and polished furniture. Everything here was soft. Curated. Safe.

He splashed water onto his face, breathing out slowly, like the day's weight might rinse away with the dust and perspiration. Age had made his hands tremble. Just a little. Not enough to notice if you didn't want to.

I stepped out of the shadow near the far wall.

He never heard me.

The knife was at his throat before his breath could turn into a scream. Blade to skin. Just enough pressure to promise what came next.

"Don't," I said softly, close to his ear. Calm. Almost kind.

His whole body locked. The basin clattered as his hands slipped from the stone. Water spilled onto the floor, darkening the rug. His pulse thudded wildly beneath my blade, fast and terrified.

559

I leaned in closer, inhaling him in. Soap. Oil. Comfort.

I felt his mind racing. Guards. Nearby weapons. *Bargains.* All the tricks that had kept him alive this long. He started to shake harder now.

"I—" he whispered.

"No," I said. "You don't get words."

I drew him back a step, forcing him upright, keeping my blade steady as I turned us toward the bed. He went easily. Too easily. This wasn't a warrior. This was a man who'd survived by letting others bleed for him.

The candle near the bedside sputtered. He reached for it on instinct, fingers stretching toward the light.

I blew it out.

Darkness swallowed the room, tight and sudden. The only sound left was his breathing.

I pressed my mouth close to his ear and whispered the last he would ever hear from me.

"I just wanted you to know it was me."

His body jerked.

"For Cira. For Frip. For Gunnr. For Temurr. *Lex talionis.*"

The knife moved once, clean and deliberate. Not messy. Not frantic. Kasuma had taught me well. How to quietly end someone who deserved it.

He made a sound that barely qualified as one. A gasp collapsing inward. His legs gave out, weight sagging against my chest as his life spilled out onto the floor.

I held him there until it was done.

When I let him fall, he landed at the foot of his bed like something discarded. No last words. No confession. No absolution.

I wiped the blade on his sleeve.

My hands didn't shake.

I looked around once more. The fine sheets. The lush curtains. Exquisite furniture.

The room built to make a man believe consequences couldn't reach him.

"They always do," I murmured, though no one was left to hear it.

I turned toward the window, already planning my exit, already gone from this place in every way that mattered.

As I slipped back into the night, I allowed myself one final truth. Not shouted or sworn. Just carried with me like a scar that finally closed.

Now you finally know what it costs to choose the wrong side.

And that bard I never got? He sang to me, in my head, one final verse...

Steel remembers every name,
Though men forget the cost of flame.
No tower stands beyond the tide—
All debts are paid. All sides are tried.

What was broken, revenge doesn't heal.
It only proves the wound was real.

Epilogue

Okay. So, if you saw me sneaking out of a tower, late at night, in Quivira... no you didn't.

But yeah. Atlantis was done. Burned, sunk, and argued over by people who weren't there and never would be. I've told the story enough times now that I can recite it without flinching, which feels like progress... or at least emotional recovery.

I went back to the Irkallan palace, Braylor at my side. I went back to people who demanded to know whether the world was ending again. It wasn't. Not imminently, anyway.

Mostly, I dealt with more trade disputes, supply shortages, and a truly heroic number of arguments about grain. This, apparently, is what victory looks like.

But I didn't hate it.

Turns out, being queen is tolerable when no one is actively trying to overthrow everything. I signed decrees. I listened to complaints. I corrected a minister who thought dragons ate gold. (They don't. Mostly.)

The crown still weighs the same, but I've stopped expecting it to crush me.

We found all but one of the Deep Guard. All the nations came together for that.

My people still call me the usurper, the demon, the dragonwitch. I no longer care.

And yes—before you ask—there was another mess to deal with. This one north of Valhalla. Past the polite edge of maps. With frost giants. And the gods, who were never gods.

I've been there.

But that's not this story.

I have a kingdom to run and exactly zero interest in explaining myself to anyone who thinks peace means I've gone soft.

Atlantis was a chapter.

Jotunland is a different book.

I'll get to that story. Someday.

Let me spend some time savoring my revenge.